His kiss grew bolder.

"So," he whispered in surprise. "Even proper Southern ladies have a fire in them. You will come to me, Fancy, before this year is out. And when you do, all promises, all agreements will be forgotten.'"

She slapped him a second time, hard as she could. He caught her hand and brought her palm to his lips. His gaze held hers as he slowly swirled his tongue across her palm, then, smiling, he stepped back. "Welcome to my home, Fancy," he said softly. He released her then, breaking the gaze that had held her captive to his whim and, whistling, he clattered down the stairs.

"I will resist you to my last breath, Coop Fletcher," she shouted and was answered only by his mocking laughter.

Also by Peggy Hanchar
Published by Fawcett Books:

THE GILDED DOVE
WHERE EAGLES SOAR
CHEYENNE DREAMS

FANCY LADY

Peggy Hanchar

FAWCETT GOLD MEDAL • NEW YORK

A Fawcett Gold Medal Book
Published by Ballantine Books
Copyright © 1994 by Peggy Hanchar

All rights reserved under International and Pan-American Copyright Conventions. Published in the United States of America by Ballantine Books, a division of Random House Inc., New York, and simultaneously in Canada by Random House of Canada Limited, Toronto.

Library of Congress Catalog Card Number: 93-90722

ISBN 0-449-14770-3

Manufactured in the United States of America

First Edition: March 1994

10 9 8 7 6 5 4 3 2 1

Prologue

"**W**HOA! HOLY SHIT!"

"What's the problem, Aaron?"

"Get Coop! Now!" Aaron Sayer stared at the rubble of rock that cut off the trail and tightened his grip on the reins.

"Whoa, now," he commanded his mule team.

They danced and sidestepped restlessly, as if sensing something was amiss. The wagon wheels rolled forward a few inches. Aaron cursed and set his booted foot more firmly on the brake.

Down along the line of pack mules and laden freight wagons, men called out a summons for Coop Fletcher, and soon a tall, lean man with a weather-beaten face and stern countenance made his way along the narrow rocky trail.

"What's the holdup, Sayer?" he demanded when he reached the lead wagon.

The teamster pointed his whip handle at the path ahead and spat nervously. "Rock slide," he said.

In stony silence, Coop Fletcher studied the tons of rock that blocked their path, then he raised his dark gaze to the line of crags and ridges above, his narrowed eyes alert, his body rigid. Aaron remained silent as Coop studied the situation. Coop kind of reminded him of a Tennessee bird dog sniffing the air.

A second path led off to the right, impossibly steep for

1

the heavily laden wagons. Aaron grew nervous just watching Coop consider that slope.

"You ain't figuring on taking the wagons down that are you?"

"If we have to," Coop answered. His steely glance swept along the exposed bluffs overhead. "We may have to."

"What makes you figure that?" Aaron asked following the direction of Coop's gaze. The sharp granite ledge wall reared barren against the cloudless sky. Aaron could see nothing to become alarmed about.

Coop shifted in his saddle. "Think about it," he said flatly. "Two days ago this trail was clear. Now, we're trapped on the narrowest part of this ledge. A couple of men up in those rocks could pick us off one by one if we try to turn the wagons." Aaron felt dread grow in him.

"And who's to say if we do manage to turn back, we won't find another rock slide cutting us off back there someplace?" Coop took out a thin cheroot and clamped it between his teeth. "There's no place to go, Aaron, but down."

"Look, Coop, I figured there'd be some hard going this trip, but this beats all," Aaron said gruffly. He hated admitting he was even the least bit afraid of taking his laden wagon down the incline, but he'd rather face an outlaw's gun than the steep mountainside.

"It's the best we've got," Coop Fletcher said, his steely gray eyes narrowing as he studied the brown whiskered face of the man on the wagon seat. "Speaking of best, I figure you can handle this if no one else can."

Sayer scratched his jaw and studied the flat mountain walls around him. "Seems like there ought to be a better way," he muttered.

"I scouted this myself," Coop said patiently. "It's the best we've got." He waited while Sayer considered the trail ahead. Coop respected the other man. He'd worked for Coop for nearly six years now, and he'd proven to be fearless but not foolhardy.

Now Aaron adjusted his tobacco wad and scratched his

hairy jaw. Finally he shook his head. "Nellie's expectin' our third child next week, and she made me promise not to take chances."

A shot rang out. A mule brayed. Drivers scrambled for cover. Gun in hand, Coop leaped off his horse and took shelter behind the wagon. Aaron had slid off his seat and was crouched in the foot space below.

"Looks like you don't have much choice," Coop said and glanced back up the supply line at the other teamsters trying to calm their teams and stay out of the line of fire. He had to act before they had a chance to think. "What's it going to be, Aaron?"

"Reckon I'm losing my nerve in my old age, Coop," he said regretfully. He nodded down the incline. "I see that way as certain death. Up here I might stand a chance against those bastards." He peered out from behind the wagon bed, studying the wagons and drivers behind him. "They ain't goin' to have much chance at makin' it down this."

"I wouldn't do it either, if I had a fine woman like Nellie waiting for me," Coop said. "But I'm not waiting here for those guns to get into position. They don't know yet what we're going to do, so we've got to act fast." Taking off his hat, he wiped at his tanned brow. His hair gleamed in the sunlight, blue-black as a raven's wing, testifying to his mother's Indian heritage. His pale gray eyes were all the more remarkable for his dark coloring. They narrowed now, gimletlike as he studied the rocky slope.

Sayer watched his boss, knowing the kind of thoughts going through his mind, the weighing of chance and skill against the unyielding mountains and the lawless men that lived and died there. Coop had been delivering goods to mining camps ever since Sayer had known him, and if any man could get supplies to an isolated camp, Coop was the one to do it. He knew these mountain trails and passes like the palm of his hand and wasn't afraid of mountain or man. Sayer wasn't surprised to hear Coop's next words.

"I'll take your wagon down," he said quietly.

Sayer swore under his breath. "What about them?" he nodded back at the other mule skinners. "Even if you make it to the bottom of this trail, what's to say they will?"

Coop's glance was piercing, cutting off any more protest. "I say they'll make it," he said softly, and Sayer wasn't sure if his words were meant as a statement or a threat.

"I'm sorry to let you down, Coop," Sayer muttered.

"You're not. Take my rifle and organize the drivers at the end wagon. Tell them to take cover and shoot back. I want those drivers covered as they head down this incline." All the time he was giving orders, Coop was digging in the bottom of the wagon, pulling out chains. "Tell the men to use their rough locks," he went on, passing the chain through the spokes and around the rim of one of the wagon wheels. Securing it to the wagon, he glanced up at Aaron.

"That's a good enough brake on a grade but not on a steep incline like this one," Aaron warned.

"It'll do!" Coop said.

"We could unload the wagons and haul the stuff down on muleback."

Coop studied the distant peaks of the Rockies. "Takes too long. It'll be dark in an hour," he said, motioning to the western light. "I don't want to be stuck on this part of the trail with a bunch of nervous mules and green drivers and God knows how many murdering bastards up in those rocks. Send the men down."

"What if they won't go?"

"They'll go," Coop said. "They won't have much taste for lead. Cover me."

"I will. Keep your head down."

Coop nodded and leaped on the wagon seat. A hail of bullets rained down on him.

"Giddap," he shouted, slapping the reins against the mules' backs. The lead wagon began its descent.

"Is he driving that dang wagon down that incline?" Hoagy Davis yelled. His prominent blue eyes seemed to bulge even more in consternation. "Is he crazy?"

"A little bit," Sayer yelled back. "You have to be to survive out here. Now get your rifles and start firing at them rocks up there, and be prepared to follow Coop."

"Ain't much choice," Davis mumbled, but he dug out his rifle from beneath his seat and checked the chamber to see if it was loaded. Word was passed back along the mule train, and the men took cover and returned the fire from above, and all the time they waited to hear the crash of wood and metal and the scream of horses.

Tense and alert, Aaron watched as Coop skillfully coaxed the nervous mules forward, his long lean body pitched backward, a booted foot riding the brake to slow their momentum. They could have used logs beneath the wheels if they had had any. They could have loaded the mules and left the rest of the supplies behind for the thieving coyotes that stalked them from above, but Coop didn't easily give up what was his. Sayer had come to understand that in the years he'd been with him. He'd never seen his boss defeated.

Coop usually overcame impossible odds by sheer willpower. His lanky, wiry body seemed to possess the strength of three men, and his keen intelligence and steely nerve made him an ominous adversary. Sayer had decided from the beginning, he'd rather have Coop on his side than against him, and he'd never changed his mind in the six years he'd remained with him. Coop was a hard, exacting boss, but he never demanded anything from his men he wasn't willing to handle himself.

Now Sayer watched Coop ease back on the brake and call commands to the mules. Shots pinged in the rocks around him, like the irritating cry of an insect but far more deadly. Coop never even looked around. Aaron fired back at the ambushers. He couldn't help a thrill of admiration for the younger man.

Half-breed or not, Coop was a man to be reckoned with. He'd made his fortune hauling goods over these mountain passes, when other men grubbed in the streams and Colorado hillsides in search of first gold and then silver. And he'd been honest and fair with every man he'd dealt with, thus earning himself a reputation among the miners and speculators that used his services. When he wasn't hauling food and supplies to the mines, he was hauling ore out, and never once had a miner's ore been diverted or lost. Such was the reputation of Coop Fletcher that other haulers had a hard time making a living.

"I'll be damned. He's doing it," Hoagy yelled when there was a lull in the firing.

Sayer nodded, unperturbed. "I never doubted he could."

"Now, he's going to expect us to go down," Hoagy said, biting off a wad of tobacco and tucking it into his cheek before offering his cud to Sayer. Sayer bit off a wad and passed it back.

"If you're afraid, I'll take your wagon down," he offered. He'd welcome a chance to repair his image with Coop, but Hoagy shook his head and pushed his hat back.

"I reckon if he can make it down, I can, too." He growled and crawled back to his wagon. The ambushers set up a barrage of bullets.

"Cover Hoagy," Coop yelled, running up the incline, his gun blazing. He dove behind the boulder where Aaron had taken shelter. Both men fired at the ledge above. Hoagy started his wagon down the slope, then hesitated.

"Get it rolling," Coop yelled, and leaping up, slapped his hat at the mules. Nervously they started the downward plunge. "Ride the brake," Coop yelled, and Hoagy automatically obeyed.

Sayer saw the look on Hoagy's face just before his wagon rolled over the edge and began its plunge. It was one of sheer terror. A bullet chipped the boulder near his head, and Aaron took cover again.

By dusk they had all the wagons down. One had been damaged on its descent, and one man was wounded. Sayer and Coop both had had to drive down some of the wagons of the green drivers. At the bottom they'd followed a flat trail, outrunning the mountain bandits that harassed them. With the mining camp warned and armed, they'd rested easy, eating a hearty if monotonous meal of beans, salt back, and bread before rolling into their bedding and falling asleep. The hard trail they'd covered that day, the last precipitous drop, even the gunfire from above was all part of their job and to be taken into little account. Some talked in quiet voices about Coop Fletcher, alternately admiring and berating him for his daring. During the night more than one man dreamed he was sliding unchecked down a mountainside with only Coop Fletcher standing between him and death.

Six days later they were back at the Bar C Ranch, just outside of Elizabethtown, without their wagons, which they'd left in the miner's camp still filled with supplies. But their string of mules and men were intact. The wounded driver was resting comfortably in the bunkhouse under the eagle eye of River Adams, the crochety, unwashed cook who alternately fed and bullied them. The other drivers had been paid in gold and now prepared to descend on Elizabethtown with a mighty thirst and plenty of tales to regale their saloon buddies. With each tale, Coop Fletcher's legend would grow a little more.

"You heading into town, Sayer?" Coop asked his pack master as he turned from giving instructions to his stable boss. The mules would be housed in the sturdy, ample barns of the Bar C Ranch and put out to pasture in the flat, high prairies beyond. Coop had nearly a hundred men working under him, but he liked Aaron Sayer the best of them all. Now the two men paused by the corral and watched stable hands tending the hard-worked mules.

"Reckon I'll go back home and see about Nellie." Sayer said, nodding to the snug bungalow set to one side away from the other ranch buildings. As Coop's right-hand man, he'd been given his own house and had promptly married a long-legged, big-busted Irish widow whose husband had been killed in a mine cave-in. That was six years before, and he already had a houseful of little ones with another on the way. "She was having some back pain when I left. I figure she may already have birthed me an heir."

"You don't want any more daughters, eh?" Coop asked

idly, loathe to let the man go. Loneliness had haunted him lately, like a coyote slinking down out of the hills.

"I figure it's time I had me a son to carry on the name of Sayer," Aaron said. "How about you, Coop? When're you going to find you a wife and start producing some heirs? You've built up a small empire here, but it don't do you no good if you get killed back there in them mountains. If you had a son to pass it on to, you'd likely feel better."

"You mean I'd stop taking chances?" Coop asked, his grin wide and spontaneous, lighting his stern chiseled features.

Sayer grinned shamefacedly. "I reckon that is what I mean," he said.

Coop clamped a broad hand on his foreman's shoulder. "You've got no call to feel bad about anything on this trip, Aaron," he said. "I always know I can depend on you."

Sayer made no response, but his expression showed his pleasure at Coop's words. Gathering up his gear, he turned away. "G'night, Coop," he called softly and stepped into the darkness, heading toward the small frame house which held noise, enough commotion to set a man's teeth on edge and more love than he'd ever thought possible.

The lights at the big ranch house glowed invitingly on the dark plateau, but Coop turned away to stare with somber eyes at the mountain peaks silhouetted against the last streaked colors of western light. Maybe Aaron was right. Maybe it was time to start thinking about a family, a wife and children. He wondered what it would be like to have a woman in his life on a permanent basis, one that sat at his table and shared his bed every night and bore his children. He thought of the women he knew in Elizabethtown and Denver, prostitutes and dance hall girls, camp followers who traveled from one mining town to another in search of men with gold and a need for a woman's flesh. He'd known his share of women, but he couldn't think of one he'd like to wake up next to every morning.

Sayer had touched on something else, a fact that Coop

had acknowledged only slightly. He had indeed built a fortune, his ranch and transporting business were outrageously profitable, but even Sayer didn't know about the mines he'd bought shares into, mines that had also produced far beyond their expectation. If Coop chose not to work another day in his life, he could live in regal comfort and still pass along a sizable inheritance to his sons. If he had sons. The thought hung in the air, needling him, drawing him toward a new direction in his life. He felt its pull and thought to resist, but some restless longing in his soul wouldn't let him.

Coop thought of Elizabethtown and the way it was changing. Once it, too, had been nothing but a raw mining town, sporting its share of saloons and bawdy houses, but in the past few years as the placer mines gave way to more expensive techniques, a new breed of men had come, bringing their families and building fine homes and hotels. He'd seen these changes and understood that a line was being drawn through the town. On one side were the men who worked the mines, laboring for someone else's profits, and the storekeepers and bartenders, gamblers and prostitutes who serviced their needs; on the other side were the bankers and financiers who reaped the greatest share of the profit and made the town grow, who put up churches and libraries and schools. They were the future of Elizabethtown, just as would be their sons and daughters. Suddenly, Coop wanted more than anything to be a part of those builders, the town officials, the professionals, the elite society. He, Coop Fletcher, son of an Indian prostitute and a drunken miner, wanted to walk proudly among those better people, and he wanted his sons and daughters to take their place beside their progeny without any sense of the shame Coop had known.

He'd do it, by God, he thought. He'd find a wife, not just any wife, but a proper lady who'd add stature and luster to the name of Coop Fletcher, a genteel lady who'd give him intelligent sons and pretty daughters. Slapping his hand against the corral fence in a gesture of resolve, he turned to survey his dynasty. Sayer had called it an empire and so it was, and he was its ruler. He had now only to find a suitable woman with whom to share it.

Chapter 1

"*O*OH, I CAN'T take no mo', Miss Fancy. My innards is so shook up, they ain't never goin' back to the right place."

"We'll be there soon," Fancy Bourne said, waving a limp handkerchief before her face in a vain attempt to create a breeze and displace some of the Colorado dust that had settled over her skin and hair. The Denver-to-Elizabethtown stagecoach rattled over the rocky trail, tossing them around inside like limp rag dolls.

"I don't know why we couldn't have been met in Denver as the letter instructed," Fancy fussed, righting herself and brushing at her dust-covered clothes. "It could have saved us this horrid trip through these mountains." And indeed the promise had been that they would be met in Denver, but when she'd arrived, a telegraph had tersely instructed her to continue on to Elizabethtown by stage.

Green eyes flashing with indignation, Fancy fanned herself and thought back over the events that had brought her to this hellish country. Since the war, conditions in the south had been such that the once prosperous and popular theatrical troupe of Montgomery and Adele Bourne had fallen on hard times. Where once they'd enjoyed royal accommodations and adulation, their audiences had dwindled to a mere handful, and most of those had been boorish Yankee carpetbaggers and their white trash female companions.

11

Valiantly they'd floundered on, believing the south would rise again and gentility and culture would reign as once it had, but the years had passed, and her father's hope had become as threadbare as their sets and costumes.

A train wreck had ended her parents' lives, and Fancy had struggled to carry on, but the rest of the troupe hadn't wanted to continue with an inexperienced nineteen-year-old girl in charge. They'd abandoned her.

Only Annabelle, who as a child had been rescued by Monty Bourne from an abusive owner, had remained at Fancy's side. They'd grown up together, more sisters than mistress and maid.

Chance alone had carried Fancy to the offices of Wheeler and Wheeler that fateful day the letter arrived. Seeking help from her desperate situation, she'd in turn been propositioned, pawed, and finally shoved into a dusty file room by Travis Wheeler when his wife made an unexpected appearance. If Fancy hadn't been so outraged, she might have laughed, for the situation was so like the French comedies their troupe had presented onstage. It was there, in that dusty file room, where mail was opened, that Fancy chanced upon the letter from a Colorado gentleman who was looking for a bride.

Now Fancy braced herself against the pitching of the stagecoach and took out the letter, much worn from her eternal reading of it. Once again she perused it, looking for the reassurance that had so captured her that fateful day.

The writer of the letter had scrawled the following in impatient slashes across the page:

I am a man of some means, healthy and in possession of all my faculties. I operate my own transport business out of Colorado, own a ranch and half-interest in several gold mines.

Gold mines! Even now the words captured Fancy's imagination. She tried again to remember everything she'd read and heard about the gold discoveries out west. Why men had traveled out here paupers and returned with vast fortunes. Sighing she turned back to the letter.

I am in need of a wife, one of genteel breeding, perhaps a daughter of one of the plantation owners. Although I am not particular as to looks, I should like her not to be too plain of face or sharp of tongue. A docile, respectable woman will do nicely. She must be of child-bearing years. I am enclosing a bank draft to cover any expenses needed for traveling accommodations and a trousseau. The wedding will be performed in Elizabeth-town upon the arrival of the bride-to-be.

The rest of the letter was given over to advice on traveling arrangements and was signed,

Cooper Fletcher, Elizabethtown, Colorado.

Fancy glanced back over the letter. The mention of the bank draft had certainly claimed her attention before and seduced her into believing this was a viable option for her. Not that she was possessed by the love of money, but any man who could so generously provide for his future wife was obviously someone to consider. That was before she'd begun this endless journey.

Carefully, she refolded the letter and placed it back in her reticule, then sat staring pensively at the barren, rocky land passing beyond the window. How easy to convince Wheeler to send her as Cooper Fletcher's bride, almost as easy as it had been to convince herself she could go through with this. Wheeler had been anxious for her to leave town without his wife finding out about his attempted infidelity. He'd been willing to write a letter to Cooper Fletcher stating she was, indeed, the gently bred daughter of poor southern aristocracy. Fancy had no experience of such a life, but she could pretend. Her whole life had been spent doing that. Though she'd never attended any of the fine finishing schools such southern belles might have done, or been in a ballroom, she could play the role of a lady to a fare-thee-well. Most importantly, she had a lively imagination and a strong will to survive.

Now as she peered at the rugged mountain scenery, she wondered if her impulsiveness had led them into more trouble than she could handle. The vast open plains, pitiful sod shanties, and the miserable huddle of buildings that constituted western towns had robbed her of her confidence. The rough, volatile men, gunfights, and stories of Indian raids had led her to believe she'd made a dreadful mistake. She couldn't marry this strange man and live in this harsh country. She'd tell Cooper Fletcher so the moment she met him. Perhaps she could convince him to send her on to San Francisco. She'd heard about the theaters there where grateful patrons threw bags of gold dust onto the stage. She'd go there and join a theatrical troupe. Would Cooper Fletcher cooperate?

She looked out the window and wondered what manner of man he could be. A hard man, she suspected. A man would have to be hard to survive and prosper in this harsh country. He'd be older, weather-beaten, like some of those men hanging around the stations, their faces bearded, their lips and teeth stained by chewing tobacco. Fancy shivered delicately.

A whimper brought her attention back to Annabelle, whose dark eyes were beginning to look scared as she clung to the hand strap in a vain attempt to stay on her seat.

"We're bound to be in Elizabethtown soon," Fancy said with false cheerfulness. Annabelle said nothing, just rolled her eyes.

"Can't be more than an hour away now," the gentleman seated across from them spoke for the first time. He'd sat dozing for most of the trip, his wide-brimmed hat pulled over his face. His dark suit, though gray with the dust of travel, was obviously of a good cut, and the watch chain tucked into the pocket of his vest was gold.

Fancy had felt only a mild interest in his identity. Now

out of boredom, she smiled sweetly. "I don't believe I caught your name, sir."

"Doyle Springer at your service, ma'am," he answered, doffing his hat. His hands, Fancy saw, were slender and brown, unmarred by the cracked nails and knobby calluses of so many men out here. His dark eyes were restless, like a man constantly looking out for trouble.

"What do you do, Mr. Springer?" she asked.

Springer grinned at the innocent question. "Where you from, ma'am?" he stemmed her flow of questions with one of his own.

"We've traveled from Alabama," Fancy answered.

"That's some trip," he observed with a shake of his head.

Fancy nodded and stared out her window at the rocky ledges and deep crevices of the mountainsides. She dared not look down. She was afraid of what she might find. The stagecoach, she noted, hadn't perceptibly slowed for the narrow ledges winding round steep drops. Now she concentrated on Doyle Springer's comment.

"Yes, we have come far," she answered wearily, "first by train as far as we could and now by stagecoach. I'm going to meet my husband-to-be in Elizabethtown."

"That's mighty brave of you, ma'am, coming all this distance with just a maid as a companion." Springer barely spared a glance for Annabelle. She remained expressionless. She'd quickly discerned Springer's ilk, and her disliking for him was no less than his regard for her brown skin.

"We've been treated with surprising, albeit rough, courtesy by every gentleman we've met thus far," Fancy said. "I've felt little apprehension for our safety." They rode awhile in silence while she studied the man across from her. There was something about him she sensed didn't quite fit the staid gentlemanly attire, some mannerisms that reminded her of Travis Wheeler. "You haven't said what business you're in, Mr. Springer," she said.

"No, ma'am, I haven't, and if you take my advice, that's not a question you ask easily out here. There's some men who might get riled at it."

"Oh?" Fancy sat back and stared at him, wide-eyed. He chuckled.

"No, ma'am, I'm not one of them. I'm an Indian agent."

"Indian agent?" Fancy's expression showed even more alarm.

"Miss Fancy!" Annabelle squealed in terror. Her eyes had gotten so big, you could see the whites all around the dark irises.

"Are—are the Indians dangerous out here?" Fancy asked.

Springer snickered, and Fancy sensed he was pleased with the reaction he'd gotten. "No, ma'am, they are not, leastwise, not now. The murderin' Cheyenne and Arapaho were pretty near wiped out back in '64 at Sand Creek. We should've killed all the murderin' devils then and there. They teamed up with the Sioux later on and attacked more of our troops at Breecher Island. But we've got 'em under control now. They've been whipped and put on reservations. That's why I'm here, to see they stay there. I'm headed to the Middle Park Mountain Range right now to talk to the Utes."

"I see," Fancy said and leaned back against the cushioned seat. Springer regarded her from beneath the brim of his hat.

"I reckon your bridegroom is right anxious to see you again, Miss—"

"Bourne," Fancy supplied. "I've—we've never met."

"Now is that a fact? You're one of them mail-order brides, then." Springer's expression was inquisitive, friendly, inviting more confidences, but Fancy remained silent, sorry she'd revealed so much about herself.

"Who might the groom be?" he inquired. "I know most of the folks in these parts, and likely as not I know him."

Fancy sat up, a smile curving her lips at the thought she might glean some information about the man she was to meet. "His name is Cooper Fletcher."

Springer's smile faded. "Coop Fletcher?" he repeated as if he hadn't heard right. He shook his head from side to side and looked at her with sympathy. "Ma'am, I'm afraid you've had a god-awful trick played on you. Coop Fletcher ain't nothing but a half-breed." His tone was scathing.

"A half-breed?" Fancy asked with some alarm. What had she done?

"Yes, ma'am," Springer was saying. "Leastwise, that's what they call him. I believe it was his mama who was the half-breed, and his papa was some ragtag miner that got shot when Coop was a kid."

"In his letter he said he owned his business and a ranch and—and several gold mines," Fancy said haltingly.

"That much is true, ma'am," Springer agreed. "But he's got Injun blood in him just as sure as I'm sittin' here."

"Why isn't he on a reservation, too?" Fancy asked, sitting up straighter and smoothing her gloves in agitation.

"If I had my way, ma'am, he'd be there all right," Springer said.

Annabelle had remained silent throughout this conversation, her delicate nostrils twitching in distaste for the Indian agent. Now she glanced out the window and pointed. "We're comin' to a town," she said excitedly.

"Elizabethtown!" Springer confirmed their hopes.

The women fell silent and stared out their windows at the jumble of wooden buildings with false fronts. Fancy's heart sank at the sight of the rough mountain town.

Coop Fletcher leaned against the hotel porch railing and watched as the buff and yellow stagecoach rolled into town. His eyes narrowed in anticipation, otherwise he gave no sign of recognition that he was waiting for the stage. Casually he took out a thin cheroot and lit it, pulling the smoke deep into his lungs. He had no liking for what was about to occur. He'd made a dang fool mistake, and on that stagecoach was the consequence of his actions in the person of a Miss Francine Bourne of Mobile, Alabama. God help him, what had he been thinking of to send off for some southern spinster, smelling and looking like dried-up old parchment, who was forced to travel two thousand miles to find a man who'd have her?

Well, he'd changed his mind. This wasn't for him. He
liked his life just the way it was. He had no need of a
woman to tell him when to come and go and where to
place his muddy boots in his own house. Aaron was the
one who'd got him thinking about a wife and heir. He drew
deeply on the cheroot and braced himself for the scene
about to follow. She'd no doubt cry and protest, but he'd
offer her a goodly sum of money and send her packing
back east on the next stage.

The team of horses came to a halt in a cloud of dust, and
the stagecoach door swung open. Coop pulled his broad
brim hat low over his eyes and pretended not to be interested in the passengers disembarking. A man stepped out
first, and Coop's alert gaze automatically took in the details
of his eastern suit and vest. The hat hid the man's face as
he turned back to the stagecoach, but something about the
tilt of his head and shoulders caused the muscles to tighten
in Coop's stomach. He should know that man but couldn't
place him. His attention was pulled to the second occupant:
a slim black woman, obviously a maid. And then a dainty
foot was placed on the coach step, a slender ankle encased
in white silk stockings was briefly revealed. In a swirl of
lace and petticoats the third passenger alighted from the
coach, shook out her skirts, and unfurled an impossibly inadequate scrap of a silk umbrella all in one smooth move,
and all the while her green-eyed gaze darted here and there
taking in the town. Coop felt the air go out of him as he
took in the slim, shapely figure, the gleaming gold hair, and
the creamy skin of her face and throat. This was no dried-
out old maid. This was the kind of woman a man dreamed
of spending a lifetime with. Coop felt a tightening in his
gut. He could feel the trap, the very trap he'd set himself,
springing closed around him.

Fancy looked around the little mountain town. Though
not as large and well-developed as Denver, Elizabethtown
with its wooden sidewalks and neatly painted store fronts

was quaint if crudely built. The sign on the building before
them said MAISON FRANCAIS, HENRI DUBOIS, PROPRIETOR.

"Regardez, c'est francaise," Fancy cried to Annabelle.
Perhaps the town was not as lacking as she'd feared.
Townspeople had gathered to welcome the stage, and Fancy
peered around, looking for the savage, dull-featured face
she imagined would be Coop Fletcher. A tall, good-looking
cowboy slouched against the porch post, his silvery gray
eyes regarding her from beneath his lowered hat brim. His
gaze was bold and much too familiar. She felt an edge of
irritation at such ill manners and with a sniff of disapproval
turned away.

"Do yo' see this Mr. Fletcher anyplace?" Annabelle
asked cautiously.

"No one that answers Mr. Springer's description," Fancy
answered. "Come, we won't wait out here in the street like
poor white trash. We'll inquire inside and perhaps take a
room to freshen up." The driver had climbed up on the
stagecoach and was throwing down bags. Fancy's trunks
landed unceremoniously at her feet. Annabelle hurried to
retrieve what she could. Fancy looked around for help, and
her gaze fell on the lanky cowboy still slouched against the
hotel post.

"Here, you," she called peremptorily, holding out a few
coins. "Collect my trunks and take them inside please."

If the shadowed eyes registered some surprise, she didn't
hesitate to note it, but mounted the wooden steps and swept
into the Maison Francais.

"Ah, mademoiselle, entrez. Bienvenue. You are welcome
to my humble establishment. *Je suis Monsieur Dubois."*

"Merci, monsieur," Fancy returned. *"Je suis venu
jusqu'ici.* Have you a *salle de bain?"*

"Oui, oui, mademoiselle. Are you not here to meet Monsieur Fletcher? You have been expected, and your room and
a bath are awaiting you. Come with me."

"Who made these arrangements?" Fancy asked.

"Why, Monsieur Fletcher, himself, *mademoiselle.* He has
been awaiting your arrival."

"But I didn't see him," Fancy said in some exasperation. "Are you sure he's here?"

"*Certainment, mademoiselle*, he was just here," the Frenchman insisted, looking about. His gaze fixed on the cowboy with the luggage and quickly shifted away. "He will show himself, never fear, *mademoiselle*."

He bustled behind the counter to collect a key and motioned her to follow him up the stairs. Fancy cast one last glance at the front of the hotel. She had hoped to see Coop Fletcher immediately so she might tell him at once she had no intentions of marrying a half-breed, but the only one who'd lingered after the stage left was the lanky cowboy who was taking his good time in collecting her trunks and bringing them in.

"Please, hurry," she ordered. "And bring them right up to my room."

"Yes, ma'am," the man answered, and she noted his voice was deep and smooth. She turned to the stairs. Annabelle followed.

"The men out here are handsome enough," Fancy commented, "if a bit inclined to slothfulness. I've never seen anyone move so slowly as that man does."

"Ummm!" Annabelle cleared her throat, and Fancy glanced back to see the cowboy was right on their heels. How had he moved so fast and silently? she wondered. Raising her chin in prim dignity, she climbed the remaining stairs and followed the short, rotund Frenchman.

"*Voila, mademoiselle!*" he exclaimed, throwing open a door and signifying the room and bathtub beyond. His beaming smile indicated his pride in his hotel.

"*C'est magnifique!*" Fancy exclaimed, more to please him than out of awe for the room. She stepped inside, followed by Annabelle, and looked around. The room was comfortably furnished with a high-back wooden bed and matching dresser with a mirror. A thick woven rug with a rose pattern covered the floor, in the middle of which sat a high-backed steel tub filled with steaming water. Fancy dipped her finger into the water and closed her eyes. "*C'est magnifique!*" she repeated with more heart than she had at first.

"*Bon!*" the little Frenchman exclaimed, bowing. "If you need anything, you have only to send your maid to me. *Bonjour, mademoiselle.*" With another bow he was gone. Annabelle turned to close the door, but the cowboy was entering with their trunks. He'd clasped one small one under his arm and loaded one on his broad shoulders. His free hand carried still another. Now he dropped them in the middle of the room.

"That will be fine," Fancy said, stepping forward with the coins to tip him. Her gaze collided with the smoky gray eyes which contemplated her with more than casual interest. He was much taller than she, and she was forced to tip her head back to study his chiseled brown features. High cheekbones and a square chin gave his face a strong character. His shoulders were broad, tapering down to slim hips and impossibly long legs. His clothes were dust covered, his boots muddy. Now that his hands were free, he swept his hat off in a stately gesture of manners. His hair was blue-black, sweeping from his brow and lying straight and thickishly long at his nape. Her gaze met his, and she drew in her breath, feeling a flush creep along her cheeks. His eyes were quicksilver, far too shrewd and arrogant.

Fancy drew herself up and held out the coins. "Here's something for your trouble," she said, haughtily indicating he should take the coins, but he only shook his head.

"It was my pleasure, ma'am." His voice was deep. He nodded to her, then to Annabelle and was gone, his long legs striding from the room before Fancy could recover enough to insist. She stared at the coins in her hand, then impatiently threw them into her bag.

"If he has no need of money, then I have," she said crossly.

"Are we low on money?" Annabelle asked, turning from her task of unpacking the dainty gowns and petticoats they'd brought, part of the trousseau Coop Fletcher had so thoughtfully provided.

Fancy nodded. "If Mr. Fletcher doesn't put in an appearance soon, Annabelle, I'm not sure how we'll pay for our rooms here."

"He'll turn up," Annabelle said. "Just you wait and see. Didn't he make arrangements for this nice room and a hot bath?"

"He did, indeed," Fancy said, feeling better at Annabelle's reminder. "And I intend to take full advantage of his largesse before it disappears as the elusive Mr. Fletcher has done." Quickly she undressed and slipped into the hot water. Nothing had felt so heavenly. She sluiced away the dust of travel from skin and hair and rose from her bath feeling renewed. When Annabelle had taken her bath, the two women lolled across the bed discussing the as yet unseen Coop Fletcher.

"Maybe that man too ugly t'show himse'f t'yo'," Annabelle speculated.

"Maybe that's it," Fancy replied. "Did you see anyone who looked hideously scarred or marked?" Annabelle shook her head. "Maybe he was watching us from some hiding place." The two women stared at each other in sudden apprehension. What manner of man was this Coop Fletcher?

A sharp knock on the door brought a squeak of terror from Annabelle, and both girls jumped, their eyes going wide.

"W—Who is it?" Fancy called.

"*C'est moi, Monsieur Dubois,*" came the answer. "I have a message from Monsieur Fletcher."

"Monsieur Fletcher? Has he been here?" Fancy called, rising from the bed and pressing her ear to the door panel so she might hear better.

"*Oui, mademoiselle.* He does not wish to disturb you, so he leaves a message, *n'est pas.*"

Fancy sighed deeply before enquiring about the message.

"Monsieur Fletcher says he will dine with you at six in the hotel dining room, *s'il vois plait.*"

"Yes, all right. I'll be there," she answered and leaned

against the door until the little Frenchman's footsteps disappeared down the hall, then slowly she turned to Annabelle. "Tonight, at six in the hotel dining room," she whispered. "He can't be so bad if he's accustomed to dining in such an establishment."

Annabelle sprang from the bed. "Yo' can wear yo'r blue and cream silk, and I'll weave ribbons through yo' hair." Nervously, Fancy dressed for her first meeting with Coop Fletcher. Suddenly she felt anxious for what he might say when she told him she had no intentions of marrying him. She'd taken his money and spent it. If only she could offer to pay him back. By the time she was dressed in the elegant gown with its wide rows of creamy lace cascading from a bustle she was a nervous wreck and could hardly hold still for Annabelle to arrange her rich golden tresses in an elaborate array of curls and waterfall chignon. The heavy gold loops of hair were twined with satin ribbons of pale blue and cream. At last Annabelle stood back and surveyed her handiwork.

"Umm-uh, Miss Fancy, yo' look like an angel. That Mr. Coop Fletcher sho' goin' t'be sorry yo' ain't goin' t'marry him."

"Let's hope he takes the news like a gentleman," Fancy said and, pinching her cheeks to bring up the color, cast a last approving glance at herself in the mirror. She looked her best tonight, and she wished she really were a young bride going down to meet the man she loved, an attractive, virile man. For some reason she thought of the handsome cowboy who'd brought up her bags. Someone as handsome as he, she thought, but as rich as Coop Fletcher had claimed to be. Sighing with regret that appearances were seldom as they were presented, she waved good-bye to Annabelle and left her room.

Standing at the top of the stairs, she looked down on the people milling in the lobby. Which one of those men was Coop Fletcher? Which one had come tonight, expecting to claim her hand in marriage? Was it the short, stocky gentleman in the mismatched suit coat and shiny pants? No, he

looked like a whiskey salesman. Perhaps he was one of the
white-haired men who looked like bankers. No, well-
dressed ladies joined them and were escorted into the dining room beyond. In one corner sat a wizened old man in
rough range attire, cracked boots, and dirty shirt. His beard
was unkempt and tobacco stained. Even as she watched, he
worked his lips and spat at a bronze spittoon, striking its
fluted side with a spirited ping. Glancing up, he caught her
gaze and winked triumphantly before shoving himself to his
feet. Fancy's heart sank.

Her desperate sweeping gaze sought out Monsieur
Dubois and settled instead on the tall figure standing at the
hotel counter. His sleek black head towered over the other
men in the room. His back was to her, but her heart began
to beat faster as if she were looking at someone she should
recognize. Some premonition should have warned her,
should have prepared her.

Monsieur Dubois glanced up. *"Regardez, c'est ici."* His
exclamation caused the tall man to turn toward the stairs,
and now Fancy saw his lean tanned cheeks, the now familiar mocking slant of a smile, the bold silvery eyes that saw
her too clearly and robbed her of her breath. The cowboy
who'd brought up their luggage came to the bottom of the
stairs and gazed up at her, his teeth flashing white against
his deeply tanned skin, his eyes glittering with approval. He
was dressed in a white shirt and black string tie. His suit
coat was of some fine, dark material, well-cut to his broad
shoulders. His boots gleamed. He was dark smiles and
bright glances, shadow and substance, thunder and lightning.

Her breath caught in her throat as she began the descent.
He said not a word, letting his expression show his appreciation for her beauty. She was unaware that the talk in the
room had fallen silent as men and women watched this
meeting between Coop Fletcher and his bride-to-be. When
she'd reached the bottom step, she stopped, her eyes level
with his. She felt the warmth of him, it burned her skin
from a foot away. It seared her soul for eternity.

"Why didn't you tell me?" she said breathlessly.

"I should have," he answered, and his voice was deep and full as she remembered it.

"Monsieur Dubois—"

"Was warned to silence. I wanted a chance to look you over first. I could hardly believe a good-looking woman like you would travel so far to marry a man she'd never met." His words were blunt. His smile was devastatingly charming. She was torn between anger and relief.

She glanced away, drawing a tentative breath. His words were easy, no stuttering, self-conscious cowboy this, no half-breed savage. She brought her gaze back to him, puzzlement showing in her green eyes. He had taken her hand, she wasn't sure when, and now she felt the strong brown fingers entwining with hers.

"Is something amiss, Miss Bourne?" he asked.

"Something someone said about you. It's nothing. They must have been mistaken." She glanced beyond his shoulder at the curious faces that openly watched them. "Could we go somewhere more private?" she stammered, and he seemed at last to focus his attention on something other than her.

"They were as anxious to see my new bride as I," he said, tucking her hand into his elbow and leading her toward the dining room. "Here in Elizabethtown, everyone knows everyone's business. Monsieur Dubois, we'll have your finest table, please."

"*Certainment*, right this way." The little Frenchman ushered them through the elegant dining room to a curtained alcove. Coop Fletcher held the chair until she was seated, then ordered a bottle of champagne. Sprawling in a chair across from her, he fixed her with his bright gaze, his glance lingering as it roved over her face and shoulders. Fancy flushed and looked away, sorry now they were seated in such a private corner.

"Forgive me for staring," he said, noting her unease. "I'm still not accustomed to my beautiful bride-to-be. Tell me something of yourself. Travis Wheeler's note wasn't exactly informative. He told me nothing of your background."

"Nothing?" Fancy could only stare at a loss for words. She had been so sure she would tell him at once that she didn't want to marry him, she'd concocted no story for him. Now she sat, dumbfounded as much by her reaction to this overpowering man as by his request. Coop was patient. He stretched his long legs to one side and waited, his expression expectant, his smile encouraging.

"I—I hardly know how to begin," she answered, playing for time.

"Begin with your parents. I'm surprised they'd allow a pretty young filly like you to travel all the way out here to marry someone they don't know."

"I—my parents are dead. Besides, I had my maid."

"Little help against the kind of malcontents we get out here, ma'am. But never mind, you're here and safe. You have me to protect you now." His smile was meant to be reassuring, but again she sensed the arrogant self-assurance of the man. Though handsome as any girl might wish for and expensively attired, she sensed some rough edges to Coop Fletcher. His gray eyes flickered across her features, measuring her against a yardstick she was as yet unfamiliar with. The silver gleam in those eyes and his words reassured her he was not disappointed in her, but she saw something else, a wariness that said he was reserving commitment. Well, that was all right. She wasn't here to make a commitment, but to break one.

"Mr. Fletcher, you've been most kind, the accommodations and all," she began hesitantly.

"I wanted the best for my bride," he said with obvious pride. He leaned back in his chair and took out a slim cheroot. Without asking her permission, he lit it and drew deeply, seeming to relax a little now that he had something familiar to do. Beneath that arrogance, he was as nervous and uncertain as she. Fancy felt better, discovering that. She was willing to gamble that Coop Fletcher didn't often reveal such things about himself.

"Let's talk frankly," he said now, leaning across the table. She caught a whiff of his smoke and coughed gently. He seemed not to notice. "I don't know why a woman of your looks and caliber came all the way out here in answer to my letter, but I've made a fairer bargain than I'd thought I would."

Anger flooded Fancy. "I beg your pardon," she began.

"I'm sorry if I've offended you with my straight talk," he cut off her sputter of indignation. "It's the way we are out here, and I don't really know any other manner. Besides, I figure we can get the business end of this behind us and concentrate on getting to know each other." His eyes narrowed as he studied the array of emotions crossing her flawless features. He noted the flush on her cheeks and the sweep of golden eyelashes as she demurely lowered her gaze.

He'd hardly been able to believe she was his when she stepped off the stage. After depositing her luggage, he'd gone for a ride to think about things. The thought of having a wife had begun to sound agreeable again. He'd come tonight to see if he'd dreamed her. He'd thought his heart would stop beating as she made her way down the stairs straight to him as if she knew she belonged to him. Now he sat affecting a nonchalance he didn't feel while he studied her from beneath his lashes.

Her skin was pale, honey kissed, her hair rich as the Colorado gold they dug from the mountains. Her nose dainty, her mouth, ah, there was the true beauty of her, the lush, pouty lips that invited a man's kiss. Then the golden lashes swept upward, the green, gold-flecked eyes met his head on, and he forgot his name and forgot to breathe. He felt his chest tighten and his groin begin to ache.

For one mad moment, he thought of snatching her up and carrying her off to his ranch tonight. He'd never felt such a raging desire for a woman. But she wasn't just any woman, he reminded himself. She was a lady, a proper eastern lady, and tomorrow she would become his wife, if he wanted her. He had a lifetime ahead to slake his need with her, but he would do nothing to dishonor her.

A need to protect rose in him, pushing aside for the moment the fierce lust she'd aroused. When a waiter brought the chilled champagne, he watched as she nervously fiddled with the lace of her bodice, then gripped her hands in her lap as if to stop their trembling. She was frightened, he realized, and well she might be. She'd endured a long journey to marry a man who was a stranger to her. Wanting to reassure her, he placed his hand palm up on the table between them.

"Give me your hand," he said softly.

"Wha—" Startled, she jerked her head up and contemplated him with green eyes so deep and mysterious they reminded him of the moss agates he'd found once in the hills.

"There's no reason to be afraid," he said soothingly. "Give me your hand, Miss Bourne."

Hesitantly, she placed her slim soft hand in his. It quivered there like the heartbeat of a tiny frightened animal.

"You can call me Fancy," she murmured. "That's what Papa used to call me, and it just kind of stuck."

"Fancy," he tried the name. "It suits you, ma'am."

She smiled, a quivering semblance of a smile, but her eyes were watchful and filled with courage.

"I promise you, Fancy," he said softly, "that you will never regret coming here to be my bride. I will always protect you. You need never fear any man, not even me."

"You are kind," she said, ashamed of her duplicity in the face of his straightforwardness. "I'm afraid I've misled you somewhat."

"In what way?" he asked. "We've hardly spoken to each other. There's much to learn in the days ahead, and although our marriage is to take place tomorrow, I swear I'll give you as much time as you need to be comfortable with me."

Her darting gaze stilled when the import of his words reached through her haze. "We're to be married tomorrow?" she repeated.

Coop nodded. "I figured it wasn't seemly for us to delay too long, ma'am," he said. "Folks might misunderstand about you being a lady and all."

"I can't marry you tomorrow. I don't know you." Fancy could barely speak her pulse was racing so.

Coop leaned across the table and peered into her eyes. "Like I said, ma'am. I'll give you time before we share a bed."

Seeing how troubled she was, he clamped his teeth against his own wishes and nodded. "Don't worry yourself about it, ma'am. Let's get to know each other better. I'll tell you about myself, and then you can tell me something of your own life." His voice was deep and soothing.

Over plates of tolerable beef steaks, he told her many things, of the years he'd spent ramroding for other outfits, of the investments he'd made, the dreams he had for his future and the future of his children. He told her about Elizabethtown and every other mining town he'd seen and how they were changing. He spoke of his hopes and expectations. He told her he'd wanted a lady, a real lady, at his side to represent him with the good folks of Elizabethtown.

"I'm building an empire," he said proudly. "I wanted a wife, a lady, to do justice to that empire."

His words might have seemed braggardly, except for the honest, straightforward way in which they were stated. Staring into his eyes, Fancy saw the years of loneliness this man had endured in his long struggle to overcome obstacles and succeed beyond most men's wildest dreams. He wanted her to be part of his dream. He wanted a lady. She'd never felt like a cheat before, but she did now.

"Tell me all about your life back east," he said, reaching across the table to take her hand again.

Fancy's mind was racing with conflicting emotions. Now was the time to tell him the truth about herself and admit she didn't wish to marry. She should throw herself on his mercy and confess she'd never intended to marry him and beg him to loan her the money to go on to San Francisco. But her thoughts became jumbled at the warm touch of his hand against hers, her resolve melted at one silver-edged glance. What was she to do? she wondered. She'd wished for a handsome bridegroom, one who would love her and care for her. She'd been granted her wish or nearly all of it. If Coop Fletcher did not love her now, she had little doubt she could make him love her, but what of her own feelings? Why this strange lethargy, this welling of emotions like a tide that couldn't be held back? Why did she stutter so before him, like an ingenue about to take her first bow upon the stage? He was handsome, it was true, and kind and— She couldn't remember the other reasons this marriage would be a good step for her. Her senses became enmeshed in the wonder of the silver-gray fire of his glance and the tanned, smooth skin above the stark white shirt collar. Would his brown skin be smooth to her lips? Would it be warm and masculine-scented?

"Tell me what plantation life was like," he urged her.

Fancy gathered her senses. "It was most difficult, especially during the war," she began, spinning her tale as she went along. "M—My father was killed by union soldiers who'd come to pillage our plantation. He fought valiantly, but he was one man against many."

"Go on," he said, gripping her hand firmly. "What was your home like?" So Fancy told him of a plantation she'd visited once. She spoke lovingly of her mother and father and the people who'd served them. She told him of aunts and uncles and cousins that didn't exist, concocting a life that had never been except in a young girl's enchanted expectations when cotton was king and the south seemed invincible.

Coop listened to her light musical voice and let his mind wander to the ranch, picturing Fancy entertaining their friends, picturing Fancy in his bed, warm and receptive.

Her words slowed and stopped altogether, and he saw the dark shadows of weariness beneath her eyes. Rising, he escorted her back to the stairs. More than anything, he wanted to climb those stairs with her and slowly undress her and cradle her rich body against his. Patience, he told himself. One more day and she'll be yours.

"Good night, Fancy," he murmured. When she raised her face to answer, he stooped and planted a light kiss against her soft, pink lips.

She looked startled, her eyes going wide and anxious, so he gave her a quick nod good night and walked away. He didn't think he'd ever done anything so hard in his life. Out on the sidewalk, he paused and drew the cool mountain air deep into his lungs. He thought of the woman he'd left inside. He couldn't get her out of his mind, and that bothered him. He'd wanted a woman suitable to mingle with Elizabethtown's best society, someone he could bear strong sons by, but he had given no thought to feeling anything for her more than gratitude and the respect a man shows a good wife. Fancy Bourne was something else altogether.

Chapter 2

"WHAT AM I going to do Annabelle? I should have told him last night I didn't want to marry him." Fancy paced back and forth across the elegant rug from window to door and back again.

"From what yo' say, that Coop Fletcher one mighty fine lookin' gentleman and mighty persuasive."

"I don't know why I didn't just blurt it out to him. I don't want to marry you. I don't want to marry you." Fancy accented the litany with a slashing sweep of her clenched fist. Her eyes were stormy with confusion, her bosom rose and fell in agitation. Distractedly she paused at the window and peered out.

"People are arriving downstairs," she exclaimed. "You don't suppose they—" She whirled and glared at Annabelle with wide haunted eyes. "They can't be arriving for the wedding."

As if on summons a knock sounded at the door.

"Don't open it," Fancy commanded. "It might be Coop Fletcher." She pressed a fist against her mouth, her eyes stark and melodramatic. Annabelle sighed and shrugged. She'd seen all of Fancy's moods and knew they were expressed more extravagantly than might be by other folks, simply because she'd grown up on the stage.

"If'n it's him, yo' can tell him what yo' want to,"

Annabelle said reasonably and threw open the door. Fancy cringed until she saw the effusive, smiling proprietor.

"Mademoiselle," he exclaimed, stepping into the room. His black eyes took in the bride-to-be, still attired in her morning dress. "Your guests are arriving," he declared reproachfully. "All is in readiness. Everyone is looking forward to this day. Ah, the flowers, the food, the music. *Le Maison Francais* has outdone itself for your wedding. Monsieur Fletcher has spared no expense for his beautiful bride. You must hurry, *ma petite mariee*." Monsieur Dubois paused and looked at Fancy expectantly. She stood as if frozen, her expression too revealing.

"Ah, *mademoiselle, c'est frousse*, how do you say, the jitters, the nerves. Monsieur Fletcher, *c'est homme par des exemples*, a good man. The best catch of ze season. Such a man, *mademoiselle*, even I would desire him." Annabelle giggled, and Fancy couldn't repress a smile.

"Ah, *c'est bon*." Dubois said, pleased he'd lightened her mood. "Now, hurry, hurry. The ceremonies start in one half hour, *n'est pas?*" In a whirlwind he was gone, his short legs carrying him from one part of his hotel to another as he saw to each detail. These Americans, these westerners, they could not get married in style without the likes of him, Henri Dubois. Humming, he hurried to the kitchen to check on the cake. Coop Fletcher had, indeed, ordered the very best, and it was up to Henri Dubois to ensure the quality was representative of his fine hotel.

With the little Frenchman gone, Annabelle and Fancy faced each other.

"What am I to do?" Fancy said. "There are wedding guests downstairs. I can't just hide here in my room."

"Yo' could go down and tell them, they ain't goin' t'be no weddin'," Annabelle offered laconically.

Fancy paced to the window once more and stamped her foot. The memory of Coop Fletcher's face as he spoke of his ranch and the town and all he hoped for the two of them together returned to her. She couldn't shame him in front of his friends. "I have to go through with this," she said at last. "Perhaps later I can explain to him, and he'll understand I only went through it to save him embarrassment."

"I expect that would make him beholdin' t'yo'," Annabelle said, and Fancy wasn't certain if she were serious or making fun of Fancy's indecision.

"Ooh, I've been horrid, haven't I, Annabelle. I was going to trick him from the beginning. It's my own fault I'm in this mess."

"Yes'm, I reckon that's true," Annabelle said flatly.

Fancy's head snapped up, and she whirled to face her maid. "You're no help at all," she accused. She stalked away and came to an abrupt halt. "My God, what will I do? I didn't buy a wedding gown. I didn't think I'd need one. Oh, Annabelle. I can't go down there in front of everyone. They'll know I tricked Coop Fletcher."

Annabelle shook her head wearily. "I been thinkin' 'bout that," she said. "You have that gold silk damask."

"Oh, that won't do," Fancy cried distractedly.

"The underdress is of white satin, and we can use that lace shawl you bought as a veil."

"Do you think it will work?"

"Yo' act like it's the best wedding dress money can buy, and it'll do jus' fine," Annabelle declared. "'Sides, we'll make you so pretty, won't nobody be lookin' at that dress anyhow."

"Hurry, then." Fancy flew to get ready for her wedding to Coop Fletcher, a man she'd known for less than twenty-four hours. She pushed away any thought of what might happen after the wedding. She wanted only to get through these next few hours without anyone knowing her true intentions. She didn't ask herself why it should matter what the people of Elizabethtown thought of her or Coop Fletcher. She was impelled to go through with this wedding for reasons she couldn't understand or explain. And having decided upon the wedding, she set about preparing for it as thoroughly as if it were a premiere performance before Jefferson Davis, himself.

The stairway and lobby had been festooned with flowers, hundreds and hundreds of flowers, some of which she couldn't name. Some were roses and daisies and alyssum. Their scent wafted up to her. Somewhere organ music played. At the top of the stairs, someone thrust a bouquet of pink roses and assorted wildflowers into her hands, and she started the long descent down the stairs. The lobby was filled with smiling strangers who oohed and aahed as she came into view. She knew the pale gold damask set off her coloring and the white satin underskirt whispered silkily with each movement. Annabelle had pinned tiny nosegays into her hair before attaching the lace shawl. It fluttered behind her as gossamer and surreal as the scene below.

Panic beset Fancy. This was not a play, a performance that would end when the curtain went down. This was for real. She felt at odds as if she'd wandered into the wrong play. This was not Fancy Bourne, daughter of Adele and Montgomery Bourne. She was a stranger to herself engaging in a role never meant for her.

Then her frantic glance met the calm smoky gaze of Coop Fletcher. He stood at the foot of the stairs as before, his head thrown back, his handsome face turned toward her, his teeth flashing white against his tanned skin. Her trembling stilled, her fears diminished, and without breaking eye contact, she descended the stairs. She was vaguely aware of Annabelle taking her place halfway down the stairs so she might watch the wedding. Then Coop took her hand, and she thought of nothing else.

His touch was cool and steady at her elbow, his glance warm and encouraging. The organ music crescendoed as they walked through the aisle of people and entered the ballroom. At one end a man in a dark coat holding a Bible stood calmly waiting for them. Like one sleepwalking, Fancy moved forward. The only steady, sure thing in all the room was the man to whose arm she clung. He stood beside her, tall and sturdy like one of the mountain peaks rearing toward the sky, dauntless, his strength unchallenged by any man present.

Fancy shivered while the words swirled around her.
Coop felt the tiny tremor and tucked her hand against his
heart, silently vowing to her the same promise he'd given
her the night before. He was her protector, her husband.
She need have no fear from any man, not even him. Fancy
remembered his words and grew easy in her mind. Her answer to the preacher's query was firm as she said "I do."
Then it was over. She could hear the collective sigh of the
strangers behind her as if they'd all held their breath until
the preacher had pronounced them man and wife.

"You may kiss the bride," the clergyman solemnly in-
toned, and Coop turned to Fancy expectantly. She thought
of the night before as she'd stood on the bottom step after
dinner. She'd known then that he desired her, that he
wanted to kiss her, but he'd refrained and she'd been grateful, but now she knew an embrace was inevitable, was expected by those looking on.

Slowly she raised her face toward him, her glazed eyes
taking in the slant and line of his features close up. He even
looked like he'd been hewn from the mountain granite, she
thought, and then his lips claimed hers, light and undemand-
ing but explosive in their power to reach her. She gasped and
drew back, staring into his smoldering gray eyes. She felt the
heat of her own emotions sweep into her cheeks and brow,
but there was no chance to examine her response, for the
guests had stepped forward to greet her and press congratulations upon them.

Coop smiled good-naturedly, introducing faces that
meant little to her, laughing at the teasing remarks, remind-
ing people to partake of food and wine. A china plate of
food was brought to her, but she couldn't eat. The organ
music was replaced by a fiddle and guitar, and the tunes
were lilting, inviting people to tap a toe or break out in an
outright dance. Some did, while some of the dowagers settled in chairs around the room to gossip about the new ad-
dition to their community and watch the livelier guests
dance.

"I'm so sorry you couldn't have waited to meet my sister," a voice said at Fancy's elbow and pinning a smile on her face, she turned to greet still another guest. "She's quite lovely and a perfect lady," a middle-aged woman was saying to Coop.

"Then I expect she'll look forward to meeting my bride," Coop said. "They'll have much in common."

The woman's stiff smile faded, and without bothering to speak to Fancy she flounced away.

"Who was that woman?" Fancy asked faintly.

"Mrs. Maida Robinson," Coop explained. "Her husband owns some of the ore mills surrounding the town."

"He sounds like he might be one of those proper citizens you mentioned last night."

Coop laughed, his glance admiring. "You're quick," he said. "Once you get to know Maida, she's not so bad, kind of snobbish like but friendly once she's accepted you."

"What if I choose not to accept her?" Fancy muttered, and when Coop looked at her sharply, clamped her lips together. After all, she wasn't planning on staying here in this town. She was going to leave as soon as she reasonably could.

Fancy shook hand after hand, nodded, smiled, and even allowed herself to be whirled around the floor until she was breathless and Coop had to come and claim her for a slow waltz. She moved, willowy and suppliant in his arms, yet he sensed some part of her was untouched by all that was happening. She was a lady, more sensitive than the rough and rowdy women he'd met in the saloons and whore-houses of the mining camps. He'd have to give her time to adjust to her new surroundings.

"Are you tired?" he asked, breaking through her quiet reserve.

"No, I—perhaps if we could go someplace quiet to talk."

"Coop, by gum, we didn't think you'd actually do it. The boys were bettin' down at the saloon that you'd back out, till this little filly come to town. So this is the little lady that came all the way from back east to hitch up with you. You're mighty pretty, ma'am."

Fancy hid her disappointment that yet another guest had thrust himself forward, just when she'd worked up the courage to take Coop aside and tell him this had all been a dreadful mistake.

"Chet Dunham at your service, ma'am. I've known Coop here since he was a boy, and you couldn't have got a better man, no sir." He clamped Coop on the back so hard Fancy expected her new husband to be sent to his knees, but Coop braced up and returned Chet Dunham's exuberant greeting.

"I wasn't certain you'd make it," he said with obvious delight. His smile was wide and almost boyish, a surprising change in his stern features. His eyes were bright with laughter and affection as he shook hands with Chet.

"The things I could tell you about this boy," Chet said to Fancy. "I don't believe I caught your name, ma'am," the rough-hewn man inquired, holding out a broad callused hand.

"Fancy Bourne," she replied, placing her hand in his. She'd expected him to carry it to his lips in a gallant gesture of respect, but he shook it vigorously, nearly snapping her wrist.

"Fancy Fletcher now, ma'am," he reminded her. "Fancy lady, Coop. Yes, sir, she's a fancy lady." He continued to shake her hand as he gazed at her with open admiration.

"Have a care with the poor girl," a voice scolded from behind him and an older woman pushed forward. She was somewhat stooped about the shoulders, but she elbowed her way past the towering men and smiled at Fancy.

"You got yourself a real beauty, Coop," she said approvingly and thrust out a wrinkled brown hand. "Geraldine Russell," she said brusquely. "You can call me Ma Russell, if you want. Every man, woman, and child west of Denver does. If you don't want to, then call me Geraldine."

"I'm pleased to meet you," Fancy said, tentatively taking the old woman's hand and shaking it gently. She'd never get used to the directness of these people.

"When did you get here, child?"

"Yesterday," Fancy replied.

"And Coop rushed you into a marriage today. He should have postponed it a day or two. No wonder you look fair ready to swoon. Here, Coop. You take this child and find a seat for her, then bring her a drink, none of that highfalutin sherry these women have taken to sippin', but a good stout shot of whiskey. She needs to get the blood runnin' through her veins again."

At Geraldine's words, Coop stepped forward, his brow furrowed in a frown of concern. "I'm sorry. Are you feeling faint?" he inquired.

"No, I'm just a little tired," Fancy answered, aware suddenly she'd been standing for hours without respite. Suddenly awkward in the face of female complaints, Coop led her to a chair and motioned a waiter forward. A glass of whiskey was pressed to her lips, and Fancy, unaware of how close she'd been to swooning, sipped, coughed, and sipped again as ordered by both Coop and Geraldine.

"There, her color's comin' back," Geraldine said, shaking her head. Her gray curls bobbed. She threw aside her dull shawl and perched on the settee beside Fancy. "Don't try to talk. Just lean back and relax a bit," she ordered, and Fancy gratefully complied. From beneath lowered lashes she studied the old woman. Although her speech and movements were quick, her faded blue eyes and weathered face revealed her years. She was dressed in a gown of fine cloth that had been in fashion nearly ten years before. Yet so formidable was her countenance that no one would dare dismiss her as insignificant.

"Coop, you go on and talk minin' and mule teams with your friends for a spell, and I'll set with Fancy."

"Are you all right?" he asked anxiously, and when Fancy nodded he turned away with obvious relief.

"Just like a man," Geraldine snorted. "They don't know what to do with themselves if their womenfolk are not up on their feet and doin' for 'em. They can live in the bush for months on end, nurse a calf back to health as gentle as a mother with her babe, but let a woman get sick, and they turn all pale and scared of us." She stopped talking then and studied Fancy.

"Tell me about yourself," she said abruptly. "Ain't many quality ladies of your caliber travel all this way just to marry a man. You got some reason you couldn't stay back east there where you was?" The question was asked with a no-nonsense air. Fancy sensed it wasn't meant to insult.

"My—My father lost our plantation and lands in the war. Then he was killed by northern soldiers, and I, well I just had no reason to stay back there. When I heard of Mr. Fletcher's offer, I decided to come out west and start all over."

"There's many a folks have done that, child, even with less prospects than you. This is the place for startin' a new life. You've got a fine man. He's one of the strongest, bravest men I know, and I reckon there ain't a man here what could bring him down, but a woman now, that might be a bit different, if you get my drift."

Fancy stared at her in bewilderment.

"Well, never you mind," Geraldine said. "You just give Coop some time to get used to how to treat a lady and give yourself time to get to know him, and everything'll work out fine. You're both healthy, good-looking young people." She nodded in satisfaction.

"Have you met Mary Peabody?" she continued when a woman approached.

"Yes, I met Mrs. Peabody earlier in the reception line," Fancy said, grateful Gerry had repeated the name.

"My dear, it's time to cut the cake," Mary Peabody said gently, and Fancy was pulled to her feet and rushed off to another whirl of events. Cakes were cut, toasts given, food eaten, presents opened, and more dances performed with more men than she cared to remember, and when it was done and everyone bid them good-bye, Fancy couldn't remember the names of any guests except Geraldine Russell and Chet Dunham.

"That's all you need remember for now," Coop said when she commented of such to him. "They're the ones who mean the most to me." Something about his simple words touched Fancy. Chet had said he'd known Coop since he was a boy, and she found herself wondering what he must have been like as a child. Were his eyes that same changeable gray, was his dark hair that sleek and thick? Had he laughed more often as a child or been somber and quiet as he was now?

"Monsieur Fletcher, the wedding, *c'est magnifique, n'est pas?*" Monsieur Dubois asked, making himself known now that the guests had departed.

"It was everything I asked for," Coop said, pulling out a thick roll of bills and peeling off several. Fancy wasn't sure whose eyes bulged more, hers or Monsieur Dubois's. "Give these to your help, and tell them how much we appreciate the job they did for us."

"*Oui, merci beaucoup, monsieur. C'est tres genereux.*"

"It's well deserved, Dubois. Thank you again."

The little Frenchman hurried away. Fancy looked at the rough rancher and miner who was now her husband.

"He's right. That was most generous of you," she said softly.

Coop shrugged. "I like to reward the people who work well for me."

"And those who don't?"

His gaze met hers, and for the first time she felt the uncompromising nature of the man.

"I get rid of them," he said quietly.

It wasn't an encouraging sign for her and what she was about to do, but she couldn't carry this farce any further. He had taken her arm and even now guided her up the stairs toward her room. Did he expect to share the room with her this very night? Did he expect to share her bed? The pulse beat in her throat, making it hard for her to swallow.

"Could we take a moment and talk?" she asked breathlessly, pausing at the top of the stairs. He studied her face in the lamplight and with a nod of acquiescence guided her toward a settee which was placed in one secluded corner.

When they were both seated he leaned back, one long arm lying casually along the settee back, his long legs stretched before him.

"Were you pleased with your wedding, Mrs. Fletcher?" he asked, and one large brown hand played with the curls above her ears. Involuntarily, Fancy pulled away, and a rich golden strand caught against his finger and pulled loose. He carried it to his lips before she shrugged away. Her startled gaze met his, then the golden lashes swept downward, the pouty lips set in a determined line, and he sighed, knowing, despite his limited experience with real ladies, that he must listen whether he was inclined to or not.

"You haven't said if the reception was satisfactory. I suppose I should have waited and consulted you on these matters. Ladies may have certain ideas on how they want such things done, but I was ever aware of your position as an unmarried lady in t—"

"The ceremony was truly wonderful," Fancy interrupted, "except that—"

"Yes, except what?" he prompted when her hesitation lasted more than a moment.

"Except that it was all wrong," she wailed, twisting her hands in her lap. Coop sat stunned. He'd ordered the best of everything and closed his mind to the outrageous costs of flowers, wine, and food. He'd fumed and fussed over such matters as pâtés and finger sandwiches and seating for ladies and even sent back east for the biggest diamond wedding ring he could buy. It rested even now on her slender finger, winking and twinkling up at him as if in mockery for his buffoon behavior. And now she was unhappy? Coop swallowed hard, set straight up on the settee, and counted to ten. When he was finished and she still sat with her slim shoulders bowed and trembling in unhappiness, he counted to ten again. Finally when he was sure he could manage a calm tone, he spoke to her.

"If it wasn't all that you wanted, we'll do it again," he said, "and this time you can plan everything the way you want."

"Oh, no!" she cried, raising her tearful eyes to meet his, and any tinge of resentment he might have harbored against her for not liking his wedding melted in the brilliant green and gold fire of her eyes. His hands shook as they reached for her. He took hold of her shoulders, meaning to pull her against him and ravish that sweet pink mouth that had tantalized him all day, but she placed her slender hands on his chest and gazed up at him with an expression that would have melted the heart of Zeus on his mighty mountain.

"You've been more than generous," she said, hiccuping, "and I—I'm afraid I've misled you terribly. I tried to tell you last night, but—but I couldn't. And then today with the wedding and all those people arriving, I just couldn't embarrass you like that."

"What in God's name are you talking about?" Coop thundered, lost in the quick, light notes of her lament. Fancy jumped and leaned away from him.

"Well, it isn't going to help if you shout at me," she said accusingly.

Coop took a deep breath. "I'm sorry," he said in a conciliatory tone. "I don't understand what you're trying to tell me."

"I've been trying to explain, if you'll just listen," Fancy began again. "I know I haven't been fair to you and you've been so generous with the wedding and the flowers and—and this ring and all, but—"

"Just spit it out," he growled, feeling alarmed now.

"I can't marry you," she gasped and fell silent. Coop sat staring at her a full minute, trying to understand what she'd said and why.

"We already are married," he explained finally, careful to keep his voice low and reasonable.

"Yes, we are, but we aren't really," she said as if it made perfect sense.

"We aren't really?"

"Not until we consummate the marriage, and of course that can't possibly happen, Mr. Fletcher, because I never meant to be your wife. I came west on your money because

I had no place else to go, and I thought if I came here I could start over again and that if—if you were a kind man you might loan me the money to go on to San Francisco, and there I could get a job and send your money back to you, every penny—"

"Stop!" His brows were pulled low over his eyes. Gray-silver ice sliced through her soul so she couldn't meet his gaze.

"I'm sorry," she said meekly.

"You had no intentions of marrying me?"

"I—I—no."

"Yet you took my money under false pretenses."

"I know I sound terrible, Mr. Fletcher, and I do hope you'll forgive me."

"Do you realize what you've done is fraud? You could be put in jail for this."

"Oh, no, not jail. I—I mean I'm not a criminal. I—I'm not. It's just that after we lost the plantation and with my father dead and all, I didn't know what to do." She fell back on her lies. "I didn't even have money for food." That wasn't a lie anyway.

His anger faded at her admission. He thought of her alone and hungry with no money. No wonder she'd accepted his proposal. He was touched by the courage it took for her to travel so far to an unknown husband. That protective side of his enlarged. He knew what it was like to be alone and hungry and frightened. One hand clamped her shoulder gently, and sensing his shift in mood, she gazed up at him.

"I didn't understand what you've gone through," he said softly. "Forget what I said about jail."

"Oh, thank you," Fancy cried, a smile of relief lighting her features. Now if she could convince him to loan her the money to go on to San Francisco.

"You're my wife, and although you may not love me now, we'll grow to love each other. I can understand that you feel some concern over our marriage, but as I told you last night, I won't force myself upon you. I'll wait until you're ready to become my wife in all ways."

"What if that never happens?" she asked in dismay, seeing her plans once again thwarted. Although she could already feel her body responding to the virile masculinity of the man seated next to her, she had no wish to be married to him.

He paused for a long moment and finally sighed. "If we should find we're not compatible, I'll pay for your passage to wherever you wish to go and give you money to live on for a time."

"Couldn't you do that now?" Fancy cried impatiently.

Coop regarded her hopeful expression and slowly shook his head. "All my friends in Elizabethtown have seen us married. I'd be hell-bent to explain why you lit out again on the very next stage." Actually, he found he cared less what they'd say as he might have otherwise. He didn't want her to leave. "Since you've used my money to come here, seems to me you owe me at least a halfway attempt to make our marriage work."

"And if it doesn't?"

"Do you find me so unattractive as a husband, Fancy?" he asked softly. His silver-edged gaze held hers, mocking, compelling, warmly disturbing.

"It's not that, I mean," she blushed and looked away, but he saw the heat in her cheeks, the shifting emotions in her green-gold eyes, and he felt elation.

"You must promise to give our marriage a try," he said. His tone sent shivers through her.

"What would that entail?" she asked.

"You will come to my ranch, act as my hostess. It won't be an unpleasant task for you, I assure you."

Fancy thought of his ranch and of the things he'd ask of her. His request was not unreasonable, and she owed him that much at least.

"You agree not to consummate our marriage unless I'm fully in agreement?" she hedged.

"Agreed," he said. "Only with your consent."

"What if I don't consent?"

"We've made a business agreement between us, Fancy. Never doubt that I'm a man of my word."

"No, of course not." She hesitated, feeling trapped and elated at the same time. This hadn't gone the way she'd planned, but in the face of his generosity she must make some concessions herself. Making up her mind she held out her hand.

"Agreed," she said firmly. Coop took her small hand in his, but instead of shaking it as she'd intended, he brought it to his mouth. She felt the hot smoothness of his lips against her skin, and a tremor raced through her. Alarm made her jump to her feet.

"You promised," she said in some agitation.

"I've promised not to force the consummation of this marriage," he answered, rising, "and I will keep it, but I didn't promise not to be attentive and loving to my new wife."

"Shall we set a period of time?" Fancy asked, suddenly nervous with this arrangement. "We don't want this to go on indefinitely."

"One year," he said promptly, his expression implacable.

"A year?" she faltered. A whole year. The time seemed interminable, but he'd been more than generous. It would go quickly. She could endure it if it meant she would have the funds to travel where she wished and start anew.

"One year," she agreed with some misgivings and turned toward her room. A new thought gave her pause, and she faced him again. "One thing more I meant to ask you, Mr. Fletcher."

"Coop," he corrected. She nodded in acquiescence.

"Tell me what a half-breed is here in your country." Her question had been innocent, only a way of better understanding those things she'd seen and heard, but its affect upon her new husband was stunning. He moved like a viper, striking before she could draw a breath, his hands gripping her shoulders cruelly, his face contorted with anger.

"Where did you hear that?" he grated.

"You're hurting me," she cried. His clasp on her loosened only a little. His enraged gaze pinned her. Thunder and lightning, she thought again, remembering that first impression she'd had of Coop Fletcher, smiling and waiting for her last night. He'd seemed gentle and kind then. But now he was frightening, and she had no idea what she'd done to bring about this change in him.

"Where did you hear this?" he demanded again.

"On—on the stagecoach. A—A m—man said you were a half-breed."

"What else did he say?" He was unrelenting.

"Th—That if he had his way you would be on a reservation with the rest of the m—these are his words, not mine—murdering devils."

"Who was this man?" His fingers no longer cut into her tender flesh. His hold on her could have been shrugged aside, but his anger still held her attentive.

"I—I can't remember his name," she whispered, and it was true, she couldn't. Too much had happened in the past few days, and her mind was shutting down, demanding rest and surcease from the uncertainty and tension of the past weeks.

Coop released her and turned toward the stairs. Gone was the gentle suitor wooing his lady. He was a grim, purposeful man who had no time for the anxieties of a mere woman. Fancy sensed his dismissal of her and felt a small thrill of anger. Daringly she stepped forward and leaned over the banister.

"Is what the man said true?" she demanded taking in his thick black hair and deeply tanned skin. "Are you a half-breed?"

He turned on her then, his expression almost savage, so she drew back, her eyes wide as if she'd just confronted an untamed animal.

"Is this the reason you couldn't stay married to me?" he demanded.

Slowly, she shook her head in denial. His expression relaxed a little then as if he believed her and liked her better for it.

"My mother was a half-breed," he said, wearily pushing back the blue-black locks that had fallen across his wide brow. "She was a prostitute in the white man's mining camps. My father was a miner, a man committed to tearing gold from the earth. He was killed in a drunken brawl when I was ten. My mother went back to her people when I was twelve. She didn't ask me to go with her. She just left one day, and I never saw her again." His voice held pain and bitterness. His shoulders slumped. Fancy thought of the young boy left alone in a rough mining camp, abandoned by his mother. How had he survived? Sympathy made her reach out to him, but her hand had barely settled on his shoulder when he shrugged it away.

"We've made a bargain, madam," he said bleakly. "A business opportunity, and it doesn't include pity. I've always paid for everything I've ever had in life. I'm not offended that I must pay to have a lady as my wife. I pay well, and I expect the best. You have one year in which to prove your worth, if you wish any more of my money." He stalked down the stairs.

"You promised to give me time. You said you wouldn't force yourself on me," Fancy reminded him, leaning over the railing as if to reach him.

He whirled again, and his features were hard set, his expression unyielding. "I'll give you time," he said, "but make no mistake, fancy lady, I intend to have my money's worth."

He left then, stalking away into the dark shadows of the hotel lobby and out into the night. Fancy slumped against the railing, staring down into the lobby. Had she made a pact with the devil himself? Twice she'd descended those stairs to go to Coop Fletcher, and each time he'd greeted her gently and with restraint, but tonight she'd seen the dark side of him. She shuddered to think which one she must appease in the year ahead.

Chapter 3

*F*ANCY WOKE SLOWLY, for a moment believing herself back in Alabama, and a pall of anxiety fell over her. She must find some way to keep the troupe going. Restlessly she turned her head, opened her eyes, and through a silky screen of golden hair tried to focus on the room around her. A noise, loud and gruff, erupted from the bed beside her, and she turned back. A man's dark head lay on the other pillow, his large, lanky body, fully dressed, sprawled across the comforter. Fancy's high-pitched scream brought a loud snort and a surcease of the noise that had wakened her. The man sat up, moaning and grabbing his head as if in sudden pain.

Fancy screamed again, leaping out of bed. Annabelle jumped up from the cot on the other side of the room and ran to throw her arms around Fancy, her wails adding to the commotion. The man on the bed sat up, his face a thundercloud.

"Shut up!" he growled above their screams, and both women fell silent. Fancy pressed her fingertips to her lips to still their sudden trembling. "What in tarnation is all this noise?" Coop Fletcher demanded, getting out of bed. He staggered and fell back, once again clasping his head. Balefully, he glared at them. "Well?"

"I—I thought you were a—a stranger," Fancy stammered, then squared her shoulders. "What were you doing in my room? You promised."

"I promised not to violate your virginal womanhood without your consent," he muttered, "but I didn't promise to sleep outside in the hallway so the whole dang town can know what a bad bargain I made."

"A bad bargain?" Fancy sputtered. "You got the best of the bargain between us, Mr. Fletcher. If it's not to your liking, we can renegotiate. I'd be happy to leave."

He raised his head and glared at her. He was unshaven, his eyes were red-rimmed, and his breath reeked of whiskey all the way across the room. She felt no sympathy for him.

"We made a bargain," he muttered, reaching for his boots. "We're sticking to it."

"Only if you promise never to come into my room uninvited again," Fancy stipulated, standing with her chin stubbornly high, her arms crossed over her breasts.

Coop looked at the rebellious girl with the swirl of honey gold hair covering one shoulder and didn't know whether to spank her or laugh at her. Fancy's curvaceous figure was cleanly outlined in the light from the window. Coop liked what he saw and almost grinned. Almost. One look at her expression told him he'd better not.

"It won't happen again," he vowed grudgingly. "I have no care to sleep with a howling banshee."

"I wouldn't have howled if you hadn't been in my bed," she snapped implacably.

"And I wouldn't have been in your bed if I'd had a choice," he snapped back. He jumped to his feet and faced her, a fierce expression on his face. Fancy was unintimidated. He had not honored the rules laid down in their agreement.

Annabelle had crept back to her pallet and huddled there watching the two of them. Like two bantam roosters fightin' over nothin', she thought.

"Coming into my bed is not one of your choices, Mr. Fletcher," Fancy reminded him. "You agreed!"

"All right. I know I agreed. And your bed and person shall remain as pure and untouched as the first driven snowfall from this moment on. When we reach the ranch, you'll have your own room, and the next time we come to town, I'll see to it that we have two rooms."

His words mollified Fancy somewhat. "Thank you," she said quietly. Then another thought struck her. "When are we going to your ranch?"

Coop had crossed to the window and stood rubbing his neck. Now he glanced back at her. "We leave as soon as you're packed and ready. When will that be?"

"An hour or so, I suppose. Look here, will you come away from that window? What will people think?"

He gave her a quizzical look, one black eyebrow rising slightly. "They'll think Coop Fletcher just spent his wedding night in his beautiful bride's bed," he snapped, crossing the room in long strides to take up his suit coat. "I have some business at the bank. I'll have a buckboard brought around in an hour for your trunks and things." Without a backward glance he left the room.

Fancy and Annabelle looked at each other in silence. Finally the maid shook her head. "Ummm, un. That's some man yo' got hold of," she observed. "I don't think he can be led 'round by the nose the way yo' done them boys back in Alabama."

"We made an agreement to stay married for one year," Fancy said, "one year only. After that he'll give me the money to go to San Francisco."

"He do that for just one year o' yo'r time, and he can't even share yo'r bed?" Annabelle exclaimed. "Maybe he's not the man I thought he was."

"Oh, Annabelle. Who's side are you on anyway? Help me get packed. God only knows how far away his ranch is or what we'll find when we get there."

An hour later, true to his word, Coop was waiting below with a small replica of the stagecoach that had brought them from Denver. Monsieur Dubois sent up a stout boy to carry down their trunks and profusely bid the new Mrs.

Coop Fletcher good-bye. Coop cut through the fuss of departure, and in little time they were on their way, rolling out of the rough little town. People along the way waved as they passed. Their elaborate wedding had made an impression on the scions of Elizabethtown.

"I didn't have time to see much of the town," Fancy remarked, peering out the window at the two-story frame houses with lace curtains at their windows. Her gaze fell on Coop Fletcher seated on a sleek black stallion. The powerful spirited animal seemed but an extension of the man. When he caught her glance, he touched the brim of his hat, his smile mocking, his silver-gray eyes inscrutable, maddingly unfathomable. He was a strange, enigmatic man, this husband of hers, and she felt the lure of a challenge. Perhaps it would be amusing to peel away those protective layers and discover more about Coop Fletcher.

The first discovery was his ranch. The trail had climbed for an hour out of Elizabethtown, then rushed downhill before leveling out in a lovely green valley that stretched away for some distance. Mountain peaks rimmed the high flat plateau to the west, but to the east the foothills gave way to flat dun-colored prairie land.

"What's out there?" she called when Coop drew near the coach.

"Texas," he answered. "New Mexico and miles of prairie and deserts and Indians."

The coach rattled on, and now there were wonderful trees rising like golden sentinels around streams and rivers that danced over rock-strewn beds. The sky was cloudless and seemed close enough to touch. The air was dazzling, scintillating. Fancy felt effervescent just drawing it into her lungs. She wanted to hate this valley, this place he was taking her to, but she was stunned by its beauty.

In spite of Annabelle's admonitions about her fair skin, she rode a good deal of the way with her head stuck out the window enjoying the feel of the wind against her cheeks and the panorama that delighted her eye and imagination.

She knew Coop was watching her and that such behavior was not altogether ladylike, but she'd been closed in too long, first in a train, then in that dusty stagecoach and the hotel room. She felt a sense of freedom like that small bird darting away from them.

Only when she caught sight of buildings in the distance did she draw back into the coach and repair the curls that had been blown loose. By the time the coach had rolled into the ranch yard, she was every inch the proper lady. But when she stepped out of the coach and looked around at her new home, her mouth dropped open in a most unsuitable manner.

From her train window she'd seen many small hovels, some little more than sod shacks which bore the name homestead or ranch. She'd been appalled at the thought she might have been lured to such a place. But her fears had been allayed somewhat when she saw the accommodations Coop had arranged for her at the hotel. She'd revised her expectations for what his ranch must be. Nothing had prepared her for this small kingdom that spread out before her.

The ranch house claimed her attention first. Constructed of cut stone, it soared from its foundations as if in competition with the lofty mountain peaks themselves. Steep roofs supported several chimneys, promising the comfort and warmth of several fireplaces within. White pillars, though not of the grand circumferences of those used on the south's plantations, supported a railed veranda which wrapped around three sides. Wide windows and high peaks added to the grandeur of the main house. At some distance away on the opposite of the yard sat the barns, which threatened to dwarf even the main house. Smaller buildings of various sizes and usages were scattered about. Fancy saw men come and go from one and guessed it might be where the hands slept and ate. Fenced corrals surrounded the barns and beyond lay flat fields of sweet meadow grass. Even from here, Fancy could see horses and mules grazing peacefully with large herds of cattle.

Coop had dismounted and stood watching her. Did she

see the beauty of this land as he did, he wondered, or was her awe measured in dollar signs? He had no way of knowing, for she made no comment, simply turning back to face him, her eyes as inscrutable as his had been earlier.

"Come," he said, taking her elbow and leading her up the porch steps. "Mrs. Oakes, Nellie," he called, and two women hurried out of the ranch house. Both wore beaming smiles that were infectious.

"This is my new wife," Coop said. "Fancy, this is Delores Oakes and Nellie Sayer."

"Welcome," the woman called Delores cried, stepping forward to take Fancy's hand and curtsy. She was of Mexican origin, and her dark eyes glittered with good-natured lights. Nellie was a faded red-haired woman, whose fair skin was peppered with yellowish tan freckles. Her sleeves were rolled up above her elbows as if she'd been caught at some task. She wiped her hands on her apron before taking Fancy's hand.

"We been cleaning the house ever since Coop sent word to us. Like as not, it won't be to your taste, it needin' a woman's touch and all."

"I'm sure it's satisfactory," Fancy reassured them. "It was so kind of you to go to the trouble."

"No trouble. That's what we're here for," Delores said.

"These two women will work up here at the big house for you during the day. Delores sleeps here in the main house, but Nellie will return to her own home at night," Coop said. "You'll have to make do with Annabelle in the evenings."

"Yes, of course," Fancy answered mildly.

"Like as not you're used to being waited on and having more help, but out here women are kind of scarce and they have to go around."

A faint smile curled Fancy's lips. "I'll keep that in mind," she said softly. Coop glanced at her, reading the humor in her eyes. She was a strange one, he thought. He hadn't known ladies were so quick-witted or could engage in bawdy humor. He grinned at her and was answered with a frown.

That was a slip, Fancy thought. Ladies didn't make such double entendres.

"Would you like to come on in? We've got some lemon-ade made. It's been chillin' in the spring and it's right cold," Nellie offered.

"That sounds wonderful," Fancy said. "Perhaps you can show me to my room as well, so I might freshen up."

"I will do that," Delores spoke up, but Coop gripped Fancy's elbow and angled her toward the door.

"I'll show Mrs. Fletcher to her room," he said gruffly.

Silently, Fancy followed him up the stairs, certain his intervention was only another sign that he meant to renege on their agreement to separate rooms. She was surprised, therefore, when he pushed open a door, indicating it was his and led her on past it.

"This is your room," he said gruffly, "for the time being."

Startled, she met his gaze. The cool shadows of the house cast mysterious phantom lights in his silvery eyes. "You promised," she said, and her voice came out little more than a whisper.

He laughed, then the humor quickly faded from his features. "This is only temporary, Fancy," he said softly, his thumb smoothing along the edge of her jaw. Her breath quickened; her green eyes flashed. He chuckled.

"Why, you great, arrogant—" Words failed her, so she brought her hand and landed it smartly against his tanned cheek. He didn't even flinch, so she brought back her hand intending to strike him again. His hand stopped her, his strong fingers encircling her narrow wrist in a grip that might have hurt her but didn't. His eyes had captured her gaze. She felt his hot breath against her cheek. Inexorably, he pulled her toward him.

She sensed his hold was not so strong she could not break it, but she was defenseless in his hands. He was go-ing to kiss her, she realized, and remembered the gentle brush of his lips in their wedding kiss. She wanted to push him away but didn't. Her gaze fastened on that well-formed mouth, and involuntarily she licked her lips, moistening them, readying them. He was so close now she could see the radiating lines of his irises, and she closed her eyes against the wave of confusion and longing that washed over her.

She did not raise her face so he might have better access to her mouth. She was not so spineless, so mesmerized as that, but neither did she fight him. His lips claimed hers, hot and firm, pressing her soft giving flesh against her teeth. She felt the swirl of his tongue against her lips and started. No man had ever kissed her like this. She tried to pull away. She was certain she tried, but his kiss grew bolder. His mouth had opened on hers, and she felt the gentle scrape of his teeth nip at her full bottom lip. She whimpered, and he drew back, his eyes glittering darkly as they gazed into hers.

"So," he whispered in surprise, "even proper southern ladies have a fire in them. You will come to me, Fancy, before this year is out. And when you do, all promises, all agreements will be forgotten."

She slapped him a second time, hard as she could. He caught her hand and brought her palm to his lips. His gaze held hers as he slowly swirled his tongue across her palm, then, smiling, he stepped back. "Welcome to my home, Fancy," he said softly. He released her then, breaking the gaze that had held her captive to his whim, and whistling, he clattered down the stairs.

Fancy stood where he'd left her on the landing while rage built somewhere deep inside her. She could have forgiven him his words, maddening as they were. She could have forgiven his kiss, disturbing as it had been, but she could never forgive him that whistle that said too clearly he could dismiss her at a moment's notice.

"I will resist you to my last breath, Coop Fletcher," she shouted and was answered only by his mocking laughter.

Annabelle came up the stairs and paused, looking at her

mistress. Silently she shook her head. "That Coop Fletcher,
I think he's mighty wily, mighty wily," she observed.

"Oh shut up, Annabelle," Fancy snapped and threw open
the door to her room. Impatiently, she stepped inside and
paused, holding her breath. The room was bare of frills and
refinement, but its rough beauty could not be denied.
Through the wide, multi-paned window was a breathtaking
view of the mountains rearing their purple crags in majestic
splendor. They were part of the room. Roughly woven rugs
lay on the pine floors, and a large bed with a heavy oaken
headboard and a matching dresser did little to fill the spacious room. A heavy rocker sat before a marble fireplace,
and she could well imagine resting there on a cold evening
while the wind howled outside.

"My, my, they sho' like everything big out here,"
Annabelle said looking around. A door opened on either
side of the room. "Wonder what's in here," she said, opening one of the doors. A smaller bedroom with the same
view was obviously meant for a maid's room or a nursery.
A single bed and dresser nearly filled the room. Annabelle
nodded with satisfaction and placed her bag on the single
bed.

Curious, she crossed Fancy's room to the opposite door,
threw it open, and peered inside. Her silence alone told
Fancy there was something amiss. In a swirl of petticoats
she hurried to investigate. This was obviously the bedroom
Coop had led her past, the room he'd indicated was his. It
was a corner room, so the windows gave a full view of the
ranch buildings as well as the mountains. Boots had been
flung on the floor. The oak dresser with its carved mirror
frame was draped with shirts and jackets. Otherwise the
room was neat.

Fancy felt her anger rise. Coop Fletcher had no intentions whatsoever of honoring their agreement. Her trembling fingers found the key on his side of the door and
in a fit of temper, she drew it out, slammed the door shut
and locked it from her side. She was tempted to throw
the key out the window, but the fear that he or one of his

men might find it stayed her. She looked around the room, looking for a hiding place, and finally she dragged a chair over to the large chiffonier. Its top reached nearly to the ceiling, and a small carved pediment hid the key quite nicely. Climbing down, Fancy dusted her hands in satisfaction. Annabelle only shook her head and retired to her own bedroom.

Once she'd splashed cool water over her hands and face and smoothed her curls, Fancy went downstairs to have the iced lemonade Nellie had promised and to look over the rest of the ranch house. To her chagrin, Coop was seated at the table, a glass before him. When Nellie saw her coming, she quickly poured a second glass and set it on the table across from him.

"Thank you so much, Nellie," Fancy said sweetly.

"You're welcome, miss," Nellie said, wiping her hands again in a gesture Fancy guessed had become a habit. "If you need me anymore, I'll be in the kitchen; just call me." She disappeared toward the back of the house.

Fancy sipped at her lemonade, aware Coop was studying her with lingering amusement. She'd give him no more reason for laughing at her, she vowed.

"I'm looking forward to seeing the rest of the ranch. It seems quite beautiful," she said conversationally. They couldn't sit in stony silence!

"It could be," Coop said, looking around. "As Nellie said, it needs a woman's touch, but then that's true of many things here at the ranch." His glance was warm on her skin. "There's no hurry, but when you're ready, I'd like you to see to redoing the place."

She wanted to refuse, to cut him down, to deny him, for he was obviously used to having his way with people. She wanted to show him that she was different, but as she gazed around the large rooms, she envisioned them as they might be with fresh paint and proper draperies and furniture. He remained silent, watching her face as she studied his home, and when at last she turned to him, he read her answer in her eyes.

"I appreciate it," he said, and the mockery was gone so she knew how important his ranch was to him. "I plan to begin entertaining here, and I'd like the house to be suitable."

"I've never done this before," she said, suddenly feeling overwhelmed by the task she'd taken over.

"Don't tell me you never helped with your father's plantation?" He thought she was being difficult on purpose. He didn't recognize her slip. Quickly she recovered her poise.

"You must remember that during and after the war there was no money with which to decorate, and before that, I was really too young to be interested in such things."

He leaned toward her. "Tell me what you were like as a girl," he inquired softly. His tone was silky, persuasive. She was learning the danger signs. Quickly she stood up.

"Perhaps I'd better look over the ranch house right away. Is there a limit to how much money I may spend?"

He drew back, his eyes going dark again. "None," he said indifferently, "as long as you can account for it."

"Of course. I wouldn't spend your money without asking for a receipt. You may have no fear I'll cheat you, Mr. Fletcher."

His somber mood passed as quickly as it had come. He smiled almost absently. "I had no such fear, Mrs. Fletcher," he said, emphasizing her name as she had his. Fancy hated the sound of it and gritted her teeth not to snap back. Now he got to his feet.

"As delightful as this has been, wife, I must leave you now. There are things that need my attention."

"Of course, Mr. Fl—Coop," Fancy said, inclining her head graciously as if dismissing an underling. If Coop Fletcher wanted a lady, she'd be one he'd never forget. The effect was spoiled by his smothered laugh. Fancy tightened her chin and got to her feet.

"By the way, I've taken care to see that the door between our two rooms is locked. There will be no use made of it in the middle of the night."

Coop remained silent a moment, his eyes measuring as

he nodded his head. "If you feel that insecure about your nightly yearnings, then perhaps it's best," he said quietly and made his way outdoors, while Fancy once again stood counting her losses. One thing could be said about Coop Fletcher, half-breed or no, his wit was sharp and quick. If he didn't make her so angry, she might almost enjoy sparring with him. Humming, she went off to investigate her new home.

Chapter 4

"**W**HY DIDN'T YOU send word to me about this?" Coop asked, studying the crushed, blood-matted prairie grass.

"I didn't want to interfere with your wedding," Aaron said, hunching down beside his boss. "I figured they was just cattle rustlers, and this was a one-time event. I thought it could wait till you got here."

"But they came back!" It was a flat statement.

Aaron nodded. "Yeah. Two nights ago I heard gunshots and rode out here to see what it was. That's when I found the mules." He rose and walked back toward the dark hunks scattered about the pasture.

"It just don't make sense. Why should they shoot the mules if all they wanted was the cattle?"

Coop stood staring out at the craggy mountaintops, striving to control the outrage building inside him. "They didn't want cattle," he said, stalking back to his horse and re-mounting.

"Why'd they come here, then?" Aaron asked, following, "And why'd they fire shots like that? Didn't they know that'd alert us?"

"The arrogant bastards wanted you to know they were there," Coop growled. "Someone's out to sabotage my shipping business."

"Christ, why put you out of business? There's more need

for transportin' in these here mountains than you can ever handle."

"Yeah, but someone wants what I've got."

"You figure that landslide and ambush on the way to the Argentine Mines wasn't just coincidental?"

"That's my thinking," Coop said. "They didn't fight enough for outlaws living in the mountains and desperate for supplies. Once we got down off that trail, they retreated."

"Maybe whoever it is wants to scare you off those Union Pacific contracts for their tracklaying crews," Aaron spat and waited expectantly.

Coop shook his head. "No, it's more than that. The Union Pacific crews are nearly finished around here. There wouldn't be much future in that."

"How about the government contracts to supply beef to the forts?"

"They would have concentrated on the cattle," Coop said. "Won't do us any good to speculate on it. We've got to stop them before they do any more damage. I want a team of men out here patrolling day and night. Hire more men if you have to; don't use the mule skinners." He glanced back at the dead mules. "Get a detail up here to bury these animals before they start rottin'. Butcher out a few of them, and send the meat to the Utes up in Middle Park."

"Yes, sir." Aaron rode beside Coop, making mental notes. He liked Coop, liked the way he went right to the heart of the matter, not rampaging around like a wounded bull, but setting out to make things right again. He was also impressed that Coop thought of sending some of the meat up to the Utes. Rumor was they were in pretty bad shape. Government supplies hadn't come through for them like they were supposed to, and rumor was the Utes were starving.

"We're going to be short of pack mules if we don't buy some more," he reminded his boss.

"Send a couple of men to Denver. Replace the wagons

we lost last month. Give them a list of supplies for the ranch."

"Want me to check with Mrs. Fletcher to see if she needs anything?"

Coop's thoughts turned to the woman established in his ranch house, and his tight expression eased a bit. She was different than anything he'd expected. She kept him off-balance a little, and he wasn't sure if he liked that or not. He'd surely gotten more than he'd bargained for, and he had little cause for complaint, except for that silly promise and her sharp tongue.

"Did you want me to check with Mrs. Fletcher?" Aaron repeated when Coop didn't answer.

"That'd be a good idea. She's redoing the ranch house, so like as not she'll want some furniture and whatnots."

"I'll get with her right away," Aaron said.

"I'll speak to her about it," Coop said. "Her order will be ready in the morning." He looked forward to another reason to engage her feisty temper and sharp wit. He grinned in spite of himself. Aaron saw the grin and said nothing more. He remembered that first flush of excitement between a man and woman. It was gone now, and Nellie had settled into a hard-working, loyal wife, but Aaron kind of missed those peppery first encounters.

The two men continued their tour of the ranch. Sixty-five thousand acres stretched before them, and all of it belonged to Coop Fletcher. He'd been buying up acreage with the first dollar he made ramroding. All profit from his transporting business and from his mines was turned into land. It had been a good investment. After the war, he'd leased his grassland to Texas ranchers driving their herds north, taking starter herds as payment. Later, when he'd fattened his herds, he'd traded them back to those same Texas ranchers, one range-fattened cow for two of their stringy, trail-weary ones. His herds had grown; his ranch was one more prosperous enterprise for a man who'd never been to school.

Coop thought of that frightened abandoned youth of ten

who'd learned to depend on his own skills to live. For two years he'd made himself indispensable to a boozy old saloon owner, running errands, sweeping up, and later keeping an eye on his till so he wasn't robbed. When the old man died, he'd joined up with one of the trail herds riding through Denver. Because of his youth, he'd been set to helping the cook and doing every dirty task a trail drive entailed. When the trail hands did let him ride with them, he always rode drag at the end of the herd, where the trail dust nearly smothered the breath from you. He hadn't minded. He'd learned his trade, and the next time out, he'd lied about his age and hired on as an extra trail hand. After that life had gotten easier, not a lot, but some.

Coop took off his hat and looked around his spread. He'd happened on this spread at the right time. After ten years of ramroding, he'd been sick of working for someone else. Using his meager savings to buy mules, he'd started his transport business. That was how he'd found this place, run down and on its last leg. The house had been half finished, the easterner who'd come with such grand plans had run out of money and heart and was only too happy to sell and head back to civilization. And this valley had become home to Coop Fletcher, who had never known the feel of a home.

Now he looked around, and his thoughts once again went to the beautiful woman who'd become his wife. She'd stay, he thought, his lips tightening in a straight line. She was right for the Bar C Ranch, right for him. He had a year to convince her to forget about their bargain, a year to woo her into his bed. And although his expertise with women of quality had been limited, he'd had a considerable number of prostitutes in the cow towns and mining camps, so that he knew once you stripped away their petticoats, women were pretty much the same. He thought of Fancy and wondered briefly if when that moment arrived between them he'd find her as accommodating as other women proved to be. The thought even crossed his mind that she might be a virgin.

After all, she'd been a protected southern lady. Maybe they were different after all.

The rest of the afternoon dragged for Coop. He'd lost his zeal for riding his land. His thoughts returned again and again to his ranch house and the beautiful green-eyed woman who waited there.

If Coop had seen Fancy, he might have been put off by her appearance. Cobwebs clung to the golden strands which had fallen about her shoulders during her work. Dirt smudged one cheek and her gown, one of the old thread-bare dresses she'd been forced to wear before Coop's generous voucher had provided for a trousseau. She'd poked into every nook and cranny of the ranch house. If she were to redo it, she wanted to know exactly what she was taking on. Nellie, Delores, and Annabelle had been her partners in crime.

Tongue clucking, Nellie had set about scrubbing the rooms they'd thrown open, rooms where their feet left imprints on the dusty floors.

"I've never seen the like," Nellie fussed. She seemed to have a personal vendetta against dirt.

"Law, that woman goin' t'kill me," Annabelle complained, collapsing on a settee beside Fancy.

"Nellie, do come and have some coffee. Delores has made us a fresh pot."

"I can't stop now," Nellie said. "I got to get finished and get back to my young'un. She'll need feedin' soon."

"You have a little one?" Fancy asked in dismay. The woman hadn't said a word before now.

Nellie nodded, and her severe features softened momentarily. "Another little girl," she said. "That makes four altogether. My man wasn't too happy at first. He had his heart set on a boy, but when the little one come, he just took her in like he done all the rest."

"But who's watching your children while you work up here?" Fancy asked. "Why don't you bring them here, or is your husband home?"

"No, ma'am, Lizbette, she's the oldest. She's six and a

half, so she helps with the younger ones. Charley, the cook, looks in on them ever now and then to see they're all right. Aaron's out ridin' with Mr. Fletcher. He's Coop's right-hand man and his best pack master."

"What's that?" Fancy asked, both because she wanted to learn as much as she could about this country if she were going to stay here a year, and because her questions might entice the tireless Irish woman to come and sit with them. Delores had already settled into an opposite chair and taken herself a cup of coffee.

"A pack master's someone who leads a pack train," Nellie answered and did indeed take the cup of coffee Delores handed her. "Coop's got several pack trains goin' out at different times. He's about the most respected packer in these mountains. Why, he just started a pack-mule express out of Elizabethtown to the Argentine mines. Aaron says he's never seen a man so set on working. He's even thinking of taking passengers into the Middle Park and to the Hot Sulphur Springs there."

"Passengers?" Fancy said in surprise. "Is he going into the stagecoach business, too?"

Delores and Nellie looked at each other and laughed. "Ain't no stagecoach could get over some of them mountain passes. Takes a pack mule to do that. Sometimes they're able to use a freight wagon, but most times they just quick freight over them passes. Last time they tried using wagons, they run into a landslide and had to go down a steep incline. Aaron said the men only did it because they were ashamed not to follow Coop."

"Is the freight business dangerous, then?" Fancy asked in some surprise. She hadn't considered anything Coop had done as being life-threatening, yet she had little doubt he'd not shirk danger.

Nellie and Delores exchanged uneasy looks with each other as if they'd let something slip they shouldn't have. "It is the job of the man to take risks," Delores said, shrugging, "and the job of his woman to wait and pray."

"Everything's a risk out here," the practical Nellie spoke

up. "If you came out looking for any kind of guarantees about safety and comfort, you've come to the wrong place. A man'll put his life on the line a half dozen times a day and think nothing of it out here. If you're a jumpy woman, you'll have a hard time of it. A man's got to be brave out here; his woman has to be braver." Nellie's pale unflinching gaze met Fancy's, and it was Fancy who looked away first.

"Will you bring your children with you when you come up tomorrow?" she asked to change the subject, and because she hadn't forgotten her anxiety at the thought of such young children being left alone. How much care would a ranch cook give in his spare time?

"We won't hardly get any work done with them about," Nellie warned.

"I like children," Fancy answered, "more than I do housework."

Nellie smiled for the first time, a revelation that brought the beauty back to her face and softened the lines of her mouth. "I reckon we can try it," she acknowledged. "They're good young'uns, every one of them."

The women went about their business then, Nellie to finish last-minute chores before returning to her children, Delores to begin supper for the ranch house.

Annabelle scooted outdoors for some fresh air before returning to her chores. She wasn't certain she was going to like this ranch life. She was used to the theater, and although she'd never (in her whole life) been a shirker, she was used to handling plush fabrics and mending costumes and painting sets. The year seemed even longer to her than it did to Fancy.

Wandering down to the corral, Annabelle was surprised to see a black man hauling hay out to the feeding pens. He seemed to notice her at once, but he made no effort to talk to her. That was all right, Annabelle thought, staring at him boldly. She had no wish to converse with a common stable hand. Sticking her nose in the air, she turned back to the ranch house, but she rolled her hips a little as she walked. Wouldn't hurt that man to know what he was missing out on, she thought mischievously and couldn't resist a peek over her shoulders once she'd reached the ranch house porch. Sure enough he was staring at her like a hungry man studying a possum dinner. Annabelle giggled and hurried inside.

When everyone left, Fancy walked through the ranch house. She'd gotten to know every secret turn it possessed, and the knowledge made her feel more at home, more accepting of its quirks. She'd never really lived in a house before. Oh, she'd been a guest a few times before the war began, but hotel rooms and small drafty apartments above the theaters had been her lot.

Now she reveled in the spacious rooms, the sense of privacy, the freedom in knowing she might do whatever she liked with them. The idea was almost scary, then she thought of the theater sets. She'd make this ranch the grandest place Elizabethtown had ever seen. She'd hang heavy damask drapes at all the windows, and beneath she'd put sheer white panels, and she'd buy silk-covered, gilt-edged chairs and sofas all to match with carved figures and crests and one of those tall mahogany clocks she'd seen once in a town house where she'd been a guest, and one of those elegant cherry tea tables with candle slides and inlay tables of walnut with neo-Grec images and medallions. Why she'd even order a pianoforte and a canterbury to hold the music and magazines.

Her imagination ran out of steam as she thought of the money involved. Besides, she turned and looked back at the long parlor with its large stone fireplace and wide windows letting in the view of the mountains and sky. What draperies would be better than that view? She was torn between her own inclination to leave things as they were and to please Coop Fletcher with the fine house she knew he wanted.

Almost on cue, the door opened and Coop entered. He had to bend his head to pass through the doorways, she noticed and repressed a smile. Coop saw the laughter in her green eyes and wondered if it were aimed at him.

"Did you stay busy today?" he asked, taking off his hat and stretching his long frame on the well-worn settee. The room seemed less spacious now that he was in it. Fancy brushed at her hair and wished she'd had time to freshen up before he'd arrived. His gaze settled on her smudged cheek, and she wasn't sure if the amused grin was at her disheveled appearance or not. Drawing a disdainful air about her, Fancy spread her limp, threadbare skirts as grandly as if of the finest satin and lifted the coffeepot and a chipped china cup.

"There's fresh coffee. Would you like a cup?" she inquired with savoir faire. One eyebrow raised elegantly above the green-gold eyes. Despite his inclination to laugh, for never had he seen a lady quite so inconvenienced by cobwebs and dirty smudges, he was charmed by her.

"I'll have a cup," he said, inclining his head, although he was more used to a shot of whiskey at this time of the afternoon. Silently he watched her as she poured out the coffee, inquired after sugar and cream as if this were the most formal of afternoon teas, and finally passed the cracked cup and saucer over to him.

"I've made several observations in my tour of the ranch house," she said, leaning back with feigned composure as he cradled the cup in his big hand. He was dressed much as he'd been that first day she saw him, wearing the rough canvas Levi's of the other ranch hands, a woolen shirt, and a cotton kerchief knotted at his throat. A well-worn, wide-brimmed hat had carelessly been tossed to one side. His blue-black hair lay close against his head, curling over his shirt collar. He looked big and capable and powerful. How had she ever mistaken him for a shiftless drifter?

He sipped his coffee and waited for her to go on.

"First of all, we must have more help. Nellie has her small children to see to. They can't be left to tend for themselves while she works up here. For the time being I've asked her to bring the children up to the main house while she works."

"That's right decent of you," he said, surprise showing in his voice and clear gray eyes.

"What else could I do?" Fancy snapped, irritated that he should think her so uncaring she could have done anything else.

"I'll send one of the hands back into town to hire another woman tomorrow," he said. "What else would you like?"

His patience surprised her. Restlessly she got to her feet and walked around the large room. "We need to paint and install better lighting, perhaps some chandeliers. I'll need a handyman for that."

"That's no problem. Daniel's a black man from your part of the country. He may even have come from your own plantation. He's good with a hammer. Anything else?"

"Thank you. That will be all to start with."

He was surprised by the simplicity of her requests. "No fancy furniture and draperies and doodads?" he asked now. "I have a man going to Denver tomorrow. He can bring back all those things."

"Not yet," Fancy hedged. "I wouldn't know yet what to buy."

Coop studied her a moment, somewhat startled at her admission. She had said the war had curtailed such expenditures for most plantation owners, but he'd expected her to have some ideas of how to go about furnishing a house. "I'll have Aaron bring back some catalogs," he offered finally.

"Oh, yes, that would be lovely," she said in obvious relief. "In the meantime, you'll have to tell me what your own preferences are concerning the ranch house."

"I want it to be the best money can buy," he said immediately. Setting aside the cup, he rose. Fancy got to her feet and faced him.

"Have you no regard for taste?" she asked.

"I leave that up to you, fancy lady," he said, grinning down at her. "That's part of your job as my wife."

"I see," she answered, turning away from the keen gaze that had suddenly grown warm on her cheeks and mouth.

"By the way," he said, pausing in the doorway. "I'd forgotten, I also won a town house in a card game a few months back. I'd like you to do something with that this summer. When the roads are too bad or we're inclined to stay in town, we'll stay there."

"Is that usual for most ranchers around here?" she asked in dismay.

"Most big ranchers," Coop said, nodding. "Don't underestimate us out here, Fancy. We may seem like a rough steed, but anyone who takes the rough edge off will see we can be broken." She sensed he wasn't talking about the ranch house anymore. He grinned, that silvery gaze capturing hers challengingly. "Of course, to a tenderfoot, we might still seem kind of wild."

"One thing I've learned, even as a lady, Coop," she said, facing him unflinchingly, "is not to be frightened of wild things whether a wild horse, a wild cowboy, or just an old ranch house that's been neglected too long."

"Maybe Nellie's right," Coop said softly. "Maybe all they need is a woman's touch." He caught her hand and carried it to his lips. His lips were firm as they brushed across her fingertips, and then he was gone, ducking beneath the too-low door frames and stalking across the porch to his horse. Fancy stood with her hand clenched against her breast, feeling the touch of his mouth against her flesh, then she fled upstairs calling for Annabelle to bring her a tub of bath water, immediately.

The next afternoon, the cowhand Coop had sent to Elizabethtown returned with the sturdy daughter of a miner. Her name was Polly, and she was a large full-bodied girl with pink cheeks and an eye for the men. As Woody helped her off the wagon seat, she managed to brush against him with her soft breasts. Blushing and stammering, he nodded to Fancy and the other women standing on the porch and quickly drove the wagon back to the stables.

"Trouble," Nellie muttered under her breath.

"She can help with the children," Fancy said, putting her arms around the slender six-year-old form of Lizbette, Nellie's oldest. When Nellie had come up to the ranch that morning bringing the sleeping baby with its tufts of red hair and the three adorable little girls, Fancy had immediately fallen in love with each of them, but as the day progressed, it had been Lizbette who'd quickly become her favorite. With the quick gawky grace of a yearling, the girl was enchanting.

The admiration had been mutual. Lizbette had been awed by the golden-haired lady who'd become the new mistress of the Bar C Ranch. All day she'd trailed after Fancy, running errands, chattering away about a number of subjects of great interest to a lively six-year-old. Freed of caring for her younger sisters, Lizbette had taken full advantage of her time at the ranch house, asking hundreds of questions about Fancy and studying Annabelle with an intensity that might have been rude in an older child. Even Annabelle had forgiven her endless chatter when Lizbette had taken up needle and thread and calmly set about helping with the mending.

"That child is a wonder," Annabelle had said, shaking her head in mock amazement. All day the women, young and old, had worked, while the younger girls had played on the floor with their dolls and been put down for naps in one of the now-cleaned spare bedrooms. Only Lizbette had remained awake to see the arrival of Polly.

Polly stood in the yard facing the four women and sauntered up the porch steps, dropped her tapestry bag on the porch, placed her hands on her hips, and looked each lady over from head to foot. "Woody said you're aneedin' another woman around here. Looks like you got plenty."

"Not really," Fancy said, holding out her hand. "I'm Mrs. Fletcher. This is Delores, who does the cooking, and Annabelle, my personal maid. Nellie comes down now and then to help in the house, but we needed someone to be here every day to do the cleaning."

"I don't do windows and such," Polly said looking around. "I hurt my back helping out some ladies, and I ain't recovered yet."

"Well, we'll not ask you to do more than you're able," Fancy said, nonplussed by the girl's attitude. "Delores will show you to your room, and you can begin when you've had a chance to catch your breath from your ride out."

Polly nodded and sauntered into the living room, leaving her bag behind. Delores looked at Fancy and, arching her eyebrows, retrieved the bag. "Looks like there's a fair amount of work to be done here," Polly called, peering into the parlor and study which opened off the main hall.

"My husband and I are newly married," Fancy said. "I'm afraid as a bachelor, he left things undone. That's why we needed an extra hand."

"I don't do floors by hand," Polly said. "My back, you know."

"We'll have to keep that in mind," Fancy replied. "Here's your room."

"Behind the kitchen?" Polly asked, looking around. "Kitchen smells bother me something terrible. All that smoke and whatnot. I've got a touch of asthma."

"We'll have to see about moving you then," Fancy said helplessly, wondering which guest room upstairs should be given to the cleaning girl.

"That's a shame," Delores said slyly. "This room is so handy to the pantry if you need a snack in the middle of the night, and it's the warmest room in the winter."

"You ain't stayin' out here in the winter, are you?" Polly demanded.

"I—I'm not sure what we'll be doing then," Fancy said.

"I ain't staying out here in the winter," Polly declared. "Them passes'll get snowed in, and there won't be no gettin' back to town afore spring."

"All right," Fancy said meekly.

"In the meantime, I'll stay here. Long's there no undue amount of smoke from cookin', I reckon I can stand it."

"Th—Thank you," Fancy said and escaped to the parlor.

"What did I tell you, trouble," Nellie said, gathering up her children. "I'll be back in the morning. I don't believe you're going to get much work out of that one."

"Thank you, Nellie. I don't know what I'd do without you," Fancy said gratefully.

"You don't have to thank me, Mrs. Fletcher, that's what I'm here for. You don't have to be so all-fired grateful to that lout in there, either. Knowing Coop, she's being well-paid to come out here and work for you." Nellie went off with her baby against her shoulder and two little girls clinging to her skirts. Lizbette shyly waved good-bye to Fancy, then ran after her mother. Fancy watched them leave, then taking a big breath turned back inside the ranch house. She almost flinched at the idea of giving Polly instructions. She looked around the ranch house. It was looking better, because it was cleaned and much of the bachelor clutter removed, but it was a long way from the grand style Coop had in mind. She began to doubt her ability to do as he wished, and she hated the thought of having to admit defeat to him. How had things become so complicated?

Chapter 5

A S IF THINGS weren't bad enough, a rider appeared the next day with an invitation from Maida Robinson for a soiree. Fancy tried her best to sort out the names and faces from her wedding. She had a niggling feeling she'd met Maida, and that first encounter hadn't been an auspicious one. Realizing the importance Coop had placed on the role she was to play in Elizabethtown society, Fancy felt even more pressured. She thought about sending her regrets, but Coop's response ended that possibility.

"You'll like Maida, once you get to know her," he said. "Her husband owns the mills outside of town. He's also involved in quartz mining. I've just contracted to haul their ore down to their mills."

"So this is an important business contact," Fancy said with a sinking heart. She'd have to go. Furthermore, she'd have to make herself most charming so Maida Robinson and all her friends would like her.

"Are you worried, fancy lady?" Coop asked, sensing her disquiet.

"No," Fancy lied. "I'm just so involved in the work here at the ranch. This is a bad time to leave."

"I thought you were ready to begin painting," Coop said, looking round at the rooms. "We'll plan to stay in town a few days while that's going on. We can stay at

76

the hotel while you look at the town house and see what it needs."

"I—all right." Fancy nodded in defeat.

He glanced at her. She'd been surprisingly easy to live with these past few days. He'd noted how she'd settled in with Nellie and Delores. He'd come upon them several times, sharing a laugh or engaging in some discussion over the things that needed to be done on the ranch house. He'd even felt rather smug to think he'd provided his elusive new bride with a project that had so captured her interest. Now he was astonished and pleased that she wasn't in a hurry to return to town. He noted her full lower lip jutting forward in a pretty pout and on impulse rose and bent to place a quick kiss on her lips. She gasped and jumped up.

"I beg your pardon," she snapped.

"That's not necessary," he replied. "I found your kiss quite adequate."

"*My* kiss! Adequate!" Her mouth opened and closed several times before settling into a prim line. "You have no right to press your kisses upon me. I haven't indicated in any manner that they're welcome."

"That's true, you haven't," Coop said calmly. "But I thought we needed a little practice."

"Practice!"

"We'll be returning to Elizabethtown in a few days, and as far as everyone there is concerned, we're happy newlyweds. I'm not figuring to tell them anything different. Our business arrangement is strictly between us. When we're in Elizabethtown, we're going to have to act like we care about each other."

"Act like we care! I assure you, Mr. Fletcher, such a role would be beyond my ability."

"That's why I figure we need to practice," he said, smiling. "Good day, ma'am." He ducked his head and was out the door before she could recover enough to answer him. She stood watching him lope across the yard and couldn't repress the smile on her lips. Annabelle was right. Coop could be downright wily when he wanted to be. In the long run the joke was on him, though. She was perfectly capable of acting any role required of her, and if Coop wanted a loving wife while they were in Elizabethtown, he'd have one.

"'Cuse me, ma'am," a quiet voice said from the doorway. Fancy turned to find Daniel waiting patiently. "Mr. Fletcher say they's work yo' want done up heah at the ranch house." A tall black man with intelligent eyes and a gentle manner about him stood waiting for her instructions.

"Yes, Daniel, I do," she said, her eyes going to the door framing. "I want all the doors in the house to be made taller. My husband has a hard time not to bump his head when he walks through."

"Yes, ma'am," the black man said, nodding and smiling. "He's a mighty tall man, even for out here."

"How long have you been out here yourself, Daniel?" she asked as he set to work tearing out the door frame.

"Ah come out here when Abraham Lincoln freed the slaves," Daniel said. "Ah figure ah ain't ever seen no part of the country 'cept that plantation where ah was born. Ah come out here to be a cowboy, but ain't too many ranchers wantin' a black man. Mr. Fletcher, though, he don't seem to mind what color a man's skin is."

"You like Mr. Fletcher, then?" Fancy asked. "He treats you well?"

"He treats me like he treats the other men," Daniel said, and his dark eyes met Fancy's proudly. His simple declaration and proud look told Fancy more about Coop and his handling of his men than anything could have done. She thought of his own battle to be treated equally despite his mixed blood and thought he would understand another man's struggle. Somehow, she felt proud and reassured by this quality in her husband. Funny, how after that first initial shock of hearing he was a half-breed, she'd given little thought to his Indian blood. Were the citizens of Elizabethtown as open-minded as well? Certainly, Maida Robinson's invitation would appear so. Suddenly, she was looking forward to returning to Elizabethtown and meeting these people who were so much a part of Coop's plans. She'd make them like her. She'd convince them she was a lady of quality and thereby show them the worthiness of a man like Coop Fletcher. Humming, she went about her tasks and gave no thought to the change her opinion of Coop had undergone.

Two days later, when Geraldine Russell's buggy pulled into the yard, Fancy had lost her confidence and was ready to weep with frustration.

Shortly after their talk, Coop had been called away unexpectedly over some trouble with one of his pack trains. Daniel had finished the door frames and gone on to other tasks, but Annabelle had become moody and irritable. Polly was no help whatsoever, claiming children made her nervous. She spent most of her time in her room, except when she resurfaced for cups of fresh coffee or buttered bread or cakes. Delores, seeing how Polly was allowed to malinger, had become difficult, refusing to work outside the kitchen. That left only Nellie and Fancy to prepare for the men to paint, and Nellie's children claimed much of her attention.

Aaron had returned from Denver with several catalogs, and in her spare time, Fancy had poured over them, looking for furniture for the ranch house, but none of it seemed suitable, and the more she looked the more she feared making a mistake. In the midst of all this confusion Geraldine came calling.

"I hope you don't mind that I've just dropped in," she said, puffing as she climbed the stairs. "My ranch is the next one down that valley, and I figured it was time I did the neighborly thing and called on you." Daniel was leading her horse and buggy toward the watering trough.

"I'm delighted you did," Fancy said, genuinely happy to see the older woman. "Delores, will you bring us some fresh coffee?"

"I'll make it, but I won't bring it to the parlor. That's not my job."

"I'll come get it," Fancy called back and, smiling apologetically at Geraldine, led her to the parlor where furniture, windows, and mantels had already been covered in preparation for the room to be repainted.

"What color are you using in here?" Geraldine asked.

"I thought white with the dark stone of the fireplace," Fancy replied, happy to have someone who might express an opinion about what she was doing.

Geraldine nodded approvingly and thumbed through the catalogs Fancy had been studying. "I see you're planning on some new furniture, too. It's about time. The man who started building this place had some grand ideas, but he ran out of money. When Coop came along he just let everything stay the way the builder had left it. With the right furniture and carpets, this ranch'll be a showplace."

"That's what Coop is expecting," Fancy said, "but—" she hesitated. "I'm just not certain what would fit in here best. Look at those mountains beyond those windows. How can I cover that view? And anything I might put in here will seem pretentious and stuffy. This house is different from those back east. There's strength and open spaces. How can I transform it into something else?"

"I believe you hit on the right idea," Geraldine said. "It ain't a matter of putting in a lot of furniture, only what's necessary. And I see what you mean about them windows. You wouldn't want to block that there view, so I reckon you're going to just pull the drapes back and leave 'em."

She grinned, and suddenly the weight of decision fell off Fancy's shoulders. "I guess that is what I had in mind," she said. "I've just been afraid Coop wouldn't like it."

"Ain't no man goin' to like what a woman does in a house, but then you didn't think much of how he had things. I guess he'll just have to get used to your tastes."

It's not that easy, Fancy thought, but tactfully changed

the subject, "We're leaving in a few days to go back to Elizabethtown for Maida Robinson's party. Will you be there?"

Geraldine nodded. "I reckon I will. Maida sent me an invite. I ain't much taken by all these fancy parties goin' on now. Callin' it a soiree sounds mighty highfalutin to me. I remember when we had hoedowns and quilting bees and barn raisings and the like. Folks didn't put on airs then, but then we was all poor. Now we're richer'n we know how to be, and we're tryin' to be more than we was before."

Fancy smiled at the old woman's remarks. "Have you always lived out here?" she asked, just to keep the old woman reminiscing.

Geraldine nodded. "I come out here with my papa and mama when I was young woman. Left a husband and baby dead of cholera on the trail. Didn't think I'd ever get over it, but I met Ryerson, and I knowed the minute I laid eyes on him, I was done with my grievin'. He was minin' out in California and made a little bit of money, but he was smarter'n some of them durn fools. He brought his money back here to Colorado and bought him some land, started a ranch. Then, dad burn, if the gold fever didn't catch up with him. They found gold out there in them mountains." She nodded toward the mountain range rearing against the sky. "He went out yonder and found himself another fortune, but he got killed in a mine slide. He left me rich as Croesus, but dad blamed alone. I'm probably the richest woman in these here parts, may even be richer than Coop himself, but it don't do me no good. Don't make me no happier than I was when I was with Ryerson and we was just startin' out with our ranch."

Geraldine paused, and Fancy sensed the loneliness and old grief in her. "I'll see about that coffee," she said, rising.

"Why there's Polly Britches, herself," Geraldine said as the hired girl sauntered by the parlor. "Polly, go get our coffee, and serve it in here." Polly paused, her mouth hanging open as she stared at the old woman. It was plain she wanted to refuse Geraldine's request but didn't dare.

"Hurry it up, Polly Britches," Geraldine snapped, and the girl took off in the direction of the kitchen.

Fancy glanced at her guest in surprise.

Geraldine chuckled. "I've known Polly since she was a little girl running around with droopy britches. She grew up to be a lazy girl like her father and a bit on the sly side. You'll have to take a firm hand with her to keep her working for you. Once she sees you can't be bamboozled, she'll be a good worker."

Polly entered the parlor at that moment with a tray bearing a coffeepot and chipped cups.

"I'll pour, Polly," Fancy said, looking over the tray. "Take these spoons back to Delores and tell her they're not clean, to send new ones immediately. Also I want some of that cake she baked this morning. It should have been on the tray."

Polly's eyes rolled from Geraldine and back to Fancy. "Yes, ma'am," she said sullenly, but she went.

Fancy and Geraldine fell to discussing the furniture choices for the main room of the ranch house, and soon Polly was back with the requested items. With ill grace she banged them down on the small table Fancy had chosen as a tea table and turned to go.

"Polly, the windows in the dining room haven't been taped yet," Fancy said crisply. "You can start on those immediately and when you've finished, clean out the fire grates in there and be sure the mantel is well covered."

"Yes, ma'am," Polly answered sullenly.

"Then I should like you to pack a few things for yourself. You'll be accompanying me to Elizabethtown to begin work on our town house there."

"Yes, ma'am," Polly said, and with a last dark glance over her shoulder left the room.

As Fancy served the coffee, she couldn't help the slump of her shoulders as she considered her next problem. "Could you tell me something about Maida Robinson and some of the other ladies I'll be meeting at this party?" she asked lightly.

Geraldine studied the younger woman and thought if she had ever looked like this golden-haired girl, she would never have feared anything or anyone. But the charm of Coop's new bride seemed to be her unawareness of her beauty.

"Well, my dear, they are as curious about you as you are about them. They know Coop wrote back east because he wanted a real lady. They're eaten up with curiosity about your background, your lineage, and your wardrobe. You dazzled them all at your wedding."

"I scarcely remember a thing about it," Fancy murmured.

"Most young brides feel that way," Geraldine comforted. "Take my word for it, you made a fine first showing. Maida has two reasons for having this little soiree of hers. First of all she wants to be the first one to entertain the new Mrs. Coop Fletcher in her home, and secondly, she wants to show off her little sister, who's not all that young and who's come all the way out west in search of a husband. If Maida'd had her way of it, Coop would have been the one, but her sister's timin' was bad."

"I see," Fancy said and was surprised to find herself annoyed that another woman had wanted to marry Coop. She should have been delighted at the thought. If Claire had arrived first, Coop would have been only too happy to give Fancy money to continue on to San Francisco, just to get rid of her. That was what she wanted, wasn't it?

"Anyway, the genteel ladies of Elizabethtown are waiting for your return, so if I was you, I'd go back in a blaze of glory with my prettiest and best. You show them the kind of stuff Coop Fletcher's wife's made of."

"That's what he wants me to do, isn't it?" Fancy said wistfully.

"I reckon it is, child," Geraldine said. "And there ain't nothing wrong with him wantin' that. He's spent a considerable amount of his time on the outside lookin' in. He's just wantin' to have a taste of the other side."

"I'll do what he expects of me, of course," Fancy said. "After all, that's why he married me." Her voice held a note of something Geraldine couldn't quite put her finger on.

"You ain't the kind of woman for a man to put on a shelf and pull out like a showpiece," Geraldine said, rising. "I took your measure that first day you stepped off the stage and ordered Coop to carry in your luggage. I said right then and there, he had gotten himself more than he'd bargained for, and I figured that's good for him. You got your hands on a fine man, Fancy. You can make this marriage whatever you want it to be, and you can make this town think and do what you want it to. Coop needs a woman like you. He don't know that yet. It's up to you to show him."

Fancy smiled at the homey advice. "Thank you for coming today," she said, taking Geraldine's wrinkled old hand. "You've eased my mind about a lot of things."

"Don't let anyone flamboozle you, girl. And if you get to needin' someone to talk to, why just come on over to the Silver Bar Ranch."

Fancy hugged the old woman and walked her out to her buggy. She stood watching as the buggy headed out at a fast clip. "I want to be just like her someday," she murmured to herself, and with new resolve went back into the house. The rest of the afternoon was spent reestablishing her authority with two recalcitrant servants and making out an order for furniture for her new home. When Coop returned later that night, he found a serene wife, a beautifully served supper, and doorways he could pass through without bowing his head.

"Are you beginning to feel at home here?" he asked Fancy as they climbed the stairs to their separate rooms.

"It's funny, but I am," she replied. "The ranch, this valley itself is so beautiful and peaceful. I've never known a place like this."

"Surely, your father's plantation was equally as beautiful," he said, thinking he should have traveled back east to claim her, then he would know more about her. He could have met her parents and all those cousins and aunts. Having no family of his own, Coop was curious about hers.

Now he turned on the landing and gazed at his wife. She'd dressed her hair casually for their evening at home, pulling it high on her head and letting it cascade freely down her back. One gold-spun curl lay on her shoulder. His large hand reached out for it. She didn't pull away as she had done before, and he fingered the curl, feeling it wind around his fingers like a silken cord.

"I've never touched hair like yours," he said softly, lifting the rich heavy tresses and letting them slide through his fingers. They fanned like liquid gold in the lamplight. Nervously, she stepped away from him, and he sensed her movement wasn't meant as a rejection of him so much as a reclaiming of herself.

"You're very beautiful, Fancy," he said softly. "But even more than that, you're warm and real. I can touch you." His hand fell on her shoulder, heavy and warm. She felt its weight. His eyes were dark-shadowed as they gazed into hers. "I never knew ladies could be like you."

"Does it matter to you so much that I'm a lady?" she asked, her voice nearly a whisper in the darkness. "Would you have wanted me to be your wife if I were not?"

He removed his hand from her shoulder and studied her face. "But you are," he said imperturbably, "just as surely as I am not a gentleman. We can't change who we are, Fancy."

"But isn't that what this is all about?" she asked. "Aren't you trying to change who and what you are? You want people to accept you as a gentleman."

He took hold of her hands and shook her slightly. His voice was gruff when he spoke. "I want people to accept me," he said, "not as a gentleman, but as a half-breed."

He let go of her, and she clasped her arms where his hands had been. "How can they forget you're a half-breed if you can't forget it yourself?"

He'd walked away from her a few steps, but at her question he turned back to her. "I don't want them to forget I'm a half-breed," he said clearly. "I want them to remember it every moment they smile at me and doff their hats to me and force themselves to do business with me. I want them to remember it when they see my beautiful wife, my fancy lady, and later when they greet my children." She moved restlessly, and his hands were there on her shoulders, calming her, soothing away her unspoken protests.

"There will be children one day, Fancy, yours and mine. We both know this bargain between us is an empty one." He pulled her to him, his mouth settling on hers. She had no time to prepare her defenses against him. Her lips were parted slightly, preparing to refute his words. Her chest rose and fell with emotions he'd awakened in her, emotions she couldn't name or understand. His mouth found hers, soft and pliant beneath his, and he took his advantage, his tongue, hot and probing, sweeping between her lips, delving into the moist sweetness, touching some untouched secret places in her very soul.

She wanted not to respond. She wanted to push him away. She wanted to draw him closer and explore the exploding forces within. She stood unprotesting, so it was Coop who pulled her closer, wrapping his arms about her slender waist, crushing her full breasts against his hard chest until the tips ached with a sweet longing. He lessened his assault on her mouth, and she whimpered, wrapping her arms around his neck, pressing against him, her mouth open, her small tongue darting out to touch his lips.

Coop felt the flame consuming his senses, like a runaway prairie fire, and trembled with need. He hadn't been near a woman in weeks. Now to feel his own wife responding to him so openly was like a hot wind sweeping over him. His hands moved over her slender back. Silently he cursed the whalebones and layers of fabric that kept her flesh from his touch. His hands swept around to the fullness of her breasts, his thumbs kneading the tender nipples through the silky fabric. Thank God, ladies didn't pack their breasts in the same stiff whalebone contraptions they did their hips and waists.

Fancy drew in her breath. His touch was impatient and painful against her virginal breasts. The unaccustomed passion had been swept away at his first touch on her hot flesh. She pushed away from him, the palms of her hands settling over her breasts in an innocent gesture that was more seductive than she could have imagined.

Coop reached for her again, then saw the look on her face, and his hands fell to his sides. For a few heated moments he'd forgotten she was a lady and unaccustomed to being handled in such a manner. But hell's fire, how was a man to break through her defenses if he couldn't touch her? Coop pushed his fingers through his thick black hair. His britches were tight and restrictive across his bulging groin. His chest rose and fell with his heavy breathing, and he strove to bring his emotions under control. God help him, he didn't think he could walk away from her now that he'd tasted the sweetness of her. His fingers itched to tear away the silk material and feel the warm smoothness of her breasts and the puckered arousal of her nipples. He could almost taste their scalding sweetness in his mouth. But she was staring at him with something akin to terror, and he had no choice but to back away.

"I'm sorry," he said gruffly. "I didn't mean to push myself on you like that."

"You—I—" Her voice faltered, and without another word she turned and fled to her room. Standing on the landing, Coop heard the key turn in the lock, and taking a deep breath, he made his way to his own room. Throwing himself on his bed, he tried to think of something else besides the woman on the other side of the wall. He could break through the door that separated them, if he so desired. He could claim his husbandly rights, and no man would fault him for it. He could, but he wouldn't. For a moment, she'd responded to him, and he'd been heady with the smell and taste of her. He wanted her more than he'd ever wanted any woman, but he wanted her the way she'd been for that brief moment she forgot herself. He wanted her giving and seeking the way she'd been then. He tossed on his bed, trying to ignore the ache of his groin. And all the time he heard the movements of the woman in the other room. His wife! Only when he heard the creak of her bed and the muffled sounds of her weeping was he able to cool his ardor. Then he felt like the world's biggest jackass for having forgotten she was a lady.

Chapter 6

FANCY'S RETURN TO Elizabethtown was far different from her first venture there. Coop, looking incredibly handsome in a dark suit and new boots and riding his sleek black horse, was a perfect counterpoint for her pale beauty. Their private coach rolled into town drawn by six horses and causing almost as much stir as the arrival of the Denver coach. With a flourish, Daniel drew to a halt before La Maison Francais, and Coop dismounted and hurried to help Fancy from the coach. She emerged as serene and elegant as a duchess, and many a man watching her arrival agreed that the name, fancy lady, suited her to a tee.

For her arrival, Fancy had chosen one of her favorite afternoon gowns of dark brown silk. Its skirt was draped into an elaborate bustle revealing a lining of an apple green, brown, and red floral pattern. The pale copper silk underskirt was fringed and pleated. Brown silk bows adorned the copper lace ruffle that fluttered at her elbows. Perched atop the pale golden curls piled high on her head was a bonnet of matching brown silk and a sweeping plume.

If her aim had been to have every head turned toward her, she'd achieved that. Every man doffed his hat at the elegant lady and envied Coop Fletcher for yet another overwhelming success in choosing a wife. The gimlet eyes of every woman were taking in every exquisite detail of her

costume, every tiny nuance of her bearing. Fancy could tell
Coop was pleased by the sensation she was causing.

Monsieur Dubois, having been apprised several days before he would once again house his distinguished guests,
swept forward with the proper amount of obsequious hand
kissing and droll flattery. His dark eyes shone with approval. Madame Fletcher was a guest of refinement and so-
phistication. Simply to have her here was to reflect the
cachet, the prestige his hotel enjoyed. And Monsieur Coop
Fletcher? Ah, a man of some crudities, that was true, but
never, never gauche. A handsome giant of a man who had
made much money in this rough country and had the good
grace to marry such a woman as the fancy lady. Ah, how
fortunate was he, Henri Dubois, that they chose to patronize
his establishment.

Clerks and maids were sent scurrying, seeing to every
whim of the Fletchers. Luggage was carried up the stairs
and deposited in the hotel's most elegant suite of rooms.
Tubs of water were filled. Irons were heated, spat on to test
their readiness, and delivered forthwith to the Fletcher
rooms before the spittle had dried away. Annabelle accepted them and set about pressing Fancy's gowns. She'd
outdone herself with Miss Fancy's hair and gowns, and the
triumphant arrival reflected on her as well. Now she rushed
about organizing the ribbons and petticoats and stockings
and white satin boots and slippers and hundreds of other
details that went into making her mistress so elegantly attired. There was an ulterior motive for Annabelle's industry.
Daniel had driven the stage into town, and Annabelle rea-
soned when he wasn't needed by the white folks, he'd have
a lot of free time on his hands. She meant to help him fill
that time.

Coop saw that Fancy was comfortably settled into their
rooms and went off to talk business with Carl Robinson and
other associates. Aaron had brought back word that an Indian agent was in town and looking for someone to freight
government supplies out to the Ute reservation. Coop was
especially interested in that enterprise. He'd see the Utes

got every scrap of what was coming to them. God knows the supplies were barely adequate to get through a winter, but when part of them were stolen or redirected to the forts and outposts, the reservation Indians didn't stand a chance.

Coop's lips tightened in anger when he thought of the plight of the Indians. Beaten by the superior strength of the white soldiers, their land stolen, their wives and children placed on arid land not fit to support a mongrel dog, they were slowly being starved while missionary teachers assailed the customs of their fathers, trying to wipe out all traces of other cultures that existed before the white men came.

Coop paused and took a deep breath. He wasn't here to pick over old bones, and he'd not achieve anything if he went into the meetings with a chip on his shoulder. Besides, he had something else to worry about. Whoever had been sabotaging his freight business had grown more bold. He'd said nothing to Fancy about the reason for his two-day trip, but he'd had to take a posse of his own men and ride out to Argentine pass. Mountain bandits had attacked another freight train, killing one of his men and making away with most of the supplies.

Right now, Aaron was traveling from Denver with a mule train of replacement supplies paid for out of Coop's own pocket. He rode with a guard of ten armed men. They could take such precautions for now, packing out mules instead of wagons so they could travel faster through the mountain passes and riding with an armed escort, but that meant double the men and double the mules for each delivery. He couldn't maintain that for long without a major loss of profits. Besides, Coop's lips thinned, he didn't intend to knuckle under to whoever was trying to drive him out of business. He intended to find the bastard and put a stop to his plans.

Coop threw away the end of his cheroot and entered the offices of Carl Robinson. He was shown at once to Robinson's private office. When he entered, two men rose and turned toward him.

Carl Robinson was a man of medium height, with sandy coloring and a pleasant face. Mild-mannered and dominated by his wife, Maida, Carl might have given an impression of weakness if one discounted the quick intelligence in the pale blue eyes. Behind his mild manner lurked a keen businessman with a rapacious appetite for profit. If he wasn't yet as wealthy as Coop Fletcher and Geraldine Russell and a few of the other old-timers, it was only a matter of time. He was the new breed of investors that had hit Colorado's mining towns, the men who hired Cornish coal miners to work the mines.

The placer miners were gone; quartz mining was the way now. New methods were being used, pounding the granite and shale mountains until they were forced to relinquish their treasures of gold and silver. Coop hated their methods and hated their philosophies that allowed them to rape a land of its beauty and treasures and abandon it when they were finished. He had little doubt that one day Carl Robinson would move his family back east and settle into some comfortable mansion along the Hudson River with no thought given to the pillaged land he'd left behind.

Without revealing by even the flicker of an eyelash his true feelings for Carl Robinson, Coop shook his soft, limp hand and acknowledged his introduction of the other man in the office.

"Doyle Springer," Carl Robinson said. "He's the new Indian agent for the Middle Park Reservation."

"I'm pleased to meet you, Mr. Fletcher," Doyle Springer said smoothly. Coop returned his handshake, but his keen eyes studied the handsome face. He'd seen this man before, but he wasn't sure where, and he had the needling feeling he should remember.

"As I sent word by Aaron, Agent Springer is looking for a freighter to carry supplies out to the reservation. I've told him no one knows that Middle Park route better than you."

"I've traveled it," Coop acknowledged. "What tonnage are you talking?"

The talks settled into the details of hauling. It was late

afternoon by the time Coop left Robinson's offices and made his way back along the street to the saloon for a shot of whiskey. He stood at the bar, lost in thought over all that had been said and trying to figure out why he had this uneasy feeling about Doyle Springer. Something nagged at him about this contract, but he couldn't quite put his finger on it.

"Whooee, I tell you," a young cowboy shouted from a nearby table. He and his buddies had been engaged in a game of poker, but now, too drunk to see the cards, they set to discussing the new arrival in town. "If I had me a woman like that, I'd just put her on a shelf and look at her. She's shore some fancy lady."

Coop's head jerked up at the words.

"I wouldn't just look at her," another man said drunkenly. "Only one thing a woman like that's good for. I'd strip off them fancy duds of hers and see if she's as fancy underneath, then I'd take me a taste of her, startin' right down at her toes and working my way up until I got to them smooth pearly breasts." He rubbed his hands over his chest in a slow circular motion that set his buddies to snickering. "After I tasted her real good, I'd—" His words were cut off by a big fist bunching his collar.

"Hey!" the cowboy yelped, struggling so his hat fell off. An open-handed blow ended his struggle. Another blow followed the first, and the cowboy slid out of his chair onto the floor. The man with the fist stood glaring around the table at the young cowhands.

"We don't want no trouble here, Mr. Fletcher," they mumbled. "Stacey there's blessed with a dirty mouth, but don't none of the rest of us think about your lady that way."

"Yes, sir," another one said. "We ain't ever seen a lady so pretty like her, and we sure ain't fixin' to insult her none. It's just that every man round about here's heard about her, her being so beautiful and all. Everyone's got so they call her Fancy Lady. Why, I even heard one of the mines up at Crested Butte got named after her for good luck."

Coop eased back, relaxing his fists. His fierce gaze moved around the circle of faces. How had his wife's fame spread in a few short weeks? Shaking his head, he bit back a grin and nodded at the fallen man. "Get him sobered up and tell him when he comes to that out here a smart man uses his eyes a lot and his mouth mighty little."

"Yes, sir, Mr. Fletcher," the young cowhand said. "I reckon he forgot that, sir."

"I reckon he did, son," Coop said softly. His narrowed gaze moved around the circle of faces. "Tell him next time he won't live to wake up."

"Yes, sir." The young cowhands reached for their unconscious buddy and half-dragged him out of the saloon. The bartender poured Coop another whiskey and slid it across the bar.

"On the house, Coop," he said, busying himself wiping down the dark mahogany wood. He cast Coop a quick glance from under bushy brows. "You ain't goin' t'stop the talk, Coop. You got yourself a mighty pretty lady there. Ain't a man in this place ain't wishin' he was in your boots."

Coop downed the raw whiskey, tossed a coin on the bar, and grinned at the burly man. Pulling his hat low over his eyes, he stalked out of the saloon and headed toward the hotel. All this talk of Fancy had gotten his mind off Carl Robinson and Doyle Springer and got him to thinking of the golden-haired woman who'd filled his thoughts too much these past weeks.

Whistling good-naturedly he strolled into La Maison Francais and climbed the stairs. Suddenly, he wanted to see Fancy again, wanted to watch the light play in her clear green eyes and see how her hair curled near her face before swirling over her shoulders in wild disarray. He wanted to smell her and touch her and, god help him, like that randy, drunken young cowhand, he wanted to taste her. Like as not she was resting now before dressing for the Robinson affair. He'd go to her room and sit on the edge of her bed and tell her how he felt and take her into his arms. He

could imagine her all warm and soft from her nap, suppliant, susceptible to his blandishments. He wouldn't give her
a chance to resist him, and by God, they'd skip the Robinson affair if it meant getting his wife, his fancy lady, in his
bed.

But when he threw open the connecting door to her
room, he paused and stared in disappointment. Disappointment that she wasn't napping in a darkened empty room as
he'd envisioned. People bustled in and out, and all under
Annabelle's imperious demands. A hotel maid was clearing
away bathwater and bringing fresh; another had an arm
load of towels. Still another had come running with a warm
iron.

Fancy stood serene and untouched by all the bustle, in
the middle of the room, clad only in a whaleboned corset,
a lace-edged camisole that barely covered the rounded
peaks of her breasts, and petticoats. On her hips was fastened a wire basket contraption covered with gauze pad-
ding. Coop could only stare at this malformation on his
wife's slender body.

"Oh, Coop," Fancy said, glancing up and finding him regarding her with an open mouth. "I'm not dressed yet. Your
bathwater will be ready in a few minutes, and Annabelle
has already laid out your clothes."

" 'Scuse me, sir," Annabelle bustled to the door and began
swinging it closed. "I've got to get Miss Fancy dressed. Yo'
bettah hurry, too, else yo' keep Miss Fancy waitin'." The
door closed on him, leaving him in the comparative quietness
of his own room.

The tub placed in his room was nearly filled now. Coop
bit back his frustration and, sagging onto the side of the
bed, pulled off his boots. Somehow, he'd envisioned something else in this trip to town. He hadn't imagined that he'd
have even less access to Fancy than at the ranch. There she
was always busy with the ranch house, here she was—
hell's fire, she was like a queen with all her drones buzzing
around. He pouted all during his bath, thinking of Fancy in
the other room, her firm breasts pushed high and full above

the tight whalebone. He longed to see her without all that rigging. She was outfitted like a Conestoga crossing the desert.

Peevishly, he got out of the bathtub, toweled himself, and dressed. While shaving he decided he'd better take some extra pains with himself if he were to be up to the privilege of escorting Fancy Lady to the Robinsons. He'd just knotted his tie, jerked it loose, and tried again, when a knock sounded at the connecting door. Impatiently, he threw it open, then stepped back and gawked.

Despite the whalebone and wire and petticoats, no Conestoga ever looked like this. Fancy smiled, the kind of smile a woman gives when she knows she's more beautiful than she's ever been, and moved forward a few steps. The lamplight from her own room turned her golden hair to a spun silk halo around her head. She wore a gown of lavender silk, trimmed with dark green velvet bows and an underskirt of pale green silk and lace flouncing. The bodice was cut low, revealing the tops of her creamy breasts, and his eyes couldn't rest anywhere else but there.

"You can't go out like that," was all he could think to utter.

"I beg your pardon?" she said, her smile fading.

"Your—uh, your dress." He nodded at its bodice. "You need some lace, a scarf, something." The words of the drunken cowboy came back to haunt him. No man could think of Fancy that way without answering to Coop, and by God, he wouldn't let her out of her room looking like that.

Fancy looked startled at his words, then she smiled indulgently. "But there is lace on my dress," she said reasonably, her slender fingers fluttering over the short ruffle of lace that only accentuated her revealed flesh rather than hiding it.

"It's not enough," he said gruffly. "You look—look like a dance-hall girl."

Now her smile wavered. Her eyes blinked against the moisture that threatened to spill over.

"You don't like my dress?" she asked softly. She'd

looked forward to seeing the glow of admiration in his eyes. The whole afternoon she'd primped and groomed herself with the thought that Coop would find her irresistibly attractive. She hadn't forgotten Geraldine's statement that Maida Robinson's sister from back east would be there. She was, no doubt, a real lady. Everything Fancy had planned for this evening had been meant to outshine this unknown woman. Now she stared at Coop with wounded eyes and waited for his answer.

"That's not the kind of dress my wife is going to wear in public," he stated gruffly. Fancy made no answer. Her lips pouted; her eyes were bright with tears. She took two steps back and slammed the door in his face.

"Fancy!" he called, reaching for the handle. She'd locked it! "Fancy, open this door," he demanded, knocking against the wooden panel.

"No," she called, and he could tell she was holding back tears.

"The dress isn't so bad. It's just a bit daring for Elizabethtown." An ominous silence came from the other side. Coop pounded on the door again. "Fancy!"

"I'm not going to the party!" came the answer.

"You have to. They're expecting us." His words were inadequate, even to his own ears. "I mean, your dress is not so bad. I like it." He stood, swearing under his breath and sweating under his suit coat. How in hell had he, Coop Fletcher, gotten into this predicament? He could ride a wagon down a thirty degree incline without batting an eye, he could tame a wild bronco, lick most men without getting bloodied, he could even bed a woman and have her moaning with pleasure before he reached his own satisfaction. He was doing business with the likes of Carl Robinson without giving an inch and making money. So how was it he was standing here on the other side of a locked door pleading with a tearful woman?

"Fancy, open this door!" he thundered. Immediately, the door was opened, and she stood on the other side, not a hair out of place, not a trace of a tear having been shed.

She was even smiling, but even Coop was not so inexperienced with women as to believe that smile was the same as it had been the first time she opened the door. He saw the dimple in her stubborn chin, saw the prim line of her mouth, and the crackle of green fire in her eyes. The ivory flesh above her bodice rose and fell as if she were striving to calm herself. Her voice was deceptively sweet as she spoke.

"Did you call me?" she asked with feigned lightness.

"Yes, I—I like your dress," he said gruffly and turned away. "We'd better go. We'll be late."

"Of course, we will be," Fancy said sweetly. "I'll just be a moment. I'll get my shawl." She disappeared within her room and returned, a lacy length thrown about her shoulders. Her low bodice was covered.

"That's better," Coop growled and was met with another docile smile from beneath her lowered lashes. Taking her arm he escorted her downstairs and out to the hired carriage which would take them the quarter mile through town to the Robinson mansion. Fancy was quiet beside him, and he had no idea if she felt the same anxiety as he. Rubbing his clammy palms against his thighs, he jumped out of the carriage and helped her down, and like a man going to his own hanging, he escorted her up to the porch. The Robinson house was built of brick, its entrance laid with slate taken from the hills. Doors were thrown open from the hall leading into two parlors, one of which had been cleared of its rug for dancing. Its pine floor had been polished to a high gloss. In the front parlor, a pianoforte dominated the bay window, and chairs had been set about for guests.

"I'm so delighted you could come," Maida Robinson said when Coop and Fancy entered and made their way along the receiving line. Carl welcomed Coop and slapped him on his back. Maida was a full-blown woman who once had been a beauty, but indolent living and a sweet tooth had thickened her waist and hips and shaped her breasts to the full curve of a dowager. She was elegantly clad in a cream and lace silk creation totally unsuitable to her figure. Her glossy black hair, the only thing to have retained its original beauty, was piled high on her head and spilled in rich ringlets over one plump white shoulder.

"My dear Coop, I've so wanted you to meet my sister, Claire, who's visiting here from the east." Maida turned to the slender, dark-haired woman standing next to her. With a rustle of petticoats, Claire turned, her pink lips parting in studied surprise, her blue eyes widening in appreciation as she gazed frankly into Coop Fletcher's eyes.

"How do you do, ma'am," he said awkwardly. "Welcome to Elizabethtown. I hope you'll like our country."

"I'm liking it better all the time, Mr. Fletcher," Claire Williams replied softly. "I've not met you before. Do you live here in Elizabethtown?"

"No, ma'am. I have a ranch outside of town. I cam—my wife and I came into town today." He turned to Fancy as if he'd forgotten her until now. Taking her arm, he hustled her forward like a mulish child. "This is Fancy, my wife."

"How do you do, my dear," Claire said patronizingly. "Maida didn't tell me how young you are. She did say you traveled here from the south just to marry Coo—" she caught herself and smiled engagingly at Coop. He was grinning back like the biggest fool Fancy had ever seen. "Mr. Fletcher," Claire went on. "How very brave of you. You must have been in desperate need to have made such a journey."

"No more so than you must have been, Miss Williams. After all, as you've so kindly pointed out, *I* am still young."

Claire's face flushed with anger. Her thin lips pinched together as she fought to regain her control and air of superiority. Finally, she smiled at Coop.

"Why, Mr. Fletcher, your bride is simply charming. I'm sure we're going to enjoy getting to know each other." She patted Fancy's hand condescendingly. "But not now, dear, I really must greet my other guests. I'm sure you'll find someone else to talk to in the parlor."

Fancy gritted her teeth and smiled sweetly at her sum-mary dismissal. "What a charming person," she said, following Coop into the drawing room.

He paused and looked around, his expression unreadable, but she'd come to know some of his moods, and his eyes, those silver eyes that saw too much and gave little away, were guarded. With a start she realized this was the first time Coop had been inside the Robinsons' house. Now he stood taking in the other gentlemen who stood talking to one another.

A crystal chandelier must have held a hundred candles and gave off a dazzling light, reflecting in the silks and satins of the ladies' gowns and the sweating bald pates of some of the men. Coop stood looking about the room, and Fancy sensed he wasn't certain of whether to stand at one side or to move forward boldly.

His hesitation was endearing to her. This was the man she'd already seen in action around the ranch, coming and going on horseback, bossing his men, troubleshooting his freight lines. Somehow she sensed he was afraid of no man, indeed, at their wedding he'd greeted these same men without hesitation, but here in this setting, he stood as if flummoxed, uncertain of his reception in spite of the invitation. At this moment, he was Coop Fletcher, a half-breed orphan, kicked around by anyone who felt like lifting a foot and not worth much in the white man's eyes.

"Darling, I'm so happy I came," she said, gripping his arm and pressing herself against his side. Coop turned to look at her as if a man waking from a dream. Fancy's smile was wide and intimate, conveying to the whole room that she and Coop shared something special between the two of them. The other guests looked at the handsome young couple, and most of them forgot his origins. They remembered he was a rich and powerful force in town and he'd just married a beautiful southern lady.

"Do you mind introducing me to some of your friends, or do you still find my attire unacceptable?" She raised one eyebrow mockingly. She'd thrown aside the lace shawl, but even at that her dress was surprisingly modest in view of

Maida's bare shoulders and the necklines of some of the other ladies' gowns. Her grin coaxed one from him. He threw his head back and laughed, a full, rich sound that caused other heads to turn, while people wondered what the handsome Coop Fletcher had found so amusing. They saw his regained ease and moved forward.

"I find you very acceptable, Mrs. Fletcher," he said in a soft tone that reached only her ears. Her smile was radiant, the look of a woman in love. Coop led his bride forward and took great pleasure in presenting her. In turn Fancy alternately charmed and disconcerted everyone with her quick, open wit and wicked repartee.

Maida's soiree was a success, due in large part to Fancy and Coop; a most colorful couple, was the general consensus. Despite the limitation of a mountain town, the party was not without its entertainment. After a supper of cold sliced venison, wild partridge, beef and ham, potato casseroles, and freshly baked bread and pies, everyone retired to the parlor, where Claire Williams seated herself prettily at the pianoforte and regaled them with several selections of Beethoven and Mozart.

"How talented your sister is," Lillian Howe gushed when Claire had concluded her recital and smilingly bowed at the polite applause.

"My little sister always was the clever one," Maida said. She turned to Fancy, her expression smug. "Do you play, my dear? We must show off your talent as well, since you're a newcomer to Elizabethtown."

Fancy was caught off guard by Maida's request. "Yes. I—do," she stuttered, glancing around.

"Then do play a selection for us," Maida said magnanimously, encouraging the others to applaud at her request.

"I—I'm not really prepared," Fancy hedged.

"Oh, we understand, my dear," Beatrice Osgood said encouragingly. "We haven't much to entertain us up here in this mountain town, so we must fall back on our own devices. If you play or sing, you must share your talent with the rest of us."

"Land sakes, we've all inflicted ourselves on one another out of simple boredom at one time or another," Geraldine Russell said, and Fancy was left with no alternative but to go to the piano. Seating herself she ran her fingers across the keys in the introduction of yet another classic piece. Then she glimpsed Claire's expectant face. Her presentation of the classic melodies had been well-done, but the audience was tiring. No matter how well she played, it would be anticlimatic now. Fancy glanced at Geraldine and remembered her words. Be bold, and don't let them back you down.

Her fingers glided over the keys, the tempo quickening. The men sat up and looked less bored. Fancy broke into a rollicking version of "A Bicycle Built for Two," her clear sweet voice filling every corner of the room and waking those bored husbands who'd dared to sleep or lapse into talk of the mines. She heard the ripple of shock go about the guests but continued with the popular ditty.

"Join me," she called, striking the chords again. Half the room joined her in singing the song again, and by the time she'd finished, all had. Before they could loss their nerve, she played the opening chords for "When Johnny Comes Marching Home Again," singing it through once at a slower tempo, so they could pick up the words. Again her sweet voice conveyed the loneliness of the southern women as they'd waited for their men to return from the war. Everyone, regardless of what their sympathies had been during the war, joined her in a livelier repeat of the song. Fancy led them through several more songs, then relinquished her place at the piano to a loud round of applause. Claire Williams's smug expression was gone now as she watched Fancy with some speculation.

The evening drew to a close, and Fancy reclaimed her shawl and bade her hostess good-bye. Coop stood at her elbow, flushed with success and too much brandy. For his sake Fancy was grateful the evening had gone so well.

"Why, you've surprised us all with your singing and playing," Claire said with mock graciousness. "Have you had professional training?" Her manner indicated that she was already every bit a part of the community while Fancy was but a newcomer, a usurper.

"Oh, my, no," Fancy said, batting her eyelids as if mortified at the very thought. "My father would have rolled over in his grave at the thought of one of his womenfolk performing professionally."

"You are so talented, my dear," Lillian Howe said. "I do hope you'll join our ladies' club. We meet every first Tuesday afternoon of the month. Why that's next Tuesday at my house. Do say you'll come, my dear. I should be so pleased to sponsor your membership."

"We'll be staying in town for a few days," Fancy said, "and I should be pleased to attend your ladies' meeting. How kind you are to invite me."

Lillian Howe flushed with success. If Maida had been the first to invite the new Mrs. Fletcher to her home, Lillian was to be her sponsor. Maida's frown only strengthened her notion she'd managed a coup.

Amid good nights, the guests departed the Robinsons' house, and Coop bore his wife back to their hotel in triumph.

"You've set the elite of Elizabethtown back on their ears," he said appreciatively as they climbed the stairs. It seemed such a long time since she'd walked down these stairs to meet him on their wedding day.

"I suspect they liked it," she said now, laughing. "They were a bit staid."

"Did you behave like this among your parents' friends?"

"Yes," Fancy answered truthfully, thinking of her father. "My father wanted me to think on my own and never to accept something simply because others had. I had to know something was right for me."

"He sounds like a man I would have liked."

"Oh, you would have, Coop. And he would have liked you." She'd paused on the top step and turned back to him. Their eyes were level. She saw the dark passion growing in his glance and felt timid. She couldn't risk letting him kiss her again. She forgot all about being a lady when he touched her like that. Playing this role was far more challenging than she'd imagined. She had to keep her senses about her. Leaning forward, she dropped a light kiss on his mouth and before he could draw her closer, whirled and ran lightly down the hall to her own door. A light quick tap brought Annabelle, and she was inside, safe. Whether from Coop Fletcher or her own passions, she wasn't quite sure.

"Yo' shor' look happy," Annabelle said. "Yo' look like the cat that swallowed all the cream."

"That's just the way I feel," Fancy said dreamily. "That's just the way I feel."

Chapter 7

*T*HE TOWN HOUSE was not nearly as grand as the ranch house, not as sturdily built, nor did it possess the wonderful view of alpine pastures and distant snow-capped mountain peaks. In fact it barely possessed a view at all, built as it was against one of the straight granite sides of the gulch. The front of the house faced onto the town with a small front and side yard with a badly neglected garden.

Fancy spent the next few days going over her new town house, directing the hired girls in their cleaning and a Chinese gentleman in the garden. In her spare time, she poured over the catalogs ordering furniture, carpets, and drapes from Denver. As with all projects, she threw herself into it, so that she was unaware the wind had shifted among the good ladies of Elizabethtown.

Coop had become involved in his business enterprises, so she seldom saw him during the day, and one night he sent a message he wouldn't be home at all. During this time, with Annabelle accompanying her, Fancy took the opportunity to learn more about the town where she would live for one year of her life and more if Coop had his way. Dressed in another gown designed to capture the admiration and envy of all the citizenry, she promenaded forth to see the town.

A large general store dominated the main street. Inside it carried all manner of things from potbellied stoves and cracker barrels to boots and baby carriages. Fancy even found schoolbooks, tobacco, and plum preserves alongside men's Stetsons and women's long johns. Next to the general store was the town newspaper. She could hear the clack and wheeze of its printer.

Hurrying past the barber shop with its shelves of shaving mugs and hair tonic bottles, and the meat market where sides of beef hung alongside a stuffed elk, she turned into a long narrow establishment. The sign outside claimed it to be Dr. Daniel McCarty's Pharmacist. Inside, various colored and shaped vials and bottles were neatly lodged on narrow shelves and behind round glass-topped counters. Cabinets of myriad small drawers graced the nooks and crannies.

Fancy paced along the plank floor studying the labels on the bottles. There seemed to be many remedies for female complaints, all of them promising amazing results and all of them created by a doctor of some sort. Stomach bitters, cod liver oil, cathartic pills, sulphur, anti-pain plaster, and worm expellers vied with herbal nostrums of squaw vine, mandrake root, and summer savory, pressed soaps, and unsweetened wheat food. An amputation kit was displayed behind one of the glass counters, its saws and pliers bringing a shudder to Fancy's slender shoulders.

She turned to leave when she spotted Lillian Howe and Mary Peabody chatting in one corner. Inclining her head in a slight bow, Fancy smiled.

"Good morning, ladies," she greeted them.

"Mrs. Fletcher," Lillian Howe said after some hesitation. Her tone was icy, her expression stiff and unfriendly. Sensing she'd interrupted their conversation and they were merely waiting for her to pass on, Fancy took the hint.

"Lovely day isn't it," she said and moved toward the front of the store. With a sniff of disapproval at the two ladies, Annabelle followed. There was no answer from Lillian or Mary, and Fancy forgot any discomfort she might have felt at the encounter in her amusement toward Annabelle. She was steadfastly loyal to Fancy. Since their arrival in Elizabethtown, Annabelle's moodiness had dissipated. Fancy'd just about decided Annabelle didn't like ranch living until she'd caught a glimpse of her maid laughing with Daniel, the black hand who'd driven their coach to town. Now as they passed a store bearing hats and other women's apparel, Fancy turned in and Annabelle followed.

The shop was filled with bolts of cloth, cards of ribbons and buttons. Annabelle's eyes went big as she fingered a red-sprigged muslin.

"What's your favorite color ribbon?" Fancy asked her friend and maid. The brown-skinned girl looked around the counters until her gaze settled on a wide red ribbon. "That would go pretty with that old red-striped gown you gave me," she said. Reluctantly, she drew away from the muslin. Fancy felt a wave of regret wash through her. Once the tickets west had been purchased and her own trousseau bought, there'd been little left of the money Coop had sent, not enough to buy Annabelle a new gown. Uncomplaining, Annabelle had taken Fancy's old threadbare dresses and set about repairing them for herself. Now Fancy watched Annabelle's face as she studied the various bolts of fabrics. How she longed to give Annabelle a gift, but she had only a few coins left from their travel money, and Coop had offered her no more. He should have seen to it she had an allowance, she thought stormily. Even when she'd placed her order for things for the town house and the ranch, he'd given the driver a purse of money to pay for the items. Now, on impulse, Fancy stepped forward.

"How many yards do you think you'd need for a new gown?" she asked Annabelle. Annabelle's dark eyes widened.

"I wasn't wantin' any, Miss Fancy," she murmured. "I was just dreamin' a little."

"Everyone deserves to have her dreams come true, sometime," Fancy said. "How many yards?"

"Four or five yards ought to be enough," Annabelle said, "but Miss Fancy, we ain't got the money to pay for even one."

Fancy glanced at the clerk, who'd been listening to them. "I'm Mrs. Coop Fletcher," she said firmly as if she were certain of what she was about to do. "I should like to buy some lengths of cloth and have the bill sent to my husband."

"I know who you are, Mrs. Fletcher," the woman answered, "and your credit is good in my store."

"Thank you," Fancy said, casting a triumphant glance at Annabelle. "We'd like five yards of this cloth and the same of that one and that one."

"Lawd, Miss Fancy. Yo' goin' t'get us both in trouble with Mr. Fletcher."

"I don't think so, Annabelle. In any case let me worry about it. I should also like some of those buttons and that lace and some of this red ribbon. Is there anything else you'd like, Annabelle?"

"Not me, Miss Fancy," Annabelle said fervently.

Fancy's glance fell on some lacy material and she crossed to it, holding it out away from her. "I'll have enough of this for curtains for the parlor," she said with a flourish.

"Yes, ma'am," the proprietress said, measuring and cutting as fast as she could. The door bell had sounded while Fancy was making her selections, and now Claire Williams and Maida Robinson stepped forward.

"Surely, you aren't buying all those things for your maid?" they said, scandalized.

"All but the lace," Fancy answered. "Don't you buy your maids material for new clothes?"

Maida sniffed disapprovingly. "We don't have personal maids out here, Mrs. Fletcher," she said primly. "The war was fought to free these poor black people, and you and Mr. Fletcher both have chosen to continue to hold them in bondage as if there'd never been a war."

"Why, Annabelle is not in bondage," Fancy said with some amusement, thinking of Annabelle's nagging, flippant tongue and sassy ways. "She can come and go as she chooses. She just chooses to stay with me. We grew up to-gether."

"Mmmmphf," Maida said. "We aren't used to the likes of such things out here. We take care of ourselves and don't require such pampering. We don't profit by the sweat of someone else."

"Why, Maida Robinson," Fancy said, feeling her temper grow, "that's a big lie." She heard the gasp of the clerk be-hind the counter but went on. "Your husband hires Irish and Welsh miners for a pittance. You hire their wives to clean your houses and wash your clothes." She wasn't exactly certain of this, but Maida had just made her too mad to go back now. "If you could convince one of them to become your personal maid and be at your beck and call every min-ute, I believe you'd jump at the chance."

"I've never been so insulted in my life," Maida Robinson said. "No one has ever called me a liar to my face and cer-tainly not a—a—young woman who's supposed to know better behavior."

Fancy could see she'd gone too far. "You're quite right to be angry," she said. "I shouldn't have called you a liar, and in truth, I didn't mean it the way it came out. I simply meant you weren't looking at things from all sides, not even for yourself."

"You needn't apologize," Maida said. "After my kind-ness in inviting you to my home, this is the way I'm repaid. Come, Claire. Let's leave this place."

Claire put her arms around Maida's shoulders protec-tively. "I don't know what part of the south you're from, Mrs. Fletcher, but ladies of quality were never brought up to behave as you just have." The two women stalked from the store. Fancy watched them leave, her spirits subdued. Claire Wiliams's words rang in her ears. Just when she'd begun to believe she could carry off being a lady, she spoiled it all by losing her temper. Annabelle came to her side, the bundles of dress material under her arm.

"Don't pay them no never mind, Miss Fancy," she said softly. "If they was ladies like they pretend to be, they wouldn't have said the things to yo' they did. 'Sides, ain't none of their business whether I choose to stay with yo' or not."

"I know, Annabelle," Fancy said, all joy in their outing gone. "But Maida Robinson's husband is important to Coop. I shouldn't have flared up at her like that. Papa always used to say my temper'd be my downfall. Come on, let's get back to the hotel."

That night Coop returned to find a much subdued wife. They went down to supper in the hotel dining room, Fancy a vision of beauty on Coop's arm, but once they were seated, he saw her expression was crestfallen.

He wasn't certain quite what to do. He'd already grown used to her vivacious chatter. Since their triumphant night at the Robinsons, she'd seemed easier with him, happier somehow, more open. Now the old wariness was in place.

"What did Elizabethtown's famous fancy lady do today to keep herself busy?" he asked, trying to tease her into a conversation.

"I did some shopping," she said tentatively. "I hope you don't mind that I charged some material for dresses for Annabelle and curtains for the town house parlor."

"Of course not," Coop said in some relief at the thought that that was all that bothered her. "I should have thought to leave you some money. I'll see that you get a household allowance from now on."

"That's very kind of you," she said somberly. "You may not want to though when you hear what I've done."

"What have you done?" he asked indulgently. Her lower lip was pushed out in an entrancing pout. He longed to lean across the table and nip at the sweet flesh.

She cast him a full glance, her green eyes gone dark and troubled. "I've destroyed your business with Carl Robinson," she wailed, and once she'd started she couldn't stop. "I truly didn't mean to. I was just so mad, and I've always spoken out when I should just keep my mouth closed," she said. Pressing one hand against her lips, she fought back the tears. Coop glanced around the dining room and wished he'd chosen a more secluded table.

"I doubt if you managed to do that," he consoled her.

"You don't know."

"Tell me."

"I called Maida Robinson a liar." Her eyes were tragic in her pale face. Coop bit back a grin.

"Why did you call her a liar?" he asked patiently and listened while Fancy told him of her meeting with Maida and Claire.

"Maida's got a temper herself, and she's a bit of a puncture lady."

"What's that?" Fancy raised her tear-filled eyes to his in puzzlement.

"She's a lady who does a fair job of puncturing someone's reputation."

Fancy giggled. Her green eyes were liquid and brilliant with sudden humor. Coop laughed with her, thoroughly enchanted by this woman.

"Don't let her hoodwink you," he said when their shared laughter had died away. "Actually, you did the best thing you could have. You backed her down. Folks out here admire someone with courage to speak up for themselves. They don't think much of meanness and bullying, and they don't root for the underdog unless they think the underdog's going to win in the long run." He paused and took her hand. "This isn't the genteel society you're used to back home. I may have done you a disservice in bringing you out here."

His words were so kind, so generous that she was touched by them. At any other time she might have agreed with him, but not now. Now she was lost in the silver gray power of his eyes and the warmth of his hand covering hers on the table between them. She didn't want to contemplate what life would be like without Coop Fletcher in it and sharing a life, even for a year, meant being here in Elizabethtown and making a place for herself. What would it be like, she wondered, to climb the stairs like a real hus-

band and wife and close the door of their room, leaving just
the two of them? How would it be to have Coop's long
arms close around her in a sweet embrace and to feel the
passion grow between them? She knew the feel of his lips,
the taste and scent of him. Her very nerve endings remembered the hard ridges of his lanky body pressed against her
own and even now woke like a slumbering child to shriek
its desires.

Coop read some of what she was thinking in her eyes,
and his grip on her hand tightened. Wordlessly, he pressed
a kiss on her palm. She felt the heat of his mouth on her
skin and closed her eyes against the wave of warmth that
flooded her.

"Fancy?" he murmured, and she drew her hand away.

"You pro—" she began, then the memory of the things
he'd said lay between them. He'd said she would come to
him. She'd be the one to open the locked door that held
them apart. She wanted to, more than anything in her life,
she wanted to, but she thought of what Coop wanted out of
his life and of the lies she'd told him. Her lashes lowered,
and he sensed her mood had changed.

"I'm tired," she whispered. "If you'll excuse me, I believe I'll retire early."

"Fancy!" Heads at other tables swiveled to look at them.
Coop cursed under his breath. This was no place to woo a
reluctant lady. The right time would come. He could be patient. He smiled at her.

"Tomorrow, Daniel and the other men will be back with
the furniture and goods you ordered. We'll unload the
things for the town house before I send the rest out to the
ranch."

"All right. I'll be ready early in the morning." She left
the dining hall, and Coop noted that many a gaze followed
her retreat. Lounging back, he lit a cheroot, waiting for the
smoke to ease the tightness in his body. He didn't know
how much longer he could go on like this. He was as randy
as a bull. He considered visiting the parlor house he once
frequented down at the other end of town, but the thought

of bedding Lillie or one of the other girls didn't set well with him. Not when Fancy was sleeping in the room next to his, warm and golden and innocent.

Sighing with regret for the way the evening had ended, he paid his bill and sauntered outside. It was Monday night, and the street was relatively quiet. Miners and hands from the few scrabble hard ranches didn't usually come into town until Saturday when all hell broke loose. As Coop walked along the streets of Elizabethtown, he thought of many things, of the years of loneliness when there'd been no soft woman's touch to gentle his own wild restlessness.

He thought now of Fancy and the tears she'd shed on his behalf. Those tears had said more clearly than words could have done that she had some caring for him. She hadn't wanted to hurt him with the Robinsons. The thought of that made him expand within himself, feel the fullness life now offered. He walked all the way to the end of town and back again before finally retiring to his own bed. Soon he thought, his bed would not be empty. It would be shared by a woman who was coming to care for him whether she wanted to or not, a woman who seemed to have forgotten he was a half-breed.

The next morning when Fancy rose, Coop was already gone. Quickly she dressed and, with Annabelle, walked to the town house. Coop had said the freight wagons with the new furniture and bedding would arrive in the morning. That would give her time to return to the hotel and ready herself for the ladies' club meeting she'd been invited to attend. She'd spent a wretched night trying to decide what to do after her run-in with Maida. Should she go and pretend nothing had happened or stay away altogether? She'd finally decided to brazen things out. She'd go and be as friendly to Maida as she knew how to be.

The arrival of the freight wagons cut off any further thought of the afternoon meeting. With Polly and Daniel's help, Annabelle and Fancy had wrought a miracle in a few short days. The small morning parlor had been wallpapered in a pale cream embossed pattern with a double border of flowers running around the top. Fancy had weeded out the heavy pieces of furniture that had overpowered the small room. Rescuing a small settee of rosewood with green tapestry, she'd placed this before the fireplace with its white marble mantel. Other odd chairs had been grouped according to their shape and pattern. Two side chairs of walnut with a carved back of birds, berries, vines, and flowers and having cabriole legs occupied a choice spot before the front windows. A plain, roughly made table sat between, its crudeness covered by a long tablecloth of lace. Fancy had sent away for a new lamp to sit on this table. Annabelle had set about at once hemming lace curtains and before long the windows were gracefully draped with sunlight streaming through the sheer panels.

The wagons delivered rugs, a new settee and matching chairs for the main parlor, and under Fancy's supervision the men soon had the things unloaded and set in place. She'd chosen a pale blue wallpaper for the main parlor, and the new rug echoed the color in a border of blue roses. The furniture was elegant yet surprisingly comfortable with its tufted backs and arms. Fancy had imagined Coop seating himself for an evening before the fire and made her choices accordingly.

Even the entrance hall had not escaped Fancy's touch. Wallpapered as it was in a Chinese design and its well-polished wooden floors and simple hall tree and table, the hall projected an image of prestige and wealth.

Fancy was at work in one of the bedrooms upstairs adding last-minute touches when Coop called out from below. Wanting to see his expression as he viewed his home, Fancy immediately dropped her tools and rushed to the stairs.

"This must be my house," he said upon spying her, "for there's my fancy lady."

"Do you like it?" she called down, leaning over the bannister.

"It's the perfect setting," he said approvingly. "But come down and see. I've brought you company."

"It's just me," called a familiar voice, and Geraldine Russell came into view, her face turned up to Fancy. "I came in early for that ladies' social. I have to go down and see Carl Robinson first about some business."

"Oh, I'm so glad you came," Fancy cried, taking off her apron and rushing downstairs. "What do you think about everything?"

"You've done a good job," Geraldine said, nodding, "yet you've kept it homey."

"I want that. I guess I tried to put in this place and the ranch the kind of things I always wanted to have in a home." She saw the puzzlement in Geraldine's eyes and smiled. "It's one thing to grow up in such a place, but you know how a woman always wants her own home."

Geraldine nodded. "I reckon I do."

Coop wandered back from the morning parlor. His eyes were filled with gratitude. "It's grander than the Robinsons' house," he declared like a small boy who'd just discovered his wagon was bigger than everyone else's.

"Wait until you see what I have in mind for the ranch," Fancy answered, flushed with success at her first attempts at decorating.

"What are the bedrooms like?" Coop asked, hurrying up the stairs to see.

"I've kept them fairly simple," Fancy said, following behind him. Proudly she led them from room to room, showing off the fresh paint and wallpapering and new rugs and furniture. The house had taken on an aura of wealth.

"There's much more I want to do here," she said shyly when they stood again in the lower hall. "Things I'll want to send for, new china and porcelain figures and pictures and fans for the walls."

"Doodads," Coop scoffed.

"Never you mind, Coop Fletcher," Geraldine said. "If Fancy chooses those things for your home, you just let her. It's her home, too."

Fancy was grateful for the older woman's support. Coop just flashed a boyish grin.

"I'll leave it up to you ladies," he said. "The next time we come to Elizabethtown we'll stay here." He glanced at Fancy. "Will you be ready to return to the ranch tonight?"

"I believe so. I have an engagement this afternoon." She smiled at Geraldine.

"We're going to a ladies' meeting," the old woman said.

"I'd better hurry if I'm going to have time to freshen up a bit before we go. I'll have Annabelle go back to the hotel with me and pack our trunks while I'm at the meeting."

"I'll stop by for you when I've finished seeing Carl Robinson," Geraldine said, following Coop out of the parlor.

Glancing around one final time, Coop smiled at Fancy and put his arms around her, pulling her close. She stiffened, not wanting to push him away in front of Geraldine, yet angry with Coop for taking these liberties, for making her pulse race so. She looked every place but at him, until she realized he was waiting for something from her. Her gaze flew to meet his. His eyes were warm.

"Thank you," he said earnestly, and she forgave him everything. The stiffness left her, and she wanted to return his embrace. A blush rose on her cheeks, and her eyes sparkled.

"Isn't that what a good wife is supposed to do?" she asked lightly.

Coop's expression became serious. "Among other things," he said huskily. His wide hands spanned her cinched waist, drawing her closer to him. Fancy's pulse thundered in her ears. He was going to kiss her, she realized and sought frantically for some diversion.

"Please, Coop. We have a guest," she said, turning her head away so his lips brushed against her rounded cheek.

"Land's sakes. Don't y'all pay me no never mind," Geraldine said gruffly. "It does a body good to see young people together."

"We'll finish this at a later time, Fancy Lady," Coop said, releasing her. Touching the brim of his hat with one finger in a final farewell, he escorted Geraldine down the walk and into her buggy. Climbing in beside her and taking up the reins, he drove off in the direction of Carl Robinson's mill.

"We better hurry if yo' goin' be ready to go when Mrs. Russell comes callin' for yo'," Annabelle reminded her. They hurried back to the hotel, where Annabelle helped Fancy into an afternoon gown of blue and gold satin damask with an underskirt of paler blue silk. The gown was stunning and set off her exquisite ivory skin and gold hair. She was just perching a matching bonnet atop her curls when a knock sounded at the door.

"Mmmm, Missus Russell's early," Annabelle said, going to answer, but a hotel clerk waited with a note for Fancy. Geraldine stood right behind him.

"I'm ready," Fancy said. "Just let me see what this is about." Thinking it might be a message from Coop, Fancy hurried to open the heavy cream envelope and stood staring at the ornate, spidery script. Her face went pale, and she remained silent.

"What is it?" Geraldine asked, alarmed at her expression.

Fancy raised her head and stared at the older woman who had befriended her. "It's from Lillian Howe," she said slowly. "She sends her regrets but withdraws her sponsorship of me for the ladies' club. She suggests it might be a good idea if I don't call this afternoon."

"Nonsense. What's this all about?"

"I was rude to Maida yesterday. That has to be the reason."

"Mmmphf, seems to me that woman run this town," Annabelle spoke up.

"Tell me what happened, Annabelle," Geraldine demanded and listened quietly while Annabelle recited their meeting with Maida and her sister.

"That Lillian Howe would withdraw her support," Geraldine muttered. "She hasn't got a lick of sense in her body or a bit of backbone. She does whatever Maida wants her to do."

"Well, I guess that's that," Fancy said, taking off her bonnet and trying not to show she was upset. The truth was she'd looked forward to getting to know the ladies of Elizabethtown better and of inviting them to tea and socials now that she had the town house in order. All her plans and hard work seemed for naught now, and the worst of it was that she was letting Coop down. She sank down on the side of the bed, her shoulders slumped.

"I'll be your sponsor," Geraldine snapped angrily.

"I can't ask you to risk your own social standing with your friends, just for me," Fancy protested.

"I ain't riskin' nothin'," Geraldine said. "I'm richer than most of their husbands, and they know it. They wouldn't dare risk offending me."

"Still, I can't force myself on them, if they don't want me."

"Fancy Fletcher, if you're tellin' me you're willin' to give up that easy, then I reckon you're not the woman I took you for," Geraldine said. "You've been doing just fine up to now in this here town. You been making them set up and take notice and helping change their attitude about Coop at the same time. If you go·slinking quietly back to that ranch, you might as well not show your face in town again."

"I can't just go to someone's house when they've asked me not to. Certainly no lady would do that."

"Pshaw, forget all this lady nonsense. Nobody out here knows for sure what a real lady is. They ain't seen many, so you can just about make up the rules as you go along."

"What about Claire Williams, Maida's sister? As she pointed out to me yesterday, my behavior was not that of a lady. She'll know I'm n—"

"They all know now, thanks to Maida's tattling tongue that you're not a lady to be insulted. You have a mind of your own, and you aren't afraid to speak up."

"That's what Coop said," Fancy whispered, then raised her head and stared at Geraldine. "He said you folks don't like underdogs unless you figure they're going to win."

"We don't like whipped puppies with their tails between their legs, that's for durn sure," Geraldine said.

Fancy got to her feet. "Well, I'm neither," she said. "And if you're willing to sponsor me, I'll be happy to accompany you to this meeting."

"Good for you," Geraldine cried, her wrinkled face beaming.

Fancy pinned her bonnet at a jaunty angle and, taking up a matching parasol of silk and lace, led the way downstairs. A buggy carried them down the street, past the stores and businesses, past Coop's new town house to the Howe residence. The women alighted and made their way up the sidewalk to the front door, which flew open well before they were there. Lillian Howe stepped out on her porch and faced Geraldine Russell.

"Missus Russell, I'm so happy to have you come to my home," she began, her manner almost fawning. Her expression hardened when she glanced at Fancy. "I reckon you didn't know that we've asked Mrs. Fletcher not to come to our meetings after all. We've found her behavior unbecoming to all the principles we hold important."

"What's that, Lillian? Honesty, forthrightness? If Mrs. Fletcher is not welcome in this organization, then I withdraw my own membership to it."

Lillian Howe's eyes widened. "We wouldn't want you to do that, Geraldine," she said slowly. "If you vouch for Mrs. Fletcher's worthiness, then I'm sure there's been some misunderstanding somewhere. Come inside, and we'll straighten things out." She threw her door open, and Geraldine and Fancy entered. Lillian's home was almost a copy of Maida's. There was little time to note details, as they were led directly to the front parlor where the other ladies sat sipping tea. The moment Maida Robinson saw Fancy enter, she got to her feet. Claire was at her side, her expression angry and disapproving.

"If that woman stays, I shall not," she said grandly. "I'll not sit in the same room with a man or woman who would call me a liar to my face."

"Oh, sit down, Maida," Geraldine said. "Far better she said it to your face than to your back as many of your friends do." Her gaze went around the room, and more than one lady looked away. Outraged, Maida sat down.

"I've never," she sputtered.

Fancy almost felt sorry for the other woman. Crossing the room, she held out a hand. "I wish to apologize to you, Maida, for my hasty words," she said sincerely. "I spoke without thinking of the consequences of my words. I offer only my youth and the heat of the moment as my excuse. You've been most gracious, and I ask you to extend that graciousness to me again by accepting my apology."

Maida was left speechless by Fancy's eloquent defense. In fact, she would have liked to continue the quarrel for a while longer, for it had made her the center of attention among her friends, but to refuse such a gracious plea would have made her the one at fault. Maida never wanted to admit she was at fault, so she smiled tolerantly and nodded with all the graciousness of a queen granting a bequest.

A palpable sigh went around the room. Yet, Fancy sensed a reserve among the ladies as she took a seat.

"Have you heard from any of your people since coming out here?" one woman asked abruptly.

"No, I have no family left," Fancy answered serenely. "My mother and father died during the war."

"Why, my dear, who raised you, then?" another asked.

"I—an aunt," Fancy said, realizing each lie only led her to more.

"And she hasn't written. Tsk, tsk."

"She's dead, too," Fancy said hesitantly, looking around the circle of curious faces.

"Then you're an orphan?" Claire Williams said sweetly. "How lucky for you that Coop Fletcher wrote back east for a bride."

"Yes, I suppose it was lucky," Fancy answered, guessing that Claire's brittle tone was meant to goad her to anger. "But when I arrived and met him, I counted myself even more fortunate. Coop Fletcher is such a wonderful man."

"But, my dear, didn't it bother you to marry a half-breed?" still another woman asked, her expression avid as she waited for Fancy's answer.

"Do you mean, did it bother me to bed down with a half-breed, even one as rich as Coop Fletcher?" Fancy snapped, eyes flashing.

"My dear, of course, she meant no such thing," Maida responded. "Everyone knows Coop's no half-breed. Why, if the truth were known he probably has very little Indian blood in him. Have you noticed what a lovely pale shade of gray his eyes are?"

Fancy's anger cooled. She was immensely grateful to Maida for speaking up in Coop's behalf until she realized that if Maida's plans for Claire and Coop had come about, he would have been her brother-in-law. Perhaps she still entertained such notions.

"I meant no offense," the original speaker said. "My name is Dorrie English, and I—well, we all just think it's dreadfully romantic that you came all this distance to marry a man you didn't even know, and now you make such a handsome couple, as if you belong together."

Maida frowned. Claire pouted. Fancy smiled forgivingly.

"You're right. It was terribly romantic. I can tell you I suffered some misgivings until I got off the stage and had my first glimpse of him. He was so handsome and gallant, taking up my luggage, making arrangements ahead for my room and a hot bath. And the wedding was perfect. My mother would have been so proud if she'd been there." Fancy wiped at an imaginary tear, then thought of Adele and Monty Bourne. Both her parents would have been happy to see her on her wedding day. The thought brought real tears to her eyes, and the ladies looked at one another and back at Fancy, clucking their tongues in sympathy.

After tea, the discussion turned to improvements to be made to the town. The ladies wielded much power and from these afternoon socials had come the plans and determination that had built the churches and school and hospital in the town. The get-together ended with a request for Claire to play the piano and Fancy to sing. She refused, begging her throat was delicate and offered a recital from *Macbeth*, which won her a warm round of applause.

"You played them like a fish after the bait," Geraldine said gleefully on the way back to the hotel. "You've already got them eating out of your hand. I predict before the year is out you'll be the leader of Elizabethtown society."

"I have no desire to be," Fancy murmured. "I only want them to like me and accept Coop."

"That, they seem to be doing," Geraldine said and chuckled under her breath. "Seems to me you spend a lot of time worrying about Coop and what he wants."

"That's part of my marriage vows, isn't it?" Fancy replied smoothly.

"I guess it is," Geraldine said, gazing at the girl in some surprise. Fancy said nothing more to enlighten her. She'd told Geraldine the truth. Part of the agreement she'd made with Coop was that she'd be the proper wife and help him become established in Elizabethtown society, then she'd be free to leave with all the money she needed to live comfortably. She was only doing her job, wasn't she?

Chapter 8

*F*ANCY WAS SURPRISED at the sense of homecoming she felt upon returning to the ranch. Immediately, she and the other women set about placing the rugs and furniture as they had done at the town house. The men had painted the walls as she'd instructed, whitewash between dark oak trim, and the mountains loomed beyond the windows. She was pleased that she'd kept the furnishings simple so they didn't detract from the beauty of the outdoors. At night with a fire on the grate and the lamps casting warm pools of light, the rooms took on a welcoming aura.

Coop found himself returning to the house more readily in the evening, welcomed by a well-prepared supper, a handsome home, and a beautiful wife. The newness of sitting in a parlor watching the lamplight glow on his wife's pale golden hair and rosy cheeks never failed to enchant him. He'd never known this type of contentment, this sense of belonging, this feeling of substance about himself. Each evening as he sat pretending to read the latest issue of the *Elizabethtown Gazette* or going over accounts, he surreptitiously studied Fancy, and a yearning for her grew, different from his previous lust. For a man who'd never known love, these new sensations were unnameable. For Fancy, who'd often played at the game of love onstage, the reality of her budding feelings was unsettling.

As each of them sat in the parlor, grappling with their

feelings, the specter of their beds, large and empty with only one slumbering within, the memory of the locked door between their rooms, nudged them toward an action they were hesitant to take.

He thought she was a lady, and though she'd responded to his rough embrace, she'd obviously been disturbed by it. He had no desire to drive her away with his unbridled passion, yet he hungered for her.

Remembering her loss of control when he touched her, the passion that flared at his kiss, she felt defensive and uncertain. Claire had already reprimanded her once for unladylike behavior. She had no wish to shock Coop with such improper responses as she had thus far. So she pulled a prim air of decorum about her, conveying by every gesture her refinement and breeding.

Coop became more frustrated and often stomped outside to light a cheroot and stare at the star-studded night sky while Fancy went back over her every word and action wondering if she had, at last, given herself away.

One night as Coop and Fancy sat in the parlor stiffly pretending an unawareness of each other that gave lie to the heat of their colliding gazes, gunshots sounded.

"What the hell?" Coop cried, jumping up. "I beg your pardon, Fancy," he said, then sprang for the hall where his gun belt hung on a wooden peg. Satin embroidery thread spilled from her lap as Fancy jumped up and followed him.

"What was that?" she asked.

He turned to her abruptly, and she was stunned by his stern demeanor. His steely gaze raked over her, but she sensed his thoughts weren't on her at all.

"Stay here," he ordered. "Turn out the lights in the parlor, and stay away from the windows. Lock this door behind me." With that he was gone, and she stood staring at the empty door.

"Coop!" She disobeyed his orders and ran onto the porch. He was already halfway across the yard, dashing toward the corral. Other men were throwing saddles onto horses. At her cry, Coop swung around.

"Get inside," he shouted, and she'd never heard him use that tone of voice to anyone before. She had little doubt he was a man used to being obeyed. Her chin came up, and she meant to call out a retort, but gunshots sounded again, this time closer to the house. Coop veered, running toward the back of the ranch house.

"Sayer!" he shouted. "Bring some men!"

Fancy drew back into the ranch house, raced to put out the lamps as Coop had ordered, and pressed herself against a wall near the front windows.

"Miss Fancy, what's goin' on?" Annabelle came running from upstairs. She nearly collided with Delores in the darkened hall, who crossed herself and uttered prayers in Spanish under her breath.

"Get down!" Fancy called and peered out. Through the lace curtains, she could see Aaron Sayer astride his horse and leading another as he rode in the direction Coop had taken. Heart hammering in her ears, Fancy ran to the side windows and crouching on the floor, peered over the edge of the sill. All was black and quiet without. She heard the thud of hooves, and Aaron was there with the extra horses. Coop moved out of the shadows and leaped astride his horse. A shot rang out; Aaron slumped in his saddle. Coop's gun spat streaks of fire. The moonlight glinted on the rumps of two horses as the riders made off. Coop reined his horse and looked at Sayer.

"I'm all right," Aaron cried, clinging to his saddle. "Go on!"

"No," Fancy cried when she saw Coop meant to pursue the attackers by himself, but he couldn't hear her through the windowpane. She stood up and pounded against the glass. The sound was lost in the flurry of hoofbeats as Coop galloped after the ambushers. Aaron glanced around at her but made no gesture. Clasping his bleeding shoulder, he shouted at the other men who were saddled now.

"Coop rode out after them. Down that way," he yelled. The men spurred their horses into a hard gallop.

"Mi Dios," Delores prayed tearfully, crossing herself repeatedly. Her broad cheeks were wet with tears.

Fancy looked at the cook and felt like crying herself. Coop had ridden after those men. He could be wounded even now. Then common sense returned, and she thought of Aaron who was already wounded and needed their help.

"Delores," she said sharply so the woman stopped her praying and looked at her expectantly. "Annabelle, come help me."

She ran to the door and threw it open.

"Is it safe to go out there?" Annabelle asked, her eyes as big as saucers.

"Coop and the men have chased the ambushers away, but Aaron needs us. Come on." The three women ran around the veranda to the side yard, where Aaron stood beside his horse, trying to keep himself upright.

"Here, lean on us," Fancy ordered, taking one of his arms and looping it over her shoulder. Delores did the same on the other side. Between the three of them they got the man inside and laid him out on one of the sofas.

"I'll get your pretty new sofa bloodied," Aaron said.

"Shh, you're more important than a sofa," Fancy said, loosening his shirt and packing her shawl against the bleeding wound. "This'll stop the bleeding until we can get some help for you. Delores, go get some hot water to wash this wound. Get some bandages and salves. Annabelle, go tell Nellie to get up here at once. Don't tell her what's happened to Aaron. You stay with her children. Stop on your way there and tell River Adams, never mind he'll know what to do."

"Yo' want me t'go down to Mrs. Sayer's cottage in the dark, all by myse'f?" Annabelle asked, her eyes wide and scared.

Fancy looked at her in some exasperation. "Just pretend you're creeping out to meet Daniel," she snapped.

"Ain't no bad men out there in the dark when I meets Daniel," Annabelle sassed.

Fancy fixed her with a stern look, her green eyes glittering. "If there are bad men out there, they won't do half as much to you as I will if you don't go get Nellie. Now run!"

"Yo' be sorry if somebody gets me," Annabelle groused, but she took off at a trot.

Fancy busied herself with unbuttoning Aaron's shirt and making him as comfortable as she could. She'd had no experience with this kind of injury and felt helpless. When Delores brought the water and bandages, she set about cleaning the wound. There was an ugly hole in his side. Aaron said little during all this, moaning only once as Fancy turned him slightly.

"The bullet didn't come out the other side," she said, looking at him with wide eyes. "It's still in there."

"Nellie'll get it," he grunted, his eyes squeezed tight against the pain. Footsteps ran across the porch, the door was flung open, and Nellie was there, her red hair streaming around her shoulders, her plain face filled with dread.

"He's all right, Nellie. He's alive," Fancy said, getting up so Aaron's wife might tend to him. Nellie never said a word, nor did she embrace her husband, but set about immediately examining the wound.

"The bullet's still in there," Fancy said, watching Nellie's rough, work-worn hands gently examine her husband's body. There was a tenderness, a familiarity in her touch that spoke volumes about the woman's feelings. And Aaron's face, which had been creased in pain and worry, was calm now.

"We have to git that bullet out," Nellie spoke at last. "I'll need a sharp thin knife."

"I know just the one," Delores cried and ran off to the kitchen.

"Scald it," Nellie called after her, then looked up at Fancy. "We'll be needin' some of Coop's whiskey. It's in his study."

"I'll get it," Fancy cried and raced to retrieve the bottle. Nellie held it to Aaron's lips while he swallowed.

"No more, Nellie," he said pushing it away. "You know I ain't a drinkin' man."

"Aaron Sayer, you're goin' to need this when I start digging at you with that knife. Now you just drink this down. For once in my life, I don't mind seeing a man of mine drunk." She held the bottle to his lips, and he drank deeply and lay back. Nellie handed the bottle back to Fancy and reached for the large, sharp knife Delores had brought. Its blade glinted in the lamplight.

"I'm going to need more light," Nellie said, glancing up at Fancy. "Can you hold the lamp?"

"What?" Fancy asked falteringly. She'd planned on hiding her face or even leaving the room. Now she looked from Nellie to the lamp. She couldn't let Nellie down. Slowly, she nodded her head. "I can hold it for you," she said. The whiskey bottle trembled in her hand, and desperately, she raised it to her lips and took a swig. The liquor hit the back of her throat like a firecracker going off on the Fourth of July. Fancy gasped and coughed.

"Better let me have that," Nellie said, taking the bottle, and Fancy wasn't sure if it were because she feared for Fancy's steadiness or if Aaron truly needed the dulling effect of the whiskey. Either way, she relinquished the bottle and retrieved the lamp, kneeling at the head of the sofa and holding it so Aaron's wound was well lit. With steady hands, Nellie took up the knife and touched the point to the wound. Taking a deep breath, she began to dig through the layers of perforated, bruised flesh. Aaron started with pain, then gritted his teeth. Sweat stood out on his brow. Blood flowed from the disturbed wound.

Fancy thought she might faint, but in the presence of Nellie's steadfastness, she wouldn't allow herself such a luxury. She turned away, unable to watch as Nellie probed the wound, searching for the bullet. A scrape of metal against metal told them all she'd succeeded. Now she worked the edge of the knife around the head of the bullet and slowly, painfully drew it from her husband's body. It fell into the washbasin with an spine-chilling ting. Blood gushed out behind it.

"That's good," Delores said, leaning over the sofa. "The bleeding will clean the wound."

"Uh-huh," Nellie said, taking up a wad of bandages and packing them against Aaron's wound. "I just don't want him to bleed to death now." Her hands were sure and steady as she finished bandaging her husband, and when she was finished, she slumped beside him, her head against his shoulders.

"I thought I lost you," she said, and her voice wavered.

"Ain't goin' to lose me, woman," Aaron muttered through his pain and whiskey fog. He grinned up at her, conveying a message of lust and desire. Nellie's plain face flushed and looked around quickly to see if anyone else had noticed.

"You ain't got no sense, you fool," she scolded as his limp hand tried to settle on her breast. "I just took a piece of lead out of you. When that whiskey wears off, you ain't goin' to be fit for anything, leastwise that."

The sound of horses in the front yard drew them all, save Nellie, to the windows and then to the porches. Fancy's heart was in her throat as she sought out the tall lean figure of Coop Fletcher. He'd already swung himself out of his saddle.

"Get some sleep, men," he called out. "We'll try to trail them again at first light." With long quick steps he turned to the house and came up on the porch. "Are you all right?" he asked, taking hold of her shoulders and turning her toward the light from the lamp as if to determine for himself she'd come through unscathed.

"I'm fine," she answered, liking the warm, protected feeling he gave her. She wanted to tell him how worried she'd been about his safety but felt shy and uncertain. "Only Aaron was wounded," she rushed on.

"How is he?" Coop turned toward the door.

"He's okay now. Nellie took out the bullet." Fancy followed him inside.

Aaron turned a lopsided grin to his employer. "Did you find them?"

Coop shook his head, took off his hat, and hunkered down beside Aaron. "We'll look for them again in the morning. Are you sure you're all right?"

"Never better." Aaron grinned. "I'm just fixin' to get up from here and go down to my place and my own bed."

"You shouldn't move around," Fancy said. "You'll start the bleeding again. You can stay here until you're better. There are plenty of beds."

Aaron shook his head. "Ain't no place like your own bed." He glanced at Nellie. "Just as there ain't no woman like your own." The whiskey haze was clearing away now, and his eyes registered gratitude for the plain woman who knelt beside him. Her hand hung on to his.

"I'll have someone carry you down to your own place," Coop said and put his hat back on.

"Ain't no need to bother them. Your wife and Delores got me in here. I reckon with you and Nellie on either side of me, I can walk on my own two feet."

"That's impossible. You've just been wounded," Fancy cried. Nellie had remained silent, now she rose and sighed.

"I reckon Aaron's as stubborn as most men, and he ain't goin' to take such things into consideration," she said. "Coop and me'll haul him down. We're much obliged for you actin' so quick-like and lettin' me know."

"My goodness," Fancy cried in amazement. "What else should I have done? Are you sure you won't stay up here?"

But Aaron was already on his feet, and Coop and Nellie were hitching his arms over their shoulders, their own arms steadying him at the waist. Delores nodded her head in disapproval as the three made their way out of the house and across the yard toward Aaron's cabin. Fancy stood on the porch and watched them until she saw a wink of light as the Sayer door opened, then closed behind them. Sighing, she went back inside. Now that the danger was past, she had a hundred questions about what had happened. She'd just have to wait until Coop returned.

Delores had already cleared away all signs of Aaron's ordeal: the pan of bloody water and discarded bandages. Only the whiskey bottle remained on a nearby table. Suddenly, she was shaking, her knees unable to support her. She sank onto the settee and thought back over the events. Everything had happened so swiftly she'd hardly had time to feel afraid for herself. Her concern had all been for Coop and of course for Aaron. Nellie had been so calm about her husband's wound, setting about to help him without tears. What if that had been Coop? Could she have behaved as bravely as Nellie had? Her tearful gaze fell on the whiskey bottle, and with shaking hands she raised it to her mouth and took a deep drought. As before, it burned her throat. She coughed and breathed deeply. When the first shock was past, she felt the burning, comforting warmth travel through her cold body.

"That's not an answer," Coop said behind her. Fancy jumped, hiccuped, and looked around guiltily.

"I was just—I—" Suddenly, she was blubbering like a baby. "I was so sc—scared," she cried. "I th—thought, hic, you were going to be killed. Then when I saw Aaron wounded like that and N—Nellie just t—took out the bull—bullet l—like a real doc—hic—tor. I—I c—couldn't ever d—do that. I'm just useless out here. I—I don't have the k—kind of c—courage it takes."

Coop held back a chuckle.

"D—Don't l—laugh at m—me," she sobbed and took another swallow of whiskey on the assumption it would stop the tears and the stuttering and would give her courage. "I—I sh—shouldn't, hic, h—have come. Hic!"

Coop's laughter disappeared as he regarded her lovely face stained with tears. Her eyes were like green stones in a creek bed, liquid and moist and incredibly beautiful. He took away the bottle just as she was raising it to her lips again.

"I never knew ladies drank whiskey," he said pleasantly.

"We don't, hic." She smiled at him and was unaware that her smile wobbled on one side as Aaron's had done.

Coop repressed a grin and, sitting down on the settee beside her, pulled her down on his lap. She came willingly, flooding his senses with the scent of warm female flesh and raw whiskey. Her head went automatically to his broad chest as if it had rested there a hundred times before. His arms tightened around her shoulders, and he inhaled the scent of her hair. His cheek rested against the silken strands. He felt her breasts soft and warm against his chest, then they jiggled as she giggled softly. Raising her head she gazed into his eyes with impish humor.

"I'm not really a lady," she whispered. "Shhh! Don't tell anybody."

"Not a soul," he whispered back. "But if you're not a lady, then what are you?"

She thought for a moment, her head wobbling. "A duchess," she said with some satisfaction, "Juliet, Desdemona, Lady Macbeth."

"Lady Macbeth?" The names were all strange and unfamiliar to Coop who'd never been exposed to the theater. "Sounds like a lady to me."

"She was a very evil lady," Fancy said, playfully counting the buttons up Coop's shirt and ending at his nose. Her bleary gaze met with his. Her green eyes sparkled. "She murdered people. Lady Macbeth did."

"You'd never murder anyone, would you, Fancy Lady?" Coop asked low and husky in her ear.

The strangest shivers were rushing over her. Slowly she thought over his question, her jade eyes registering a myriad of emotions and thoughts Coop was not privy to. Finally she shook her head, her demeanor growing serious.

"I would never murder anyone," she said tearfully, "but I've told t—t—terrible lies."

"You? My fancy lady?" Coop whispered. "I don't believe it."

"I have. You wouldn't want me if you knew."

"I'll always want you, Fancy," he murmured. His silvery gaze was warm on her skin. His words touched the deep melancholia that had claimed her these past weeks.

"Will you?" she asked prettily, her light mood hiding the hidden fears.

"Always!" he breathed, and then unable to contain his desires any longer, his head swooped down, his mouth claimed hers, hot and moist and demanding.

Fancy felt his kiss all the way to the tips of her toes. She returned it with all the emotion she possessed in her clamoring body. He didn't care that she'd lied. He wanted her anyway and she wanted him, wanted his kiss to continue forever, his big hands to always slide over her body the way they were now, skimming her breasts, pressing against her waist, smoothing over her slender back, possessing her, claiming her as his lady, his fancy lady.

An ache began deep at the center of her, a void that begged to be filled, and she sensed that this big, wild man could fill that void as no one else could. Her fingers swept through the blue-black locks that had captured her from the first, her hand swept along his lean jaw to the warm hollow of his throat. Her head rested now against his shoulder, and she leaned forward to place her tongue against that smooth brown skin, tasting him as she'd once thought of doing when she first became his bride. She was his wife. She could give herself and take back pleasure from him, and she wanted to, longed to. She gave her mouth to him, in a frantic kiss no less demanding than his had been. Coop felt the flame of it to the roots of his hair. His long arms crushed her slim body to his chest, his big hands fumbled with the bustle and petticoats, wanting to feel the sweet round curve of her buttocks. He swore. The contraptions ladies donned!

The thought washed over him like a plunge in an icy mountain stream. She was a lady. The whiskey had taken away her inhibitions for now, but what about in the morning? She'd hate him if he took advantage of her now. But God almighty, how was he to walk away from her now, when she was warm and willing, as seductive and acquiescent as any Saturday night whore he'd known? Shock waves killed any lingering desire. How could he compare a lady like Fancy to a whore? He ought to be horse whipped.

Abruptly he got to his feet, spilling her off his lap onto the floor.

"Ouch!" she cried, landing on her behind and looking up at him belligerently. "Why'd you do that?"

"I think it's time we get you to bed," he said, reaching down to grab her under her arm and lift her to her feet. Fancy stood weaving, gazing at him whimsically.

"All right," she said agreeably and fell forward into his arms.

"I've got you," Coop said, scooping her up in his arms. Her body was limp, giving no resistance and no help. She lay in his arms, humming some little tune he didn't recognize while he carried her up the stairs and set her on the edge of her bed. She fell straight back. He couldn't leave her like that in her clothes, he thought in irritation. Where was Annabelle? Nowhere around when she was needed. She was probably out in the barn with Daniel. Coop felt a flash of unreasonable anger for the lucky Daniel. Then shutting his mind to the thought of his wife's soft, inviting body, he stripped away her clothes and tucked her into bed. All the while she hummed the little tune.

Chapter 9

*T*HE MORNING AFTER is never pleasant, Coop could have told his wife, especially for a lady who's never partaken of strong spirits. He stood outside her door listening for any sign of life and finally, concerned by the dead quiet on the other side, opened the door and went in. She lay with one arm flung over her brow, the other rested on the pillow. The covers had been tossed aside, so her breasts were bared. In her abandoned position, the pert nipples mocked him. One leg was free of the covers and lay long and sleek. Coop leaned over Fancy, taking in the fair skin, the smudge of gold lashes against her cheeks. Without the distraction of those green eyes, he was delighted to find a faint smattering of golden freckles across the bridge of her nose. Without her airs and haughty demeanor, she appeared more childlike and imminently vulnerable. She moaned and rolled away from him. Fearful of waking her and subjecting himself to her searing condemnations for entering her room, he left as quietly as he came, but he carried the image of his wife with him as he set about with his men, breaking a string of wild horses they'd captured.

Fancy rose with a headache that defied description. Annabelle was unsympathetic, still miffed at being sent off to fetch Nellie in the dark when the gunmen might still have been around. Nellie was at her own cabin preoccupied by her husband's wound. Delores was in the kitchen. Fancy

tried not to think about Coop and where he might be as she
settled herself on the porch with a glass of lemonade and a
fan. She would not, she decided, move until her head had
stopped aching.

From the porch she could see the corral where the men
worked training wild horses. Coop's tall lanky figure towered over them all. The sunlight was dazzling, but once her
eyes had adjusted, Fancy found her headache was leaving
her. Drawn out of a need to see her husband this morning
and to find out his reaction to a drunken wife, she slowly
wandered down to the corral. Coop was just saddling a
beautiful stallion of a reddish white color.

"That there's called a red roan, ma'am," a voice said
next to her, and Fancy glanced at a wiry, sandy-haired man.
"Frank Avery at your service, ma'am."

Fancy nodded in recognition. She didn't particularly like
this man. His gaze was insolent, almost a leer.

"Why is Coop mounting that rein like that?" she asked,
referring to the strap he'd run from the horse's bit down between his front legs.

"Well, you see, ma'am, this here horse is a mighty mean
one. He bucks off ever' rider, pert near, that's tried him.
Coop's fixin' to try and break him, and the horse can't rear
up with his head tied off like that." He snickered. "Reckon
ole Coop's not wantin' to get thrown, if he's usin' the martingale. That's a city man's way of breakin' a horse."

"Have you broken many horses, Mr. Avery?" Fancy
asked sweetly, not liking this man's criticism of Coop.

Avery shrugged his thin shoulders. "I've done my share
in my time," he said.

"But you chose not to try and break this one?" she inquired. Frank studied her pretty face with its sweep of
golden lashes, the pouty mouth, and heard the dare in her
voice.

He hesitated a moment, wishing she hadn't come down
to the corral. He had no desire to ride the Red Devil as the
hands had dubbed this horse. Everyone had kind of agreed
to let the boss do it, but now standing here beside the fancy

lady herself, smelling her perfume, seeing the swell of her breasts beneath the fabric of her gown, and the derisive challenge in her green gaze, he threw away caution and swaggered a little.

"Wasn't much of a reason to get my britches dusted before, but I reckon if you'll be watching, I'll do it." He sent her another significant glance, pulled his hat brim down, and climbed into the corral. The other hands set up a whooping, and Coop looked around.

"Well, Avery, what are you up to?" he asked.

"I figured I'd ride the red roan, if you don't mind," Avery said and resisted an urge to look back to see if the fancy lady was watching. She would be. It was her dare.

"This is the one they call the Red Devil," Coop reminded him.

Avery shrugged his shoulder. "You know what they say. There ain't no hoss that can't be rode."

"And there ain't no man that can't be throwed," Coop said pleasantly. He stepped back, a grin lighting his craggy features, but his eyes were stern. "This is an exceptional piece of horseflesh," he warned. "I want the horse broken, not damaged."

"You've got it," Frank said, letting his cockiness hide the seething anger at Coop's orders. "Take off the martingale," he ordered to the men holding the bridle. Billy Dee looked at Coop for confirmation. Coop regarded Avery a few moments more, then nodded his head. The line was removed, and Coop stepped back.

"Good luck, Avery," he said.

Avery brushed his sweaty palms against the side of his pants and quickly stepped into the saddle. The roan was still at first as if unaware anyone had mounted him. The men holding the bridle waited nervously to see what the horse's reaction would be. All along the rail fence cowboys moaned in disappointment that the roan was giving in so easily.

Then suddenly the horse jumped straight up, jerked its head, and reared, its hooves striking at the air in outrage at its loss of freedom. Avery hung on, knowing he was making a good showing for the lady, then readied himself for the jolting landing when the horse came down. The Red Devil had been an apt name; the horse charged around the corral, bucking and snorting. The hands on the fence whistled and exchanged bets.

"Waltz with the lady!" they called, egging Avery on.

The horse was tiring beneath him, Avery could tell. Unwilling to give up the spotlight just yet, he kicked the horse's sides with his stirrups. Winded, the roan squealed in pain and began bucking again. Avery kept applying the spurs. He saw Coop's face in a blur, scowling, his mouth open as he yelled some more instructions.

Avery knew Coop was yelling at him to dismount, but some deep anger kept him going. Once he got off the horse, he was just another hired hand, having to do what a half-breed boss told him to, but up here on the back of this red stallion he was his own man. No one could tell him what to do.

He kicked the winded horse again, digging in his spurs viciously. The roan became crazed. Bucking, it rammed into a corral fence, sending the rail sitters running for their lives. The big roan reared, pawing at the fence, and came down hard, its legs tangled in the railings. Avery heard the bone crack just before he leaped off and rolled to a stop near the fence where Fancy stood. Avery looked at her smugly, but her expression was horrified and accusing. Without sparing another glance for him, she ran around the corral to the cluster of men gathered around the roan.

The roan was down, its sides wheezing. One leg lay at an odd angle. Coop knelt beside the horse examining the damage. Slowly, Avery got to his feet and brushed the dust from his clothes. No one had checked to see if he was hurt, he thought resentfully. They seemed to think more of horseflesh than they did a man.

"How bad is it?" Aaron was asking. He'd finally escaped Nellie's mothering and come down to the corral to watch.

Coop looked at the white bone splinter and shook his

head. "He's done for," he said and ran a hand over the roan's heaving sides. His palm was smeared with blood. Getting to his feet, Coop looked around. Spying Frank Avery, he stalked across the corral and without a word doubled up his fist and socked Avery in the jaw. Avery went down hard and lay still, holding his jaw, his eyes angry as he glared back at Coop.

"I told you to ride him easy," Coop roared. "You should have stopped riding him when he hit the fence the first time."

"I thought I could break him," Avery whined, afraid to get up and meet that big fist again.

"I can't have a man around the place who won't listen to orders," Coop said. "Get your gear and see Aaron for your back pay. I don't want to see you on my place again."

Fancy stood watching her husband's reaction, stunned at such ferocity. This was the dark side she'd seen the night of their wedding, the night she'd asked him about being a half-breed. For the first time, she realized no one crossed Coop Fletcher. He was a mean and hard boss. There were no second chances. She shivered, wondering what she'd said the night before when she'd had too much whiskey to drink. She remembered babbling about being a lair. Had she confessed everything? Was he going to send her packing as well?

White-faced she watched as Coop spun on his heels and walked back to the downed horse. He drew his gun from his holster and aimed it at the suffering animal's head.

"No!" Fancy cried, flinging herself at Coop. She had the sensation of having thrown herself against a brick wall. A shot rang out. The horse screamed in pain and flailed with his legs.

"You little fool," Coop shouted. His long arms wrapped around her, swinging her to one side away from the thrashing hoofs. His shot had gone wild, ploughing into the horse's belly. The roan screamed again. Blood streamed from this new wound. Fancy cried out and hid her face against Coop's chest.

"You can't just shoot the horse," she cried. "It wasn't his fault he fell."

"His leg is broken, Fancy," Coop said angrily. "He's no good to anyone, not even himself. If we don't kill him, he'll suffer even more." Coop's arm cradled her to one side, while he leveled his gun and aimed again. The report was loud and sharp in the hushed air. The animal's scream was cut off, and he lay still in the dust. Fancy felt as if the top of her head were coming off. She pulled away from Coop and glared at him in disbelief.

"How can you kill a living creature like that?" she demanded.

"It's one of the hard lessons of the west, Fancy," he said. "Surely, your father had to put down a horse now and then back on your plantation."

She wasn't listening. Eyes brimming with tears, she backed away from him. He saw the disgust and fear in her and tried to take her arm, but she shook him away. He was aware of his hands watching.

"Fancy, you don't understand the way of it," he said lamely, but she only whirled and ran away from him, heading down toward the stream. Coop took a step after her, meaning to follow and help her understand, but Nellie was there placing her work-worn hand on his arm.

"Leave her be for now, Coop," she advised. "Part of this is a hold-over from last night with the shootin' and all. I'll go down and sit with her a spell."

"Thanks, Nellie," Coop said and turned back to his men. Their faces were somber, and they avoided Coop's gaze. All of them were glad to see Frank Avery go. A swaggering braggart, he'd talked more than he'd worked, and they hadn't liked the way he'd handled animals before. Now they set about hauling the dead horse away from the corrals and barns to someplace where he could be buried.

Frank Avery packed his gear and prepared to leave, but as he entered the barn to claim his horse, his gaze fell on a new cowhand who'd been brought in recently. Billy Dee was young and shy and the butt of many of the jokes in the bunkhouse, but he'd handled it all with good humor, and the men had come to like the young cowboy. Frank stood watching the young man work, mucking out the stalls, remembering all that had happened outside at the corral. Finally, he meandered over to Billy.

"Howdy, Frank," Billy said, halting to wipe his sweaty face. "I'm sorry what happened to you earlier."

"Don't think nothing about it, Billy," Frank said evenly. "I'll get me another job someplace. They're always lookin' for experienced hands. Just you be careful you don't get on the wrong side of the half-breed."

Billy started nervously and looked around. "I heard he don't like to be called that," he warned. "Besides, it was his mother who was the half-breed."

"An Injun squaw, nonetheless," Frank said and spat into the stall. "No wonder he got himself a fancy lady for his wife."

"Yes, sir, she's sure something," Billy Dee said.

"Where d'you reckon she come from, a woman like that?" Frank Avery asked speculatively. "One of them northern states likely."

"No, sir," Billy said. "That there's Miss Fancy Bourne. She was an actress back in the south."

"Are you sure, Billy?" Avery asked, narrowing his eyes.

"Yes, sir. My pa and ma took me to see a play with her in it. Her ma and pa were actors, too. I ain't ever likely to forget somethin' like that. She's shore something."

"She sure is," Avery agreed. "Well, so long, Billy Dee. Don't take no wooden nickels."

Avery mounted his horse and rode away. All the way into town he mulled over the information Billy had given him. He didn't know yet how he could work it to his advantage, but there'd come a day and he'd be ready.

Nellie followed Fancy down to the creek bank and sat down beside her, not saying a word, just letting her presence ease the other woman's spirit. Fancy sobbed like a child, without reservation, and when she was done, she raised her head and wiped at her eyes with the backs of her hands like a child does. Nellie shook her head. She was mighty young to have come so far on her own to a strange land. Coop was a wonderful man, but Nellie guessed that he, like most men, hadn't the patience and insight to deal with a lady. He'd lived here his whole life. He wouldn't understand how a girl might find this rough country overwhelming. Nellie remained silent, while Fancy sat with bowed head studying her thumbs and sighing now and then.

"I acted rather badly, didn't I?" Fancy said at last. She raised a tear-streaked face to look at Nellie. "I try to be all that Coop wants me to be, but somehow I always manage to fail."

"I wouldn't say that was so," Nellie said, pulling a blade of grass and chewing it. "He seemed mighty proud of the way you took care of Aaron. And when he says your name, well, he gets a look in his eyes, kind of soft and scared looking at the same time. If you ask me, I think your husband's mighty in love with you."

"You don't know, Nellie, you don't understand," Fancy began, then clamped her lips together. She didn't want to admit to anyone the agreement she and Coop had made, that the look in his eyes was just part of the role they were playing for one year.

"I think I understand a little bit," Nellie said. "This is a hard country out here, hard on a woman especially. If you're not prepared for the way things are done, you might think we hold life in mighty short regard, but that ain't so. This land makes you be practical, and a lame horse ain't goin' to be no good for anyone. It was bad luck for the horse. Coop held that roan in some store. Think he planned on breaking it and giving it to you. It would have made a mighty fine riding horse for a lady." Nellie looked at Fancy.

"There're too many Frank Averys in this world, men who are callused to the sufferin' of other beings. Coop ain't one of 'em. He may have seemed hard, shootin' that horse the way he did, but it was an act of mercy."

"I know that now," Fancy said and sighed deeply. "I just don't know if I can last a year in this country."

"Pshaw, you'll last a year and twenty more besides," Nellie said, getting to her feet and shaking her skirts. She'd allotted as much time as possible for soothing feelings. "Reckon I'd best get on back to the house and start supper for my young'uns. Don't be too hard on yourself or on Coop. You got a good man, a steady man. You can always be proud of men like Coop and Aaron and some of the others." Without waiting for a reply she stalked back up the bank and headed toward the small cabin that housed her world.

Feeling better, Fancy meandered along the banks of the creek, tossing rocks into the sparkling depths sometimes and pausing just to look into space at others, while she pondered all that Nellie had said. Fancy respected the hardworking Nellie. She wasn't a woman given to gossip or speculations. If she said a thing was so, Fancy sensed she could trust it was. And Nellie had said Coop cared for her, that he loved her. Fancy stopped, staring off at the distant mountain peaks, while she pondered the fact that Coop might love her. And how did she feel about him? She shouldn't be going on like this. She was leaving in less than a year. So what would it matter how Coop and she felt about each other? Except these feelings inside her had been growing ever since that first day she saw Coop Fletcher, powerful feelings she couldn't just ignore. They troubled her at night when she lay alone in her bed and during the day whenever she caught a glimpse of her husband's rawhide figure or heard his voice.

How had she come to this? This shivery yearning that grew inside her every day, making her dress more carefully when she knew Coop would be home in the evenings, that made her pinch her cheeks and moisten her lips when she knew he was about to appear. She'd spent her whole life in the theater where feelings and emotions were her stock in trade. She understood that a sweet smile and a flutter of eyelashes denoted something far different than an air of indifference. If she could manipulate her behavior to fool her audiences, she could not fool herself.

She had feelings for Coop such as she'd never known before, feelings that nagged at her and troubled her long after she'd put out her lamp at night. She wanted to feel him near, to have him touch her as he had before. She wanted to feel his fire and his passion. Furthermore, she wanted to return it.

Finding no answer to her troublesome thoughts, Fancy walked along until the creek ended into a clear pool in a coppice of gold-leaved aspen. Thick bushes provided a screen of privacy. Fancy stood feeling the trickle of sweat between her breasts and impulsively unbuttoned her bodice and drew off her gown. It was discarded in a heap on the grassy bank and was followed by her chemise, petticoats, and pantaloons. When she stood naked and golden beneath the innocent blue sky, she poised on an overhanging rock and dove into the still, green pool.

The water was wretchedly cold. She gasped and nearly sank to the bottom, then she got her breath and forced her arms to flail at the water. When she'd swam to one end of the pool and back again, she'd begun to warm up a bit and enjoy the bracing swim. When she was tired, she climbed up the bank and stood sluicing the water off her skin and hair with her bare hands. A sound made her crouch and whirl, her gaze darting here and there, seeking the intruder to her oasis.

Coop stood a short distance away, his hat in one hand, his silver eyes dark with passion. She made no token effort to protest, no effort to cover her body. Her wet hair streamed around her, casting a watery sheen over her sleek golden limbs. Coop came down the embankment to her, his big hands going out to take hold of her arms and pull her against him. She went willingly, her face raised to his, her lips slightly parted, waiting for his kiss. She could feel him trembling as he encircled her waist and pulled her high against him. Her feet left the ground, and she automatically wrapped her legs around him.

His kiss was savage, his touch demanding as his hands cupped her buttocks and pulled her closer. He could feel the heat of her body through his clothes and cursed that he'd have to release her to remove them. But for now he claimed her sweet lips, his tongue delving deep to taste her. Her arms wrapped around his neck, and she returned his kiss, openly and without reservation. When his large warm hands moved up her back, she shivered, moving her body against his, so he felt the soft, hot peak of her nipples. His thumbs caressed the sides of her full breasts, then the swollen, tender nipples themselves.

She gasped against his mouth, drew a breath, then moved against him in a rhythm that was ancient and pagan. His hands slid along her tiny waist and the flaring hips and the long sleek line of thigh. She was more beautiful to touch than he'd ever thought possible. He tried to move her aside so he could get to the buttons of his britches, but in her innocence she mistook his meaning and clamped herself harder against him. Coop let his knees bend and sat back on the bank. She was sitting in his lap now, her long graceful legs spread out on either side of him.

"Coop, do you love me?" she whispered against his cheek. "Nellie said you loved me."

"I love you, Fancy," he whispered. "You just need to move a little so I can get my pants open."

"Oh, I'm so glad," she whispered. "I love you, too." She wriggled closer to him. Coop was frantic with need for her. He kissed her again, nibbling at her soft lower lip, sucking on its fullness until she moaned with pleasure. With his arms under her arms, he lifted her back slightly so her breasts were fully exposed to him. Lowering his head, he took one nipple into his mouth, rolling it gently between his teeth, suckling while she writhed against him. His hands swept down to the moist core of her and caressed the hard bud, feeling her stiffen at his first touch, then relax against him as he continued to suckle and caress until she was panting. Gently, he placed her on her back on the grassy bank. Her hands clung to him as he rose to remove his clothing.

"Don't leave," she cried gently.

"I won't," he whispered and swiftly drew off his gun belt and unbuttoned his pants. He'd just shucked off his boots when he heard horses passing in a dead out gallop. Something was wrong. He didn't know what, but he could tell the sense of urgency in the riders. Cursing, he drew his boots back on.

"What is it?" Fancy asked, sitting up and looking at him. Her hair tumbled forward, hiding her breasts. With her knees drawn up, her mound was modestly shielded from his eyes, yet her position was more provocative than any previous ones, for there was innocence in her movements. She had no idea how sensuous and desirable she was at this moment.

"Something's wrong," he said, fastening his trousers. Her expression was crestfallen, embarrassed, and now her arms were folded in front of her to cover her nakedness. He bent to drop a kiss on her unresponsive lips. "I have to go," he said. "But I'll come to your room tonight."

He didn't ask. He simply told her and then he left, running up the bank, his thoughts already on his ranch and its needs. She felt rejected.

Slowly she redressed thinking of their encounter, and the more she thought of it, the more shamed she was by her wanton behavior. He must surely know by now that she wasn't a lady and never had been one. She'd acted no better than a trollop. Mortification burned her cheeks. When she was certain her clothes were fastened properly, she pulled her long wet hair back and quickly braided it. Coiling the braid into a bun at her nape, she jabbed her pins back in. With her hair and clothes in place, she marched back to the ranch house, her lips pursed in a prim line.

Coop was late coming home that evening. "Rustlers hitting us again," he grunted as he sat down to supper. Fancy had already eaten what little food she could force between her lips. Now she sat listening to Coop's conversation, responding lightly, playing the role of a lady as she never had before. He made no reference to their afternoon tryst at the creek. When he was finished with his meal, he rose and picked up his hat. His expression was apologetic.

"I have to make arrangements with Daniel Stone," he said. "I have a supply train going out tomorrow, and I'm making him pack master."

"Oh, Annabelle will be pleased," Fancy said happily. Then she thought of how moody Annabelle became when Daniel wasn't nearby. "Well, she ought to be pleased," she amended. "You're a fair man, Coop, to give him this chance."

"He's earned it," Coop said. He hesitated again. "I'll see you later." His silvery glance was warm on her face. She knew he was referring to his promise to come to her room tonight. Blood filled her cheeks, and she couldn't meet his gaze. Nor could she utter a reply. Apparently none was needed, for he strode from the ranch house and disappeared toward the corrals. Thoughtfully, Fancy carried the dishes to the kitchen, where Delores was cleaning up, her fat brown arms buried up to her elbows in sudsy water.

"Thank you, Delores. Supper was delicious tonight."

Delores glanced at her plate and snorted. "I see how you liked it," she said. "Tomorrow, I make chili and tamales. This is real food you will like, senora."

Fancy laughed and left the kitchen. The evening stretched long and empty for her. She wandered through the ranch house taking in the changes she'd made. She was proud of the things she'd done. The house glowed with a rich patina of care and love. The only thing it lacked now were children. Fancy paused. Funny that she should think of children now, tonight, when Coop had promised to come to her room and when she was torn between admitting him or sending him away. She thought of the afternoon. How depraved she'd been, without reservations, without shame. Surely, he'd guessed then she wasn't a lady. But then what made a lady? She was a virgin. Was that so different than a lady?

The hours passed, and she wrestled with her dilemma. She would turn him away, send him packing, reject his advances, rage at him for seducing her by the pond. She would be outraged and reiterate the terms of their agreement. She'd send him packing with his lust intact, then smugly she'd go to her bed, still a virgin and, as far as he knew, still a lady.

But the memory of the fire he'd built between them nagged at her, inviting her to imagine what would have happened if the horsemen hadn't passed by. She wouldn't turn him away, she decided. She was his wife, and he wished to claim her. But she would be docile, passive, respectable. He'd know he had a lady in his bed.

Finally, the hour grew late, and Coop hadn't returned. Miffed that he should remain so untroubled by their promised encounter, she went up to bed and spitefully locked the door behind her. Leisurely, she prepared for bed, imagining her enjoyment when he tried her door and found it locked against him. He would learn not to take her for granted. She sat near the window gazing out at the mountains rearing dark and untouched against the moonlit sky. Coop was like those mountains, she thought, untouched by the frailties of others, unneedful of a woman's tender touch. He'd wanted her this afternoon by the creek, because she'd been there. If it had been some other woman, would he have desired her in the same way? Would he have kissed her and caressed her, bringing her to a moaning, gasping need for him? He was used to the game of passion between a man and woman, but she was not. What acquired a monumental importance to her seemed of little consequence to him, otherwise he would be at her door even now, trying to enter and reclaim the passion they'd almost shared this afternoon.

Her hair lay silken and smooth around her shoulders, her brush rested in her lap as she looked at the moon-rimmed mountains. She felt like weeping and wasn't sure why. Then a knock sounded at her door, and she sprang up, her heart racing, her breath coming in small short gasps. She wouldn't answer, she thought. Now was her revenge. The short knock sounded again.

"Fancy?" his voice came, gruff-edged, the very sound of it unreeling some tightly wound coil within her. On unsteady legs she crossed the room and unlocked the door.

Chapter 10

"**F**ANCY?" HE WAS a dark shadow in the darkened hallway. Only the moonlight coming through her windows illuminated them. She heard the breathless question in his voice, and her heart thundered its answer. He sensed her feelings. They echoed his own. He stepped into the room and gathered her into his arms, rocking her slightly.

"I thought about you all afternoon," he said huskily. She smelled the clean outdoors scent of him, the mountain wind, the prairie grasses, leather, and even the stream where he must have bathed. The scents were heady, wild, and masculine, aphrodisiacal. His lips closed over hers and she was lost, answering his kiss in spite of herself. He swept her up in his arms and carried her to the bed. Gently, as if she were some fragile porcelain, he placed her against the pillows. He towered over her, gazing down at her supine form. Fancy could barely breathe.

Slowly, his hands stroked over her, pausing at her soft breasts. Through the thin stuff of her nightgown, his thumb moved in lazy circles over her nipples bringing them to hard, throbbing buds. She sighed with pleasure, then she remembered the vow she'd made not to betray herself. A lady mustn't feel pleasure at such things. Coop wanted a lady, and she wanted to be that lady. Yet how could she not feel pleasure as his hand slid down her flat stomach, smoothing over her aching mound to her long thighs. His hands cupped her foot as if it were incredibly small and delicate to him. Then his hands, swift and sure, glided upward, taking with them her thin nightgown.

"I want to feel your flesh, Fancy," he whispered. "I don't want anything between us." She drew a quivery sigh, enraptured by his touch.

"And I want you to feel my flesh," he said huskily, loosening his belt and pushing his britches off. The shirt and boots followed. His skin was dusky in the moonlight, with mysterious hollows of darkness. She lay against the pillows, her hair fanning about her, her great green eyes gazing up at him innocently.

"Look at me, Fancy," he urged. "Before this night is out, we'll know every inch of each other's bodies. We'll know how the other gets and gives pleasure." Her gaze swept along the slope of shoulders, the curve of muscles gilded by the moonlight pouring through their window, the blue-black hair, and silver gray eyes that could see her very soul. She saw the tapering waist and slim hips and the powerfully muscled thighs, but her gaze was caught by the bulging rod of manhood, and some nerve deep in that womanly core of her responded.

She wanted to touch him, to spread her legs and feel him against her. She was a virgin and had no real knowledge of how and what transpired between a man and a woman, but she knew the yearnings of her body would lead her to what it wanted. She wanted him in a way she'd never wanted anything else in her life. She couldn't stay still. She groaned and turned on the bed, her hands went to her breasts, to brush against the swollen nipples, to feel their heat, to deny their need, her need.

How could she do this? she wondered. How could she give and not take back from the passion and fire he offered? Yet she must if she were not to lose him in the long run. Coop came to her then, seeing her hands pressed against her breasts in a virginal pose. He lay beside her, and she felt the smoothness of his skin and was captivated by it. She'd thought he'd be rough beneath his clothes. His muscled body was sleek and masculine. She felt the heat of his arousal against her thigh and drew in her breath. She wanted to touch him there. As if he recognized her desire, he took her hand and placed it against his chest. She felt the whipcord muscling, the taut skin and flesh.

"This is who I am, Fancy," he whispered. "A man who desires you above all others. Don't be afraid. Touch me." He slid her hand along his flesh, down to the wiry tangle of curls. Fancy started, and then he'd placed her hand around his engorged member. She felt its smoothness, its throbbing hardness, and all resistance melted. Her legs relaxed and parted.

Coop chuckled. "My fancy lady," he whispered against her ear, and she jerked her hand away. His lips claimed hers time and again. Fancy tried to maintain her detachment, but it was quickly slipping.

"Oh, help!" she thought and shut her eyes tightly. Her body had grown tense, resistive, and Coop wasn't sure why. Patiently, he wooed her, delaying his own desire to build her own. She seemed willing enough, but she was so passive. She was a lady, he thought. She wouldn't know about such things. He'd have to teach her. This was a job he was going to relish.

But try as he might he couldn't seem to ignite her to the sensuous fervor he felt. His own hunger had become intense. He slid his mouth along her creamy skin, suckling her breasts as he'd done that afternoon. He could hear the quick intake of breath. He was reaching through that incredible reserve of hers.

But she was too elusive. Just as he thought he'd captured the very heart of her erotic spirit, she slipped away from him, and he held a prim and proper lady in his arms, a lady who was willing to submit to him but offered no part of herself. Frustration nagged at him, but the sweet perfume of her body, the exotic taste of her mouth, the soft, slender womanliness of her drew all thoughts from his mind but seeking that final release. He entered her, felt her stiffen against his invasion of her virginity. Slowly, he plundered the thin veil that held him from her, then he was through, and he plunged against her body, feeling a wild yearning, such as he'd never known before.

He reached the apex without her and felt a deep sorrow that she hadn't shared in the experience. He could feel her body trembling beneath his and reluctantly moved away.

"Did I hurt you?" he asked gently.

She only nodded a reply. He sensed she was crying.

"Why, then?" he asked, catching a tear on his finger.

"I'm all right," her voice was small and lost.

"I'm sorry," he whispered, cradling her against his chest. "I shouldn't have rushed you. You weren't ready."

"Yes, I was," she whispered against his chest. She was still trembling, her repressed sobs making her body jerk against his in a most tantalizing way. Coop tempered his rebudding desire. He'd done something wrong. He wasn't sure what, but she hadn't been happy. He didn't want to repeat his mistake. In truth, he'd never run into this before. All the women he'd bedded had been perfectly happy with his lovemaking or so they'd said. Now he wondered what he should have done in making love to a lady.

"I'm sorry," he whispered against her temple. "Do you want me to go?"

Her arms hugged him convulsively. "Don't leave me," she pleaded, and he settled into her bed, pulling her closer and wrapping the covers around them both. She was shy lying flesh to flesh. He could feel the resistance in her body, yet she didn't pull away. They lay that way long into the night. Finally, she sighed deeply, turned and curled herself into a ball, her arms crossed defensively across her chest.

Coop longed to move his cramped muscles but didn't want to wake her now that she slept. So he lay watching the shadows move around the room as the moonlight moved across the sky. How he longed to be outdoors now, out in the mountains with the crisp cold air biting through his clothing. There he knew who he was and what he could do and be. Here in the bed with this slender girl, he was lost. Was he a man for having bedded her, or was he a heel? Had he not heeded the signs she gave him? He'd felt her reluctance, but he'd also glimpsed the same fire she'd displayed at the creek that afternoon. What had happened between then and now to make her change?

When the moonlight had disappeared and the first gray light of dawn lit the distant mountain peaks, Coop eased himself out of Fancy's bed, dressed, and made his way down to the corral. Lighting the first cheroot of the day, he drew the smoke deep into his lungs. Of all the things that plagued him, freighting government supplies to the Utes in the Middle Park and finding the man responsible for the attacks on his freight trains and ranch, solving the riddle of his wife's unhappy response was the one that claimed his attention. He'd never met a woman like her, never touched skin so satiny smooth, never looked into eyes so deep and green, never seen a woman with such sass about her. She was in his thoughts too much, riding with him on the range, sitting beside him on a freight wagon, dancing on the edge of every minute of his day and night.

Coop cursed out loud and threw away his cheroot. He ought to be feeling great about now. He'd just spent a night with a woman he'd desired ever since he first set eyes on her. Instead, he felt like he'd just created the biggest blunder of his life. Hellfire! When he'd gone to the prostitutes, he'd never given a thought to them once he'd left them. Why couldn't he do the same with Fancy?

The answer was too clear. She'd claimed some part of him he'd never given before. The admission frightened him, yet he understood it had added an extra dimension, a deeper resonance to their lovemaking. He felt more complete than he ever had, and even as he stood here cursing the devastation she'd wrecked on his peace of mind, he knew he would want her again, tonight and every night of his life. Shaken at the intensity of need this woman, this fancy lady had awakened in him, Coop rousted his men and set them to work. One look at his face was enough to let them know something was amiss, so they left him alone, observing that sometimes he shook his head and cursed himself roundly.

Fancy woke alone in her bed and lay thinking of all that had occurred the night before. Had she behaved properly? Did Coop still think she was a lady? Her thoughts turned to herself and the unassuaged desire. How could she endure this night after night without responding to him as she wished? Innocent as she was, she sensed there was supposed to be more, even for ladies. How could she pretend to be unmoved when his touch set her afire? She needed to talk to someone. Tears slid down her cheek as she thought of her mother. Adele Bourne would have eased her fears and helped her understand what she must do.

Suddenly, she thought of Geraldine Russell. She'd been a friend. Could she advise Fancy in this delicate subject? Fancy wasn't sure she could even broach it to her, but she had a strong need to try.

Jumping out of bed, she washed and dressed and hurried out to the corral. Coop was mounted on his black stallion, overseeing the harnessing of mule teams to freight wagons. Someone hollered at him, and he looked around. Seeing Fancy, he came to her at once, sliding off the sleek animal.

She was shy, unable to meet his gaze after their night together, afraid of what she might find there, condemnation, disappointment? If she had glanced up she might have caught the shimmer of admiration that appeared and was gone from his gaze. Instead, she studied the ground and his dusty boot tips.

"Good morning," he said quietly, and his tone drew her gaze up to meet his. His silvery eyes were flat and stern. His lean cheeks and craggy features were somber. She glanced away.

"Good morning," she answered. "I—I was thinking I might go over to visit Geraldine's ranch. She's invited me several times, but I've never gone."

"I'm kind of busy today. Can it wait?"

"No! I—I mean I'd like to go now."

Coop studied her averted face, then nodded tersely. "I'll

have Billy Dee harness the buggy for you. He'll drive you
out to the Silver Bar Ranch and go on to Elizabethtown for
supplies and mail. Will that give you enough time to visit?"

"Yes, that would be perfect," Fancy cried, relieved Coop
wouldn't be accompanying her. To sit beside him for the
long drive would have been unbearable. "I'll get my things
and be right back."

Without giving him a chance to say anything else she
whirled and ran toward the ranch house. Coop watched her
go. She looked like a young girl today. She hadn't donned
the wire bustle and endless petticoats that hid her figure. Her
gown was a simple blue-flowered print that he liked. Her
long golden hair hung down nearly to her waist, bouncing
and moving with her every running step.

He thought about following her into the house and taking
her in his arms, but his men sat waiting for him, and he
wasn't sure what kind of reception she would give him this
morning. Would she be passive as last night or receptive as
she'd been at the creek, or would she reject him altogether
as she'd done before?

Coop remounted, wondering how a grown man could
stand out in the hot sun in front of all his men and moon
after a slip of a girl, a prim little lady that didn't know how
to kiss a man properly much less respond to his lovemaking. Disgusted, he rode back to the empty freight train and
gave final instructions.

The Silver Bar Ranch was a low spread cluster of neat
buildings. The yard and corrals were clean, and no men loi-
tered anywhere. The few who were about seemed intent on
certain chores. All of this was a testimonial to Geraldine's
ability to manage a ranch and hands. Geraldine herself was
down by one of the corrals hunkered down examining a
horse's hoof. When the buggy rolled into the yard, she rose
at once and came to greet Fancy.

"Am I interrupting your work?" Fancy asked, climbing
down out of the buggy.

"Lands sakes, no," Geraldine said. "I got a horse there

that's lost a shoe. My hands can take care of it. Come up on the porch, and we'll have something cold to drink."

Fancy waved good-bye to Billy Dee and followed Geraldine to the low ranch house with its deep, shaded porch. Geraldine sank into a wooden chair next to a weather-beaten table and motioned Fancy into one across from her.

"We'll sit out here. I expect it'll be cooler," Geraldine said. "Besides, I'm like you. I like the view."

"It's beautiful," Fancy said, looking at the panaroma stretching before her. Chilled tea was brought immediately by a smiling girl, who disappeared as quickly back inside. Fancy and Geraldine sat chatting about inconsequential things, and Fancy despaired of ever being able to broach the subject that troubled her most. Finally Geraldine set down her empty glass and fixed Fancy with a friendly but stern glance.

"Out with it," she said.

"What?" Fancy looked at her startled, then flushed. She shouldn't have come. This subject was far too intimate, and Geraldine would just never understand.

"I know you didn't ride all this distance just to drink my tea," Geraldine said.

"I came to visit you," Fancy answered, stalling.

"Pshaw, not with a face as long as yours is," Geraldine snapped back. "You come here cause you needed a friendly shoulder. Well, you got one."

Fancy might have been put off by Geraldine's abrupt manner, but she'd grown used to the old woman's ways. Besides, the pale blue eyes were warm with concern.

"I don't know how to begin," Fancy said in a low voice.

"The beginnin's a good place," Geraldine declared. "Come, child, whatever's troubling you can't be that bad."

"You just don't know," Fancy said. "I've been such a fraud." Without meaning to, she plunged into the whole story about her past in the theater, finding Coop's letter, and deciding to come west parading as a lady. After that it was easier to speak of her first night with Coop and how hard it had been to maintain the facade of a lady.

Geraldine listened quietly. "I guessed as much." She nodded.

Fancy raised her tear-streaked face and stared at her. "You did? How did I give myself away?"

"One of those songs you sang at Maida's that night. You claimed your father taught it to you, but that song wasn't around during the war."

Fancy couldn't help laughing. "How could you have known that living way out here?"

Geraldine grinned. "I went back east a couple of years ago, and the song was just being sung in the theaters."

"Oh." Fancy's shoulders sagged. "I wonder how many other mistakes I've made."

"Not many that I can see, and I've been watching you," Geraldine said. "You handle yourself real well. I'd say Coop got himself that lady, quite a fine lady at that."

Tears of gratitude stung Fancy's eyes. "Thank you. But I feel like such a fraud, and after last night, well, I just don't know how much longer I can maintain this decorum."

Geraldine chuckled. "God bless you, child. Men don't want ladies in their beds. They want 'em in the parlor but not in the bedroom."

Fancy stared at Geraldine in consternation. "You mean—" Her glance flashed over the old woman's wrinkled face and untidy gray hair. "I don't mean to be—I mean, are you sure?"

Geraldine leaned forward and took Fancy's hand. "I didn't always look like a sun-dried old prune," she said. "Once I was quite beautiful. I had two husbands, and neither one of them ever had cause to go looking elsewhere for what he wanted in his bed. You go back to Coop and you forget about being a lady tonight. You respond to him with all the love you feel for him and you'll get the same back. You have my word on it."

Fancy bowed her head to hide her tears of relief.

"You must love that man a powerful bit," Geraldine said.

Silently, Fancy nodded. "Then tonight after you've made love and you're laying in his arms all warm and relaxed, you tell him the truth about your background. You can't build a relationship with lies."

"I know that now," Fancy said, raising her head. Her face glowed as if lit by sunshine from inside. Geraldine knew what caused it. Hadn't she been young and in love once? Everything was felt more intensely then.

"What about Maida and the ladies of Elizabethtown?"

"Far as I can see, it ain't none of their business. They'll never hear a word of what was said here from me."

"Thank you," Fancy said thoughtfully. "I don't think they'll ever quite accept me."

"They've started already. One thing you might do is donate something to the town. That always impresses them."

"But what?" Fancy cried. "Isn't that like buying a place for yourself?"

"Coop's got the money, and he understands the way of things out here. It was just a thought." They turned to other topics then and spent a pleasant afternoon visiting.

When Billy Dee returned with the buggy, Fancy hugged Geraldine. "Thank you," she whispered and hurried to the buggy. Geraldine watched her leave and sighed. That slip of a girl could have been her own daughter. Geraldine almost felt like she was. In that fierce old heart was born a protective love for Fancy that boded evil for anyone who sought to hurt her.

As soon as she returned to the ranch, Fancy ordered a tub of water heated, hauled the buckets to the small room set aside for the tin bathtub, and spent a long while luxuriating in the warm scented water, dreaming of the coming night with Coop. She rose from the tub, flushed and eager for her husband. She ordered a special supper prepared, then took extra care in dressing herself. She left aside the wire frames of the bustle, sensing Coop didn't like them. Without the supporting frames, her skirts formed a graceful train. Leaving her clean shiny hair unbound, she simply tied it back with a ribbon, then hurried to wait on the porch for Coop's arrival. He came from the stables, knocking his hat against his leg to rid it of dust. When he caught sight of Fancy, his eyes lit and her heart soared. In his glance was all the encouragement she needed.

"Hello," she said and was surprised at how breathless she felt. She wanted to throw her arms around him and kiss him but was too timid.

"How was your visit with Geraldine?" he asked, pausing on the bottom step so their gazes were level.

Fancy couldn't help a slight blush. She glanced away to recover herself, then her eyes met his, dancing with green lights. "It was most enlightening," she said almost playfully. He was captivated by the small dimple that played in one cheek. How had he missed that before?

"Supper's ready," Fancy said with self-conscious wifely concern, "and a hot bath is waiting for you."

"Thank you. That sounds mighty inviting." His dark eyes shone with such mysterious lights, she knew he was thinking of their night ahead.

"B—Billy Dee brought the mail back from Elizabethtown. I put it on your desk."

"I'll look at it later," he said, not wanting to be distracted from his wife, who was unaccountably pink and warm. He sensed some vibrant chord about her and wanted to explore it, but Delores came out onto the porch.

"Dinner's ready," she said brusquely and headed back inside.

"I suppose we'd better go in," Fancy said. "I had her prepare some special dishes, and she'll be awfully mad if we let them get cold."

Coop followed her into the dining room, where a linen cloth had been laid and candles provided a soft glow. Fancy set up a bright chatter, while she herself served him, hovering over him like an anxious mother over a difficult child. Coop sensed her nervousness. When supper was finished, she rose and gathered up some dishes.

"Why don't you relax a little before taking your bath? We can always warm it up for you."

"Thank you. I believe I will have a smoke," Coop said, rising.

"Of course, you just smoke and relax," Fancy said quickly. She was like a butterfly flitting around the table, unable to light anywhere and unsure where to go. With a final baffled glance at his wife, Coop made his way to his study where he lit the last cheroot for the day and leaned back in his leather chair to savor it. But the perplexing attitudes of his wife bothered his peace of mind, so finally he turned to his desk and the stack of mail. There were more catalogs from Denver, statements from his mining partners, requests for his services in shipping freight, and a letter from Alabama. Coop turned it over and read the return address. It was from Travis Wheeler, the lawyer who'd arranged for Fancy to come out west. He would always feel grateful to the southern lawyer. Eagerly he tore open the flap.

"Coop?"

He looked up. Fancy stood in the doorway, a towel over her arm, her green eyes wide and sparkling. "Your bathwater is ready. We reheated the water. I thought if you're ready, I—I might wash your back—the way I did Papa's when I—was a girl."

Coop stared at her flushed face. There was the same shyness to her that he'd seen last night, but now a certain boldness peeked through in a most tantalizing way. The prospect of having Fancy wash his back was too intriguing to ignore. Coop threw the letters back on the desk and got to his feet. His eyes shone with sensuous anticipation.

Fancy felt bolder now, surer of what she was doing. She took Coop's big hand and guided him to the room where his bath waited. His silvery gaze locked with hers as he began slowly removing his clothes. She realized he expected her to look away. Recklessly, she stepped forward and began unbuttoning his shirt, letting her hands trail across his chest enticingly, lingering over each fastener until she felt him tremble with impatience. His large hands traveled up her sides and reached for her breasts, but she brushed them aside. Her gaze turned coquettish, flirtatious, impudent as her fingers paused at his waist. Coop could feel the swelling below his belt and groaned.

"We need to wash away the dust of your hard day," Fancy reminded him softly, watching his eyes to see what effect her words had on him. She'd been so caught up in her concern over her reactions she hadn't concentrated as much on Coop's the night before. Now she felt exhilaration at his responses to her.

Taking pity on his obvious state of arousal, she quickly pushed the shirt away from his shoulders and matter-of-factly loosened his pants. Her fingers slowed as they fumbled with the buttons of his trousers, then they were loosened and she was able to push them over his hips. They fell in a heap at his feet, but she paid them no mind. Her gaze was fixed on his rod, hard and throbbing. Fancy felt her chest tighten with the effort to breathe, and an aching began deep in that secret womanly place.

Turning away, she fussed with the washcloth and soap. Glancing over her shoulder, she glared at him with mock sternness. "If I'm to wash your back, you must get into the tub," she ordered primly.

Grinning, Coop kicked aside his pants and climbed into the tub, settling into the hot water and straightening his long legs out.

"Well," he said, holding out both hands.

Hesitant now, she approached the tub, her eyes big and glistening. Coop's eyes challenged her all the way. Kneeling, she dipped the washcloth and worked up a soapy lather. Starting at one brown muscular shoulder she slid the cloth over his skin. Coop closed his eyes, reveling in the nearness of her, reveling in this small wifely duty she performed for him.

Fancy saw the tension ease from his face, and she applied more pressure, leaning forward to soap his back and even across his chest. Then she brought fresh water and washed his hair, her slender fingers massaging his scalp. She was unaware that in her efforts she'd wet the front of her gown. The thin cotton material clung to her young breasts, outlining the pert nipples and darker aureoles.

Coop opened his eyes and stared at the tantalizing sight bobbing mere inches from his face. When he could bear it no longer, he reached forward, in a spray of water, and grabbed her about her slender waist, pulling her against him, while his teeth closed around her firm breast. Fancy's startled scream turned to a low moan of pleasure as Coop suckled her.

When she thought she could no longer bear the exquisite pleasure pain, he released her and reaching for the bucket of water poured it over himself rinsing away the soap. He stood grinning at her while runnels of water slid over his sleek body and into the bath. Bemused, Fancy could only stare at him, thinking he looked like some half-wild mountain spirit.

Coop tossed the empty bucket to one side and stepped out of the tub. Without bothering with a towel, he scooped Fancy up in his arms and strode out of the room.

"Coop, you're naked. What if someone sees you like this?" Fancy protested halfheartedly. Delores came out of the kitchen, caught one glimpse of her boss's naked backside, and scurried back to her own domain. "Delores!" Fancy said weakly.

"Forget Delores," Coop said.

"You can't just walk around without clothes on," Fancy whispered above her giggles

"This is my house. I can walk around any way I want to," he growled, mounting the stairs.

"Delores may never cook for us again," Fancy teased.

"It's not food I'm needing, lady," he said huskily and stopped any further protestations with a kiss.

Fancy was breathless by the time they reached his room. He threw her on his bed and reached for the buttons of her gown. "I won't be as slow as you were," he grunted, half ripping the gown from her body. Fancy's hands were there helping him, tearing away the layers of petticoats, tearing away the layers of pretension forced on her by a society that said if she were to have any worth, she must be a lady. Here, now, in Coop's arms was the worth she sought for herself, the absolute giving of herself, the hungry seeking for herself.

He was surprised at her fierce response. No longer was she the proper lady. All he'd sought the night before and found elusive was there now, given in full measure. He tasted her lips, her breasts, her sweetness, her passion and fire. She was pure headiness in a man's blood. Her small soft hands reached for him, touching, teasing, promising, and giving so he was lost in the glorious capitulation, the astonishing wonder of this woman called Fancy.

Chapter 11

*F*ANCY WOKE TO the sensual brush of Coop's lips against her own. She groaned and wrapped her slender arms around him, sleepily returning his embrace. Coop chuckled low in his throat.

"Don't tell me my fancy lady is a sleepyhead in the morning," he teased gently. Her body was warm from sleep, her skin as soft and fragrant as a rose petal. He couldn't seem to get enough of her. His large, warm hands smoothed down her naked body, lingering suggestively at the plush mound between her thighs. Automatically, her knees relaxed, parting slightly to allow him access, but when his hands explored her, she couldn't repress a moan of pain. Immediately he drew back.

"I'm sorry," she whispered. "It's all right."

"No, my sweet lady," he whispered fiercely against her temple. "I've used you too hard. I have to give you time to heal, but I thank you for your generous gift." Reluctantly, he drew away and began to dress.

Fancy felt bereft without him. She curled on her side, her lips pouting prettily. "How long will it take for me to heal?" she asked innocently.

Coop glanced at her and laughed. "No time at all," he said. "You may be better by tonight."

"Tonight?" Fancy couldn't keep the delight out of her voice.

"Tomorrow night at the latest," Coop said, bending over her to place a light kiss on her pink lips.

"Tomorrow night! That's too long," Fancy murmured between kisses. Her lids were heavy with sleep.

"Go back to sleep for a while, Fancy," he said and tucked the covers high under her chin. His eyes were soft and glowed with love for her. With a sigh Fancy settled beneath the covers.

Coop watched her for a moment, noting the smudges of exhaustion beneath her eyes, the swollen pinkness of her lips. If he looked closely, he was sure he'd find other evidences of their night together. Sighing contentedly he rose and made his way downstairs.

He had to search for his hat. He'd left it in the study, distracted by Fancy's offer to help him bathe. Now he retrieved it and, seeing the pile of mail on the desk, settled himself down to business. The letter from Travis Wheeler lay on top. His thoughts still on the small warm body upstairs in his bed, Coop ripped the letter open and read it, then he reread it, his face going hard, his eyes narrowing to steely slits. He sat for a long time, taking in the lawyer's letter, asking himself what it all meant. Finally, he rose and slowly made his way upstairs to his room where his wife, his fancy lady, lay innocently sleeping.

The door flew open with a bang, starting Fancy from the lovely rosy dreams that enveloped her. Frightened she sat up, thinking her dreams had turned to a nightmare when she saw Coop's face. His eyes, those same eyes that had shone with love for her, were now narrowed and dark with anger. He stood staring at her while she groped to clear her mind.

"Coop?" she whispered. "What's wrong? What's happened?" An anxious nagging began in the back of her mind, a reminder that she had failed to do something that was terribly important.

Coop only stared at her a moment, then slowly raised his clenched fist with the crumpled letter. "Can you explain this?" he asked, and the quietness of his tone was more frightening than if he'd shouted.

"I don't know what it is," she said hesitantly, "so how can I explain?"

"It's a letter from Travis Wheeler. You do know who Mr. Wheeler is, don't you?"

Fancy felt as if a mountain had just fallen on her. "Coop, I was going to tell you the truth."

"When?"

"Last night, but I—you distracted me."

"Last night!" His tone was scoffing. "I should have guessed when you made this big turnaround from a shy, innocent maiden to a lusty wanton. This has all been an act to you, hasn't it?"

"No, Coop. It wasn't."

"But you are an actress!"

"Yes, but—"

"An actress!"

"You needn't say it like that," she cried, smarting at his cutting tone. "I'm a legitimate actress in the theater."

"You were an out of work actress in a two-bit, moth-eaten troupe that finally went under."

"All right!" She sat up on her knees and glared back at him. "Maybe I wasn't born on a plantation. I didn't have a rich daddy or a mammy to watch over me when I was a baby, but that doesn't mean I couldn't be a lady."

Coop was stalking now, from one side of the room to the other like a caged mountain lynx. "Don't expect me to buy that, lady," he stormed. "I've been had, conned by a pretty piece of petticoat." He paced back and forth, his fists clenched in a most threatening manner.

"I—I am sorry I lied to you," she said contritely. "Many times I tried to tell you the truth."

"Yeah? When?" Coop flared. "The night you first blew into town and I asked you about yourself. That was the perfect time to tell me, or maybe you tried before the wedding, or maybe after the wedding when you were negotiating a deal for yourself."

"I did try," Fancy cried, "but you're so pigheaded at times, it's hard to get you to listen."

"Pigheaded. More like a donkey's ass for being taken in by the likes of you. How many times have you played this little game?"

"Never before," Fancy cried, "and it wasn't a game, a con as you call it. I was desperate. I needed—"

"I've heard all about how you needed food and a roof over your head. It doesn't work anymore, Fancy. Why didn't you just find some sucker there in Alabama, or were they about to run you out of town?"

"Run me out of town? Why would they?" Fancy asked, perplexed at the turn his thinking had taken.

"Isn't that what they do with undesirable women, with dance-hall girls and prostitutes?"

Fancy's mouth dropped open, her cheeks reddened, and she glared at him. "You think I'm a prostitute?" she shrieked, getting to her feet and running to within a few inches of him. Her hands were planted on her hips, her face was mutinous. In her bare feet, she only came halfway up his chest. Her golden hair fell over her shoulders in tangled, enticing disarray. If he hadn't been so angry with her, he might have laughed, but he was still smarting at the thought he'd been had. Besides she was screaming at him now, words that ran together in a tangle of angry sounds.

"I'm an actress of the classics," she shouted. "I can recite Shakespeare and the Greek classics. I speak French fluently and know how to do all manner of things. The *Southern Enquirer* said I was destined to be a great actress in my time. I may not have been educated in one of those highfalutin girl's finishing schools, but I know how to conduct myself in any parlor."

"It's not how you conduct yourself in the parlor that's bothering me," Coop shouted back. "It's how you conducted yourself in the bedrooms and how many."

Her small hand smacked him across his tanned cheek. "You're hateful, Coop Fletcher, the vilest, most hateful man

I've ever met. I'm sorry I came to Elizabethtown to marry you."

"I'm sorry, too," he shouted.

They fell silent and glared at each other.

"I'll pack my trunks and leave immediately," Fancy said with deadly calm.

"I'll have someone drive you to Denver to catch the stage."

"Denver?"

"I don't want you in Elizabethtown. I don't want anyone to know what a fool you made of me."

"What a fool you made of yourself, you mean," she snapped. "I do, of course, expect you to pay me the money you agreed upon."

"You expect me to give you money, after the way you've tricked me and swindled me out of money already spent? Not a penny, not a penny more," he roared. "I expect you to repay me the money I sent for travel and trousseau."

"I can't pay you back. Where am I going to get that kind of money?" Fancy cried incredulously.

"Earn it," he said, stalking toward the door. He whirled and glared at her, his lip curling in disdain. "Earn it the way you would have had to back east."

"Oooh, you," Fancy picked up a vase and sent it sailing past his head. It crashed against the door frame.

"Like everything else about you," he sneered, "your aim isn't true."

"I hate you, Coop Fletcher," she shouted after him, but he was already bounding down the stairs.

Fancy slumped on the bed. Now she knew what she'd forgotten to do. Geraldine had warned her. Tell Coop the truth about herself. Don't let him find out for himself. Well, she'd failed to do as she should. God knows she'd tried and worried over it these many past weeks, but he had no right to call her such names, to brand her a prostitute. Hadn't he found her a virgin? Hadn't he remembered that at all?

Coop was remembering just that, wondering if it were true. He'd heard tales about some of the New Orleans whores and how they used a bit of fish gut filled with blood to declare themselves virgin again and again. How did he know Fancy hadn't done the same thing? Yet, he remembered the resistance of her maidenhead, the tearing of that veil that proclaimed her innocence.

Perhaps she was telling the truth. He hadn't given her much chance to explain her side. She'd said she was desperate. Yet she could have told him any time since she'd come to Elizabethtown. Why hadn't she? Had he been too unkind to her, had he been demanding and severe so she might fear him? No, he'd given her a free hand to run his ranch and his town house, sending to Denver for furniture and geegaws to make any woman envious. He'd wooed her and pampered her. He'd even loved her.

Riding absently about his ranch, Coop thought of the ecstasy he'd known in Fancy's arms the last two nights. He'd loved her almost from the moment she stepped off the stage, but last night had sealed that long-denied emotion. He could not deny it now. What was he to do? he pondered.

He'd send her away, by God. That was what she wanted. He'd even give her the money she wanted. Anything to be rid of her. Then he thought of her eyes, crystal clear, green and gold, shimmering with laughter, and he wanted her there beside him. He wanted to touch her hair and her skin. He wanted to hear her laugh.

Then fury, a sense of betrayal claimed him. How dare she come with her pretty smiles and scented skin, her sass and laughter and make him love her, when to her it was a game, a way to while away the time until she could take his money and leave? He wouldn't let her get away so easily. He'd make her pay for her deceptions.

He rode his horse until its coat was glossy and its breath was labored, then he turned it back to the ranch. The sun was straight up, and few hands were around the corrals. Coop tied his horse off near the water trough and made his way inside.

"Miss Fancy, I ain't goin' back," he heard Annabelle say.

"You have to," Fancy was saying. "If he doesn't want me, he won't want you, either." She was bent over a trunk. At the sound of his boots against the plank floor, she whirled, then motioned Annabelle away. Without hesitation Annabelle ran down the stairs, Coop guessed to go to Daniel. No wonder Daniel had given up nagging him about driving freight. He'd become content to stay around the ranch working in the stables.

"I'll be out of here soon," Fancy said, and he forgot all thoughts about Annabelle and Daniel.

"You can't go!" he growled.

"I beg your pardon?"

"You can't go," he repeated.

Fancy glared at him. "Who do you think you are to tell me I'm to go or not go? I'm leaving. We agreed this morning."

"I didn't!"

"You ordered me to go."

"That was before I thought about it," Coop said, pacing back and forth and thrusting his chin out in a show of belligerence.

Fancy stared at him in exasperation. "Well I—I've thought about things, too, and nothing has changed. I'm leaving." Fancy blinked back tears. They must surely be the last, she thought, for she'd already shed enough since this morning.

Coop looked at her stiff back. Golden tresses, glistening and lush, spilled down her back. His fingers itched to bury themselves in the satiny curls. He clenched his fists and looked away, scowling angrily. How could he be so angry with a woman and want her at the same time?

"If you leave now, you won't receive one penny of the money I promised you at the beginning of our agreement."

Fancy paused in the frantic stepping from chest to trunk and back again, her arms filled with petticoats and ribbons. She glared at Coop, her head high, her attitude haughty.

"I didn't expect an uncivilized half-breed to stand by his word," she snapped and tossed the wad of silk and ruffles

into her trunk. If she'd glanced at Coop's face, she would
have known how perilously close she came to annihilation
with her careless words.

Coop's fists clenched, the muscle in his jaw jumped as
he gritted his teeth and fought for control. He felt like throt-
tling her for her superior airs. Even as he fought for control, he crossed the room in angry strides and, grasping her
elbow, swung her about. One large hand grasped her chin,
holding her face so he could stare into her eyes. She
gasped, haughtiness giving way to a clutch of fear.

"So, here we are," he snarled, "a whore and a half-breed
with a promise made between us. Which one of us is willing to keep his word? You? I guess not. You've been waiting for the first excuse to hightail it with my money. Well,
if you want my money, you have to work for it, just like
I did. No one gives anything free to half-breeds or whores."
He let go of her then, shoving her a little so she staggered
backward and had to quick-step to keep her balance.

She glared at him with hatred. "I don't want your
money," she cried. "I don't want anything of yours."

"Then you have money for travel? Money to live on?"

"You know I haven't."

Coop walked around the room, calming himself. The sun
lit the distant mountain peaks like a herald's trumpet. He
felt the call and longed to be there. Any other time he
would have left this house with its close walls and troubling truths, but the woman held him. The silence stretched
between them. Finally he spoke, his tone flat, almost uncaring.

"Our original agreement was that you would stay here as
my wife for one year. At the end of that time, if we weren't
happy with the arrangement, we would terminate it and you
would be given a sum of money to return east and live on
comfortably. The offer still stands."

Fancy gasped as the meaning of his words sank in. "You
mean you still want me to stay?" she cried. Her face was
lit with joy. She could forgive the bitter words between
them, if he would only forgive her lies. But he stood

aloofly gazing out the window, and his next words took the joy from her heart.

"You're an actress. I'm hiring you to continue your role as a—lady." His tone grew ironic. He glanced over his shoulder and found her standing white-faced and quiet. Only her lips trembled a little. "You will continue to act as my wife at all functions in Elizabethtown. You will conduct yourself at all times as a lady. No one need ever know you are not what you claim to be. At the end of one year, you may go wherever your heart desires, and you will carry with you the sum of ten thousand dollars."

"Ten thousand dollars!" It was a fortune!

He turned to face her then, his smile derisive, scornful. "I thought talk of money would suit you. Do you agree?"

She studied his face, looking for some sign of the caring he'd shown her throughout the night, but his expression was closed, his eyes hard as steel.

"Do you agree?" he repeated impatiently.

"I—I don't know. I'd have to think about it."

"Why? You didn't think about it when you first came to Elizabethtown, and we were strangers then. Has so much changed since then?"

Yes, she wanted to cry out. I love you now, but she remained silent, her green eyes gazing at him searchingly. Finally she nodded her head and turned away.

"I agree to stay here for one year," she said. "We will, of course, continue as we have been in separate rooms."

"If that's what you wish," Coop said, nodding. "But ten thousand dollars is a lot of money, and I expect more than playacting. The door between our rooms will be left unlocked, and when I have need of a woman I'll come to your room instead of riding into Elizabethtown to visit the whores there."

His words were meant to cut. They did. He had no idea how deeply until she turned to him and he saw her beautiful face crumbled in anger and despair. She lashed out at him, her soft hands striking him about the shoulders while her sobs filled the room. He caught her to him, pinning her arms between them until her struggles stopped. Her whole body shook as she took a deep breath.

"I hate you," she sobbed. "I'll always hate you. How can you want to bed a woman who hates you as I do? There can never be love between us."

"That will make little difference to me," he said flatly. "I've never known love from a woman."

She fell silent and stared up at him. She wanted to cry out, "I've loved you," but she saw the cynicism in his face and knew he wouldn't believe her.

Her gaze, so troubled, so alive touched him as always, and he lowered his head to kiss her lips. Her mouth was passive beneath his. He drew back.

"Remember," he said mockingly, "I expect full measure for my money. In the parlor you can pretend to be the great lady all you want, but in my bed, you'll be the whore you are."

"Never. You'll never know satisfaction with me," she cried, trying to free herself from his grip, but he pulled her close again.

His mouth settled on hers, demanding and punishing. His tongue dueled with hers, subduing as always. When she lay quiet and panting in his arms, he laughed.

"I have no fear about what will happen between us, Fancy. You can't hide your true nature from me." He let her go then.

"I won't stay," she threatened and heard the emptiness of her words.

"Yes, you will," he said.

"You can't keep me here."

"I won't try. You'll stay on your own accord." His gaze held hers a moment more, then he was gone, running lightly down the stairs, then there was the clatter of hooves as he rode away. As always he could walk away from her, just forgetting her as if she were of no importance to him. She wouldn't stay. She'd leave this very day. She rushed around the room gathering her belongings and throwing them helter-skelter into her trunks, until exhaustion and common sense claimed her and she sat on the edge of her bed weeping in resignation. She must stay, not because she was dependent on Coop Fletcher for money, but because, God help her, she loved him. She couldn't walk away from the promise of a year with him. In a year she could show him he was wrong about her. In a year she could make him love her, too.

Still, for all her hard won resolve, she wouldn't capitulate too easily to this stubborn man who had claimed her heart. When Coop returned home well after dark and made his way upstairs, he found her doors locked. A well-placed boot broke through the thin panels separating her room from his. Fancy lay rigid, waiting for him to come to her bed, but he never did, and the next morning when she woke, she found the door between her room and Coop's had been taken away altogether.

Chapter 12

"*H*E'S A HARD man," Geraldine Russell said, shaking her head until her gray curls bobbed. "I disremember at times how he was brought up and all. He ain't ever had a woman he could trust in his whole life. His ma run off and left him when he was still a younker, and the only other kind of women he's known since has been whores and the likes he finds in them gold camps. That makes a man hard."

"But he wasn't like that at first." Fancy sniffed. She'd long since cried herself out on Geraldine's shoulder, gasping out between sobs all that had occurred. "He was kind and generous. Now he's cold and hateful."

"Be patient with him, child. If you truly love him, you'll win him over. I've seen the way he looks at you. He ain't as cold to you as he seems."

"I think he hates me now."

"If he hated you, he wouldn't be wantin' you to stay for a year," Geraldine said. Fancy stared at her with tearful eyes. Geraldine pursed her lips knowingly.

"He didn't want you to leave. It ain't the money he's worried about. He don't feel the same way about money as most folks. He never had it when he grew up, so he never developed that love of money. He saw it as a means to what he wanted, respectability, acceptance, love, commodities he ain't had much of in his life."

176

Fancy sat back. "You make me see him in a different light," she said softly. "You make me want to stay."

"You wanted to stay when you come up here, child. You were just lookin' for a reason to salve your pride. Love is a better reason than any I know of."

"You're right." Fancy wiped at her cheeks and raised her chin. The green lights danced in her eyes. "I'm going to make him such a good wife, he'll beg me not to leave."

"And then?"

"I'll have to decide if I'm going to stay or not." Fancy glanced at Geraldine out of the corner of her eyes, then hugged the old woman. "I can't give in too easily. He's treated me pretty shabbily."

Geraldine laughed, a gusty, all-out guffaw. "Coop's going to have his hands full," she said, then her face turned serious. "You just remember this, Fancy. You're good for him, and he's good for you. You belong together. Now you have to fight for your man with the only weapons a woman can use, understandin', loyalty, and tenderness."

"I will," Fancy vowed. "I'll be everything he wants me to be and more. He wants a wife who's a lady, one those pompous hypocrites in Elizabethtown will admire. Well, that's what I'll be. I just have to find a way to make them see I'm here to stay."

"Like I said before, donate something to the town. That's always a big thing here in Elizabethtown."

"A school!"

"Got one."

"A church!"

"Got too many."

"A hospital?"

Silently Geraldine shook her head. "How about a fire station? They sure need one of them."

"Mmm, no." Fancy's eyes widened as a thought came to her. "A theater! I'll build a theater."

"You mean an opry house?"

"Yes, an opera house. Elizabethtown doesn't have one of

those. Then we can send for acting troupes to come and have plays and musical festivals and—and—"

"Whoa!" Geraldine said.

"Isn't it a good idea? Won't it work?"

"It's a splendid idea," Geraldine agreed. "But before we start hirin' actors, we'd best set about gettin' this thing built."

Fancy's high spirits faded as she faced the reality of what she wanted to do. "I don't have any way to pay for an opera house to be built," she said despondently.

"Pshaw, Coop can pay for it. He's got more money than you'd ever imagine. He can haul the materials down from Denver what we can't find around here."

"We could put Daniel in charge of building the opera house. That would show people around here that an ex-slave is a good man, too."

"I swear you take on more causes than any one woman I ever seen. You go home and talk to Coop tonight."

"He'll say no."

"He won't. If you tell him in the right way. Give him a chance, Fancy."

"I love you, Geraldine," she said simply. "Thank you for listening to my troubles." The old woman's pale eyes watered.

"Now you got me bawlin' like a dang fool," she snapped, dabbing at her eyes.

Fancy laughed and hugged her. "That's not so bad."

Geraldine stopped fussing. "No, there's worse things than lettin' your feelin's show. You get on back home to your man now and act while the gate's still open."

Fancy returned to the ranch in better spirits. That night she approached Coop in his study. He'd thrown aside his hat, and his blue-black hair hung over his forehead. She wanted to smooth it back but knew such gestures wouldn't be welcomed now. Instead she faced him with a haughty regal air, her chin high, her green-eyed gaze cool and aloof.

"What is it, Fancy?" Coop asked with a show of impatience. But the irritation was for himself for responding to her icy beauty. Her hair was piled high on her head, making her appear taller. Her slender figure was dressed in a simple dress of green-printed muslin, with a sheer white cotton lawn underskirt. She looked immaculate, untouched by the heat. His fingers curled into the palm of his hand to ease the tension that laced through him whenever she was near. "I have work to do."

"Yes, I see you have," she answered. "I won't be long." She took a breath which swelled the soft ivory mound above the neckline of her bodice. Coop gritted his teeth. For the last two nights, he'd fought himself not to go to her.

She took her time in crossing to a chair, seating herself on its edge and spreading her skirts just so. Finally she met his gaze with the same detachment.

"I need some money," she said simply.

Coop felt deflated. What had he hoped she'd say? "You have your account at the bank. Just draw on that."

"But I need quite a lot of money," Fancy said.

Coop stared at her. "How much?"

"I—I don't know really. Several thousand, I suppose."

"What do you need it for?" His voice was suspicious, his eyes narrowed into speculative slits, and suddenly she was disinclined to tell him about the opera house.

"It's a secret," she said instead and waited for his reaction.

"Let me get this straight. You want me to hand over several thousand dollars to you without knowing what it's for?"

"That's right."

"How do I know you aren't planning to run off with as much money as you can get?"

"You don't know. You'll just have to trust that I intend to stay and honor our agreement." She waited while he debated. Both seemed to know this was an important moment between them. She shouldn't have done this, she thought. She'd done nothing to prepare him to believe he could trust her. She should have tested him on something small.

He shouldn't trust her, he thought. Why should he believe she'd stay, once she had a large sum of money in her hands? Yet, could he keep her prisoner here for a year? If he gave her the money and she left, then he'd know once and for all that his suspicions about her were correct. And if she stayed—! The thought was intoxicating.

"I'll see that you have access to the money you need," he said shortly and cursed himself for a fool. He returned to his figures. Fancy stayed where she was, feeling elation, feeling hope stir. His had been an act of trust, and she wanted to throw herself at him and tell him what it meant to her, but he was already frowning over the ledgers. She rose and waited, but he didn't look up. With a swish of skirts she crossed to the desk. He could smell her perfume, all heady and light, like the sweet wild mountain flowers in the spring. He couldn't think, couldn't make the figures add up. His pen hovered over the page, and a splotch of ink fell.

"Dad-blame it," he roared and liked the sound of his voice filling up the silence between them. He raised his head and glared at her as if it were her fault.

"I could do that for you, if you'd like. I'm very good with figures." He only stared at her. "I kept track of the ledgers for my father's theatrical troupe."

"And it failed, as I recall," he said sternly.

She blanched at his insult. "How can you justify such a remark when you've just allowed me access to several thousand dollars of your money?" she asked quietly. "That doesn't sound like good business to me, Coop Fletcher." He made no answer. She turned and calmly made her way to the door, the bustle of her skirts swaying with each step. Suddenly, he understood why women had adopted such a ridiculous style. They were meant to drive men wild with seductive persuasion while maintaining an unbreechable defense.

The door closed quietly behind the sassy swishing behind

and Coop took a deep breath, pushed all thought of Fancy out of his mind and turned back to his hated task of balancing the books. One problem with becoming a rich man was that there was more and more such work. He thought of Fancy's offer. Perhaps he had been too hasty, but he would have had to endure her bending over the desk while he fought off the enticing allure of her body so near. He slammed the ledgers closed and, grabbing up his hat, stalked into the hallway on his way to the front door. A lamp was glowing in the parlor, and Fancy sat calmly working at her needlework. He paused remembering those early weeks when she first came to the ranch and they sat in the parlor together, reaching toward each other. At least he'd thought they were. Perhaps he had been the only one reaching out, needing; maybe it had all meant nothing to her. He cursed and she looked up, her eyes wide and startled looking.

"Did you want me?" she asked innocently, and he clenched his fist around his hat brim.

"I'm leaving early in the morning," he said gruffly. "We're taking government supplies to the Middle Park to the Indians."

"How long will you be gone?" He thought he detected a note of disappointment in her voice, or was that his imagination?

"Nearly a week," he answered. He worked his hat brim some more, unaware he was ruining it. "If you want to work on the ledgers, I'll show you what I need done when I get back."

"I'd be happy to work on them, if you trust me," Fancy said evenly.

His head jerked up, and he glared at her. "Why shouldn't I trust you?" he demanded tersely.

"I don't know, Coop. Why shouldn't you trust me?" He knew she wasn't talking about the ledgers now, and his lips thinned. He hated to think he may have acted hastily toward her. He hated to think the words he'd hurled at her had been unnecessary. Without answering, he rushed out of the house and strode down to the corral. Hanging over the fence rail, he watched the moonshine on the mountains. No wonder men thought there was gold up there, no wonder they searched. The mountains themselves enticed a man onward with their beauty so he was blinded by their hidden dangers, their perfidities. He thought of Fancy and slammed his palm against the rail, impervious to the pain of splinters. One thought had hounded him these past few days since Travis Wheeler's letter came, one thought had driven him to a frenzy, now he turned back to the house. A black fury settled over him. He'd know the answer to his question, by God, this night, he'd know.

Fancy wasn't in the parlor. Her needlework lay forgotten on the settee. A single lamp burned. Delores would extinguish it before going to bed. Coop's face was a rigid mask of fury as he took the steps two at a time. He went straight to her door and without knocking threw it open.

Fancy whirled, her expression filled with alarm until she saw who the intruder was. She'd already dressed for bed, and she stood in her thin lawn gown with its chaste ribbon and lace trim. Her long hair was unbound and had been brushed to a bright sheen. She still held the brush in her hand as if he'd caught her at her task. Drawing a deep breath, she put the brush aside and forced herself to look at him.

"Did you want something, Coop?" she asked quietly, her gaze direct and calm, much calmer than she felt.

He advanced into the room a step or two and paused, fixing her with his compelling gaze.

"How many?" he asked.

"I beg your pardon?"

"How many men had you before I did?"

Her face blanched. Her eyes glittered with anger.

"How many do you think?" she asked in a low, taunting voice. "One, two? Maybe ten or a hundred. How many men do you think I've had?"

"You bitch!" His long arms reached out for her. She tried to dodge him, but he was too fast and too strong for her. He caught her shoulders and pulled her up, shaking her so her hair flew around them. One hand closed around her throat, and she ceased fighting, staring at him with wide tragic eyes. There was no pain in his grip, the pain was in his eyes. She saw it and relented.

"I've never been with any other man but you," she whispered shaking her head. "None."

He gazed deep into her eyes as if trying to reach her very soul, then he jerked her forward. His mouth, hungry and unyielding, melded with hers. At first she tried to push him away, tried to fight him, but his hot kiss tamed her, held her captive, weakened her resolve for vengeance, cooled her anger, and inflamed her senses. She clung to him, glorying in the feel of his hard, unyielding body against hers. She wanted him with a passion that threatened to consume her. She returned his kiss as fiercely as he gave, her arms wrapped around his neck, played through his hair, slid down the sloping muscles of his shoulder, his trim, rock-hard back to his buttocks and around to seek the rod of his manhood. Their melded bodies were a barrier to her questing hands. She moaned her disappointment against his mouth, and he shoved her backward onto the bed. His hand reached for the tail of her gown, flipping it high, exposing her tapering legs and the golden nestle of curls at their juncture. Her hips writhed on the bed as she pulled the gown from beneath her and flung it away.

Coop was already undressing, tossing his clothes carelessly across the room. The lamplight cast a soft glow against his dusky body. Then he straightened. Her gaze darted from his smoky glance down to his hips, and she drew in her breath as she saw evidence of his arousal. She held out her arms, welcoming him. Her body opened to him, readying itself for this pleasurable assault.

He took no time to caress her. There was no need to see to her needs. She rode a high wave of passion at his side. Grabbing her legs he raised them high and plunged against her. He wanted to give her pain as he felt pain, but her body was too sweet, too satiny smooth, too giving in its womanly secrets, so his ruthless assault turned to something else. His hard body still plunged against hers with the same intensity, but now he sought to give pleasure, too.

He cupped her face between his hands and watched the changing emotions in the green depths of her eyes. He wanted to see her reaching for the peak as did he, and he wanted to see her eyes when she reached it. Together they traveled in a land only true lovers know, moving together, reaching, finding an ecstasy found no other place but in a lover's arms. They reached the mountaintops, all gilded with the gold of moonlight, they soared over the valley floors so far below where mere mortals walked. But for a while, a brief ecstatic moment they flew with the gods. And when their flight was done, they drifted back to earth and lay cosseted in each other's arms.

Fancy was smiling dreamily, her arms holding Coop as tenderly as a babe. He lay against her satiny breast, feeling his body cool and with it his passion and his trust. He raised his head and looked at her. Her smile was warm, intimate. It spoke of the special moment they'd just shared. He wanted to weep. He used anger to hide his despair.

"No blushing shyness this time," he commented, drawing away from her and reaching for his clothes. "No bumbling innocence." His words were a condemnation.

"What do you mean?" Fancy whispered, her eyes were wide and troubled.

"Your true nature has shown itself, Fancy Lady. An innocent virgin wouldn't respond as you just did."

She felt as if he'd struck her. Sliding off the bed she wrapped herself in a sheet and faced him. "How would you know what a virgin does or doesn't do? You've never had one before," she stormed. "All you've ever known are whores and camp followers."

His head jerked up. "How do you know about such things, unless you were one yourself?" he snapped.

"I don't have to be a horse's ass to recognize one," she answered. "You wouldn't recognize an act of love if you saw one."

"Love?" he scoffed. "Don't try to tell me you love me. You're only in this for the money."

"If you truly thought that, why did you agree to give me the thousands I asked for earlier?"

"I was a fool," he snapped, drawing on his boots. "I may change my mind." He was dressed now and turned to her. Her bottom lip was trembling, but her eyes were nearly black with rage. He wanted to kiss her again. He wanted to throttle her. He wanted to run away from the pain she brought him just by standing there. He made his retreat, turning at the door to stare back at her.

She got the final word in. "Don't come to my door again, Coop Fletcher," she said stonily. "You won't find what you found tonight."

"A whore is always a whore," he said and closed the door behind him. The darkness surrounded him, so he stood for a moment trying to adjust. From beyond the door he heard a sound like a lost calf mewing for its mother. He'd made her cry. Regret washed over him. His fingers tightened on the doorknob, and he thought of going back in to comfort her. That was what she wanted. She was manipulating him, wrapping him around her finger with her sensuous body and pretty womanly ways.

He snatched his hand away and stalked down the hallway to his own room, but he remembered he'd removed the door between their rooms. He'd have to lay in his bed all night listening to her weep, thinking about her sweet body only a few feet away. Without opening his door, he turned toward the stairs, made his way to the bunkhouse and settled his weary body on a hard cot. This was better, he thought. He had to rise early with his men to begin his trip. But the moon had passed its apex and was sliding down the western sky toward dawn before he finally slept.

Chapter 13

S HE WOULD LEAVE, Fancy decided. She wouldn't stay with a man who used her then hurled ugly accusations at her. He'd left without even coming to tell her goodbye, without even attempting to make things right between them. Well, she would be gone when he returned, but when she tried to pack her clothes, the tears came and she collapsed on the bed in a hopeless muddle while Annabelle unpacked her trunks.

"These clothes been in an' out o' these trunks so often, they 'bout wore out," she said accusingly.

"What am I going to do, Annabelle?" Fancy asked piteously.

"Yo' got to make up yo'r mind if yo' going to leave him or stay," Annabelle said stoically.

"If I leave, will you go with me?"

Annabelle paused in her unpacking. Slowly she shook her head. "I reckon I won't, Miss Fancy," she said reluctantly. "Me and Daniel's already got an understandin'."

"Oh, Annabelle. I'm happy for you. Truly I am."

"The only thing we waitin' for is for Daniel to save enough money to buy some land. We goin' t'start our own ranch."

"Isn't that a big undertaking?" Fancy asked, envying her friend's glowing face.

"Oh, we won't have a fine place like this is, prob'ly

never will. We goin' t'start small and build as we can. We figure we'll have us a few young 'uns, and they can help with the ranch. Oh, Miss Fancy, why yo' cryin' again?"

"I—I'm not crying, really, Annabelle. I'm just so happy for you and Daniel." Fancy wiped at her eyes and smiled at the brown-skinned girl who'd come so far with her. "I'll miss you so much."

"If yo' stay, we won't be so far apart. We'll come visit once in awhile like yo' and Miss Geraldine do."

Fancy shook her head. "I know, I know, but I'm just not sure if I'll be staying past a year."

Annabelle shook her head. "Whatever trouble between yo' and Mistah Coop, yo' got to give it a chance to get bettah. It won't if yo' just run away."

"You don't know, Annabelle, the terrible things he believes about me. He thinks I only came here to get his money."

"Mmmm, poor man."

"What do you mean, poor man?" Fancy flared up. "He's insensitive and pigheaded and just plain mean."

"He's no such thing, Miss Fancy. He's a good man, but he ain't been gentled. He's like one of them wild hosses he tames. Daniel says they call the baddest ones a wassup, an outlaw hoss. That's what Mr. Coop reminds me of. He's an outlaw what's been chased and treated bad, and now he don't trust nobody. He only expects the worst."

Fancy stared at Annabelle. "I swear between you and Geraldine you'd make him a saint," she said, jumping out of bed. "He's just a stubborn, hard-hearted man who doesn't believe the truth when it's told to him."

"Yo' got t'admit yo' didn't always tell him the truth," Annabelle reminded her gently.

"Well, I—I couldn't. How did I know how he'd take it if I did? He might have sent us right back on the next stage. Where would we have gone?"

"If yo'd a told Mistah Coop the truth that first night he come callin' on you afore yo'r weddin', he would a married yo' anyway. I seen that look in his eyes even then."

"What look?"

"The look like a young'un gets when it's Christmas an there's somethin' under the tree for him he's always wanted and he can't believe it's really his."

"Oh, that," Fancy said, oddly deflated. "A lady!"

"It wasn't just that he was seein' a lady," Annabelle admonished. "He looked at yo' like he was seein' the angel on top of the Christmas tree."

Fancy paused, remembering the day she walked down the stairs to become Coop's bride. He had been so protective then, treating her as if she were fragile porcelain, and later even though he forced his kisses on her, he wasn't mean or frightening. She wanted that Coop back, not the one who came to her room driven by lust. Another thought came to mind, and she whirled to look at Annabelle.

"Get my lavender silk gown with the green bows. I'm going into town today."

"My goodness, yo' change yo'self around faster than anyone I know," Annabelle grumbled, but she went to the armoire to retrieve the specified gown and all the petticoats and wire bustles it required.

Geraldine and Daniel accompanied her. First they went to the bank, where with beating heart, Fancy inquired about her personal account. She was elated, then touched to see that in spite of their argument Coop had made arrangements for her to draw the large sums she would need. He'd passed the most crucial test. Then it occurred to her that perhaps she was the one being tested. Humming under her breath she returned to Geraldine. Coop would see she wasn't running off with his money. She was here to stay as long as she could.

They spent the rest of the day looking for a site for the opera house and finally decided on a place at one end of the town away from the other frame buildings.

"Build it of bricks, Miss Fancy," Daniel advised as they walked around the site.

"Can you handle bricks, Daniel?"

"Yes, ma'am," he answered. "I did many of the small buildings for Mistah Victor back on his place."

"Then make it of brick," Fancy said. "I want it to be the finest opera house ever built."

"Yes, ma'am. I'll do that," Daniel said, beaming with pride.

Word had already spread by the time they drove back through town, and several people called out to them.

"It's working already," Fancy said.

"Told you it would," Geraldine answered. "It ain't that folks are greedy. They just like to know you mean to be part of the community."

"I'm here to stay, Geraldine, as long as Coop'll have me."

Geraldine studied the dark circles under the girl's eyes and shook her head. How young people could get themselves into such a tangle of nerves, she didn't know. It seemed so simple to her. Coop loved Fancy, and Fancy loved Coop. They ought to quit fighting and get on with living. She'd tell Coop so, the next time she saw him.

Coop was giving a lot of thought to living. His big fist clenched around his forty-four as he squinted his eyes against the sun. They were being followed by someone and had been for the past five miles. Coop cast an uneasy glance at Aaron. They'd paused to rest the mules before beginning the next grade, and his pack master looked back along the line of wagons.

"I don't like this," Aaron said, bracing a foot against the brake and biting off a mouthful of tobacco. "Do you reckon they're really back there? Maybe we're just gettin' fanciful."

"Someone's back there," Coop said and brought his nervous mount under control. "I spotted them against the skyline once. It's almost like they want us to know they're back there."

"Why would anyone want to steal this freight? It's just a bunch of blankets and flour for the Utes."

"Maybe they don't know that," Coop said, but he'd been bothered by the same question. It should be obvious to any fool they were following the trail to the Middle Park, and there was nothing there but a few hunters and the Indians.

"Maybe it's the Utes, followin' to make sure we get there with their supplies."

"Maybe," Coop said, but he didn't really think so. Neither did Aaron. It just helped some to think they had a friend at their back rather than a pack of wolves.

"Let's get the wagons moving," Coop said and waved the teams forward. The air was filled with the cries of teamsters and the snap of their whips. The wagons moved forward, slowly at first as they climbed the grade, then picking up speed as they reached the top and started down the far side. The trail ahead was fairly well established. Coop rode close to Aaron's wagon.

"I'm riding back a ways just to see what's back there," he hollered. "Keep the wagons moving, no matter what."

"You taking anyone with you?"

"It's better if I go alone, less chance of being detected."

"Take it easy, Coop. The men who hide out in these mountains are killers."

"Send word back to the drivers to arm themselves and be ready," Coop answered, and with a final salute from his hat brim, turned back down the trail. He'd noticed a place some distance back. If he made that he could watch the trail without being observed. As quietly as he could he made his way down to the deep natural corridor in the rocks. Riding his horse in as deep as he could, he climbed into the rocks above so he could look down on the trail. Stretching out on the rock, he settled himself to wait. It wasn't long before he heard them moving up the trail.

There were a dozen of them, and they made little effort to remain undetected. Apparently, they felt they had nothing to fear from the teamsters. Coop remained quiet and out of sight as they rode by, trying to sort the words from their careless laughter. Some of them were drunk, he guessed, and all were in high spirits over the coming attack on the pack train. Boastful and unrepentant, they called to one another, betting on the number of men they would kill.

"We ain't leavin' no survivors," the head man called. He wore his hat pulled low over his face and rode a piebald. "No survivors, no witnesses." Coop would remember that laugh.

His hand tightened on his gun, and he gritted his teeth to keep from springing up and firing on them. Once they'd gone past, he retrieved his horse and followed. The hunted had become the hunter, he thought grimly. He followed them much closer than they had him, and they never guessed he was behind.

As the pack train labored up an incline, they struck, swooping down on the men. Coop heard the first shot and put his horse to a full gallop. The outlaws had fanned out facing the train, their guns blazing a volley of fire on the wagons. One mule was down, the rest screaming in terror. The drivers were returning their fire as best they could. The outlaws were still unaware Coop was behind them.

Taking out his forty-four, he began firing, slowly and methodically, and with each blast from his pistol, a man went down. The other outlaws turned and stared at him in consternation, then kicked at their horses trying to run for cover, but there was no place to go. They were caught between the crossfire of the teamsters and Coop's deadly aim.

Haphazardly they returned his fire, figuring he was one against many and therefore the weaker offense, but they hadn't reckoned his relentless accuracy. Three more men fell in the get-away. Only two out of a dozen rode away, one of them on the piebald. Coop chased after him for a short distance, then brought his mount to a halt. There was no sense in risking the black, riding pell-mell down that trail. He rode back to his pack train. The men stood up and cheered.

"What you want us to do with these bodies?" Aaron asked. "Leave 'em for the buzzards?"

"Better not," Coop said. "We have to use this trail again, and I don't have a fondness for riding past a man's bones.

Throw them on the wagons, and we'll take them on into the Middle Park to bury them."

"Better'n they deserve," some of the men grumbled, but they kept their voices low. If Coop said he didn't want to leave them, they wouldn't leave them. They respected his decisions.

They cut out the dead mule and hauled it off the trail, then moved some of the boxes and kegs to another wagon to lighten the load for the short team. In little time they were on their way again. The only evidence of violence on the trail was the body of the dead mule left behind.

A party of Utes rode out to meet them. "We heard the shots," said an Indian called Littlefield. He'd once acted as a guide for hunters who came to the Middle Park. Now he had retired and concerned himself only with the affairs of his people. Although he wore the white man's clothes, he was adorned with a necklace of bear claws, and his long black hair was parted in the center and braided in the ways of his people. His gaze was direct, his manner unhurried.

"We had a little trouble," Coop said, indicating the limp bodies on one of the wagons.

Littlefield and the others examined the bodies and turned back to Coop. "These are very bad men," he said. "They have come to our valley many times, and always they bring whiskey and rob the Indians and use their women. But you have not got their leader."

"The one who rides the piebald."

"The spotted pony," Littlefield said. "He is called Reynard. He is the worst of them. He tells the others what to do."

"Well, he doesn't have any men left to command now," Coop said.

Littlefield shrugged. "He will find others. Jackals run in a pack. They will return to our reservation, and when they do, we will stop them, even if we are punished for killing a white man." Littlefield's face was stern, and Coop knew it would do little good to remind him the law would punish him. White man's law had done little to protect the Indians, so they were fast losing respect for it.

With Littlefield and his men as escorts they made their way to the Indian camp, a huddle of tepees sporting ratty buffalo skins. Coop's lips tightened as he remembered how the once proud tribes had renewed their tepee skins every year. Now they ran to greet the wagons and helped unload the barrels and crates of supplies the white father in Washington had sent them to live on. With a cry of triumph they opened a barrel and stood staring at it in dumbfounded surprise.

"Coop!" Aaron called. "Come over here."

They studied the opened barrel.

"What the holy hell—?" Coop stared at the barrel of rocks.

"Somebody's playing a trick on us," Aaron said.

"Or on the Utes," Coop muttered. His gaze met Aaron's. "No, you're right. The trick was played on us. Remember how Springer insisted these crates and barrels be loaded by his men? He barely allowed you to supervise. Then the attack on the train. This shipment was never meant to reach the Utes. We were supposed to be killed back there on the trail and the wagons sent over the ledge. No evidence, Reynard said."

"If we hadn't been alert, they would have killed us, too," Aaron said. "What do we do?"

"Yes, Fletcher. What will you do? Our people cannot eat rocks," Littlefield said. Coop looked around the circle of hostile faces.

"We'll see that you get food," he promised. "I'll personally send you enough goods and heads of cattle that will hold you over until our government straightens this out."

"The warm moons draw to an end soon. There will be no time for the white father to send us more food from Washington. Soon the mountain passes will be filled with snow."

"Your food supplies are here in this country somewhere,

Littlefield, and I promise by all that's holy I'll find it and deliver it to your people."

"Perhaps the evil men who represent your government have already sold it to the miners who dig at the mountains."

"I'll find out," Coop said. "We'll take back a couple of barrels with us to show the officials what has happened."

"The Utes will wait for Fletcher's words," Littlefield said. "But if the first snow falls on the empty bellies of our children, we will leave the reservation and find our own food."

The braves behind Littlefield cheered his words, their eyes angry at yet another betrayal by their white brothers.

"I'll be back before then," Coop said and climbed into his saddle. The drivers who were tired and had expected a rest once they reached the Park said nothing, simply climbing up on their wagons and shouting at their teams to edge them back on the trail. They had little desire to stay in the Park when the Utes were riled up.

Three days later they were back in Elizabethtown. Coop sent the rest of the wagons on to the ranch, then motioned Aaron to follow him. They were headed to the sheriff's office, when Coop pulled his black to a halt. Aaron did likewise with his mule team. The barrel of rocks they'd brought from the Indian reservation rested in the back of the wagon.

"What is it, Coop?" Aaron asked, braking his wagon.

Coop nodded to a spotted pony tied to the rail before a saloon. "There aren't too many piebalds around here. You head on down and get the sheriff. I think I'll take a look see in here."

"Have a care by yourself, Coop. That fella's like a snake. He can wiggle out of tight spots, and he'll try to kill you in the bargain."

"I can handle myself. You just go get the sheriff and show him what we found in those barrels."

Reluctantly, Aaron whipped up his mules and proceeded

down to the sheriff's office. Coop tied off his horse and climbed the steps to the saloon porch.

"Coop!" A light familiar voice called to him, and he turned in time to see Fancy coming along the boardwalk toward him. "You're back," she cried, real pleasure in her voice. His thoughts were so centered on the man inside the saloon, he could barely pay attention to her words and smile. Some part of him noted she hadn't left. He felt a swell of joy at the sight of her.

"I have something wonderful to show you," she cried, running to grip his arm. "The surprise I didn't want to tell you about before you left. We've started already, Coop, and you're going to be so proud."

"Fancy, go away."

"What?"

"Get out of here. This isn't the time or place."

Her ebullient spirits died away. He saw the hurt in her eyes, but he'd already caught a movement inside the saloon door. Roughly, he shoved her away. "Go! Get out of here now!" he shouted, one hand already going for his gun. He only had a moment to see her outraged face and the flurry of petticoats as she whirled and stalked away.

A shot rang out from within the salon. Coop leaped for cover beside the open door. He couldn't risk blindly firing into the saloon. He might hit some innocent bystander.

"Reynard," he shouted, "give it up. You can't get away." His words were answered by several more shots.

The staccato beat of a woman's high-heeled boots against the plank walk had ceased. Coop risked a glance and saw Fancy standing open-mouthed, staring back at him. Even as he looked at her, she took a step toward him. He waved her away. Another shot came, splintering the doorjamb next to his head.

"Coop!" Fancy screamed and began running toward him. A hail of bullets were whining through the door now. Coop looked from the open door back at Fancy. God almighty she'd run right into the crossfire. She was at the edge of the saloon porch when he dove for her, grabbing her around the waist and rolling with her in the dust. Bullets pinged around their heads as two men rushed out of the saloon and ran for their horses.

One was Reynard. He leapt on the piebald and fired wildly along the street. People screamed and ran for cover. Coop tried to bring his arm up to level his gun, but he was tangled in Fancy's petticoats and ribbons. She was screaming in his ear and clinging to his neck with a death clutch.

"Let go of me, Fancy," Coop shouted, but she only clung tighter. Reynard was on his horse now, and seeing Coop was on the ground, he laughed and took aim. Coop heard a rip of cloth as he forced his gun hand up and fired off a shot. Reynard's laughter turned to a scream of pain, and he lurched in his saddle, clutching his shoulder. Without looking back, he kicked the piebald in the belly, and he and his sidekick galloped off down the street.

"Fancy, let go of me," Coop roared and, when she'd done so, leapt to his feet, but her skirts caught in his spurs as he tried to run. By the time he got to the middle of the street, Reynard and his partner had disappeared, hell-bent for safety in the mountains. Aaron and the sheriff came running up.

"What happened?" Sheriff Wright demanded, his pistol at the ready.

Coop shook his head. "A man named Reynard and his sidekick just shot their way out of that saloon. He's the head of a gang of outlaws that's been robbing my pack trains. We killed about ten of his men back up in the mountains three days ago."

"You say he got away?"

"Yeah," Coop shook his head and glanced back at Fancy who still knelt in the dirt, her hands clasped to her mouth.

"Where's Doyle Springer?"

"He's not in town right now. He headed back to Denver three days ago." Sheriff Wright drawled. He was an earnest man who'd come from Missouri seeking his fortune and stayed on because he hated to go back home a failure. He was a good lawman for a quiet town where nothing much happened, but he was out of his element here in the wild mountain towns.

"Did Aaron show you those barrels?" Coop asked.

"Yeah, he did, Mr. Fletcher. But I don't reckon there's anything I could rightly do about it. Springer works for the federal government, and I'm just a deputy appointed by the town mayor."

"You're a lawman who's supposed to uphold the law for everyone. Springer or one of his men stole the supplies meant for the Utes and substituted rocks. Those people up there are about to starve unless we can get some food to them before the snows set in."

"We've got lots of time, Mr. Fletcher," Sheriff Wright said soothingly. "This is July."

"In a couple of months, you could have all those mountain passes closed," Coop flared. "I've seen it happen. If we don't do something to see the Utes have the food they need to winter over, they've threatened to leave the reservation. Maybe you'd better send word back to Doyle Springer."

"Yeah, all right. I'll do that," Wright said. "I'll deputize someone and send 'em out right away."

Holstering his forty-four, Coop stalked back to Fancy and, taking hold of her elbow, jerked her to her feet. "What are you doing here in town?" he demanded. "Why aren't you out at the ranch where you belong?"

People had come out on the street now that the shooting was done, and they listened avidly as Coop Fletcher reprimanded his wife.

"I beg your pardon. I wasn't aware I needed your permission to leave the ranch," Fancy snapped, brushing the dust off her torn gown. She was still shaken by their close brush with death.

"Well, if you'd been at the ranch where you belonged, you wouldn't have been here in the way when I'm trying to capture an outlaw."

"I can't help it if you can't hit what you shoot at," she answered. "I didn't come here to be insulted or because I even wanted to. I thought you were about to be killed. My every thought was for you, but do you appreciate it, oh no, you yell at me as you do for everything."

"Look, I'm sorry. I didn't mean to yell."

"I'm sorry, too," Fancy said sweetly. "Sorry that man's bullet didn't reach its mark." She unfurled her parasol, which was slightly bent on one side from her roll in the dirt. Her face was smudged, her clothes streaked with dirt, but there wasn't an onlooker there who didn't know she was a lady as she stalked away from her belligerent husband. Many a chuckle was had that night as the tale was related over supper tables about Coop Fletcher and his high-spirited, high-stepping fancy lady.

Without a backward glance, Fancy made her way to her carriage and instructed Daniel to take her back to the ranch straight away. Coop watched them drive away and was sorry for his temper. If she'd stayed they might have had supper at La Maison Francais and spent the night at their town house. Now he motioned Aaron to follow and, retrieving his horse, made his way out of town for the long ride home, and all the way, he wondered how he might make amends.

Chapter 14

THERE WAS NO sign of the buggy or of Fancy when he rode into the ranch yard, but Daniel was letting the horses into the pasture. Coop took his time wiping down the black and feeding him, discussing business with Aaron and relating to his men what had occurred in town.

"I want you all to be on the lookout when you're freighting," Coop advised them. "I don't know why Reynard has singled out our freight trains, but he seems to know when we're hauling freight and where to."

"Reckon he's workin' alone, Coop? If so, we pert near wiped out his gang. We may have run him off for good."

"I'd like to think that was so, Evans," Coop answered, "but I just don't know. Besides, he can recruit more men. These mountains are full of disgruntled miners who wouldn't hesitate to join up with the likes of Reynard."

"I ain't sure I want to go out there again, if we're goin' to run into a string of polecats every time," another man said. "Them mountain trails is dangerous enough without bullets whizzin' by our heads."

"I can't blame any of you for feeling that way," Coop answered. "All I can tell you is that we'll take extra precautions, more ammunition, guards, and the like. We'll even see about reinforcing those bootjacks, just to give you extra cover, but ultimately, if you're attacked, you're going to have to fight back." He paused and looked around the crowded bunkhouse. "If any of you feel you don't want to face that, then see Aaron and pick up your pay, and you won't be thought any the less for it."

A couple of men gathered up their gear and shamefacedly left the bunkhouse, the rest returned to their card games and whatever other activity had occupied them before Coop showed up. They were a pretty rough lot and knew what freighting to the mining camps meant. They were used to facing dangers of one sort or another. If bears or four-legged mountain cats didn't jump you, then law of man said the two-legged variety of polecat would.

With his business taken care of for the moment, Coop could find no other excuse not to return to the ranch house. To stall a little more, he sluiced off the travel dust down at the creek. The sun was setting over the distant peaks, streaking the sky with brilliant color. Coop stopped to enjoy the display before climbing the porch steps. The ranch house was quiet. A single lamp burned in the parlor, and from the door of the study came a fine line of light.

"What the hell?" he growled and stomped across the entrance to the door. One booted foot kicked at the door. It flew inward, striking the wall. Fancy sat at the desk, the ranch ledgers spread before her. At his entrance, her head snapped up and she sat calmly staring at him. His blue-black hair was damp from his bath and still clung to his neck. His gray eyes were like the creek in the moonlight, liquid silver that moved with every nuance of emotion. She could drown in his eyes.

"What are you doing?" he demanded.

"The books," she answered casually.

"I haven't shown you how I wanted them done," he said accusingly.

"I looked at your back pages and proceeded in the same

manner," she said. "Would you like to examine my work? Perhaps then you'll feel less distrustful."

He strode across the room and stared down at the opened books. She'd brought everything up to date, the figures written neatly and entered correctly. He studied several entries, looking for an error, but there were none. She waited patiently and had the grace not to look smug.

"It isn't that I distrust you," he began gruffly.

"Of course not," she said disbelievingly and rose from behind the desk.

"It's just that—"

"Don't thank me," she replied airily. "After all, have you ever stopped to think I might be doing this just to find out your true worth?"

"And have you?"

"Actually, I do have a much better idea of your investments and such." Fancy turned to face him. "You're really quite wealthy. Geraldine says you're richer than she is, and she's the richest woman in the district."

"So that's why you stayed," he said, suddenly feeling deflated.

"I suppose you could think that, if you wanted to," she said, and he didn't hear the bitterness in her voice.

Coop looked at the slender back and stiff shoulders and sensed he'd hurt her. "What did you want to show me this afternoon in town?" he asked much as one would a pouting child.

"This afternoon?" Fancy asked innocently, casting him a quick glance. "Just a pretty hat I was thinking of buying."

"Is that all?" His anger rose again. "You know you nearly got yourself killed."

"Oh, but you were there to protect me. How fortunate for me." His anger melted at her words, so sweetly spoken.

"I'm sorry I yelled at you afterward. I was just so—"

"Scared?" Fancy's smile wasn't friendly. So that was the way of it, he thought.

"Yeah! I was scared," he answered, the muscle in his jaw

jumping. "I was sacred you'd get your fool head blown off before I could send you away."

"You really needn't worry about me and my fool head," Fancy snapped. "It wasn't me he was aiming at. And I was scared, too. Scared he'd plug that thick hide of yours."

"You mean before you could get your hands on a bigger share of my wealth."

"There! You've said it again," she rounded on him, her green eyes snapping, her little rounded chin fairly quivering with indignation. "I forgave you the first time you made such a remark, but I will not forgive you this time. You are a—as stubborn as those mules you use to haul loads over the mountains. You wouldn't recognize the truth if it reared up and kicked you in your backside."

"You're a great one to lecture me on truth," Coop growled, leaning forward, his hands braced on the desk. "I haven't heard a true word out of your mouth since you came here."

"If I'm so bad, then why do you want me to stay?" Fancy challenged him from the other side of the desk.

"I don't want you to stay. You can leave anytime," Coop said, but his roar held less volume, less certainty.

"But if I leave now, I must go without money to travel or support myself. If you really wanted me out of your life, you'd give me the money now, just to be rid of me." Fancy's expression was triumphant, as if she'd made a telling point. Coop felt his anger grow.

"I did leave money for you at the bank," he said quietly.

She blinked, then blinked several more times as if she'd gotten something in her eye. "You left that money for me so I'd leave?" she asked, and her voice went high and reedy as if she were about to cry. "I thought you left it there as a test for me. I didn't think you really wanted me to go." She turned toward the door, gathering her skirt in her hands as if preparing to run away.

"Fancy!" That single word seemed to galvanize her to action. With a single cry she ran out of the room and up the stairs. Coop stared at the empty doorway, wondering how the hell he'd said and done everything wrong again.

"Fancy!" He followed her up the stairs to her door and listened to her weeping on the other side. He couldn't stand the sound of a woman weeping. It did things to his insides. Disgruntled, resenting the feelings of guilt, he stomped to the stairs, then paused.

"I'll be damned if I'll sleep in the bunkhouse again tonight," he shouted to no one in particular. With a great show of bravado he marched into his room and took off his boots and shucked off his pants. There was no sound from Fancy's room. The weeping had stopped.

He lay on his bed, his weary muscles unable to relax and enjoy the luxury of a mattress. He thought of Fancy lying in the next room, pretending she hadn't been crying, still feeling hurt by his meanness, and he had been mean. She'd made him mad, and he'd taken out his frustration over the Indian supplies and Reynard's escape on her. He wasn't being fair. Look what a job she'd done on his books and the ranch and everything she touched. And she hadn't left. She'd stayed. That first moment of seeing her in town had caused such elation, he'd almost forgotten about Reynard inside the saloon. He'd been that grateful to see her again. His long legs kicked at the covers as he tossed on the bed. Finally, he flung aside the sheet and walked to the doorway of Fancy's room. He sensed the tension in the air as if she knew he was there.

"I'm sorry I made you cry," he said roughly.

"You didn't," she said quietly from her bed. He could picture her curled up on her side, all warm and pink and glowing, and desire stirred in his loins.

"I thought I heard you—from the hall," he began.

"No. I was laughing," she answered lightly.

"Laughing?" Coop stood there nonplussed. "At me?"

"At something you said."

"I'm glad you find me so all-fired funny."

"Not that funny," came the cool reply. "But sometimes I find it better to laugh about things."

"I see." Coop took a couple of steps forward, then backward. "Care to tell me what was worth laughing about?"

"No."

"Well, if it was something I said, maybe I should know, so I can say it again and keep you amused."

"That's not necessary, Coop. Good-night."

"Good night!" He wished the door were still there between them. It would have given him immense satisfaction to slam it. He got back into bed and thought of her huddled in her bed laughing at him, even now, she was probably amused by a rough cowboy, a half-breed who was trying to make out like he was a gentleman with a lady for a wife. Well, the joke had sure been on him. He didn't care how much she laughed as long as she kept her share of the bargain in public. He tossed and turned some more and finally, from sheer exhaustion, fell asleep.

The next morning, Fancy surprised him by appearing downstairs before he'd left to join his men.

"I forgot to tell you last night that I've invited several people out to the ranch next Saturday for a—what do you all call them, a shindig?" she said lightly. She looked fresh and beautiful and had obviously slept well through the night. He wanted to strangle her and sweep her into his arms at the same time.

"This Saturday?" he repeated gruffly, giving himself time to bring his emotions under control.

"That is all right with you, isn't it? You said you wanted me to entertain your friends."

"Who all did you invite?"

"The Robinsons and Mrs. Robinson's charming sister, Claire," Fancy replied. "You do remember Claire, don't you? She's the one who came from back east looking for a husband. Maybe after the year is up, you can take her for a wife. She's such a lady, and I thought this way you could look her over and get to know her well enough so you won't make the same mistake you did with me."

Maybe a horsewhip applied to that sassy backside would tame her tongue, Coop thought and smiled wickedly.

"I can see the thought pleases you," Fancy said, flitting about the room restlessly adjusting cups and saucers and whatever else fell under her hand. "I'm sure you'll see at the end of one year that I have fulfilled my agreement with you quite nicely." Coop stood up so abruptly, his chair spilled backward. Fancy turned and fixed him with a questioning gaze.

"I'm going to Denver on business," he said gruffly. "I won't be back until sometime tomorrow, late."

"Denver?" Fancy cried in anticipation. "May I go with you?"

He shook his head. "Not this trip, Fancy. This is business."

"I see," she said quietly, and all the color drained from her face. She had little doubt he was going to Denver to visit the pleasure houses there, but she wouldn't show him how much the thought bothered her. "Until tomorrow, then," she said with a wide grin. The minute he left the room, the grin faded, and she went around with a somber face the rest of the day. Not even planning for the party seemed to give her much pleasure. That night she slept poorly, tossing in her bed while images of Coop embracing some other woman tormented her. When she rose the next morning her face was as somber and lackluster as his had been. Annabelle shook her head in disbelief and wondered why two nice people like Mr. Fletcher and Miss Fancy couldn't work out their differences and admit they loved each other.

"Rocks were shipped to the Utes?" Doyle Springer said incredulously. His pale blue eyes met Coop's without wavering. "But what happened to the blankets and cloth and flour we sent them?"

"That's my question, Springer," Coop said. "We hauled those barrels up the mountain exactly as your men loaded them on my wagons. I went along on that trip, so I know my men guarded the freight. No one got to it at night or any other time. Those Indian supplies disappeared somewhere here in Denver, and those crates were filled with rocks and debris to hide the theft."

"Oh, come now, Fletcher," Doyle Springer said getting to his feet. "You sound as if you're accusing me of taking supplies from my own Indians."

"Someone took the supplies, and I'd be willing to bet they're already being carried over those mountain passes on their way to the mining camps at a tidy little profit."

"I don't like what you're saying here, Fletcher," Springer said. "If there are to be accusations, how am I to know you didn't steal the supplies yourself and sell them to the mining camps? You have better access to those camps than I have. After all you're the one who's got the mules and drivers."

"Getting hold of drivers is not that hard out here," Coop said, "especially if you're not particular who you hire. Have you ever heard of a man named Reynard, Jason Reynard?"

"I don't believe I know him," Springer said, his gaze uneasy now.

"He rides a piebald, a spotted pony."

"No, I don't remember a man like that."

"He's the leader of the gang that attacked my wagon train on the way to the Middle Park. No one else knew where we were going or what we were supposed to be carrying."

"He's the one who attacked your train? He wouldn't have done that if he'd already robbed you of the goods." Springer smiled at his reasoning, then assumed a more somber air. "This is a serious matter, Fletcher. As a government agent to the Utes, I have a responsibility to see those supplies reach the Indians. I hired you to do just that. The goods were loaded on your wagons, and now you come tell me that the goods did not reach the Indians. I'd say if anyone has some explaining to do here, that person is you. I shall most certainly launch an investigation into this matter."

Coop's face was pale with anger. "Let's hope between

the two of us, we turn up something," he said, "because I don't intend to let things rest as they are."

"Nor shall I, Fletcher," Springer stated. "Those supplies had better turn up, or you'd better have a good explanation."

"My men will witness that no one tampered with that freight, Springer," Coop said. "Let's hope you can produce witnesses to prove I received it." Whirling, he stalked out of the Indian agent's office.

When Coop was clear of the office, Doyle Springer ran to the back door and spoke to a man waiting outside. "He's just going out the front. Follow him and see what he does."

With a nod the man pulled his hat low over his eyes so only his dark stubbled jaw showed and slipped around to the front. Too intent on his mission, Coop wasn't aware he was being followed at first. He stalked down the street toward the train station, to the nearby warehouse where the government supplies for the Indians had been stored. This was the starting point, the place where the supplies had started. It was from here that his men had picked up the supplies. Coop intended to talk to the loaders and get some answers. The first man he approached was Odell Hudson, who seemed to guess he'd never rise above his current position of warehouse boss, therefore he poured heart and soul into it.

"Those supplies were kept separate from the rest of our crates," he said, his watery blue eyes blinking in time with his bobbing Adam's apple. "That was the way Mr. Springer wanted it, and that's the way it was."

"Did anyone else have access to the crates and barrels while they were here?"

Odell shook his head. "They might've," he said, swallowing so his Adam's apple jumped alarmingly. "The supplies were in here nearly a week afore your drivers got here to take them out."

"What kind of access did Mr. Springer or anyone else have to the warehouse during that time?"

"Wal, he had a key, ask for one, but he never used it."

"How do you know that?" Coop asked quickly.

"I never saw him around here during the day."

"What about nights?"

"We have a watchman that stays around here nights, old Maurice Lyle."

"Where can I find him?"

"I don't rightly know where he lives. He'll be back here tonight," Odell said, blinking his watery eyes.

"I'll come back then," Coop answered.

Denver nightlife was a lot livelier than Elizabethtown's. Coop made his way down the back street where saloons and parlor houses vied with each other, offering drink and women and delights unimagined. For the first time he had a sense of being followed but couldn't catch sight of anyone. Finally he turned into a saloon.

There were still two hours of daylight, and he hadn't eaten all day. With a glass and a bottle of whiskey, he chose a back table, ordered a meal be brought, and settled back to watch and listen. This saloon was near the train station and the warehouse. Anyone working in those two places would likely stop in here for a drink.

A man sidled into the bar, looked around until his gaze fell on Coop, then quickly turned to the bar. Ordering a whiskey, he deliberately kept his gaze from Coop's direction and finally left the bar, moving as if he didn't want to be noticed. Coop wondered about him briefly, then dismissed him. For the next hour he listened without appearing to pay any attention to men around him, but he heard nothing about the warehouse or Springer's government supplies. He was about to leave when a woman with blond hair piled untidily on top of her head stopped by his table. She was slim, but her breasts were large and lush beneath the flimsy low-cut gown she wore. She smiled, and for a fleeting moment he thought she looked like Fancy.

"Hello, cowboy. Are you lonesome?" she asked in a low, husky voice that promised much. She leaned against him, letting him feel her soft full body. Her scent came to him, womanly, musky, enticing. For a full minute he stared at her, considering taking her upstairs to one of the back rooms for an hour of forgetfulness and satiation, but she smiled again, raising her chin saucily, and he saw Fancy standing there, half clothed, forcing a smile in the hopes of winning a customer.

"No, thank you," he said, lunging upward. The woman was shoved backward.

"Hey!" she shouted. "You don't have to get so rough with a lady."

"A lady?" he repeated automatically.

The woman's head came up, and she met his gaze with a curl of her lips. "A lady!" she said. "Don't you know one when you see one?"

Coop couldn't keep the grin from his lips. "I'm sorry, ma'am," he said, throwing a few bills on the table. "These are for you. Thank you anyway."

"Thanks, cowboy," the woman said, snatching up the bills and shoving them into her bodice. "If you change your mind, come on back and ask for Norma."

"I'll remember that," Coop said over his shoulder, then turned back to her. "Do you know anything about the guard down at the warehouse? Maurice Lyle?"

"Old Mory?" Norma said. "He ain't much of a watchman. He's drunk half the time. Give him a bottle, and he ain't much good for anything."

"Thanks anyway," Coop said with a little bow. He made his way back along the darkened streets, pausing now and then to study the dark shadows behind him while he pretended to concentrate on lighting a cheroot. When he was certain no one was following him, he walked down to the warehouse.

Everything was dark. There was no sign of a watchman in the little shack that had been provided for him. Coop stuck his head in. A half-empty bottle of whiskey sat opened on a bench. From what Norma had said, Old Mory wasn't likely to leave that for long.

Coop left the shack and looked around. Some sixth sense was nagging at him, and he'd learned to listen to such things. Pulling his gun, he moved into the shadows of the building and made his way around the corner. The shadows were deeper here, blending with a cluster of trees and bushes and abandoned rail cars on sidetracks. Stealthily, Coop made his way along the wall of the warehouse until his foot nudged something soft. Kneeling, he felt in the dark, his hand encountering a body.

Glancing around, Coop struck a match. An old man in worn clothes that no longer fit his thin, wasted body, lay crumpled on the ground. Coop took hold of his shoulder and rolled him over. Circles of blood indicated he'd been shot several times. His pale eyes stared sightlessly at a world that no longer mattered to him.

Coop took a deep breath. This was obviously Maurice Lyle, and whatever story he had to tell had been forever silenced. A shot rang out, thudding into the warehouse wall. Coop blew out the match and rolled to one side away from the old man's body while more shots rang out. Whoever had shot Old Mory was still out there. Coop had made himself a sitting duck.

Now, with his gun at the ready, he crawled on his belly along the wall to the edge of black shadow and waited. Whoever was the shooter, he was in that clump of trees, Coop guessed. He waited and watched. The gunman was impatient. He shot again. Coop saw the flash of his gun and aimed his forty-four at it and fired. A yelp of pain, followed by a scurrying through the bushes let him know he'd hit someone. He fired again, although he had little hope of hitting his adversary. Springing to his feet, he made for the edge of a flat car, then from there angled toward the trees. By the time he was in their protective covering, he couldn't hear anything. The killer had gotten away.

Coop tried tracking him, but there was little chance in the dark. Working his way back to the main street, he stopped at the saloon, peering into its dingy interior in the vain hope the shooter had run in there, but no one seemed to be suffering a wound. Coop turned away from the door and stopped a cowboy stumbling along the boardwalk.

"Where's your sheriff's office?" he asked and followed the cowboy's direction to report a murder.

It was late by the time he made it back to his room, and his trip thus far had been unsatisfactory. He tossed on the strange bed, thinking over all the events of the day, remembering Doyle Springer's accusations. Coop's suspicions about the agent increased. If those supplies were switched, they had to have been with the agent's knowledge and cooperation. But how was Coop to prove it? And what about the Utes? If they didn't receive food and blankets before summer's end, they would leave the reservation. Blood would be shed. The Indian wars had been brutal enough the first time around. No one wanted a second series.

Finally his troubled thoughts turned to Fancy. He imagined her curled in her bed, her long hair fanning out on the pillow, her body warm and weighted with sleep. He thought of the first night he made love to her and the second night, when she came to him without pretensions, without reservations. That night had been all a man could hope for, a dream to sustain a man through lonely nights. She'd been giving and passionate and unafraid. He longed for her now, just to feel the satiny smoothness of her skin, smell the flowery scent of her body, taste the sweetness of her mouth. How could he even consider going to a woman like Norma when Fancy waited for him at home?

He'd end this division between them. He'd tell her he didn't care that she'd lied to him, that she'd come only for his money. He wanted her. God help him, he loved her and he'd plead with her to stay with him. He'd forget her past. He had to. But as he fell into a troubled sleep, the whore, Norma, came to him, her lips painted red, her eyes full of lust, her breasts bared. Taking her full, heavy breasts in her hands she taunted him with them, teasing him until he ached to taste their sweetness. He reached for her and found not Norma, but Fancy with a painted face and bared breasts. Her red mouth was opened wide as she laughed at him. The brittle raucous sound woke him, so he sat up in a cold sweat to find the sun had risen and a new day had begun.

Chapter 15

*F*ANCY HAD NOT been idle. Besides preparing for the shindig at the ranch, she'd also driven into Elizabethtown to oversee the progress on the opera house. She was amazed at how quickly such additions went up, even those built of brick. She'd enlisted Aaron in the ordering of brick, and he'd set out at once with several wagons to bring the needed building supplies. With a finish date in mind, Fancy wrote to an agent in Denver requesting any theatrical troupes who arrived there to make a side trip to Elizabethtown. Unfortunately, Fancy would be able to present only a limited season before the snows made traveling in the Rockies too difficult for outside troupes. After that they would have to depend on local talent for the long weary winter months.

When she'd finished with her business, Fancy made her way to La Maison Francais, for a luncheon with the ladies' club. Monsieur Dubois greeted her profusely and personally escorted her to the large round table reserved for the cream of Elizabethtown's society.

"*Bon appetit*, Madame Fletcher," Monsieur Dubois said, relinquishing her hand and bowing elegantly.

"Fancy, what a stunning gown," Elise Rogers gushed. "My dear if only I could wear something like that."

"But you could, Elise, dear," Fancy said lightly. "You have a lovely figure."

"When will your opera house be completed?" Maida Robinson asked.

"Daniel tells me it will be ready for use by the first of August," Fancy replied.

"If it doesn't fall down around our heads," Agnes Wright quipped. "My dear, whatever possessed you to use a black man to build it? He can't know what he's about."

"Actually, he does. Daniel is quite intelligent and skilled at his work. I suspect he comes from a plantation not unlike our own. Our slaves were trained to do many things."

"Well, I suppose if you're used to relying on black help, you might have confidence in what he does."

"I do have supreme confidence in Daniel's work. Did I tell you he and Annabelle are getting married at summer's end?"

"How romantic for them," Elise said.

The talk swirled around Fancy. She'd become a favorite of the women because she was lively and often irreverent, so that although the ladies pretended to be scandalized, they secretly laughed at her comments.

"You poor dear, is your husband still angry with you?" Claire Williams raised her voice so it could be heard above the light chatter. Everyone fell silent and turned avid eyes toward the two women. Many had wondered about the scene between Coop and Fancy when Reynard had escaped, but none had dared ask her about it.

Now Fancy fixed Claire with a serene smile. "He was terribly angry with me for a time," she answered lightly. "He was so frightened that I might have been hit by that awful man's bullets. But I managed to soothe his ruffled feathers." She smiled, raising one eyebrow in a way that left little doubt as to how she'd managed that. The women giggled, blushed, and glanced away. Many wondered what it must be like to have the darkly handsome Coop Fletcher angry with them and then to turn that anger to passion. Some shivered and thought of their own lackluster husbands and envied Fancy Fletcher.

Everyone had been invited to the shindig at the ranch, so

as the lunch party broke up, there were reassurances that
they would be attending. Fancy left early so she might return to the ranch before dusk fell. Coop and Aaron both
had been adamant about that. Other than that restriction,
she'd taken to driving herself to town whenever she
wished. Now as she rolled through the wild countryside,
she remembered the first time she traveled through here.
The stunning beauty of the mountains and valleys had not
lessened their impact on her. A bird started up from a quivering bush, and she recognized it as a Whiskey Jack, the
westerners' name for a Rocky Mountain Jay. There were
other things that claimed her attention. Graceful tamarisks,
curving their slender branches against the wind, an unexpected redbud tree, and high on a distant ridge the majestic
figure of an elk, his regal head sporting horns with many
prongs. Fancy was so captivated that despite the late hour,
she pulled her horses to a halt and stared at the noble animal. She wasn't sure how long she sat watching the elk. It
had remained unmoving as if frozen by her very presence.
Only when she blinked against the gathering shadows did
she realize how late the hour had become and whip her
horses to a brisk trot.

   She was busy telling herself she was really quite all right
being out after dark, she had only to follow the trail and it
would lead her right to the ranch, when the horses came to
an abrupt halt, shaking their heads as if to rid themselves of
their bridles. One neighed and pranced sideways, causing
the buggy to rock dangerously.

   "Whoa!" Fancy called, trying to steady them, then applying a light whip. "Giddap," she shouted as she'd heard the
teamsters yell at their mules. The horses didn't respond,
dancing nervously and pulling against their traces so the
buggy lurched backward. Fancy fell forward, barely catching herself against the front pad. In spite of herself, a cry
escaped her lips and the reins fell from her hands. An ominous roar could be heard over all and out of the waning
light a large bear lumbered forth. The horses reared,
screaming in terror, and started off at a gallop. The buggy

pitched from side to side, so Fancy had no chance to regain her balance. She was thrown to one side and felt the buggy tipping on the uneven trail. She screamed just as the door beneath her gave way and she went tumbling out of the buggy and rolled down the slight incline.

The buggy righted itself and bumped along behind the fleeing horses.

"Come back," Fancy cried until she heard the low, deep-throated growl somewhere along the trail. The grizzly was still up there. Her cries would only draw him to her. Frantically she looked around for a place to hide.

In the deepening shadows, she could see nothing that offered a haven. Helplessly she pressed herself against the sloping ground, hoping the bear wouldn't trouble himself to move off the trail to look for her. She could hear snuffling sounds above.

It seemed she was there for hours, holding her breath, straining her ears to hear any sign of the bear's approach. The ground was hard and rocky beneath her, and her muscles trembled from the effort not to shift.

Darkness fell, deeper than any she'd experienced at home or at the ranch. She'd never been far away from the welcoming glow of a lamp. Now even the stars seemed to reserve their light, and the moon had not yet risen. It had been some time since she last heard sounds from the trail.

Tentatively, she raised her head and peered above her. Then slowly she moved her cramped muscles and began the climb back to the trail. Now and then she paused to listen. She envisioned the huge grizzly patiently waiting for her to appear so he could attack.

"Silly, he's gone," she muttered to herself, and mustering her remaining courage she climbed back to the rough mountain trail. Standing aright, she peered to her left and to her right. It was easy enough to discern which way to the ranch and which to town. She stood debating which was closer and finally, coddling the hope that the horse and buggy might have ceased their mad dash and were waiting on the trail somewhere made her turn toward the ranch.

Cautiously, she set out, glancing over her shoulder every now and then as if fearful of the grizzly following her. Once she thought she heard him lumbering along the trail and flattened herself against the granite walls, her hands pressed against her mouth to still any outcry. When she was certain the trail was empty, she set out again, shaking with fatigue and fear.

"How'd it go, Coop?" Aaron Sayer came out to greet his boss.

"Not good," Coop said, sliding out of the saddle and leading his horse to the watering trough. He'd ridden him hard, coming all the way from Denver and bypassing Elizabethtown. Now as he tended his horse, currying him and giving him feed, he told Aaron of the things that had happened in Denver.

"You mean he's going to blame you for the missing supplies?" Aaron demanded, his expression angry and disbelieving.

"He's going to try," Coop answered, hanging up his bridle and looping his saddle over a rail in the barn. "He's not going to get far. I told him I had men who'd vouch for those kegs not being touched by anyone but his own men."

"What'd he say to that?"

Coop turned to glance at Aaron. "Didn't scare him. He's got something up his sleeve. In the meantime when I tried to question the watchman at the warehouse, he was murdered by the same bushwhacker who tried to kill me."

"Sounds like Doyle Springer's the one."

"Yeah, that's how I reckoned it," Coop answered and slouched against the fence. The windows of the ranch house were softly aglow with lamplight. He pictured Fancy sitting in the parlor with her skirts spread wide, her golden head bent over her needlework, her soft mouth pursed as she concentrated. He thought of how her green eyes seemed to darken when he entered the room and her cheeks stained with color. He wanted to go to her now, but something held him back, some part of that dream he'd had the night before and the whore named Norma who'd really been Fancy. Now he turned from the sight of the ranch house.

"I figure Doyle Springer's behind the attacks on the wagon trains and on the ranch."

"Even that last attack?" Aaron asked. "Don't make sense if he'd already taken the supplies."

"Makes sense he'd want to cover up what he'd done. What better way than to drive the wagons over the mountainside and kill off the drivers? No witnesses, Reynard said."

"The bastards!" Aaron exploded. "He'd leave my Nellie and the little ones alone just to cover his filthy tracks."

"The worst of it is, what will the Utes do when they aren't sent supplies to last them through the winter? You can't hardly blame them for not wanting to sit quietly and starve to death. Without supplies, that's what could happen. If they choose to go off the reservation, there could be bloodshed on both sides."

"And all because that lousy bastard wanted to line his pockets. I don't know why the government assigned a gambler to be Indian agent anyhow."

"What did you say?" Coop asked, jerking his head up.

"I said—"

"He was once a gambler?"

"Yeah, when I first came out here. He got run out of Denver for cheatin'."

"I remember him now," Coop said. "He used to meet the trail hands at the cow towns, taking them for what little money they made. I never gambled with him, but he caused some problems with our crew. He killed a couple of our hands. Witnesses declared it a fair fight, said our men drew on him first."

"Yeah, that's the way he operates," Aaron said. "Usually they did, cause they were tired of bein' cheated. Anyway, he disappeared for a spell. This is the first time I've seen him in these parts for more'n six years."

"He's back with a new game," Coop muttered, "but he's still cheating."

"Just watch him, Coop. He's as dangerous as a snake about to strike. You never know for sure when, you just know he will."

Coop nodded. "This information can't help Springer's case if we get it to the right people." He glanced at Aaron. "Keep it under your hat for a while. We've got some of Springer's men on our payroll."

"Are you sure about that?"

Coop nodded. "It's the only way he can know so much about our shipping schedules. Keep your eyes open, Aaron."

"I will." He nodded as Coop walked away toward the ranch. "By the way," he called, "the Mrs. rode into town today, and she ain't back. I don't think she was expectin' you, so she probably stayed overnight."

"Thanks," Coop said and tried to ignore the surge of disappointment. He didn't want to admit how much he was looking forward to seeing Fancy again. He went into the empty ranch house and automatically glanced in the parlor door as if the vision he'd had earlier had somehow placed her there for him.

"You are home, Senor Fletcher," Delores cried. "We did not expect you. I'll warm you some supper."

"That's not necessary," Coop said. "Just heat some water for a bath." The fat cook hurried off to comply. Coop made his way to the study where he poured over the ledgers, marveling at Fancy's clear figures and accuracy. He gained comfort just from imagining her seated here working. When the water was heated, he filled the tub, shucked his clothes, and settled into the warm water. Memories of Fancy washing his back haunted him as he lathered soap and scrubbed himself. His groin was aching with need for her, and by the time he'd stepped out of the tub and toweled himself off, he had just about decided to ride back into Elizabethtown and spend the night with her there. A ruckus downstairs drew his head up. Wrapping a towel around his lean middle he stalked out onto the landing.

"What the hell's going on?" he roared.

Aaron Sayer stood in the hallway. "You'd better come down, Coop. It's serious."

"Son of a bitch!" Coop muttered and drew on his britches and boots. He envisioned more dead cattle or some other atrocity perpetrated by Reynard and his scum. Without taking the time to button his shirt, he punched the tails into his pants and reached for his holster and gun. Within minutes he was downstairs on his porch and bellowing for Aaron. He didn't have to wait for his foreman to step forward and explain. A badly winded team of horses and a buggy stood in the ranch yard.

"Fancy?" he half whispered. "Fancy!" he roared.

"She didn't come in with them," Aaron hollered from the corral. "I've got the men saddling up now." Coop took off toward the barn at a dead run. No one spoke. The men grimly saw to their saddles and their guns, checking their ammunition. Traveling through the mountains at night wasn't necessarily the healthiest thing to do. No man thought not to go. A helpless woman was out there somewhere, and her chance to live depended on them. No one looked at Coop's set face. His eyes were narrowed, his mouth clamped shut in a straight unyielding line. The only times they'd ever seen their boss look like that, someone had gotten hurt.

Delores stood on the porch uttering a shrill litany of prayers to the black sky and crossing herself. Nellie ran up from her cabin, and both women stared blankly at the men as they rode out of the ranch. In every heart was fear for the sight that would greet the riders. Fancy was a frail, beautiful butterfly. Would they find her crushed and forever stilled? Coop rode at the front of his men, and his thoughts were black with dread and recrimination.

Fancy blundered along in the dark, uncertain where the trail was leading her. One side was faced by the granite walls of the mountains, the other was open, falling away in a gentle incline in some places but a sheer drop in others. Out of fear of falling over a mountain ledge, she hugged the granite walls, stumbling over fallen rocks and detouring into every crevice and cavelike dip in the wall. At some point it occurred to her that she'd left the trail to the ranch and was climbing to some unknown destination. She'd heard stories of how people became lost in the mountains and were never heard from again. Now she stood staring around her, trying to penetrate the dark shroud of night, trying to get some bearing on where she was. The mountains were as silent and cold as a tomb. As long as she'd kept moving she hadn't noticed the dropping temperature, but now she shivered, feeling the goose bumps on her bare arms. It was madness to go on when she might be moving away from the trail. She might never find her way back again. Moving backward to one of the indentations she'd passed, she crouched on the rocky path and pulled the back of her skirts up over her shoulders for additional warmth. Achieving some measure of comfort, she leaned her head against the granite wall and sat thinking of Coop. He was still in Denver, no doubt even now finding pleasure with a woman of the night, while she sat here on this mountain, alone and afraid. It would serve him right if he never saw her again. When they found her body frozen and pale, but still beautiful, he would weep to think how he'd treated her. So thinking she finally fell into a restless sleep.

They covered the trail in a little over two hours, using flares to light every inch of the way, calling out until their throats were sore, still they continued until the first light of dawn. The men sagged on their horses, but Coop seemed not to notice. He drove them along the trail. Now that daylight had come, they searched beyond the trail for any sign of Fancy.

"Sir, I found something," Billy Hudson cried, and Coop galloped forward, his heart pounding while he tried not to think what he might find. He skidded to a halt in a shower of stones and glowered down at the young cowhand who held up a piece of cloth.

"This here sure looks like a piece of Miss Fancy's gown," Billy said.

Coop got off his horse and climbed down the rocky incline. He snatched the dirty rag from Billy's hand and held it up. Without a doubt it belonged to Fancy. Wildly Coop looked around, but there was no sign of a small woman.

"Spread out and search," he called, and he himself searched along the incline, looking for any other sign she was there.

"Coop!" Aaron pointed to the rocky ground a little further down. Coop scrambled to where he was. "Looks like a boot print," Aaron said. They studied the small print.

"Fancy's." Coop said. "She was climbing back up to the trail." He raised his eyes to the trail above. "Why didn't we find her?"

"She could have wandered off if she tried to travel in the dark," Aaron offered, then because he was a straightforward man, he couldn't help but to continue. "She could have fallen into one of the canyons along this trail."

Coop's eyes were bleak. Without a word he climbed back to the trail and, leading his horse, walked along the rocky path studying both sides, dreading what he might find when he peered into the yawning chasms.

With the first rays of light, Fancy woke and looked about her. She was surprised at how high she'd climbed off the main trail. Now she retraced her steps, stumbling forward with determination to regain the trail. Once she found it, she turned toward the ranch. Aaron would have sent someone out to look for her by now, or she might run into other travelers who would give her a lift. The sun rose and became hot overhead. Without her parasol, she could feel its burning rays on her face. She would never grow used to the intensity of the changing temperatures. Her feet had begun to ache long before she caught sight of the ranch, but she continued putting one foot in front of the other. When she topped a familiar ridge and looked down on the ranch spreading out in its emerald valley, she thought she'd never seen anything so beautiful. Laughing and crying she ran along the trail, wanting only to reach the ranch house where Delores and Nellie would soothe her and bring her something cool to drink and listen to her adventure and laugh at her fears. But the distance from the rocky trail to the ranch was greater than she'd anticipated, and she had to slow down and limp along the best she could.

No one seemed to notice when she walked into the yard. Few men were about. The ranch dozed in the noon heat. Fancy limped up on the porch and took a deep breath before opening the front door. The cool interior of the ranch welcomed her. She closed the door behind her and leaned against its panel, savoring the joy of being home again. She could hear voices from the kitchen and guessed Delores and Nellie were visiting. She wanted to join them but wasn't sure if she had that much energy left. Eventually, she pushed away from the door and made her way along the wide hall toward the back of the house. The voices were clearer now. Someone was crying. Fancy pushed the door open and peered into the kitchen.

Nellie sat at the kitchen table, her head bowed, her face somber. Delores wept copiously into her apron. A feeling of alarm spread through Fancy. She stepped into the room and swallowed against the dryness of her throat.

"What's happened?" she croaked. "Why are you crying?"

Both women looked up at her, their faces pale as if they'd seen a ghost.

"Senora Fletcher," Delores cried.

"Thanks be to God, Fancy, you're alive," Nellie said, rising. The two women hesitated a moment as if unable to believe their eyes, then both flew to her. Fancy felt as if her knees might give way any moment. Nellie took one arm and looped it over her shoulder and helped her to a chair.

"What happened to you?" both women demanded. "We thought you were dead."

"Water," Fancy whispered. Delores hurried to bring a dipper, dripping with cold water. Fancy took hold of it with both hands and drank deeply. Nothing had ever tasted so wonderful.

"Senor Fletcher and his men are out looking for you, all night," Delores said, unable to contain her joy at seeing Fancy.

"Coop is back from Denver?"

"He came in last night," Nellie said. "When your horses and buggy showed up without you, they set out at once to search for you."

"But I didn't see them along the trail," Fancy mumbled. She was dead tired and wanted only to lay her head down.

"We'll have to send word to let them know you're safe," Nellie said, going to the front porch so she might hail a passing hand.

"Come, I make you a bath, and then you go to bed and rest. You have had a frightening experience," Delores said. Fancy offered no resistance as the women helped her strip away her torn and dirty gown and placed her in a tub of warm water. She lolled there, nearly falling asleep. She wasn't sure how long she'd been at her bath when she heard a tremendous thunder of hooves in the ranch yard. Almost before they'd stopped, steps sounded on the porch, the front door was flung back.

"Fancy!" Coop shouted, running through the house. At last the door to the bathing room was flung open. Fancy peered over her shoulder.

"Hello, Coop," she sighed. Her smile was lazy, sleepy, contented, her voice a purr, pure sensuality. Her hair was swept up on top of her head in a wild tangle that left her slender throat and shoulders bare. Her lids were lowered over her green eyes, and she stretched and yawned like a sleek, pampered cat. He wanted to snatch her up and hug her. Instead he reverted to the only thing he knew. Anger.

"Where the hell were you?" he shouted. His brows were pulled low, like black slashes in his face. His eyes were mercury, his mouth a thin grim line.

"Why, Coop. Are you angry with me?" she asked in surprise. She felt so tired her brain couldn't focus, couldn't sort out the truth of things.

He didn't catch the helpless vacant look in her eyes. He didn't realize how close she was to the end of her rope. He paced the room, snatching off his hat and running his hand through his black locks in a habitual gesture. He'd gone out to rescue her, suffered the hell of believing her dead, and here she sat in a tub of suds looking like a fragile doll.

"My men have been out there all night riding that trail looking for a silly woman who hadn't the sense to stay in town when it got too late or to have a driver on these rough trails. Are you intent on testing my patience? Do you enjoy scaring me to death?"

His tone and words cut through her weary fog. In a blaze of anger, she rose from the tub, water sluicing from her ivory limbs. She reached for a towel and held it in front of her. It covered very little.

"I'm not a silly woman," she said hotly. "A grizzly bear spooked the horses. Even the best horseman would have been hard put to handle them, and afterward, I admit, I got lost in the mountains, and it wasn't until morning when I could find my way again, and I—I walked all that distance, and I was afraid the bear might come b—back. Instead of bawling me out you should be happy I'm a—alive." She began to blubber and didn't want to. "I was s—scared, too," she said and hiccuped. She looked like a little girl standing in the water, and even as Coop glared at her, she began to sway.

"Fancy!" His long arms reached out and caught her, lifting her free of the tub.

"So tired," she mumbled. "So scared and so tired."

"You little fool," Coop said, but his voice wasn't angry now. It was warm and loving. His big hands pulled the towel from her and gently dried her body, her limbs, and even her feet. When she was dry and rosy from his buffing, he reached for her nightgown, a gathered white cotton affair trimmed in virginal lace and ribbons, and pulled it over her head. When he was finished, he gathered her up in his arms and carried her up the stairs to his bedroom, where he placed her on his pillow and stood back. She curled toward him, missing his warmth. Coop stood staring down at her, at the golden smattering of freckles across her pert nose, the sweep of golden lashes against her cheek, and the tumble of hair. One tiny foot peeked out from beneath the hem of her nightgown. Coop stared at her and felt his heart shudder with dread at the thought of what could have happened to her. She was home safe, though, and he'd never take a chance with her life again. His men would be advised that no matter what her demands, she would travel with an escort at all times.

Unable to bear being away from her for any longer, Coop shucked off his clothes and lay down beside her. Instantly she curled toward him, seeking his warmth and strength. One slim leg kicked free of the restraining nightgown and lay across his. Her arms went around his chest and all the while her lids were closed, though her pink lips curved in a smile and she moaned contentedly. Coop swept her against him, feeling the small perfect body, so yielding and suppliant, feeling the warmth and sweetness of this woman who'd come to claim his heart so effortlessly. She was his fancy lady. He rested his cheek against her silken hair, and the nightmares of the night were forgotten. She was safe here in his arms, and he'd never let her go.

Chapter 16

*F*ANCY WAS FLOATING on a cloud. She'd never felt so warm and secure. She never wanted to leave this place. Through billowy clouds of contentment she floated to the edge of wakefulness and lay with her eyes closed, reveling in the hard sinewy strength of the body next to her. Sighing, she wriggled closer and wrapped her arms around a lean flat waist. Her hand encountered a hard, pulsating member and she paused, trying to sort out what it might be. Knowledge came with a rush. She jerked her hand away. Her green eyes came open, and she stared at the broad contours of a male body. Her cheek rested on a sleek muscular back from which emanated the heavenly warmth. Coop Fletcher was in her bed! He sighed and mumbled something in his sleep.

"Norma!" he called out. "Don't go."

Fancy listened to his mumblings until they became clear to her. Then with a cry, she sprang away from him and sat up, looking around. She was in Coop Fletcher's bed! Memory returned, and she recalled how he'd stormed in on her while she bathed. As usual, he'd been angry with her about something. So how had she come to be here in his room, in his bed, cuddled next to him for all the world as if they'd—! While he mumbled the name of some other woman. Her eyes grew wider, and her lips pursed in anger.

228

"Oooh, you tricked me!" she shouted, flouncing off the bed.

Groggily, Coop raised his head. He'd been having that nightmare again, and it had left him confused. The late afternoon sun streamed through the window causing him to blink and bury his head under the covers.

"Well you should hide your head," Fancy snapped. She stood in the middle of the room in her white nightgown. Her golden hair was a tangled swirl over one shoulder, her eyes danced with green fire. Coop raised the covers from his face and concentrated on focusing his gaze on her. She looked like an avenging angel standing there with her hands on her hips, her chin jutting, her eyes flashing.

"What's wrong?" he muttered. "Come back to bed."

"Come back to bed?" she repeated in outrage. "H—How dare you say such a thing to me after what you've done?"

Coop sighed and pushed the cover to his waist and sat up. "What's got you all riled now?" he demanded.

"You, you monster," Fancy snapped, "you—you womanizer, you whoremonger, you libertine."

"Libertine? What in hell are you talking about?" Coop demanded. "I just spent all night searching for you, because you were fool enough to get yourself thrown out of your buggy. Now you repay me by calling me names."

"I'm not talking about what happened last night," Fancy snapped. "I'm surprised you were even home to look for your lost wife. I would have thought you were still in Denver in Norma's bed."

Coop went deadly still. "How do you know about Norma?" he asked quietly.

"Aha, then you don't deny it," Fancy said. "You can't, you—you lecher. I hate you." She stormed toward her room and turned to face him. "The thing I hate most about you is that after bedding God only knows how many whores in Denver you came back here and took advantage of me when I was exhausted and frightened and at my weakest moment to lure me into your bed. You're truly despicable, Coop Fletcher. I never—never want to speak to you again.

I don't want to live with you or share your bed or—or anything." Fancy disappeared into her room. Beneath her fire and flash, Fancy was heartsick.

Coop stared at her in consternation, slowly taking in her words and their meaning. He was nonplussed, standing at the side of the bed, a sheet wrapped around his middle. His face was angry, angular lines, his brows black slashes, his eyes glinting slits, then slowly the anger left him and his features relaxed. Gripping the sheet about him, he strode across the room to the dividing door. Fancy was pacing back and forth, the full white gown whirling around her ankles as she moved. When she saw him standing in the doorway, his face lit by a grin, she paused and glared at him, her arms crossed over her chest.

"What do you want now?" she demanded.

"You're jealous," Coop said and couldn't repress a triumphant grin.

"What?" The single word was a shriek of denial.

"You're jealous," Coop repeated. "You think I went off to Denver to sleep with another woman, and you're jealous."

"I am not jealous," Fancy said stiffly, drawing herself up. "To be jealous, you must first care for someone. I do not, nor have I ever cared about you, Coop Fletcher, therefore I couldn't possibly care if you slept with a whore or not. I simply object to the fact that you came back here and—and tried to take advantage of me in my weakened state."

"I don't believe you've ever had a weakened state," Coop snapped, his irritation rising. He hadn't liked her declaration that she didn't care for him. His ego had been enormously inflated at the thought she was jealous, now here she was puncturing it with her sharp tongue. He took a few steps.

"As for last night, how am I to know you really were lost in the mountains? Perhaps you spent the night with another man and only pretended to be lost when you found out we were looking for you."

Fancy stared at him enraged, then an impish light appeared in her eyes. "Why Coop, how quickly you've found me out," she said sweetly and felt a thrill of triumph as he stood with his mouth opening and closing like a fish out of water. Then his eyes turned black, and he strode across the room, his face twisted in rage. His large hands took hold of her shoulders, his grip biting into her tender flesh until she nearly cried out.

"If I thought that were true," he snarled, "I'd break your pretty neck."

"Why?" she challenged. "Would it be so different from what you've done in going to Norma?" Her green eyes gleamed as if she were about to cry, but that little chin was stubbornly resistive. He sensed she was genuinely hurt and felt contrite that he'd teased her.

"There was no Norma," he said, loosening his grip.

His sudden gentleness was nearly her undoing. Her eyes filled with scalding tears, but she refused to let them spill over. "Then why do you whisper her name in your sleep?" she asked. Coop studied her face, then stepped away from her, his lips a thin line, his eyes dark with his own pain.

"She was a woman I met in a saloon, a whore who offered herself to me. She reminded me of you."

"No!" Fancy cried out. The tears poured down her cheeks as she stared at him. Then she turned away, unable to see the condemnation in his eyes. He made no sound in leaving her room, but she knew he was gone. All that was life and joy seemed to have fled the room. She sat for a long time at the windowsill thinking over all the angry words they'd hurled at each other. How had things gone so badly between them? How could she ever prove to Coop that she wasn't what he thought? Annabelle heard her hopeless weeping and came to sit beside her and try to calm her.

"Oh, Annabelle, why does he believe the worst about me?"

"It seems to me there are only two kind of women out here," Annabelle observed. "They's the kind what can be found in the saloons and parlor houses. They pleasure a man, but he don't think about makin' one of them his wife.

The other kind is like Miss Maida and her sister, Miss Claire. They're just purdee ladies right down to their toes."

Fancy raised a tear-stained face to Annabelle. "Haven't I been like that since I came here?" she demanded.

"Yes, ma'am, Miss Fancy," Annabelle reassured her. "Only thang is, Mr. Coop, he knows yo' weren't born to that. Since he only knows two kind of women, he must figure if yo' wasn't born to be one kind, yo' must be the other."

"Surely, he can't be so narrow-minded as that," Fancy said, feeling her temper rise.

"Maybe so," Annabelle said.

Fancy jumped to her feet and paced the floor, her lips tightening in determination, her eyes glittering. "I'm about to show him a different kind of woman," she snapped. "And when I get through with him, he'll wish he had the old Fancy back."

"What yo' goin' to do?" Annabelle asked, rolling her eyes.

"I'm going to give Coop Fletcher his lady, and then I'm going to give him his whore," she snapped. "Tomorrow night is the shindig at the ranch. That's a good place to begin."

"Don't do nothing foolish," Annabelle remonstrated, but Fancy turned a deaf ear. She was planning revenge on Coop Fletcher, revenge and a new education in the ways of women.

The day of the shindig dawned golden and clear. The sun rose in the east and took its vaunted position in the sky. For the extra cooking, Fancy had hired assistants for Delores. With a dignified air, the Spanish cook had kept her helpers jumping. Numerous pies had been baked, along with great loaves of bread and pans of beans sweetened with brown sugar and molasses. There were also vats of chili, and a side of beef had been put to roasting the night before. Each hand took a turn at the handle that kept the meat slowly turning over the fire. By midday, its smell made the mouth water.

Barrels of beer had floated in the cold mountain stream throughout the night, so now as the cowboy fiddlers tuned up, the barrels were hauled down to the ranch yard and set up. A side table had been set up with bottles of whiskey, and inside in the parlor, Fancy had made arrangements for wine and sherry and lemonade to be served to those ladies who had no wish for anything stronger.

Guests began arriving at noontime. One of the hands spotted the first carriage on the trail some two miles away and sounded the alarm. Fancy gave a last inspection to her simple, yet elegant gown of white lawn trimmed with white lace. Even her bustle had been kept unadorned, and the modest train was pulled to one side and buttoned to her skirt so she might move freely. A wide-brimmed bonnet adorned with flowers was at the ready to shield her from the sun. The burn she'd acquired from her ordeal in the mountains had turned to a soft golden glow, but she had no wish to become as brown and wrinkled as Geraldine.

As she headed for the stairs she heard a curse from Coop's room and hesitated for a moment before lightly knocking on his door. The wooden panel was yanked open, and an irritable and sweating Coop stood on the other side, a badly mangled tie in one hand.

"Do you need some help?" she asked lightly.

The anger left his face as his gaze swept over her. "How do you manage to look so cool and beautiful at the same time?" he asked.

"I'll take that as a compliment, and thank you, kind sir," Fancy said, curtsying lightly. "Let me see what I can do with this." She took the tie from his hand and slid it beneath his collar. She had to stand on tiptoe, swaying toward him slightly. He could smell her perfume, flowery and exotic. With her arms raised, her breasts jutted forward against the starched filmy material of her dress, looking innocent and seductive all at the same time. His gaze fell on the curve of her cheeks, rose-hued as if she were troubled by the nearness of him, the curve of her lips, pink and moist. Her tongue crept out to moisten the full bottom lip, making it look even more kissable. Her lashes were lowered as she concentrated on knotting his tie, and when she was finished she raised her lashes and met his gaze. The shock of green fire reverberated through his body clear to his toes. She held his gaze for a moment, then swayed and moved away.

"Shall we go down and greet our guests?" she asked, taking up a parasol she'd propped against the wall. Coop slipped into his jacket and held out his arm. With a demure smile that revealed that elusive dimple, she took his arm and glided down the stairs beside him. She looked every inch the lady, virtuous, genteel, dainty. Coop felt his heart swell with pride to have her at his side. The ugliness of the quarrel between them seemed to melt away. He forgot she wasn't a lady born and bred. She was his fancy lady, and she was all he wanted. The first carriage rumbled into the driveway, followed by a steady stream of others. Fancy's gay parasol wove among their guests as she greeted each one, saw that they had refreshments, guided them to other friends so no one stood alone or neglected.

"This is a humdinger of a party," Geraldine said. "Reminds me of the kind we used to have when I was a girl."

"That's what reminded me of it," Fancy admitted. "We've had so many stuffy affairs lately. I thought it would be good if everyone let their hair down for a day."

"I like your thinking, Fancy." Geraldine was off to get a cup of beer. Fancy turned to her other guests.

"Who invited him?" Coop growled when Doyle Springer rode into the ranch yard. Startled, Fancy looked at Coop.

"I thought he was a business associate of yours," she said in surprise.

"Was," Coop snapped. "I don't want him here."

"Well, I can hardly order him to leave after I've invited him," Fancy said. "We'll have to make the best of it. I'm sorry. I didn't know."

"Maybe you should have checked the guest list with me before you sent it out," Coop said, turning away.

"Perhaps I would have if you hadn't been so busy going from one place to another without giving me a chance to ask you anything," Fancy snapped. Coop looked at her in astonishment. She was right, of course. He'd seldom been around in the past weeks, deliberately staying away from the ranch and Fancy. She'd carried on, and he had no right to criticize her now.

"I'm sorry," he said going back to her. His dark hair fell over his brow as he bent over her. "You've done a damn fine job."

Fancy's cheeks pinked at the unexpected praise, her gaze meeting his in an effort to determine his sincerity. "My only wish is to please you," she said in the same light manner she'd used all evening, and he wasn't sure if her words were part of her role as a lady or if she meant them. Before he could question her further, someone called for her, and with a last flirtatious glance she was gone in a swirl of flower-scented petticoats.

Coop was surprised at the interest Carl Robinson and the other merchants, miners, and financiers had in his ranch and his arrangement of his shipping business. They walked among his barns, inspected his stock, his mules, his wagons, noted his hands and nearly every detail of his ranch and nodded their heads in approval. Coop was an astute business manager, they saw, and their confidence in him grew. Expansively they slapped him on the back, pressed cigars upon him, and reassured him he would have their shipping business. They needed a responsible freighter to get their ore from their mines to the refineries and on to the railroads in Denver. Flushed with success, Coop looked around for Fancy and saw Doyle Springer walking toward his barns. He turned to Aaron.

"Doyle Springer's here," he said in a low voice. Aaron's carefree grin disappeared.

"God almighty, what's he doin' here?"

"Fancy invited him."

"Like opening the door to the chicken pen and invitin' the fox in," Aaron said, shaking his head.

"She didn't know," Coop defended his wife. "Just keep an eye on him while he's here. Don't let him poke around too much."

"Right. I'll set Billy Dee on him. He's like a blood-hound, worries you to death at times."

"Sounds good." Coop moved off through the crowd. Aaron went off to find Billy Dee, who was surprisingly reluctant over his new task.

"I should have had Miss Fancy ask him," Aaron muttered. "He's plumb took, and he'll do anything she wants." Coop grinned. Fancy seemed to work her magic on all of them.

Fancy was equally as busy escorting the ladies to her parlor, seeing they had a room to refresh themselves, conducting a tour of the redecorated ranch house and instructing Delores and Nellie as to food and refreshments. Maida and Claire walked through Fancy's home and exchanged glances with each other, but Fancy had caught a look of longing on Claire's face. This might have been hers if Fancy had not arrived first and married Coop. If she only knew how troubled our marriage is, Fancy thought, and wished the picture they presented to these people was the real one. How happy she would be if Coop loved and cherished her as his wife, instead of reviling her and comparing her to whores like Norma.

"My dear, you look unhappy about something," Maida said, and Fancy forced a smile to her face.

"I was just thinking how proud Papa would be if he were here," she said softly. "But then I mustn't bring a sad thought to this day when I have so many new and wonderful friends in my home." She smiled sweetly at Claire. "Won't ya'll come into the yard? I believe we're about ready to serve food."

They all trooped outdoors to the long tables set up beneath the trees. Starchy white tablecloths fluttered in the breeze. Even Nellie's daughters had been put to work with branches, fanning the air above the tables to keep away the insects. Everyone seated themselves, and huge platters of beef were carried around by Delores and her assistants.

Talk turned to matters of family and events in Elizabethtown. Glasses were filled, and laughter and talk flowed easily. When the last crumb of pie had been eaten, the tables were cleared and men and women moved to the portion of the yard where boards had been laid down to form a rough dance floor. With the fiddles singing, toes started tapping, and some of the older couples swung into an old-fashioned hoedown. Soon even Maida and Carl were trying the steps. The fiddles seesawed into a waltz, and Fancy looked around for Coop. At last she spotted him near the corrals. He and Claire Williams were leaning over a rail talking. Claire was peering up into his face admiringly, her pretty mouth curved in a smile. Coop's shoulders were thrown back in a manly swagger, and he said something that sent her into gales of laughter. Fancy turned away and deliberately busied herself with her guests, but her heart felt sore and bruised. Coop thought Claire a real lady and seemed unable to see her pretensions. Well, she'd encouraged him to get to know Claire better, she couldn't be angry now that he was. But she could. She was angry and hurt. She'd spent the whole day proving to Coop and all his friends what a lady she was. Now as the dancers grew tired, she moved toward the fiddlers. After a brief discussion she turned to her guests.

"I have an old song my mother taught me when I was a child," she said. Everyone clapped and cheered her on. She sang the haunting refrains of "Greensleeves," her high, clear voice holding on the evening air, drawing each guest closer. When she finished she bowed and moved off the dance floor to give anyone else a chance to perform who might wish to do so. One thing had become very clear in her time here, the westerners were not shy in sharing their talents, no matter how unskilled. It was just this wholehearted willingness to add to the fun of an evening that broke the ice and drew them all closer as neighbors and friends. Geraldine Russell moved onto the stage and lent her crackling old voice to a tale of a cowboy and his pony that set them all to laughing.

Fancy saw Coop and Claire had joined the fringe of the crowd and moved toward them.

"That was truly beautiful," Claire said sweetly. "Have you performed on the stage before?"

"You've asked me that," Fancy reminded her, "and I'm afraid my answer must remain the same."

"Ah, I see. It's just that once when I was a girl, my father took me to a theater in Atlanta where a young woman, I believe she was the daughter of the man and woman who owned the theater. Anyway, she came out on the stage and sang this same melody, but it was no sweeter than your rendition."

Fancy felt the breath squeeze out of her chest as she fought for composure. Waving the fan before her face so only her eyes showed, she smiled serenely. "How very lovely of you to make such a comparison," she said. "But my papa would fairly have died if a daughter of his went on the stage."

"Ummm, yes, of course," Claire answered.

An awkward silence stretched between the three of them, one that Coop suddenly felt compelled to fill.

"Ah, do you know the song, 'Claire de Lune'?" he asked Fancy.

" '*Claire* de Lune'?" Fancy repeated, looking from Coop to Claire.

"I was telling dear Coop how much I love that song. My mother sang it to me when I was little."

"I'm afraid I don't know it," Fancy said stiffly.

"Ah, well. I remember that young woman in Atlanta sang it quite well." Claire's smile was mocking.

"If you'll excuse me, I must see to my guests," Fancy said, tired of this woman and her snobbish ways.

"Are you sure you want to leave your husband with me?" Claire asked playfully, casting a quick glance at Coop from beneath her lashes. Her red lips were curved in that false smile that she affected so often.

Fancy studied her for a moment, and a genuine humor showed in her eyes. "I have no fear of leaving my husband with you, Claire," she said serenely. "After all, you are a lady, aren't you?"

Claire's smile disappeared. Fancy didn't dare look at Coop. He'd remained silent through most of the conversation. Now she felt angry with him for allowing Claire to use him to bait her. He wouldn't know a real lady if he stumbled over one, she thought angrily.

The rest of the evening passed quickly. The fiddlers struck up a final waltz, and Coop came to claim her. Leading her out on the makeshift dance floor, he smiled down at her.

"This was some shindig, Fancy," he said. "Thank you."

She was touched by the sincerity of his words and almost forgave him his behavior with Claire, almost. She smiled at him warmly, pressing herself close to him. To onlookers they seemed a couple very much in love.

Claire Williams stalked away from the dance and, entering the ranch house, walked through the rooms, restless and impatient with the way things had gone. If Fancy hadn't arrived in town first, Claire might have had a chance with Coop, then she'd be mistress of one of the finest ranches in Colorado and the wife of one of the richest men in the territory. Bitterness twisted her features as she walked through the beautiful house. Envy and spite guided her feet upstairs where she opened doors and peered into private chambers. When she saw that Coop and Fancy had separate bedrooms a ray of hope built, then she noticed the doorless opening between the two rooms. She imagined Fancy and Coop locked in an embrace and felt alone and spinsterish.

Wrathfully, she turned to Fancy's dresser and armoire. Beautiful gowns of silk and satin hung there. Frustration born of repressed emotions tore at her. Reaching for a pair of scissors she jabbed at the gowns, tearing and ripping at the delicate fabrics until they hung in shreds. Reason returned to her and she stepped back, staring at her handi-work, then smiling widely, she closed the armoire doors and returned the scissors to the dresser. Humming under her breath, she let herself out of the room and made her way back to the party.

Chapter 17

THE DANCE LASTED well into the night. The moon rose and generously cast its light on them. Even Maida seemed to have relaxed her iron temperament and was dancing with her husband. The waltz ended, and Coop released Fancy, staring down at her as if seeing her for the first time. His eyes smoldered with desire, and she felt an answering shiver in her own body. Fanning her flushed face, she glanced away, not wanting to reveal to their assembled guests the depths of her longing for her husband.

"Last dance," the fiddlers called out.

"Give them boys a bottle of whiskey, so they can play some more," Geraldine hollered. A bottle was passed among the players, and they struck a lively tune they hadn't played before. With hoots and hollers most of the ranchers moved onto the dance floor. Even some of the hands who'd held back hurried to dance while the women formed a circle to watch and clap their hands.

"Don't want to try and dance in this one," Geraldine puffed. "Things are apt to be kinda rough with these fellas tryin' to outdo one another."

Fancy stood watching in amazement at the lively foot-stomping and knee-slapping the men engaged in. Even Carl Robinson and some of the more sedate businessmen were pulled or pushed onto the floor by their wives and taking a swig from the passing bottle joined in the high jinks, vying with one another for the most spectacular steps and kicks. Coop was right in the middle of them all, his somber air put aside, his head thrown back, his teeth flashing in a smile as he leaped and cavorted. In awe, Fancy watched him, seeing a side of Coop she hadn't met before. The fiddlers seemed to have found a new burst of energy, playing tirelessly while the men cavorted around the floor.

"My goodness, don't they ever grow tired?"

"Not now," Geraldine called over her enthusiastic clapping. "These old saddle slickers are like a horse with plenty of bottom. They ain't never goin' to tire down."

Finally though, the fiddlers put aside their instruments and the men limped off the dance floor. Coop threw his arms around several men and urged them all to the ranch house porch where Delores and Nellie had set great pots of coffee. While they swigged down a final cup of coffee their wives gathered their belongings and checked the children who'd been bedded down in the wagons and buggies. Fancy stood aside, watching her guests readying themselves to leave. One and all thanked her for a lovely time.

"My dear, I believe you're fast becoming a true westerner," Maida Robinson said cheerfully and kissed her on the cheek. Fancy felt as if she'd finally earned a badge of courage.

Geraldine grinned as she hugged Fancy. "What'd I tell you? They've all come to accept you, even Maida."

"Thank you for being here," Fancy whispered, kissing the wrinkled old cheek. Coop came to take Fancy's elbow, and they stood watching their guests depart.

"I've had a lovely time," Claire said, smiling prettily at Coop. Her glance at Fancy was enigmatic, strangely triumphant. Fancy was glad to see the dark-haired woman climb into her sister's carriage and ride away.

A thin sliver of dawn lay on the horizon by the time everyone had left. The yard was empty save for the hands clearing away the dance floor and tables.

"Leave it," Coop called. "See to the animals, then get to bed for four hours of sleep." The hands set up a cheer and

headed toward the barns and bunkhouses. Coop turned to
Fancy.

"You look tired," he murmured.

"I am," Fancy admitted and turned toward the ranch
house. She was practically swaying on her feet. She'd
planned this night to end far differently for Coop and her,
but she was too tired to execute her plans. Suddenly Coop
was beside her, lifting her in his arms and walking across
the yard.

"You're tired, too," Fancy protested, but couldn't resist
sagging against his broad chest. It was heavenly to be carried by him like this. "I can walk," she muttered halfheartedly.

"I'm sure you can," he said in a low, husky voice. "I
believe you can do anything you set your mind to."

"Even be a lady?" she asked sleepily, her head was resting against his shoulder.

His laughter rumbled. "Even that!" he whispered.

She remembered him mounting the porch steps and entering the house, but she was fast fading when he reached
her bedroom and placed her on her bed.

Sighing contentedly, she curled on her side. She could
feel Annabelle undoing the back of her dress, but it was
Coop's voice that ordered her to turn so the dress and petticoats were removed. When she was stripped down to her
light cotton camisole and pantaloons, she was tucked under
the covers. The pressure of the light against her closed eyes
disappeared, and then a hard masculine body slid into bed
beside her, pulling her close, cradling her.

She felt a flood of heat against her breasts and belly. Her
slender legs were entwined with long masculine limbs and
slowly, with a passion flaring to life somewhere deep inside
her, she fell asleep only to dream erotic images of Coop
and her together. She moved in her sleep, trying to get
closer to him, trying to still that aching longing that flared
deep in the moist inner core of her.

She woke with the pressure of Coop's mouth against
hers. His hand cupped her breast, his thumb moving in laz-

ing circles over her nipple. She groaned and his kiss deepened, his tongue swirling over her lips until she yielded and he tasted the sweetness of her. She was breathless and trembling when he released her. Her arms encircled his neck, her fingers feathering through the gleaming dark hair, smoothing the brown skin beneath his earlobe, sliding down to touch his nipples. They were hard and peaked as she knew her own must be. Her hands explored further, sliding over his ribs, testing the curve of muscles, the broad back and taut buttocks and back to that hard curving prong that caused her breath to catch and her body to ready itself.

"I love you, Coop," she whispered. "I love you." She gave herself to him. Her sweet mouth opened for his plundering, her breasts swelled beneath his touch, her slender body arched, her thighs falling away as he stroked her. His fingers explored her, readied her, and then he rose above her and plunged against her pliant body, reaching deep inside her, past richly moist and satiny flesh to that center of her that made her gasp and cry out, urging him on.

Time and again, he moved against her, trying to hold in abeyance his own pleasure until he felt that first throbbing pulse against his rod and he could hold back no longer. She felt the convulsive impact of their mating and was lost to herself and the world without. She was with Coop, and they were journeying to a special place only they, together, could reach. She saw the blazing light and shut her eyes at the brilliance of it while her body shuddered beneath his.

Never again would he know such ecstasy, he thought. It was so all-encompassing, it must be given to a man and a woman only once in a lifetime. He felt the roaring, giving of himself into her body and gasped for breath, fearful for a moment that blackness might overcome him. He clenched his teeth and held on, feeling the sweat covering his body, and at last the dark mist cleared and he was able to breathe again. He collapsed against her, his limbs trembling at their exertion and lay still. Only later did he realize that the moistness against his shoulder was Fancy's tears.

"Have I hurt you?" he asked.

She shook her head, her brilliant smile answer enough. Still entwined, still connected, they drifted into sleep. Much later, Coop rose and stood over the bed studying the dainty woman sleeping there. Her lips were swollen from his kisses, her eyes shadowed by fatigue, her golden hair spread around her like a shimmery veil. One bare shoulder, ivory smooth and soft, showed from beneath the covers. Tenderly he pulled the covers around her and lightly kissed the pouty lips. She stirred, then settled into sleep again, one small hand curling childlike next to her cheek.

He went away then, because he needed to think, needed to reclaim some portion of himself that wasn't completely besotted by his beautiful wife, needed to remind himself that he was Coop Fletcher and other things were important besides the feel and smell and glory of a small feminine body.

Fancy slept well past noon. Only the lemony sunshine pouring into her windows reached through her contented slumber. Slowly she woke, arching her body, testing it, feeling its soreness, and smiled remembering the passion she and Coop had shared. She lay thinking of all that had occurred the past few days and of her anger at the thought he'd slept with a Denver whore named Norma. She was sure now he hadn't, and she was equally as sure that he cared for her as she did for him.

During the velvety darkness of night, they seemed to have put away many of their differences. She felt elated, confident about their future. She turned her head and gazed around her room. She would no longer stay here. She would move into Coop's room and this room, though large, would make a wonderful nursery.

They would have several children, for she intended never to refuse Coop when he came to her. They would make love anytime he wanted, and from their love would grow their children, the heirs that Coop wanted. Their children would never know the hardships Coop and she had known. They would be safe and protected and loved and someday would inherit their father's riches. The people of

Elizabethtown would know the Fletchers were a fine old family. No one would question that she was a lady and Coop a gentleman. The future appeared so rosy, so perfect, she was loathe to put aside her daydreams and rise and dress, but Annabelle was bustling into the room.

"I thought yo' was never goin' to wake up," she said.

"I'm not sure I have, Annabelle," Fancy said, stretching contentedly. "Life seems like such a wonderful dream."

"Yes, ma'am, Miss Fancy, it is. You and me done landed in a happy place." Annabelle bustled around pouring her water to wash and gathering up her dress and shoes. Coop had dropped them helter-skelter, but Annabelle made no comment. She knew how it was when a man was impatient. She thought of her tall Daniel. For all his gentle, easy ways, when it came to loving he was a veritable tiger. She hummed beneath her breath.

Fancy watched Annabelle's happy face and sat up. "Annabelle. I don't want you to call me Miss Fancy anymore. I'm just plain Fancy, and you're not my maid. You're more like a sister to me."

Annabelle stopped working and stared at Fancy. "I knows that," she said soberly. "But like I tol' yo' befor', it's better if I calls yo' Miss Fancy. That way, cain't nobody say I'm an uppity nigger."

"No one here's going to say that anyway, Annabelle. We're not in the south. We're westerners now. Out here people can put aside their old fears and prejudices."

"Maybe," Annabelle said, nodding. "Maybe not. I'll just take mor' time and decide that for myself. In the meantime, I'd better act like yo'r maid. Who else yo' got to pick up yo'r things?" She swung open the doors to the armoire and stepped back, her mouth dropping open.

"Lord, almightly, Miss Fancy," she gasped and turned to stare at Fancy with wide tragic eyes.

"What is it?" Fancy asked in growing alarm.

"All yo'r beautiful gowns."

"What about them?" Fancy rose from the bed and crossed to the armoire. Her face went pale when she saw her shredded gowns. The act was one filled with such hate, she couldn't at first comprehend its meaning.

"Who would do this to yo' gowns, Miss Fancy?" Annabelle asked.

Fancy turned away, clutching her stomach. "Coop," she whispered.

"No, Miss Fancy. He wouldn't do nothin' like this."

"He was angry with me." Fancy thought of all that had occurred the day before, of her knotting Coop's tie and the two of them going down arm in arm to greet her guests and of the night, with Coop carrying her to bed and Coop making love to her. She turned back to Annabelle.

"You're right. He wouldn't have done this. No matter how angry he would become with me, he wouldn't behave like this." She crossed to the armoire and fingered the once beautiful gowns, her mind whirling.

"This looks like somethin' a woman might do," Annabelle said, "a mean-tempered woman."

"Claire Williams," Fancy said and met Annabelle's outraged gaze.

"That lady from back east?" Annabelle asked disbelievingly.

"One and the same," Fancy said, pacing back and forth. "She was the only one here yesterday who would bear me such ill will."

"What yo' goin' to do, Miss Fancy, accuse her?"

Slowly Fancy shook her head. "No, that's what she wants me to do. How many of the gowns can be mended?"

"I don't know, some of them's mighty bad."

"Let's go over them," Fancy said turning to the armoire. Together they inspected the damage. Two gowns had to be discarded altogether. Some could be mended and worn around the ranch while others had received very little damage which could be repaired and camouflaged under bows or lace. Annabelle set to work at once, her skillful fingers working magic on the abused garments.

When Fancy went down for supper with her husband, she was beautifully gowned as always and serene, except for the blush that tinged her cheeks whenever her gaze met his. They dawdled over supper, neither of them hungry, each remembering the wonder of the night before, and hid their impatience for the coming night in small talk about the party and their guests.

"I never thought it important to show off my ranch and freight operation," Coop said, "but everyone was mighty impressed with what he saw. I've already received new shipping contracts."

"That's wonderful," Fancy cried, proud that she'd been able to help her husband. She hesitated, loathe to bring up an unwelcomed subject. "Can you tell me now, why you didn't want Doyle Springer at the ranch?"

Coop sighed, but in light of their new acceptance of each other, he told her of all that had occurred with the agency supplies for the Utes.

"Those poor people," Fancy cried. "Can't you do something to see they don't starve?"

"I've sent over sixty head of my own cattle," Coop said, "and I ordered some flour and goods from Denver, but that's not enough to hold them through the winter."

"I'm sure Geraldine would contribute if she knew what was happening," Fancy said. "I'll speak to her about it tomorrow." She paused thinking of the slippery Doyle Springer. "How could that man have the audacity to come here after making an attempt on your life?"

"He must assume a role of innocence," Coop said. "When it comes right down to it, it'll be his word against mine and my men."

"I wouldn't believe a word he says, especially after what he said about you on the stagecoach," Fancy stormed. "I only invited him because I thought he was an important business associate. I should have known."

"What did he say on the stagecoach that's got you so fired up?" Coop asked in some amusement at his firebrand wife.

So she told Coop of the conversation she'd had with Doyle Springer when she first came to Elizabethtown. For the first time, he was able to shrug aside the white man's hated accusation. He smiled at Fancy and sought to change the subject.

"Claire Williams is quite a lady, isn't she?" he said innocently and missed the angry arch of Fancy's brows.

"Do you think so?" she asked lightly.

"Well, certainly," Coop said in surprise. "Don't you think so?"

"I suppose it depends on what you're looking for in a lady," Fancy answered, and this time he caught sight of the angle of her chin and wisely fell silent. But the damage was done. A new stiffness lay between them, and he'd be damned if he knew what had brought it on. Conversation between them languished, and finally Coop rose and made his way to the porch to smoke a cheroot. Darkness had fallen over the valley, and the moon sat big and cheeky in the sky. He wished Fancy would come out on the porch and sit with him for a while, but he could hear her inside talking to Delores. Sighing, he tossed his cheroot away and walked out to the barns to check things out. He stayed overly long, reluctant for some reason to cross back to the house. He dreaded the thought that the old animosity had won sway between Fancy and him. Finally when a single light gleamed in an upstairs bedroom he walked back to the house and climbed the stairs to his room.

Fancy heard him coming and held her breath waiting to see which room claimed him. When he entered his own room and crossed to his bed without even approaching the door to her room, she bit her lower lip in vexation. A soft light glowed from his room, but she felt hesitant to enter. She'd caused this, her with her eternal pride and quick temper. Sitting there, she wondered how to break this new reserve between them. Geraldine had said once that men liked a lady in the parlor but something quite different in their bedrooms.

Smiling mischievously, she rummaged through her nearly empty closet, scattering silk petticoats and lace covers, picking only the briefest articles of clothing. When she was finished, she checked in the mirror and nodded in satisfaction. Taking out a straw bonnet, which she seldom wore for the feather was far too ostentatious, she settled it over her upswept curls, then stepped into a pair of high-heeled pumps. Standing before the mirror she practiced a few grinds and bumps with her hips. Her cheeks were stained bright red from her daring plans. She hesitated no longer, least she lose her nerve.

Standing to one side of the open door she extended one slender leg, bare save for the lacy garter resting just above her knee. Making her voice husky and bawdy she began singing a dance hall song that had been the rage before she came west.

"Frankie and Johnny were sweethearts," she sang and heard an oath from the other side. She was certain she'd gotten his attention. Swinging around the edge of the door, she arched her body in its skimpy attire and swung into a full rendition of the song.

"Lordy, how they did love." Coop's face was rigid with surprise. Her gaze was bold and impertinent as it met his. Twitching her hips from side to side in exaggeration, she made her way across the room to him, shedding bits of lace and articles of clothing as she went. By the time she'd finished her song she was standing before him, nude except for the high-heeled shoes and the feathered hat. Her eyes were sparkling with laughter, but he denoted a touch of uncertainty.

She stood before him, waiting. "I'm not a lady like Claire," she said softly. "Will I do?"

His arms closed around her, lifting her high against him, burying his face against her small perfect breasts, then lowering her against his body, feeling the soft sweetness of her as his mouth claimed hers.

"You'll do. You'll do right nicely," he whispered against her mouth. His hand swept away the hat, and her hair tumbled around her shoulders. He picked her up and placed her on his bed, then stood back to look at her. She made no move to cover her nudity, letting his hungry gaze rove unchecked over her body. Slowly, sensuously, she raised her arms above her head and stretched, knowing the arching of her body would have its affect on him. He growled and began taking off his clothes.

Fancy smiled, reveling in the power she exerted over him. With the same feline grace, she raised one leg and kicked off her shoe, then the other, letting her legs fall gracefully back to the bed. Raising one knee she rocked it from side to side much as a matador might titillate a bull with his cape, and all the while her green eyes shone with a bewitching light that mesmerized him.

He tossed his clothes aside and stood before her, a tall, proud man, his body the color of shadows and sun, burnished by the winds and heat of the mountains and prairies, his strong back and muscular shoulders as unyielding as the mountains themselves, his silvery eyes filled with intelligence and a vision of builders of dynasties.

If she stood unadorned, giving wholeheartedly, all that she was and ever would be, so, too, did he, offering her his hopes and dreams, his passions, his visions. Gone was the playfulness of the moments before, here was the pledge, the commitment, one to the other. It mattered not if they were lady or half-breed. They were a man and woman who'd sought their destiny and discovered it in each other. This was their coming together in heart and spirit.

Their lovemaking was gentle, as if they were lost in the wonder of each other, then having sealed their commitment with the bonding of flesh against flesh, they grew lighthearted. Fancy sang her song again, and he laughed and claimed her again, finding new dimensions of pleasure in the slender body, awakening untouched realms of passion within her. And when they sat in the window watching the golden rays of sun light the distant peaks of the mountains, they knew they'd made a bond that could never be lightly broken.

Chapter 18

*I*N THE WEEKS that followed, Fancy stayed busy with a round of teas and socials in Elizabethtown and with overseeing the construction of the opera house. She might have revealed her secret concerning the opera house to Coop if he hadn't been so busy and preoccupied. When he was back at the ranch, there seemed to be too many other things to say between them. Coop gave her a new colt which Fancy promptly named Ebenezer.

"Ebenezer?"

"I like the name."

It was easy to laugh together. A truce had been declared, and they were intent on learning more about each other.

"Tell me about your family, your real family," he said one rare afternoon when they had stolen away for an hour or two and lay in an alpine meadow resting from their lovemaking. So she told him of the Bourne Theatrical Group and about her father who had taught her Latin and French and mathematics and her frail gentle mother who'd taught her the finer points of being a lady. She told of the years they'd traveled like genteel vagabonds from one town to the next, of the fine receptions they'd received before the war and of the state of impoverishment left by the war.

She told him of funny times in the theater that left him chuckling and gazing at her with new admiration. She told him of the train wreck that claimed her parents' lives and

of her struggle to keep the theatrical troupe going and of
how they abandoned her because of her youth.

"All except Annabelle," she said. "She's been loyal
through everything."

His eyes darkened with sympathy and then anger when
she revealed how desperate she and Annabelle had been
without money for food or shelter and of her trip to the office of Travis Wheeler who offered to make her his mistress.

"If I'd been there, I would have killed him," he growled,
clenching his fists.

"But you were there, darling," Fancy cooed, and for the
first time told him the story of how Wheeler's wife had appeared and Fancy had been shoved into a dusty anteroom
where miraculously she'd found Coop's letter.

"Thank God you did," he said, reaching for her and
burying his face against her breasts. He shuddered to think
how a mere happenstance had brought her to him.

"Of course, I wasn't sure I'd meet your qualifications,"
Fancy teased, "since you asked for someone not too plain
of face or sharp of tongue."

"You're right, you didn't qualify," he muttered and tick-
led her ribs, causing her to giggle and roll away from him.

"I believe you asked for a docile, respectable critter," she
teased from the foot of the blanket, her green eyes glittering
mischievously.

"Come here, you little sage hen," he yelped, leaping for
her. He captured her and set about tickling her until she
screamed for mercy, but by then his large hands had moved
up to cup her breasts, and she lay still and breathless beneath him, her eyes as green and changing as the meadow
grass blowing in the breeze. They made love and in silence
rode back to the ranch, feeling closer than they ever had.

She asked him about his background, and at first he
wouldn't speak of it, fearful she might yet look down on a
dirty half-breed kid who'd never had love or loyalty from
anyone his whole life long. But she didn't flinch away from
him when he told of eating white-man's garbage to survive

or of the hard years that followed when he always had to prove his right to be treated as a man with his fists or his guns. She only wrapped her slender arms around his neck and planted tiny kisses along his jaw, until he forgot his bitter past and found glory in the here and now with Fancy.

It was a time of happiness for them both. If they could have gone on without the rest of the world pushing in, Fancy would have been pleased, but she knew she owed Coop more than the pleasure of their bed.

The morning after the party, she packaged up one of the gowns that had been damaged beyond repair and sent it off to Claire Williams. A note accompanied it.

My dear Claire, I know how much you've admired this gown and thought you might enjoy it. Best Regards, Fancy Fletcher.

Then she had her buggy brought out, and with Billy Dee as her new bodyguard, she set out for the Russell ranch. Geraldine met her in the yard.

"Lands sakes, you're up and about early after that shindig you threw," the old woman called.

"I needed some of your black devil's coffee and some advice," Fancy said, alighting.

"Come on in, I got plenty of both." She fixed Billy Dee with a sharp eye. "You got a shadow now?"

"Coop insists," Fancy said.

"Well, son, you go over to the bunkhouse and you'll find a pot of coffee and some company for yourself."

"Thank you, ma'am," Billy Dee said, tugging at his hat respectfully.

Geraldine ushered Fancy inside, and the two women sat talking for a full hour. Geraldine laughed and slapped her knee when she heard how Fancy had sent her torn gown to Claire Williams and clucked her tongue in concern when she heard of the problems Coop was having with the Indian agent. She pursed her lips and narrowed her eyes, then offered her advice. When Fancy climbed back into her buggy and waved good-bye, she had a much better understanding of the ways of folks in Elizabethtown. She knew she'd been given the information not to flaunt or use unwisely or spitefully, but to help her make her way for Coop and herself.

Fancy had no real idea how quickly rumors could spread in a territory as wide-flung as the rough mountainous region. She hadn't realized how starved for news people were and once they had their hands on a bit, how natural it was for them to share it. By the time she rode into Elizabethtown for the ladies' social, the streets and shops were buzzing with the rumor concerning Coop and the lost government supplies meant for the Indians.

"Ain't like stealing," some said, "if'n it was goods meant for the Indians."

"He's a half-breed, hisself, which just goes to show you can't trust them lyin', thievin' Injuns."

Others voiced their confidence in Coop. "I ain't seen a more honest man. He wouldn't have taken the supplies."

Some canceled their shipments with Coop. Mine owners who'd never had anyone bring in the ore the way Coop's freight trains did shrugged their shoulders at the tales and continued business as usual.

Fancy was the one who bore the brunt of these new rumors. When she entered La Maison Francais, she was greeted by silence in the lobby, and when shown to the parlor room where the luncheon and musical entertainment were to take place, no one rushed forward to greet her as they normally would have done. Nonplussed, Fancy's gaze swept around the room. Just a week before these same people had partaken of the Fletcher hospitality. Now they stood aloof and assessing.

"Howdy, Fancy. We was waitin' for you," Geraldine called and clumped across the room to take Fancy's hand. "You look pretty as a picture, don't she?" The old woman hugged Fancy and whispered in her ear. "You got a passel of trouble here, child." Geraldine turned to the rest of the room. "Claire, how come you ain't wearin' that pretty gown Fancy sent you?"

Claire Williams's face went chalk white, and she glanced around the room at the avid faces of the other women. "I—I," she stuttered.

"Like as not you had to let it out afore you could wear it," Geraldine continued. "You ain't got that itty-bitty waist like Fancy has."

Fancy had recovered herself, and now she smiled sweetly at Claire. "I'm sure that's not it," she said smoothly. "But you are taller than I, dear Claire. You'll have to let down the hem, won't you?"

Claire smiled sickly and nodded. "Yes, that's it," she said, and her gaze couldn't meet Fancy's.

Looping an arm through Geraldine's, Fancy bent low to say something only the old woman could hear. "What's going on here?" she asked.

"Rumors about Coop," Geraldine replied, and Fancy laughed as if she'd just said something wonderfully funny. Inside her heart was pounding with outrage. There was no chance to question Geraldine more, the other women were watching too closely.

Fancy sauntered to the tea table filled with tiny sandwiches and finger cakes. "Umm, this looks wonderful," she cried and taking up a plate, piled it high with food. Accepting a cup of tea, she settled on a settee next to Maida. The woman looked shocked that Fancy had taken such liberties. Only Maida's closest friends were welcomed to sit in such an exalted position, but Fancy seemed utterly oblivious to her faux pas. Spreading her skirts prettily, she glanced around at the other ladies, smiling brightly.

"Is Claire playing the piano today?" she asked expectantly.

"Yes, of course," Maida said stiffly, then thawed as she thought of how much they'd all come to enjoy Fancy's company. "My dear, there are some questions regarding your husband's—ah—business practices."

"Really?" Fancy asked, raising her eyebrows in mock surprise.

"Yes, it seems that when he shipped government goods to the Utes in the Middle Park, the goods disappeared. Some believe he may have sold the supplies to the miners in one of the outlying camps for a tidy profit." Maida's face was not filled with malice as she waited for Fancy's reply. She'd come to have a genuine regard for this lively girl, and she'd always thought Coop an interesting man despite his mixed blood. Now she and the other ladies waited for Fancy's defense of her husband. They weren't to be disappointed.

Carefully, Fancy placed her tea cup on the small marble-topped table and raised her green gaze to the room. Her expression was calm, even serene as she faced them.

"I thank you, Maida, for bringing this directly to my attention," she began. "So many times, such vicious rumors are allowed to build behind one's back without giving the accused a chance to repudiate them." She paused and took a tiny breath to still her trembling. It wouldn't do to let them see she was upset.

"I have little need to defend my husband," she said. "Most of you know him. You've been to our ranch, and you can see Coop Fletcher has no reason to steal from anyone, least of all the Indians who will surely suffer if new supplies aren't sent to them. Coop's resources are considerable, and he's already sent cattle and some supplies at his own cost to the Indians to insure they aren't starving.

"As for Doyle Springer," Fancy's eyes flashed her disdain, and she got to her feet and took a position behind the settee, her hands gripping the carved back. Though small of stature, so dignified was her demeanor that she seemed much taller to the women, and her gaze was direct and challenging so her onlookers turned away before she did. "Must I demean myself by speaking of this man? He was first a gambler and was run out of many towns because of his cheating. How he came to be named Indian agent is beyond my comprehension, but so he is. He spends little time on the reservation, preferring instead the comfort and society of Elizabethtown or Denver. He has no answers to Coop's questions as to what was actually shipped, and when Coop went to Denver to question the warehouse guard, the old man was killed and an attempt made on Coop's life. You all know of the day Reynard shot his way out of a saloon here in Elizabethtown. Coop has named him as the man who attacked his supply train, and he believes Reynard works for Doyle Springer. Now ladies, you know as much of the truth as I do."

"You brave little thing," Elise cried, coming forward. "You must be terrified for Coop's safety."

"Yes, I am," Fancy said, "but I have confidence in him."

"Come, have some tea, my dear," Maida said, patting the settee beside her.

The women gathered round to discuss this new information, many of them declaring loudly they never once suspected Coop Fletcher who was a fine gentleman. They commented on his generosity in sending food to the hungry Utes, and a committee was formed to gather cast-off clothes, blankets, pots and pans, and food stuffs to be sent to the reservation as well. Feeling virtuous at their philanthropic gesture they sat back to enjoy the musical afternoon.

Claire played rather badly, but they were in a generous enough mood not to hold it against her, and the social ended on quite a pleasant note. The ladies returned to their homes and that night at supper regaled their husbands with first-hand information they'd obtained from Fancy Fletcher, and thus, public opinion was swayed in Coop's favor once more.

Three nights later, a raid was made on the ranch.

Coop and Fancy lay in a deep sleep, exhausted after their lovemaking. The sound of rushing hoofbeats and gunshots stirred Coop from his slumber. Fancy sat up, gripping the cover around her bare shoulders.

"What is it?" she cried.

"Stay down. Don't light the lamps," Coop instructed, pulling on his trousers and boots.

"Coop, don't go," Fancy cried, knowing he wouldn't heed her plea.

"Stay away from the windows," he instructed hurriedly, "and no matter what you think you hear, don't come outside."

"I won't," Fancy said, but he was already pounding down the stairs. She heard the door bang closed behind him and leapt out of bed. Despite his admonitions, she had to see what was happening, dragging a sheet around herself she crouched before a window and peered down into the yard. Mounted men were everywhere, their guns blazing. Some carried torches, and even as Fancy watched one of them tossed his flaming brand into a barn. It flared up at once, testifying it had landed in hay or something else equally as flammable. The high-pitched cry of horses drew the ranch hands to the barn, where silhouetted by the flames, they were cut down by a hail of bullets.

Dear God, where was Coop? Fancy thought and raced across the room to find something to put on. She was in Coop's room, and her hands fell on a pair of trousers and a shirt. Quickly she pulled them on, muttering when they slid down her hips. Frantically she looked for a belt, and grabbing up a silk tie from her robe, tied the waist so it stayed in place.

"Miss Fancy," Annabelle cried, running in from her room. "What's goin' on?"

"Men are attacking the ranch. Stay down," Fancy yelled. Throwing on one of Coop's shirts, she knotted it at the waist even as she ran downstairs in her bare feet. Annabelle was right behind her. Delores was crouched in the downstairs hall, crying and uttering prayers of supplication.

"Delores, Annabelle, get buckets and start filling them with water in case they fire the house," Fancy cried, giving the shaken woman a shove. "Hurry." She didn't hesitate to see if they obeyed but rushed to the door and threw it open. The yard was a bedlam of fallen bodies, screaming horses, and blazing guns. Even as she stood there a bullet thudded into the thick oak door. Fancy slammed it shut and whirled, looking around the house. She couldn't stay in here, when Coop was out there fighting for them all.

Racing to the back door, she let herself out into the undisturbed quiet and slipped along to the corner of the house. Most of the fighting was taking place in the front of the house, so no one noticed as she darted from the house toward the barns. In the dark, with her heart pumping from fear the barns seemed miles away, but she zigzagged from puddles of shadows, from tree to tree, from horse trough to shed, and finally to the back of the barn. Some of the hands were there, leading the horses into the pastures away from the burning barn.

"Ebenezer," she cried when a hand led the sleek colt from the barn.

"He's all right, ma'am," the cowhand said. "You'd better get back to the house. It ain't safe for you to be out here."

"Have you seen Coop?" Fancy asked.

"Miss Fancy? What are you doin' out here?" Daniel asked. His dark face gleamed with sweat from the heat of the fire.

"Is all the stock out?" someone yelled.

"All clear," Daniel yelled and took hold of Fancy's arm. "I got to get you back to the ranch," he said, taking out his gun.

"Wait, have you seen Coop?"

"He's around somewhere, ma'am," Daniel said, "but it ain't goin' t'do him no good, if he knows yo' out here in this. You'll distract him, and that could get him killed."

"All right, I'll go back to the house," Fancy shouted over the roar of the fire. "You don't have to go back with me."

"I'd better," Daniel said and angled toward the ranch house. Fancy followed him. They crouched behind the water trough contemplating the long uncovered distance to the house. Fancy shivered, wondering how she'd made it. Now Daniel cast a quick glance at the front of the house, then motioned her forward. Crouching, he led the way. So many shots were sounding, she didn't realize one had hit close, until she saw Daniel stumble and sprawl forward.

"Daniel," she screamed and ran to him. A man on horseback galloped toward him, his gun aimed at her. When the man saw her long spill of hair and small face he raised the barrel toward the sky and sat looking at her.

"Well, well, what have we got here?" he sneered. Fancy recognized the man who had shot at them in Elizabethtown. Jason Reynard!

"Coop Fletcher's fancy lady," Reynard said and leveled his gun at her. His pale eyes glittered with madness. Desperately Fancy looked around.

"There ain't nobody around to help you, Fancy Lady. Coop's trying to fight off my men and save his barns. I'm going to burn him out tonight." His laugh was a cackle of glee. Fancy felt the cold barrel of Daniel's gun. It was caught under him. Frantically she tried to work it loose without Reynard noticing.

"You can't beat Coop," she shouted at the man on horseback. "You haven't done it yet, and you've tried. You just aren't the man he is."

"That half-breed," Reynard sneered. "He ain't worth nothing. He's just a worthless Injun."

"He may be a half-breed, Reynard, but he has more courage and more brains than you'll ever have," she taunted, and with a final tug the gun came free. She could see the spittle on Reynard's lips, the mad light in his eye, and his finger tightened on the trigger. Without thinking she snatched up Daniel's gun and aimed it. She'd never used a gun before. She was shocked at the weight of it in her hands. It wobbled, but she used both hands to steady it and pulled the trigger.

Reynard jerked in his saddle and stared at her in shock. He seemed not to know what had hit him. Then fury twisted his features, and he tried to bring his gun up, but the nerves, muscle, and bone in his shoulder were shattered. Blood gushed from the wound, wetting the front of his shirt, and his pistol tumbled from his hand. Fancy raised the gun again, pulling back the hammer. With a cry, Reynard kicked at his horse, causing it to rear and prance backward. Sawing at the reins, Reynard kicked again, digging his spurs into the horse's belly.

With a cry of pain, the horse started toward the front of the house. Fancy pulled the trigger and had the satisfaction of seeing Reynard duck and his hat go flying. She wasn't certain if she'd hit him again or not.

Throwing aside the gun, she sat staring after his departing figure while reaction set in. She'd never used a gun before in her life, and now she'd shot a man, and although he'd ridden away, he might yet die from her wound. Fancy's hands were shaking, then she saw blood, Daniel's blood on them, and she put away her sensibilities. Daniel was wounded and might be dying. She leapt to her feet and ran to the kitchen door of the ranch house.

"Annabelle," she screamed. "Daniel's hurt."

"Daniel! Oh, Lawd, no," Annabelle cried and followed her outside. It seemed the noise had diminished in the front of the ranch house and was moving off down the trail, but she couldn't be certain. The two women knelt over Daniel, trying to assess the damage.

"Get him in the house," Annabelle cried.

"No, don't move him yet," Fancy said. "He's lost a lot of blood. We have to get that bullet out. Remember Aaron and Nellie. I'll get Nellie. You get a knife and hot water."

"I cain't leave him," Annabelle cried, cradling Daniel's head in her lap.

"Wait there, wait!" Fancy cried and took off in a run for Nellie's small house. The windows were dark, but she knew Nellie and her girls were hiding until the shooting was done.

"Nellie!" she cried, pounding on the door. "Come quick, we need you." Without waiting for an answer, she ran back to the ranch house. Her bare feet were numb with pain, but she couldn't stop. There was too much to do. Several hands were wounded or dead. She ran back to the kitchen door and yelled for Delores to come with pots of water and bandages, then she ran to the bunkhouse. Tables had been cleared, and wounded men laid out on them. The bunkhouse cook, River Adams, was working on some of them, while the others lay moaning, waiting their turn.

"Daniel's lying in the side yard, wounded," Fancy said to two cowboys, and they took off at a run to bring him in. Distraught, Fancy looked around for Coop, but he was nowhere in sight, not even among the wounded men. Fancy didn't know whether to be relieved or not.

"Have you seen Coop?" she demanded of two men who limped through the door.

"Yes, ma'am, he and bunch of the hands took off after them bushwhackers. They've got 'em on the run."

"He's all right, then?"

"Yes, ma'am. Near as I could see." The young cowboy swayed, and Fancy noticed for the first time his bloody sleeve.

"Come, lie down," she directed. In a matter of minutes, all four women were busy washing and binding wounds. And all the while she thought of Coop and listened for the sound of riders returning, but there was none. The night remained still except for the moans of the wounded and dying men.

Chapter 19

*T*HREE MEN DIED in the night raid; seven more were wounded. Fancy worked beside the other women and River Adams, tending the wounded. At daylight, she sent Billy Dee to Elizabethtown to bring back the doctor. Those able hands who hadn't gone with Coop were armed and mounted, riding the perimeter of the ranch while other men sat atop rooftops and other strategic places in case another attack was made. One by one they came in for coffee and a quick meal of beans and pork and biscuits. Somehow between his nursing duties River Adams had managed to whip up some food.

"Reynard was wounded when he rode out of here," they said, talking to the wounded to make them feel better. "I reckon whoever shot him scared the bejesus out of him, so he hightailed it."

"Good thing, too, cause we was outnumbered and takin' the worst of it," another man said, swigging down his coffee and grabbing his rifle again.

"Wonder who it was shot him?"

No one knew, and Fancy said nothing. She was sick at heart. Nothing had been heard of Coop and the rest of the hands. At the sound of hoofbeats on the main road, she ran out on the porch, but the riders were only Billy Dee and the doctor.

"Did you hear any word of Coop?" Fancy demanded,

running out to meet them. Annabelle led the doctor to the wounded men, and Billy Dee stood holding his reins, scuffing his feet in the dust.

"I talked to some men in town, Miss Fancy," he said slowly. "They said someone rode in town requesting the sheriff's help, and he took his posse and rode out."

"Was he going to help Coop and his men?" Fancy demanded.

Billy Dee shook his head. "No one knows for sure," he said, not meeting her gaze.

"What is it, Billy Dee?" she demanded. "What is it you're not telling me?"

"Well, ma'am, the sheriff's posse went off to the north toward Denver. I figure if Reynard is runnin', he's goin' to hide out up in them mountains. The sheriff wasn't goin' anywhere in the right direction."

"Do you know where Reynard would have gone, Billy Dee?" she asked, laying her hand on his sleeve. He shuffled his feet and reddened under her gaze. He'd never seen anyone prettier than Miss Fancy, and even though she stood there in a pair of man's trousers and a man's shirt with her hair all down around her face, she was still the rarest sight a man could look at.

"Billy Dee, if you know, you must tell us. Coop wouldn't have sent a man into town for help unless he needed it."

"Maybe it wasn't Coop who sent for help," Billy Dee said, "since the sheriff rode out the other way."

Fancy released her grip on his sleeve and paced back and forth; finally she spun to face the young cowboy. "You know the direction Reynard's gang took. You know he would hide out in the mountains. How do you know that?" Her green gaze pinned him, her glance stern, her soft pink mouth a thin, purposeful line.

Once again Billy Dee looked away. Abe White had joined them, and Billy Dee looked from him to Fancy. "Go on, boy, tell Miss Fancy how you happen to know what Reynard would do," he roared, drawing the attention of the other men. They left their posts and unabashedly listened to the conversation.

"Tell me, Billy Dee," Fancy said sternly, "and we won't hold it against you."

"I'm sorry, Miss Fancy. I didn't mean to bring nothing like this down on your heads," the young cowboy said. "I—I didn't have nobody to ride with when I was younger. Jason Reynard let me join up with him and some of his men. I didn't much like the way they done things, robbin' and killin' the miners and travelers through them passes."

"You little bastard," one of the men yelled.

"Quiet," Fancy ordered, and the men fell silent. "Go on, Billy Dee."

He was sweating now, his young face scared-looking and defenseless. "Reynard didn't much like the way Mr. Fletcher got his wagons through and his men fought back. It made Reynard mad, so he hit on a scheme to have somebody come here and git a job and spy on Mr. Fletcher, so he'd know when to hit the supply trains."

One of the drivers stepped forward and gripped Billy Dee's shirt, his fist rolled up, ready to punch him.

"Stop it," Fancy shouted. "I gave him my word he wouldn't be hurt." Reluctantly, the driver released him.

"That's one thing I found out around here," Billy Dee said, and he was nearly crying now. "When Mr. Fletcher or you, Miss Fancy, give your word about something, you keep it. I didn't want to give Reynard information about your operations, but he threatened to kill me, said I was gettin' too pampered. Then I started giving him wrong information. When he tried to hit the supply train goin' up to the Middle Park to the Utes, I told him a different route, but he didn't trust me no more. It slowed him down some, so he couldn't git in front of them wagons and set a trap." The drivers exchanged glances with one another, remembering how ineffective the attack had been.

"I'm sorry, Miss Fancy. I didn't mean none of this to happen. I tried to make a break with Reynard, but he wouldn't let me."

"Billy Dee, you can redeem yourself now, if you'll lead us to the place where Reynard hangs out. Coop may be there, and he's undermanned."

"I'll try, Miss Fancy," he said, wiping at his eyes.

"Stop your whining, boy," Abe White said, cuffing the boy in the back of the head. "Take us to that polecat's hideout, or we'll make you wish you was back with Reynard."

"There'll be no violence against Billy Dee," Fancy ordered, facing the men. "Get your horses and extra ammunition and meet me back here."

"You ain't goin', are you, ma'am?" one of the men asked.

"That's my husband out there needing help, and I'm not sitting here wondering."

"It won't be safe out there, ma'am. You're a—well, you're a lady, and you ain't used to those rough mountain passes. And there'll be shootin'."

"Don't tell me what I'm used to. As for the shooting, well, if you want to know who shot Jason Reynard, you're looking at her. Now get your horses and guns and meet me back here."

Nearly a dozen of them rode out of the ranch yard, led by Billy Dee. Fancy followed, the heavy, unwielding weight of a pistol strapped to her slender waist. The men rode hard, and they were right, she wasn't used to the rigors of a mountain trail, but she made no complaint, only gritting her teeth against any discomfort and urging her pony on. He was a sturdy mustang, surefooted and used to the trails.

"This may just be a wild-goose chase, ma'am," Abe White said when they'd paused once for Billy Dee to get his bearing.

"It may be," Fancy acknowledged, wiping at her brow, "and it may not be. We can't take a chance it's not." The afternoon sun was slanting low against the mountains. Soon it would be dark, then they'd be forced to bed down until daylight. She already understood the dangers of blundering through the mountains after dark.

Suddenly, a volley of shots echoed across the peaks. Fancy looked at Abe, who swore. " 'Scuse me, ma'am," he said with a grin. "I think we've found them."

"Let's go," Fancy cried, kneeing her horse. They rode single file along the trail, following Billy Dee until the sound of shots was nearer. Abe White raised his hand.

"We'd best walk from here," he said. Everyone dismounted and took out their weapons.

"Maybe you better stay here, ma'am," Abe said gruffly, but Fancy was already shaking her head, and tiny as she was he knew he hadn't a prayer's chance of making her stay back. Cautiously Fancy and the men fanned out and climbed into the rocks. When they got high enough they could see Coop and his men penned down in a ravine, surrounded by Reynard's men. Abe motioned his men to be quiet and take position. When they were ready, he gave the nod to begin firing. Fancy took out the pistol she'd brought and, not quite certain what she was doing, proceeded to aim and fire until she was out of bullets. By the time the smoke cleared, Reynard's men were heading for their horses.

"Get after 'em," Abe called and turned on Fancy. "Stay here, Miss Fancy!" he ordered, and she knew this time his advice was good. She took cover behind a boulder and watched as the men raced after Reynard and his outlaws. She strained to see Coop and felt her heart leap in her throat when she saw his tall figure racing after a fleeing outlaw. He leveled his long pistol and fired, and a man went down. In a matter of minutes, the mountains were cleared. Reynard's men scattered. Many lay crumpled in their final embrace with death. When all was clear and Coop and the rest had given up the chase, Fancy rose from behind the boulder and made her way down to Coop. She thought only of her joy in seeing him alive as she ran to him and threw her arms around his neck.

"What in God's name are you doing here?" he demanded, gripping her shoulders tightly.

"We came to save you."

"Save me?" he exploded. "You little fool, don't you know you could have been killed?"

"So could you have. Besides, I had my bodyguard with me."

Coop rounded on Billy Dee, landing him a blow that knocked him to the ground. Billy Dee lay staring up at him with tragic eyes, his lip bleeding. Fancy sprang to his defense.

"You can't be angry with Billy Dee. He's the one who showed us where to come," she shouted.

Coop stood back, letting his fist uncurl as he stared at the fallen man. "Just how did you know where to come?" he asked, and Billy Dee quailed under his glare.

"There's a lot of explaining to do," Fancy said. "Let's go back to the ranch first."

"All right." Coop stepped back, then pointed his finger at Billy Dee. "But your explanations had better be satisfactory, or you'll have me to answer to. Mount up." The men moved to their horses. Once again Coop Fletcher was in charge, and not a man there thought to question his authority.

They arrived back at the ranch well after dark, weary and hungry. Delores and Nellie had prepared food for everyone. Fancy took no time to stop and eat but went directly to fill a bath for herself. With a sigh of relief she slid down into the scented water and let her body relax. The past hours had been filled with terror and tension, but now Coop was home safe and she could relax. She half dozed, then she remembered Billy Dee and stood up in the tub.

"Finished already," said a voice behind her, and she swirled.

Coop sat on a chair watching her, his eyes narrowed, his face lined with fatigue.

"I was just thinking of Billy Dee. Have you questioned him already?"

Coop nodded wearily.

"What are you going to do with him?" Fancy asked, sitting back in the water, but her eyes were anxious as she met his.

"The boys have decided to give him another chance," Coop said and started undoing his shirt and pants.

"What about you?"

"I agree."

"I'm so happy," Fancy said, feeling a load lift from her shoulders. Smiling, she moved over to make room in the tub for Coop. "Thank you for being so kind to him. He's just a kid, and he didn't know how to get away from Reynard."

Coop wrapped his arms around her and settled her on top of him. She could feel his member harden against her leg and looked at him in surprise.

"I need you, Fancy," he said in a low voice, and she opened to him. Her silken arms slid around his neck, her sleek body lay on his, her soapy breasts brushing against his flesh tantalizingly. She straddled him, then she moved slowly and seductively against him, making him forget his anger over his dead men and Reynard's attack, helping him to find the forgiveness for Billy Dee.

Now when people talked of the fancy lady, they spoke of her courage and her pride and her prowess with a gun. Sheriff Wright had found nothing in his ride to the north and only later discovered he'd been duped. Now in vengeance, he organized a posse and set out to hunt down Reynard's gang. With the posse on their trail and no further information coming about the freight train schedules, Reynard was crippled. Coop's trains went through without trouble. The only question that remained was Doyle Springer and his repeated claims that Coop had stolen the Utes' government supplies. The Utes had been disdainful of the wagon loads of clothing and food sent by the citizens of Elizabethtown and threatened reprisals if their supplies were not forthcoming before the end of summer.

Fearful of additional attacks on the ranch house when he wasn't there, Coop insisted Fancy stay at their town house in Elizabethtown, so she bundled up Nellie and her girls,

Delores, and Annabelle, and they all trooped into town. Once Fancy would have jumped at the chance to live in the town house, but now she'd grown used to the ranch and the open spaces and the rearing mountains. Town living made her feel hemmed in.

August the first came, and the opera house was finished. Its red brick walls rose regally at the end of the street. Its trim and window boxes were painted a crisp white.

The Fay Templeton Opera Company was arriving from Denver to perform the *Pirates of Penzance*. There would be two shows a day, and the lovely young singer would perform solo on her Spanish guitar as well. Furthermore, in two weeks, when the opera company's engagement was finished, the popular James and Louisa Lord would travel from Kansas to perform for two weeks. A new play each night had been promised.

The people of Elizabethtown were delighted. The only theater they'd seen in years were the ragtag variety shows which stopped off and played in the saloons, and the female performers joined the all-male audience for dancing and drinking. They were judged little more than prostitutes by most good ladies of Elizabethtown. Now to think they would have a real opera house with legitimate plays and operas pleased them all and increased Coop and Fancy's standing in the community.

Coop had been away on one of his freighting runs, but he'd promised to be present at the opening. He was still unsuspecting of Fancy's role in the building of the opera house. Fancy was beside herself with nervousness as she dressed for the opera. Coop still hadn't arrived, and she feared he might have forgotten. She'd planned so carefully for this evening. Even Nellie and Aaron and Annabelle and a much healed Daniel were to go, sitting in a premium box Fancy had reserved for all of them.

For her night at the opera, Fancy had chosen a white lace gown worn over an underskirt of pale pink silk. The bodice had been studded with tiny pearls, and ropes of pearls had been fixed in her hair. Her bustle ended in just the tiniest hint of a train, which trailed gracefully and still left her hands free.

The clock had crept closer to the hour, and Fancy was beside herself. Where was Coop? He'd promised, and she felt sure he wouldn't renege on that promise unless he'd run into some trouble. She pictured him lying beside some mountain trail, wounded and bleeding while she pranced around in her finery for the people of Elizabethtown, people who meant nothing to her if not for Coop.

"They're here," Annabelle hollered up the stairs, and Fancy felt her heartbeat ease somewhat. Racing to the landing, she peered down at the men. They were dirty and tired, but Coop grinned up at her and sprang up the stairs to plant a kiss on her soft, opened mouth. Standing back, he looked at her in astonishment.

"How could I have forgotten how beautiful you are?" he wondered. "Yet every time I come back to you, I'm in awe all over again."

"You're starting to sound like a poet, my love," Fancy whispered. "Would you rather skip the theater tonight?"

"And miss the chance to walk in with you on my arm?" he asked lightly. "I'll be ready in time."

"Your bath is drawn, then. Hurry," Fancy cried. Nellie was ushering Aaron to a tub as well. In no time the men were ready and assembled in the downstairs parlor. Coop was breathtaking in a dark suit and white shirt that contrasted sharply with his dark good looks.

The tired lines seemed to have disappeared, and he held out his arm for Fancy and escorted her to the buggy which would take them all to the theater.

"Elizabethtown is gettin' mighty fancy," he said as they made their way to their boxes. Aaron exchanged an amused glance with Fancy and said nothing. They'd had a risky moment there when they drew up before the opera house, hurrying Coop in before he had time to notice the name over the doors. Aaron had seldom seen anyone put anything over on Coop, and he was proud to have been a small part of this surprise.

An orchestra of sorts had been assembled in front below the stage, and their lively tunes set a mood of elegance and romance for the evening. People entered, oohing and aahing at the fine detail and rich velvet curtains and chandeliers. There was a certain proprietary air about them as they took in the plush cushioned seats and well-lit stage. This was their opera house, oh, it might say Fletcher on the outside, but it belonged to all of them.

All the seats were filled, and a low pleasant hum filled the air, accompanied by the orchestra music. Then the red velvet curtains parted, and Maida, looking her most commanding, stepped out on the stage. The ring of gaslights cast a dramatic aura around her as she calmly waited for the auditorium to grow quiet. The musicians lowered their instruments, and the hum diminished. When she was certain every eye in the house was on her, Maida stepped forward.

"Good evening, ladies and gentlemen," she said. "As president of the Elizabethtown Ladies' Society, it gives me great pleasure to welcome you tonight. Our new opera house is a most gracious gift to our town from Mr. and Mrs. Coop Fletcher." One gloved hand indicated the box in which Fancy and Coop and their guests were seated. Coop looked stunned.

"Surprise, darling," Fancy said. "This is why I needed all the money, the money that you never once asked me to account for."

"Stand up and take a bow, folks," someone called from another box, and Coop and Fancy stood up to an enthusiastic round of applause. After bowing several times, Fancy and Coop sat down, and Maida once again waited for the audience to grow quiet.

"Thanks to the kind efforts of Fancy Fletcher, we are pleased to offer a most noteworthy presentation," Maida continued.

Fancy had ceased to listen to the introduction for the Fay Templeton Opera Company. She was watching Coop's face, which had gone all stiff and stern. With sinking heart, she realized he had not been pleased by her surprise, and she couldn't understand why. Unable to contain her anxiety, she leaned forward and peered into his face.

"Coop, have I done something that offends you?" she whispered. He looked into her green eyes and forced a smile.

"No, I'm just surprised is all," he said, taking her hand and tucking it under his arm. When she tried to speak, he shook his head. "Shhh. I've never been to an opera before. Let's listen."

So Fancy sat with sinking heart wondering why her husband wasn't pleased with what she'd accomplished while Fay Templeton thrilled the audience with her vivacious acting and clear sweet voice. Politely, Coop watched the lively tale of a pirate king, and during intermission, he moved among the theatergoers who extended their congratulations on the theater's success. His teeth flashed often as he smiled and talked, but Fancy sensed something was dreadfully wrong.

At last the curtain was rung down, Fay Templeton had dazzled them all with her guitar solos, the last encores had been cried, and people filed out of the theater and into their carriages. From the theater they adjourned to *La Maison Francais*, where a cold supper had been set out in the ballroom and the theater orchestra continued to provide music.

Fancy couldn't help feeling that thrill of excitement when the comic-opera troupe arrived to mingle with the guests. How often had she seen her father and mother make their grand entrance to just such after-theater parties. She clapped enthusiastically, remembering the excitement, the drama, the exultation. Eyes sparkling, she turned, looking for Coop, and found he was watching her with a guarded expression. Quickly she crossed the room to him.

"Oh, darling, hasn't this been a wonderful night?"

"Pretty heady times in the theater," he said flatly and watched the changing emotions on her face.

"There's nothing like an opening night and the accolades

afterward. I wish I could make you understand how wonderful it all can be."

"I think I do," he said and moved away from her. She was troubled anew by his tone but had no time to dwell on it, for her duties as one of the hostesses demanded she come forward and present her thanks to the troupe. Seth Crane, the leading man, made a pass at her, Fay Templeton flirted outrageously with all the husbands, one of the bit players became tipsy and had to be escorted back to her room. All in all, it was a glorious evening. Aaron and Nellie and Annabelle and Daniel had long since returned home, so by the time the party was over, the moon had nearly finished its nightly round and the streets were dark. Back at their town house, Coop helped Fancy out of the buggy and saw her inside before taking the buggy on to the stables. By the time he returned, Fancy was undressed and in bed, her golden lashes already resting on her cheeks as she dozed, her long hair fanning around her, her fancy clothes put aside. Coop stood staring down at her. She looked like his Fancy now, but she hadn't earlier. He'd seen a dazzle in her, a glow, an excitement that the theater seemed to awaken in her.

"Fancy?" he whispered softly, kneeling beside her and smoothing back the silken gold strands.

"Ummm?" she mumbled.

"Fancy!" His tone was more insistent. "Are you happy with me, Fancy? Truly happy? Or do you miss the theater?"

"Ummmm!" she sighed and rolled away from him, sprawling in abandonment to sleep. Coop sat watching her awhile longer, and his questions hung in the air unanswered. Finally, he rose and made himself ready for bed, pulling Fancy's small warm body next to his to ease the sudden cold, lonely spot in his soul.

Chapter 20

IN THE WEEKS that followed, the Fay Templeton opera troupe regaled the citizens of Elizabethtown twice a day, seven days a week with the *Pirates of Penzance*. People came to see it over and over. Then just before they'd begun to tire of it, the troupe presented *Olivette*, another comic-opera that had everyone laughing and applauding anew. The dust had barely cleared behind the departing Fay Templeton Opera Company than James and Louisa, Louie as she was affectionately called in the theater, arrived with their entourage of actors, sets, and costumes. The ladies' society was lined up in front of *La Maison Francais* to welcome the Lords, who did indeed very nearly resemble royalty in the rough and tumble world of traveling players.

"I understand their plays contain much useful moral instructions as well as entertainment for the audience," Elise said, quoting what she'd read in the *Rocky Mountain Sentinel*.

"I heard they never use foul language and their plays are of the highest character," Agnes Wright said, straightening her hat and veil.

Fancy remained silent as the two heavy coaches drew to a halt before the hotel. James Lord, a tall, bearded man, stepped out of the coach and helped his wife out. The women on the porch waited with bated breath as if about to meet royalty. Louisa Lord stepped down, shook out her skirts, glanced around with a curious eye, and smiled graciously at the assembled ladies. She was a slight woman, much less commanding than one might have supposed for a stage actress, but her golden tresses were swept up into an intricate coiffure, and her hat and gown were satisfyingly elegant. Extending a thin regal hand, she acknowledged the greeting of the ladies' society. Fancy and Maida acted as hostesses, welcoming the Lords and their troupe.

The bit actors were alighting from the other coach now. Suddenly, a gay voice called out.

"Fancy! Fancy Bourne!" Startled, Fancy turned around just as a woman with bright red hair and a carefully painted face waved to her.

"I knew it was you. It's me, Carrie Wing."

Fancy instantly recognized one of the bit players from her father's old troupe. Carrie had been one of the first to leave the troupe after Fancy's parents were killed. Now she flounced out of the coach and rushed forward to grip Fancy's hand and give her a familiar hug. "It's just like old home week," she cried. "Are you in a troupe out here?"

Fancy was aware of the members of the ladies' society standing in dead silence on the porch, avidly taking in all that Carrie said. Fancy knew before she turned the disbelief and condemnation she would find in their faces now that the truth about her background had been revealed. Just like that, in a blink of an eye, she thought, a whole new life can be wiped out.

Carrie Wing stood staring at Fancy. "You're awfully elegant now," she said brightly. "You must have had a bit of good fortune."

To her credit, Louisa Lord sensed something was amiss and took steps to smooth things over. "Carrie," she snapped. "Join the others and see to your luggage."

Carrie's face grew red at the sharp command. With a final puzzled look at Fancy, she turned away, then defiantly faced Fancy again. "I'm sorry," she said. "I thought you were someone I knew." Without waiting for a response, she flounced away.

"Why how extraordinary," Elise said. "That woman thought she knew you, that you were one of them."

"She did call Fancy by name," Agnes said.

Maida remained silent, staring at Fancy as if she were a stranger, but Claire's face was bright with triumph. Facing them all, Fancy could see the truth slowly dawning on their faces. Once again, Louisa Lord took control of things.

"I'm really quite tired," she said. "I hope the rooms here are satisfactory."

"*Oui, madame,*" Monsieur Dubois said, rushing forward. "*C'est magnifique!* I promise you will be very pleased. *La Maison Francais* is the best hotel in the west."

Maida and the other women turned their attention to the Lords, pressing bouquets upon them and following them into the hotel lobby while they were checked into their rooms. Fancy didn't follow the crowd. Standing on the porch, she wondered what would happen now. Would Coop want her to leave, now that her secret had been discovered? She should have known she was courting disaster when she built the opera house and brought in theatrical troupes, but her love of the theater had blinded her to that possibility. Now, feeling cold and abandoned inside, she made her way along the boardwalk to the opera house. It welcomed her with a well-remembered richness of smells and mystery. She made her way to the stage. Through the dim lights from the high small windows, the brass gaslights gleamed. The new oak floor echoed her footsteps. The sound was lonely in the empty theater. A chair sat at center stage, and she sat in it looking up at the riggings for backdrops and curtains. This was a place she remembered well, the backstage of a theater. Her whole life had been spent in this atmosphere and something of it had called to her over these past few months, yet now that she was here, it held less enchantment than she might have supposed.

She'd been so intent on her role as Coop's wife and as a true lady around Elizabethtown, she'd almost forgotten who she really was.

"There you are, Fancy," a voice said, and Louisa Lord stepped out of the shadows. "May I call you Fancy?"

"Yes, of course," Fancy said, wiping at her eyes. She hadn't been aware she'd been crying.

"I understand you and your husband built this opera house?"

"Yes, we did," Fancy said, rising from the chair and striving for an even tone of voice.

Louisa Lord looked around, nodding in approval. "It's one of the finest theaters we've seen here in the west. You have done a good job. I think only someone who has been in the theater herself could have thought out all of the things needed." Her gaze was frank and slightly amused.

"Yes, I was in the theater once," Fancy said. "My mother and father were Monty and Adele Bourne."

"Ah, yes. I remember them. When I was very young and just starting out, they were most kind to me." Louisa's smile was generous and understanding. "The ladies in town, they didn't know you were once in the theater?"

Slowly Fancy shook her head. "I came here pretending to be a lady, because that was what my husband wanted."

"I see." Louisa paced around the stage, whirling now and then to peer out at the empty chairs. Fancy knew she was determining her marks, the places she would stand to deliver her major soliloquies.

"Well, I'll leave you," she said turning away, but Louisa's voice stopped her.

"We are short a player for one of our productions. Would you care to take the part?"

"Me?" Fancy asked in astonishment.

Louisa shrugged. "Why not? We often use local people in our plays for bit parts or backstage. They love it. If the truth be known, most people have secret aspirations for the stage, even those who belittle it and its players."

"I'm not doing that," Fancy said. "But I think I'd better not act with you."

"Ah, your husband might object."

Fancy thought of Coop and opening night. How aloof

he'd become since then, and she often caught him watching her with a puzzled look on his face.

"I'm sorry. I just can't," she answered. "Thank you for asking."

"We'll ask some of the other good ladies of your little club," Louisa said, and Fancy thought her tone and words were not so much meant to belittle the ladies' society as to help Fancy put them all in proper perspective. Had she come to let them rule her thoughts and actions too much? It wasn't because she cared about them, but she'd wanted so much to please Coop. In the long run, she'd only disappointed him, and now with her secret out, to be gossiped about and speculated about, she'd damaged his standing in the community even more.

"Perhaps if you faced everyone head on and told them what you've told me, perhaps it would be better," Louisa said now as she watched the warring emotions in Fancy's face.

"It wouldn't make any difference now," Fancy said sadly. "I must go. I wish you well in your performances here."

"You won't be here tonight?"

"No, I think it's best I don't attend."

"Oh, my dear young woman. You have much to learn about people and about yourself."

"I think I've learned all I need to know for one day," Fancy said and ran backstage and out the side door. She couldn't bear to have anyone see her now, all weepy and defeated. Slowly she made her way to the town house and fell into Annabelle's arms.

"That Carrie Wing never had 'nough sense to walk 'cross a stage," Annabelle said indignantly. "I don't know why a fine company like the Lords took her on."

"It doesn't matter now, Annabelle; all is lost. When Coop hears my secret is out, he'll send me away."

"Not that man, Miss Fancy. He loves yo'."

"He desires me," Fancy said. "He wants me as I am in his bedroom, but he wants a lady in the town parlors. No doubt that Claire Williams is planning her wedding to him right this minute."

"Then she goin' t'be mighty disappointed," Annabelle predicted, and Fancy hugged her friend in misery.

High in the mountains, Coop and his drivers pulled their rigs to a halt and stared at the trail ahead. His wagons were loaded with food supplies and blankets meant for the Utes. He'd raised the funds himself from his associates and put a large sum into the pot himself. Besides the wagons loaded with food supplies and warm blankets, he'd driven up two hundred head of cattle, enough to keep the Utes in meat through the coming winter. Now he looked around impatiently. He'd sent a message three days before that he was arriving in the Middle Park with food, but no Indians were in sight.

"Coop!" Aaron called and motioned to one end of the park. Littlefield and his men rode into sight. Coop took a deep breath of relief and rode forward to meet the Ute leader. By late afternoon the meeting with the Utes had concluded, a peace pipe had been shared, supplies had been accepted, and Coop felt certain the Utes could survive the rigors of winter without starving, and all danger of an Indian uprising was past.

"Coop Fletcher is good man," Littlefield said with a final salute and sprang on his horse. Motioning to his warriors, he led the way to the southern end of the park. Whooping, the braves fell into line behind the wagons of goods. Coop watched them go. He was tired and longed for his bed with Fancy beside him.

"Now we go after Reynard," Coop vowed and looked back at his men. "Let's head back to the ranch," he ordered, and they turned their pack mules and retreated up the trail.

"Miss Fancy, aren't yo' goin' to the theater tonight?" Annabelle asked. "Don't let them highfalutin folks take the backbone out o' yo'."

"Not tonight, Annabelle," Fancy said listlessly. "I just don't have the heart to pretend anymore."

"But that's what yo' good at, Miss Fancy, and yo' good at makin' others believe what yo' want 'em to."

"I can't believe anymore, Annabelle, so how can I make others believe?" she answered. "Besides, I'm tired of trying to make someone love me for what I'm not."

"Yo' talkin' 'bout Mister Fletcher now, ain't yo'?" Annabelle asked shyly.

"Yes, I'm talking about Coop now," Fancy answered. "Someone's at the door, see who it is, and tell them Miss Fancy regrets she's not receiving this evening."

"Yes, ma'am." Annabelle went away but was soon back.

"They's a man out there, Miss Fancy. He looks something awful, and he says they's been a gunfight in the mountains and Mister Fletcher been hurt!"

Fancy leapt to her feet. "Where is he?"

"I lef' him on the doorstep," Annabelle said, leading the way. Fancy followed, her face pale with fear.

"Where is my husband?" she cried when she saw the man standing in the shadows. "Is he alive?"

"Yes, ma'am, he's alive all right," the man said. "But he's wounded, and he sent me to get you. Wants you to come to him."

"Wait, I'll get my wrap and some bandages. Annabelle, quick—"

"Yes, ma'am?" Annabelle said, staring at Fancy who was standing stock-still.

"Coop didn't send for me. He'd never put me in danger like that," she said, staring at the man. "Who are you?"

The man stepped forward into the light, a crafty smile lighting his sharp features.

"Reynard!" Fancy said, gasping.

"At your service, ma'am," he said, bowing slightly. His pale eyes shifted with a cruel light. Whirling, Fancy ran for the hall table where she knew Coop kept an extra gun, but Reynard grabbed her by the hair and yanked her back, one hand coming up to deliver a stinging slap.

"Miss Fancy!" Annabelle squealed. Reynard pulled his gun and aimed it at the terrified woman. Fancy lurched against him.

"Run, Annabelle, run," she cried, and Annabelle disappeared through the door to the kitchen.

"Stop, you black bitch," Reynard roared and fired at the door. The wood splintered beneath the impact, knocking half the panel out, but Fancy could see that Annabelle had gained the back door and was free. Fancy struggled against the gunman's hold, and he twisted her arm cruelly until she was forced to her knees in pain.

"You'll never get away with this." She gasped. "Coop will kill you for coming here."

"Coop's dead. I killed him myself." Reynard smirked.

"Liar!" Fancy cried. "You aren't man enough to kill him." He couldn't be dead, for if he were she would know. She would surely stop breathing herself.

Reynard raised his fist to hit her, but a shadow crossed the hall and a voice rang out.

"Reynard!" He whirled. Doyle Springer stood in the entrance. "I told you, don't hurt her," he said quietly. "I have plans for the fancy lady. Take her back to my quarters."

"What about Fletcher?" Reynard whined. "He's after me."

Springer looked around the elegant town house. "Burn it down," he ordered. "That'll stop him long enough for us to get free of here. If you see him, kill him."

"So, he's not dead," Fancy said, looking at Reynard with mocking laughter in her eyes. "I knew you weren't man enough to kill him. He'll get you, Reynard and you, Springer. He's known all along that it was you who stole the supplies from your own Indians."

"He may have guessed that, my dear, but he can never prove it," Springer said. "Besides, he'll be so devastated over the death of his wife in a fire, he won't think about the Utes or me."

"What are you going to do with me?" Fancy asked, suddenly fearful for her own life.

"Oh, you needn't worry," Doyle Springer said. "You're worth more to me alive than dead. I figure we'll travel up north some until things cool down in these parts. I thought I'd go back into gambling, and you? Well, I've heard the truth about you. You were just an actress."

"I see the news has gotten around since this afternoon," Fancy said bitterly.

"I don't know 'bout this afternoon, fancy lady, but I've known about you for some time." He laughed. "Ever since that shindig you threw out at the ranch, I've been laughing to myself about the way these local yokels got taken in by you. You fooled everybody, pretty lady, and I figure you can do the same again somewhere else. We'll be a team and work together."

"You must be mad," Fancy said, twisting in Reynard's grip.

"Be careful with your tongue, fancy lady," Springer said, coming close to her and gripping her chin. "I don't want to mar that beautiful face, but I won't have a sharp-tongued woman around me. Now you just go along with Reynard until I make a stop off at Carl Robinson's office, and we'll be on our way. Take her." Doyle jerked his head toward the door. Reynard wrestled Fancy to the door, while she struggled against him. From the corner of her eye, she saw Doyle Springer pick up a lamp and smash it against the floor. The flames spread hungrily across the carpet. The frame house would burn in minutes. Fancy stopped struggling then and let Reynard lead her outside. Frank Avery was waiting.

"You got the fancy lady!" he shouted gleefully. Fancy shot him a look of pure disgust.

Reynard vaulted into his saddle and yanked her up on his lap, laughing suggestively while he settled her buttocks against him. His breath was foul. Fancy turned her head away from him and sat stiffly between his arms. She smelled the stench of his clothes and unwashed body. Taking back streets they rode away from the fire and dismounted at the back of a boardinghouse.

"Come on now," Reynard said, yanking her off the horse and shoving her toward a back door. Wildly, Fancy looked around for help, and the last thing she glimpsed before being shoved indoors was the blazing town house she and Coop had shared.

Chapter 21

"COOP, LOOK DOWN there," Aaron yelled, and Coop followed the direction he pointed. They'd sent the other men on to the ranch and detoured to Elizabethtown. Now with a curse, Coop kicked his horse into a straight-out gallop.

"It's the town house," he shouted. All four men made their way toward the blazing building. The citizens of Elizabethtown had been alerted, and men ran to form a bucket brigade. They'd be little use against the fire's head start. Saloons and parlor houses and even the theater emptied as the alarm went out. People poured into the street.

"Watch it, the fire's spreading," someone yelled, and the bucket brigade gave up trying to save the Fletcher house and began wetting down the adjoining buildings. The town house was fully ablaze, flames shooting from the collapsed roof.

Heart pounding with fear, Coop galloped into town.

"Fancy!" His cry was heard over the roar of the fire, and people turned to look at this man with the horror-stricken face.

"Mistah Fletcher," a voice cried, and Annabelle shoved her way through the onlookers. "I'm so glad to see yo', sir," she said. Coop was off his horse, reaching for her, looking over her head for a glimpse of Fancy.

"Where's Fancy and Nellie and the kids? Tell me,

Annabelle!" He shook her slightly, so she placed a hand on his arm to calm him.

"They all right, leastways I think they are. They ain't caught in the fire."

"Where are they?" Aaron asked, dismounting and coming to join them. "Where are Nellie and the kids?"

"They went back to the ranch this afternoon. Miss Nellie say she tired o' town livin'." Aaron sagged with relief.

"Did Fancy go with them?" Coop demanded, willing that it be so.

"No, Mistah Fletcher. She stayed here to meet that new theatrical troupe."

"Then she's at the opera house," Coop raised his head and looked at the people filling the street.

"No, I'm trying t'tell yo', Mistah Fletcher." Annabelle shook his sleeve. "That bad man that attacked the ranch. He come to the house. He said yo' was hurt and wanted Miss Fancy t'go with him, but she caught on. That's when he come on in and drew a gun and that Mistah Springer arrived and told him t'burn down the house. They were goin' t'kill me, Mistah Fletcher, but I run out the back door." She began to cry. "I left Miss Fancy there by herself with those men."

"Don't cry now, Annabelle," Coop said impatiently. "Did you see which way they went?"

Annabelle swallowed back her sobs and nodded. "I snuck around t'the front of the house, and Mr. Springer, he said he was going to Mr. Robinson's office. He had something to get there, and he told the other men to take Miss Fancy back to the boardinghouse and wait for him."

"Why didn't you say that in the first place?" Coop yelled, looking along the line of frame constructions. With nothing to stop it, the fire was roaring along the row of buildings.

"The whole town's going," Aaron yelled, trying to hold the frightened horses, who pranced and neighed in terror at the fire.

"Let 'em go," Coop hollered. "We've got to get to

Fancy." He ran down the street toward the boardinghouse. Aaron and Billy Dee were right behind.

From the window of the boardinghouse, Reynard and Frank Avery watched the fire spread.

"It's headed this way. Let's get out of here," Avery said.

"Springer told us to wait here," Reynard said, fingering his gun nervously.

"I ain't stayin' here and gettin' caught in a fire," Avery whined.

Reynard leveled his gun at Avery. "You'll do what I tell you. We wait for Springer."

"All right!" Avery eased back and leaned against a wall watching Reynard with a leery eye. Fancy sat on the bed listening to the two of them and wondered how she could escape. The raging fire illuminated their room with an eerie glow and lit the savage contours of Frank Avery's face. Fancy shivered. Both men were like vipers, waiting to strike when the other wasn't looking.

"What's that noise?" Avery said starting up, his pale eyes gleaming in the firelight.

"What? I didn't hear anything," Reynard said. "You're just jumpy."

Watchful, Avery leaned back against the wall. "There it is again. Someone's out there. Maybe it's Springer."

Reynard lowered his gun and went to the door, swinging it open and peering out into the empty hallway. "Springer?" he called, but there was no answer.

"There ain't nobody out there," Reynard said, closing the door. His face went still when he saw Avery had pulled his gun and had it aimed right at his chest. "Put that gun away," he ordered.

"That's the last order you'll ever give me, Reynard," Avery said and pulled the trigger. The impact of the bullet knocked Reynard against the door. He hung there a moment, his face registering shock and pain, then slowly slid to the floor, leaving a trail of blood on the wall behind him.

At the first sound of the shot, Fancy turned away, hiding her face and trembling. She'd never seen such cold-blooded murder. It horrified her that any man could take a life so casually. The room was silent. Slowly she turned her head and looked at the dead man, then at Avery, who was smiling.

"Now you're mine, fancy lady," Avery said, and in the reflected orange glow of the fire, his face looked distorted and evil. Fancy couldn't keep the fear from showing. Avery laughed and leaned closer to her. "You ain't so stuck up about old Avery now, are you?" He grabbed her arm and jerked her to her feet. She stood swaying, her head turned so she wouldn't have to look at the face of the killer.

"We're gettin' out a here," Avery said, "before that fire gets to us." Callously he kicked Reynard's body out of the way and threw open the door. Jerking Fancy along behind him, he made his way down the narrow hall. The boarding-house was empty and ominously shadowed. At the top of the stairs Avery paused, then jerked Fancy forward, wrapping his arm around her waist and shielding his own body with hers. He pressed his gun against her ribs and stood waiting.

Swallowing convulsively, Fancy tried not to cry out, tried not to whimper, but her face was wet with tears. From terror-stricken eyes she peered into the darkened shadows of the stairwell. She could see no one, but the sound of someone stealthily climbing upward was audible above her ragged breathing. Avery dug the gun into her ribs, and she cried out in pain.

"Don't come any closer. I'll kill her," he called. There was no answer from below.

Coop! Coop was down there, Fancy thought elatedly. He'd come for her. The footsteps continued upward at a steady pace, and finally the head and shoulders of a man emerged in the eerie orange glow.

"Where are you going, Avery?" Doyle Springer asked. His tone was pleasant, but Fancy could feel Avery's body jerk nervously.

"I'm gettin' out of here," Avery said. "The fire's spreading."

"Where's Reynard?" Springer continued his climb, his arms hanging at his side. He was unarmed. Avery relaxed a little, moving Fancy off to the side while he faced his boss.

"Reynard got scared. Took off on his own. Said he'd meet you at the old place."

"But you stayed," Springer said quietly. "You weren't frightened off by the fire?"

Avery shook his head. "Fire doesn't scare me. Did you get your money?"

"How do you know I was going for money?" Doyle Springer asked.

"I just figured. You're finished with this town, and you're fixin' to leave with her and all."

"You're right about that," Springer said. He'd attained the top stair now and stepped up on the landing beside Avery. "I'm finished with my operations in this town. That means you'll have to go, too, Avery."

"I'm ready, Mr. Springer. It's gettin' too hot for me." He paused, awareness sweeping over him. Avery tried to bring his gun up, but Springer grabbed his arm, blocking him while he pulled a small derringer from his pocket and fired it point-blank into Avery's chest. The gunman sighed in a last denial and tumbled down the stairs. Without a glimmer of regret, Doyle Springer watched until Avery's body reached the bottom and became still.

"It's unfortunate, my dear," Springer said, tucking the little gun back into his suit coat, "that you've had such an unpleasant beginning in our association. I promise you, it will get much better." He held out his arm to her as if about to escort her to a church social. "We'd best be leaving now. There's nothing to keep us here, and the fire is spreading rather rapidly."

"You horrid man," Fancy gasped. "Do you think I'd go with you? You've destroyed the town, you've murdered and stolen and lied."

"Yes, rather unpleasant tasks, but sometimes a man has to do such things to achieve what he wants."

"What do you want?"

"Money!" Springer said simply. "Being an Indian agent didn't appeal to me. I was able to realize a much bigger profit by selling the government supplies to someone else. It was absurdly easy. The people in this town were trusting fools. Your husband was the only one who gave us any trouble."

"Surely you can't think money is justification enough for all the havoc you've brought this town?"

"Maybe that's an issue we can debate later," Springer said, "but now we'd better leave. Don't force me to be tough with you, fancy lady. Hitting a woman is another unpleasant task I've performed when I've had to."

His gaze was implacable. Fancy knew he'd never leave her behind. Slowly she made her way down the stairs with Doyle Springer right behind her. The shadows were darker below, and she felt as if she were descending into hell. Then she reached the bottom step and felt a hand grip hers where it rested on the banister. Startled, she wondered if Springer had grabbed hold of her, but he was too far back. She barely had a chance to take a breath before she was jerked forward into the black shadows.

They found the boardinghouse. Coop paused outside, aware if he barged in he could be risking Fancy's life. A lone rider came up the street, and he ducked down. Who would be coming here when the fire had drawn everyone else up the street? The rider stopped in front of the boardinghouse and dismounted. In the glare from the fire, Coop could make out Doyle Springer. His hand tightened on his gun, then eased off. Much as he wanted Springer, he wanted to be sure Fancy was safe first. Slowly, he made his way to the back of the house and entered through the kitchen. The house was dark and silent. Coop tiptoed toward the front hall. A shot rang out, and he hugged the wall, his gun ready. He heard a body tumbling down the stairs, and his fear for Fancy overrode his need for caution. He hurried to the front hall, almost charging forth to examine the falling body, when he heard a woman scream at the top of the stairs. Crouching in the shadows, he listened to the voices above. Doyle Springer was forcing Fancy to do his bidding.

Coop waited, willing Fancy down the stairs to him, remembering that first time she came down to meet him looking like an angel and the day she walked down the stairs as his bride. Now he readied himself, his eyes straining through the dark shadows. When his hand touched hers, he felt a new strength. She was alive and unhurt. He swung her off the stairs out of harm's way, and his pistol blazed. Doyle Springer hadn't expected him. He grabbed hold of the banister, trying to keep his legs under him, but blood bubbled at his lips as his punctured lungs labored to breathe, then slowly he let go of the banister and plunged downward to rest beside his hired gunman.

"Coop!" Fancy cried, throwing herself at him.

"Thank God, you've alive," Coop whispered, holding her close. "When I rode into town and saw the fire, I thought I'd finally lost you."

"I'm all right, darling. You came in time. I didn't know what I was going to do. Springer was trying to make me leave with him."

"I know, you're safe now," he cradled her to him, both of them lost for the moment in the knowledge of how close they'd come to losing each other. Then reality intruded.

"Oh, Coop, the fire! It's spreading."

"I have to go help," he said, and she nodded. "I want you to gather up the women and children in the street and take them down to the opera house. It's brick and should be the safest place for now."

"Yes, all right. Be careful, Coop. I love you."

He paused and gripped her hands one last time. "I love you, Fancy," he said softly. Then he pulled her through the door and into the street. One last kiss and he was gone, running toward the fire. Fancy looked at the milling, frightened people. Some were weeping as they saw their homes catch fire. As the buildings flamed up, red hot sparks rained down on them, so they were in danger of having their clothing catch fire. She ran toward them.

"Women and children, get back to the opera house," she called, hurrying through the crowd. "Mothers, take your children to the opera house. It's brick. It won't burn." Some of the dazed women began to move, gathering up their frightened children and moving down toward the opera house.

Fancy came face-to-face with Maida. "All women and children should go to the opera house. They'll be safe there," Fancy said. "Will you help me get them rounded up?"

Maida only stared at her a moment, then nodded and began weaving her way through the people, spreading the message there was a safe place for them at the opera house. Claire Williams simply stared at Fancy and made no offer of help. Her look was insolent and superior.

"Fancy," Geraldine called, pushing through the crowd. "Are you all right? Annabelle said Reynard and his men kidnapped you."

"They did," Fancy answered. "It's a long story. I'll tell you later. Right now we need to get everyone down to the opera house where they'll be safe."

"I'll help." The old woman went off, and soon there was a steady line of women and children straggling down to the theater where the Lords and their players stood watching the fire.

When everyone was safe inside, Fancy looked around. The windowpanes glowed with an orange-red light, and as the fire drew closer, the panes shattered from the heat.

"We'll be trapped in here," a woman cried hysterically.

"No, we won't," Fancy said quickly to stem the spread of panic. "This building is new. The wood is green; the exterior is brick. We'll be safer here than anywhere. As for the windows, we just need to wet some cloths and hang them over the windows so sparks can't get inside. Now who wants to help?" Maida and the rest of the ladies' society stood up.

"Where can we find fabric heavy enough to keep out any sparks?" Maida asked.

Fancy looked around. "We'll use the stage curtain," she cried. "Let's get it down." With the concerted effort of all the ladies, the curtain was pulled down and cut into squares for the windows. They were then wet with water put out for the actors and actresses. Someone found a hammer and nails backstage, and the nimblest young boys were enlisted to stand on their mother's shoulders and nail the dripping cloths in place. When all the windows were covered, the theater was dark and the young children were sobbing with fear. Frantic mothers tried their best to quiet their cries.

"Light the gaslights," Fancy cried, and one of the stage-hands hurried to the stage.

"What are you doing?" Maida and some of the women called.

"We're putting on a show," Fancy cried.

Louie Lord caught Fancy's glance and nodded her head in agreement. "Everyone quiet. The show is about to begin."

The Lords and their troupe were dramatic actors, but each and every one of them offered some small skit to divert the fears of their audience. They sang and danced and did pratfalls, and when they tired, Fancy called on members of the audience. Geraldine Russell was the first to come forward and regale the children with tales of how things had been in the west when she first came. Fancy wandered to the front windows and drew aside the wet velvet to peer into the street. The fire had nearly burned itself out along one side of the street. They'd lost half the town. Wearily the men stood back and watched the last frame building collapse in on itself. Where was Coop? she wondered, and tried not to be afraid for him. She thought of his declaration of love. At one time, it was all she would have needed to make her happy, but now she wondered how he'd feel once he knew her secret was out.

The children had grown tired of Geraldine's stories, so Fancy mounted the stage and looked at the soot-stained faces. She'd come to know many of these people, knew their secrets, their dreams, their weaknesses, and their strengths. She was part of them and they a part of her. Suddenly she was glad her secret had been found out. She wanted to be a whole and real person, not the fancy lady. She wanted them to know her as she was.

The upraised faces waited expectantly. The door at the back of the theater opened, and some of the men trooped in. Fancy raised her chin and put her hands on her hips.

"Do you know what I did when I was a little girl?" she asked, and the children called out happily, urging her to tell them. She told them of being born to parents in the theater and of dancing onstage when she was just a little girl barely big enough to walk. She did a little dance to illustrate her tale and sang funny little songs she'd learned so long ago in the theater. She left nothing out.

"Then I came here to Elizabethtown to live," she ended her story. "And I learned something very important. I learned that if you want people to care for you, you have to tell them the truth about yourself."

She saw Coop standing at the back of the theater. Claire Williams was clinging to his arm.

"I'm so sorry for you, Coop," Claire said softly. "I've known the truth about her for some time, but I just didn't know how to tell you."

"I've known the truth for some time, too, ma'am," he said and grinned.

"I came to love a man very much," Fancy went on, knowing she was leaving herself open to ridicule and scorn, but knowing she must do this. "And I've been happier than I ever was in the theater. Now we have a town to rebuild, and we must all be brave and truthful and giving. We'll make the town better than it was. I'm going to be here working alongside all of you. I'm part of this town, part of the people, and I won't go away. I'm not a fancy lady. I'm just a woman called Fancy."

She stopped talking, because the tears were blinding her eyes. She'd caught sight of Coop making his way down the aisle to her, his soot-blackened face filled with pride. She couldn't breathe as she thought of what this meant to them all. Would he accept her now that the truth about her was known? Coop climbed the stairs and met her center stage. His silver-gray eyes stared into hers.

"I love you, Mrs. Coop Fletcher," he said and swept her into his arms. His mouth claimed hers. He smelled of smoke and fire. The audience sent up a cheer, and when he released her she turned to face them. She wasn't aware her face was as smudged as Coop's now, but the townspeople only laughed and clapped harder.

Tears sprang to Fancy's eyes. She'd spoken the truth. There was much hard work for them all in the days and weeks ahead. Not all the town could be rebuilt before the snowfall, but they'd do their best, and people would share. The town would pull together, closing itself around its own, and suddenly, as surely as she felt Coop's arms were around her, Fancy knew the town accepted her as she was. There were no more secrets to be told. Well, one secret, and that one only for Coop.

"Well, Fancy Lady," he said, his breath hot against her ear. "What new surprises have you got in mind for us next year?"

"Maybe it's time we filled up that big old ranch house," she said softly, eyes shining. Coop stared at her in consternation.

"You mean—"

"Umm—huh!" Her final secret was told.

Coming to bookstores everywhere next
winter . . .

WILD SAGE

by Peggy Hanchar

Published in paperback by Fawcett Books.
Read on for the opening pages of
WILD SAGE . . .

Chapter 1

"**C**OMANCHES!" CALEB HUNTER uttered the one word like a curse and spat between his teeth, a further indication of his loathing for the line of horsemen silhouetted on a distant ridge. Captain John Wright glanced at his tracker.

"Could be Kiowas," he said. "They're too far away to see their markings."

"I can smell them." Caleb slouched in his saddle, one hand resting easily on the pommel, the other gripping the reins. His tall, whipcord-lean body seemed at ease, but Captain Wright wasn't fooled by Caleb's stance. He knew from experience that Caleb was a coiled spring capable of striking faster than a mad sidewinder. He also knew he could rely on Caleb's information about the menacing line on the horizon. Caleb Hunter was the best damn tracker around, better even then the half-breeds the army usually employed and a damn sight more reliable. Once they'd earned enough for whiskey, the Indian scouts would often disappear into the mountains for a few months, returning only when they were broke, hung over, and half starving.

Caleb never seemed to need a rest. No one knew much about him, except that he hated Indians, all Indians, but the Comanches most of all. No one knew why exactly, although rumors abounded. No one had ever found the courage to question him about his past. The secrets lay sealed behind weather-beaten features seemingly carved of stone, and flinty gray eyes that could look at a man in such a way that made his blood run cold. Captain Wright had seen more than one man back down from a fight with Caleb, intimidated by his rock-hard demeanor. Those who hadn't backed down learned the hard way and never came back for a repeat lesson.

In a land of tough, hard men, Caleb Hunter stood out as the toughest and meanest, yet Wright had never seen him pick a fight with anyone or shoot a man in the back. If anyone had asked him who were Caleb's friends, he guessed he would have to say he was the one and only man close to him, yet even he didn't really know anything about the loner. And Caleb Hunter was a loner. He had no family. Sometimes, Captain Wright imagined he had been fashioned of Texas clay and mountain granite, receiving the breath of life from a hot prairie wind.

Rumor had it he was only fifteen when he killed his first redskin and was in turn wounded and left for dead among the mutilated bodies of his family and the charred remains of their ranch. There were a lot of rumors about, true or not, but one rumor everyone trusted was the one about the mechanical skill with which he killed the redskins. With unemotional detachment he sought out their haunts, running the Comanches to ground even in the Cross Timbers, where they believed themselves to be safe. Caleb found them and killed them. Only once had Captain Wright looked in Caleb's face on such an expedition, and the hell he'd seen mirrored in his eyes had caused him to look away. If ever a man lived in torment, Caleb Hunter was that man.

Now Captain Wright turned his attention back to the line of warriors on the distant bluff. In the blink of an eye, they'd disappeared, drawing back down the hill on the opposite side.

"Let's go after them," Wright said, signaling to his men to prepare to ride.

"Wait," Caleb said and leaning forward flicked a match head against his boot and lit a cheroot.

"They're on the run. They must think they're outnumbered," Wright persisted.

Caleb shook his head and pulled his sweat-stained, broad-brimmed hat lower over his eyes. "They didn't run," he said in a low flat voice. "They'll play with you and your men awhile, tiring out your horses, making you careless, then they'll attack."

"How do you know?" Wright demanded.

"I know." Caleb drew the smoke deep into his chest and slowly let it out. His eyes were keen beneath his hat brim. Trail dust lay in the creases of his cheeks and near his eyes. His jaws were unshaven, containing several days growth. There was a tense anticipation about him, yet he smiled, a savage grimace that boded no good for anyone.

Reluctantly, Captain Wright lowered his hand and gazed at the empty horizon where dust still hung in the air like a curtain testifying to the passing of their enemy.

"We'll do it at our time and pace," Caleb said. "Turn your men and ride toward that distant ridge back there. That's where you'll find your Comanches."

"Are you sure about that, Hunter?"

Caleb's glance was derisive. He turned his horse and with a sharp prod set it to cantering toward the ridge they'd just left. Captain Wright sat warring between his choices, his men watching silently. How they all longed to dash over that hill in full out pursuit of the Indians, but if what Caleb said was so, the Comanches wouldn't be there. They'd be at the regiment's back. Wright nodded to his assistant, and the order was given. Wheeling his horse he followed Caleb Hunter.

The men sat in a neat line, their horses turned to their rear, their weapons unsheathed and ready. The foothills had gone silent, as if the hills and prairie held their breath waiting for what was about to happen. The Indians came silently.

They were closer here, and Wright and his men could pick out details in their dress.

Their lances could be seen first, poking out along the ridge like stiff barren stalks drying in the wind, then came the heads of the Comanches, some of them wearing their war headdress. Their painted buckskin shields reflected the sun. Bits of cloth and hawk feathers, deer hooves and eagle feathers decorated the rounded discs in various symbols and meanings. Even the manes and tails of their mounts had been woven with bits of cloth and feathers. They came forward stealthily.

"Son of a bitch!" Caleb Hunter said under his breath, and his knuckles grew white on his rifle butt.

"What is it?" Captain Wright asked and felt the hair at the back of his neck tingle.

"It's our old friend, Two Wolves," Caleb said without taking his gaze off the head Indian.

The Indians came on as if they hadn't yet caught a glimpse of the line of soldiers, then a war chief wearing the honored buffalo scalp headdress, came to an abrupt halt and held up his hand. As if connected, the line of warriors obeyed him instantly. For a full minute the leader known as Two Wolves glared down at the soldiers; then with a wild, savage cry he led the line of screaming Comanches down the ridge toward Captain Wright's regiment.

Army horses snorted with terror at the sudden rush of noise and animals, but the men brought them under control with an impatient jerk of the reins. They were brave men, experienced in Indian fighting and not easily routed.

"Fire when ready," Wright cried and a volley of shots echoed across the valley. Caleb Hunter took little notice of Wright or his men. He waited until the mad dash brought the savages closer, his rifle cocked and aimed at the leader known as Two Wolves. Closer the warrior came, his lance raised high, the whites of his eyes, fierce and menacing in his painted face. As the war chief stood up in his saddle to throw his lance, Caleb's finger tightened on the trigger. His shot nearly spun the warrior out of his saddle. Caleb aimed again, but Two Wolves was no longer in his saddle. Caleb wasted no time looking back on the ground. He knew the wounded Indian lay in a sling against the side of his horse, only a heel holding him in his saddle.

The battle raged around them. Comanche horsemen reached the line of soldiers and engaged in a bitter fight. Caleb paid little attention to the sound of mortal combat, the cries of men dying. He thought only of the Comanche leader streaking away from him. He sighted along the barrel of his rifle and fired again. The tough little Indian pony stumbled, then regained its feet and ran toward the open prairie. Caleb prepared to fire again. This time the little pony went down, and the Comanche clinging to its side flung himself clear of the floundering beast. Taking shelter behind his horse, Two Wolves lay studying the battle behind him. Caleb drew a bead on him again and fired. The bullet kicked up dirt near the warrior. He drew back, his fierce dark eyes glaring at Caleb. The gaze of the two men locked in deadly combat. Pinned behind his dead pony, the Comanche war chief could do little. He was used to fighting from horseback and now he'd been dismounted, but his hate-filled glare promised vengeance.

Some silent signal had been given. The Comanches rallied their men and galloped away. Distracted, Caleb fired at their departing backs, taking down three men in as many seconds. When he glanced back at the dead Indian pony, Two Wolves was no longer there.

The gunfire died away followed by an instant of silence before the soldiers sent up a cheer. "They're on the run. We ran the bastards off, sir," they cried jubilantly.

Captain Wright grinned and holstered his gun, looking around to find Caleb. "You were right, Hunter," he called. "How'd you know they would double back?"

"Like I said, Captain, you can smell a Comanche. When I couldn't smell them anymore, I knew they'd moved downwind." Caleb's gaze never wavered from the backs of the fleeing Indians. Two Wolves, mounted on a fresh pony, was leading his warriors up a ridge. When he reached the top he whirled his pony and glared back down at the white men. Raising his lance over his head, he let out a blood-curdling shriek that brought shivers to the bloodied men below. Caleb knew the wild cry was meant for him. Raising his rifle, he sighted along its barrel and pulled the trigger. The lance splintered in Two Wolves's hand. In a cloud of dust, he whirled his pony and disappeared over the ridge.

"Shame you missed him, sir," Nye Garrett wiped his sweat stained face and peered at the horizon.

"I didn't," Caleb said and sheathed his rifle.

"Why didn't you kill him, when you had the chance," Captain Wright snapped. "He was their leader."

"This wasn't the time," Caleb said. "I want to look into Two Wolves's eyes when I kill him."

"How come you hate this Comanche so bad?" Nye asked, remounting. He was still a young man, but years in the army riding the trails and fighting had prematurely aged him. His brown hair had long since turned gray at the temples. Only the lithe, spryness of his trail-hardened body gave some clue to his true age.

The men around Caleb grew quiet, silenced by the hard-bitten gaze of the tracker. Most doubted he'd answer Nye. They were surprised when he pushed back the rim of his hat.

"A few years back I rode with Murray's rangers, when a band of renegades started attacking homesteads south of here. They were a bunch of rebellious young Comanche bucks out to make a name for themselves. I saw the evidence of their handiwork. Men disemboweled, women raped and left cut in a way that—" he stopped talking. "They took no prisoners, not even children, but they scalped 'em. Have you ever held a baby that was scalped and left to die in his own blood?" Caleb gathered up his reins and looked around at the circle of stark faces.

"Comanches take scalps, but there's no real honor in it. It's just a symbol of the battles they've fought. Taking the scalp of a baby wasn't necessary for him to make a name for himself, but he did it anyway. Someday, I'm going to take his scalp, and I want him alive when I do it."

Their moment of jubilation was ended. Caleb's stark narration had brought them back to the reality of the foe they sought. If the Comanches had ridden away from them this day after only a short skirmish, they had a reason. Some of the men counted themselves lucky; some longed to ride back to the safety of the fort. Only the wounded would be sent back. The rest would go on. Silently they waited for Caleb Hunter, not their captain, to give them new orders.

"Now we go after them," Caleb said. "We follow them far enough back so they don't suspect we're there. We're goin' all the way to their village."

"Into the Cross Timbers?" a man cried, whether in dread or disbelief, Captain Wright wasn't sure, nor did he care. His gaze was locked with the bleak, fierce gaze of Caleb Hunter. Slowly, Wright nodded in agreement.

"See to the wounded," Wright called. "Assign a

detail to take them back to the fort. The rest of you, prepare to mount up and ride."

Exhilaration over razing the Comanches was gone. Each man thought about the Cross Timbers, the desolate wooded area of West Texas that was a hiding place for Comanches and Mexican bandits alike. If one didn't get you, the other surely would.

Also by
Peggy
Hanchar

Available in bookstores everywhere.
Published by Fawcett Books.